WHEN NOTHING ELSE MATTERS

KATHERINE JAY

Contents

To my characters, Dylan and Summer.
Thank you for screaming at me to write this story.
Without that, I never would have become an author.

Prologue

Dylan – Twelve Years Old

She's here again. I know I shouldn't look. As the quarterback, the coach needs me to focus, to lead this team, but I can't help myself. I didn't think she'd show today, considering the weather, but there she is, long blonde hair stuck to her face and clothes soaking wet from rain. For the last three weeks she's been in the same position—hiding in the tree line, watching my football team train. Alone. She doesn't look older than ten, so at first, I thought she was the younger sister of a teammate, but no one else has mentioned her. She always arrives midtraining and leaves before it's over, like she doesn't want to be seen. But she has to be here for someone, right?

I try to keep my eyes on the play but keep stealing glances her way. She must be more confident today, because for the first time, she's stepped out from the trees and is standing by the fence. Now that she's closer, I manage to catch her eye. She's watching me, not the team. *Me.* And I gotta say it feels good to know that. Because at twelve years old, I finally understand the appeal of girls. I used to think they were annoying, but now, I get it. And every part of me is now focused on her, training forgotten.

"Heads!" Someone yells from behind me, but I stupidly ignore it. *Big mistake.*

Thump. Direct hit. *Dang, that hurt.* Rubbing my head, I look back at the team before shaking off my thoughts and running to my starting position.

"Head in the game or the laps are on you!" the coach yells, and my team collectively boos as they set up for the next play. For the next twenty minutes, I ignore the girl and play my best, determined to give it my all, even showing off a little. *Okay, maybe not completely ignoring the girl then?*

I'm in my element, showing everyone how it's done. Every throw, every move, every second. I'm not going to be the reason for the extra laps today; someone else can deal with that. I'm focused now, or at least, I'm trying to be, until we set up for the fourth run of the same play, a play I know inside and out. Confident in myself, I check out the girl near the trees, and then all focus is lost.

I watch in horror, frozen, as the girl falls to her knees in the slosh as a man towers over her. From what I can see, he's tall and solid, so while she's trying to use her strength to pull away, she's helpless against him. The rain makes it hard to see properly, but it's impossible to miss when he rips her to her feet and drags her toward a car. She doesn't scream, doesn't make a sound. She just lets him drag her without even fighting back. *Why isn't she screaming?*

It seems I have a split-second decision to make. I look back at my teammates to see if anyone has noticed and see that they haven't. I'm just about to alert Coach when I glance back to see the girl cry out in surprise when the man slaps her across the face. That cry finally snaps me out of my shock and kicks my ass into gear.

"Hey!" I yell. "Let her go...Stop! You're hurting her..."

The man doesn't react, but his movements become faster and less violent. He can definitely hear me, and yet, no one else is moving.

Without a plan, I take off in a run, knowing I need to reach her. *But what am I going to do? I'm a kid.* I need backup. Without stopping, I yell over my shoulder.

"Someone help...by the fence...help her!" *Why hadn't anyone else noticed?*

I feel like someone has answered my prayers when I see Dad's car pulling into the parking lot. As soon as he spots me, I wave frantically and point in the girl's direction.

"Dad, help her. Please!" The panic in my voice is enough to rattle my dad into action.

"Get your hands off her!" he yells as soon as he spots what I'm seeing. "Hey! I'm talking to you!"

He's running now too. I'm fast, but I got my speed from him. He'll catch them. He has to. My eyes remain focused in the girl's direction. The man now has her in the car and is making his way to the driver's seat. No! Yelling and loud footsteps start up behind me. Finally, others have noticed, but no one will reach them in time. I reach the fence just as the car speeds out of the parking lot, and seconds later, my father follows. I hadn't even noticed he'd gone back to his car. Relief hits me.

There's nothing more I can do. Dropping to the ground in a heap, I rest my head in my hands and take a deep breath. It's only then that my teammates catch up.

"Who was that?"

"What happened?"

"Does anyone know them?"

"Do you think she's okay?"

The questions are firing, but I have no answers. I have nothing left. When the coach reaches my side, I brace myself for the lecture, but it doesn't come.

"You did a good thing, kid," he says as he squats down in front of me, patting me on the back. "Alright boys, show's over. Off to the locker room. No laps tonight."

Cheers ring out at his words. The girl is clearly forgotten as everyone heads back across the field, met by their concerned parents.

I look back toward the parking lot and can't help but think about the questions my teammates had asked. *Who was she? Who was he? Is she okay? At least I could answer that one. She will be. Dad will find them. I know it. She'll be okay. She's got to be.*

With a sigh, I get up and follow the team back to the locker rooms, completely unaware that what I just witnessed would not be the worst thing to happen that day.

Chapter One

Dylan

My eyes glaze over as I stare at the face in front of me. The girl's lips are moving, and she's animatedly talking with her hands. Whatever she's saying seems important to her; it must be, considering how wide her eyes are and how expressive she is. But I can't say for sure. I'm not listening. Just like I hadn't listened to the two girls who were standing here before her. I need an exit strategy, and fast. It's not that she's not attractive or interesting, because I've met her before and can confirm that she's both of those things. I would have happily chatted to her all night if that's all she wanted. But it's not. That much is clear. And because of that, I need out.

I have a girlfriend. In fact, despite being a senior in college, a time when many seem to let loose, I'm rarely without one. It's something I'm not ashamed to admit. I love being in a relationship. There are no games, no questioning what someone wants, no stress about when to call, what to say, who they've just been with. Okay, that last one was a little harsh, but you get the drift. The physical bonuses don't hurt either. In fact, I'd say they're pretty high on the relationship pros list. In summary, I'm a relationship guy, and I'm currently taken. Granted, this relationship is new, but it's not a secret. Everyone knows I'm with Gemma, and yet, here we are.

I smile and refocus, so I can offer a polite excuse to leave. But before I get the chance to speak, her eyes drop to my lips as she seductively licks her own. *Shit! Shit!*

"What did you say?" I yell, to no one over her shoulder. "I can't..." My eyes meet hers again, and I offer an apologetic smile. She pauses and looks around, a little flustered. "Sorry, I'm being summoned by the guys. It's a boys' night." I shrug before walking away.

That was a close one. Was it a dick move? Yes, but it had to happen. I don't know why I keep ending up in this situation in the first place. Actually, I can probably guess. First, through no fault of my own, I have a reputation as a player. How that happened when I've never once done anything to support that claim? Who knows. But I'd wager it might have something to do with two of my exes cheating on me and then both declaring I was to blame. And maybe I was, but not for reasons people assumed.

I myself have never cheated. I've also never confirmed or denied the rumors. Once I've moved on from someone, I *move* on. No use dwelling on the past and ending up with a he said, she said situation. Instead, I just let people believe what they want to believe. Which unfortunately leads people to assume that my being in a relationship doesn't mean I'm off the market. And second, I'm too nice and always look for the good in people. I don't see the situation until I'm already in it. Like now. And even though I just heard my name and *asshole* uttered under her breath, I still walk away with my head held high, knowing I saved her from embarrassment by not making a big deal out of what she was doing. *Nice guy, right here.*

It takes a ridiculously long time to get to my friends. There must be at least a hundred college students squashed into this place and all of them seem to know who I am, yet I couldn't name ten percent if my life depended on it. I'm currently walking through Huntington House—or as we all call it, the Ball House. It would be better described as a manor over a house, because unlike most college student accommodations, this one has grounds with a large swimming pool, spa, and pool house. Not to mention a sweeping deck complete with daybeds, mood lighting, and well-maintained gardens. Who maintains them is anyone's guess. The house itself is a huge red-brick structure with a dark pitched roof and obnoxious white pillars framing the entry from the floor to the second story. It doesn't look like the home of a bunch of rowdy football players, but that's exactly what it is. Some of my closest teammates live here, and tonight they're throwing a party.

Speaking of teammates...they're all staring at me as I approach. I was technically lying about the boys' night, but since none of the girlfriends are here, it's only a small fib. Even if it *was* a boys' night, they'd never stop me from hooking up. *If* I wanted to. In fact, I'm going to guess that at some point one of them is going to say or do something to prove exactly why some girls still throw themselves at taken men.

"What is wrong with you, Mathers? That chick was hot and a sure thing," Luke says with a look of pure astonishment.

And there it is. I thought I'd at least get a sip of my beer before it happened. "That might be true, but I'm with Gemma." *Information he knows.*

"But Gemma's missing in action, *again*," he reminds me, like that's a good enough reason. *Douche.*

It may not seem like it but Luke is actually a friend. He's a good guy to have around but has no morals when it comes to women. He'll learn the hard way, I'm sure. Unfortunately, he has one thing right. Gemma is MIA again. This isn't her scene. She's more of a quiet get-together type of girl. And if she was going to party, it definitely wouldn't be at a huge college rager. Or any frat parties or sports team parties or...doesn't matter. Point is, she doesn't party. Surprisingly, her aversion to sports parties is something I like about her—that she's not sports obsessed. Because let's face it, a lot of girls want me 'cause they think I'll make the big bucks as a pro football player. Like that's all I'm good for. Yet, despite what many believe, it *doesn't* define me.

Anyway, I don't hold the partying thing against Gemma at all, but it sucks because it means we're rarely out together, thus creating the need for me to remind people. I'm. Not. Single.

"Wouldn't matter if she was on-a-milk-carton level missing; she's still my girlfriend," I explain to Luke.

He laughs. "Whatever, man—let's get drunk."

That I can agree to. With only two weekends left before our training schedule ramps up, we are making the most of our freedom.

Discussion among the boys eventually moves away from my relationship status and turns to sports. We spend the next hour on that and other mindless chitchat, which finally allows me to relax and enjoy myself.

This, *this*, is why I'm here. I've spent too much time away from these boys. They're my family, and I'm lucky they haven't ditched my ass lately. I'm going to spend more time with them. I was kind of consumed by my last girlfriend—something I promised myself I'd try not to do again, and Gemma is very supportive of that.

To show just how dedicated I am to these guys, I offer to get the next round of drinks. Sure, they're free, but it's the thought that counts, and at least they don't have to move from their seats.

As I pass the dance floor on my way to the bar, a petite hand locks onto my arm, stopping me in my tracks. *Here we go again.*

I turn around, ready to flick her away, but freeze when my eyes lock on the girl in front of me. I'm instantly drawn to her. She looks so familiar, and yet, I'm almost certain we've never met.

She's devastatingly beautiful and difficult to turn away from. I say devastatingly, because she's gazing up at me through long lashes with a look that tells me she could destroy me in a heartbeat. Her mesmerizing eyes hold the promise of ruin to anyone who dares to want her, while failing to hide a hint of insecurity, just enough to remind you that she, too, is breakable.

Wisps of her long blonde hair fall around her face, and it takes everything in my power not to reach over and play with the strands. She must have read my mind because she reaches up and brushes the locks behind her ear, providing me with an excuse to focus on her features, to take in her alluring soft-pink lips and the light dusting of freckles that cross her perfect little nose.

My heart picks up speed as I stare, that little flutter proving why I'm not a player. I've always needed to *feel* something. Random hookups hold no interest to me. I want this feeling...crave it, even. *Fuck! This is bad. Didn't I just finish saying I was a good guy? I am. I am.* She stands confidently in front of me while my mind is going crazy, trying to decide what I should say to her.

"So, are you?" she asks.

Huh?

"You're on the football team, right?" she asks again, trying to coax an answer. I've heard this question multiple times tonight, and since it's the worst pickup line ever, I usually nod and walk away, but in this case, I allow it. I'm about to answer when she adds, "So, you know Nate?"

Nate? She wants Nate. I inwardly deflate. Girls have been throwing themselves at me all night and now...*not important.*

"Sorry, I thought you were on the football team. Forget I asked," she snaps when I still don't answer.

Speak, dickhead. "Yep. Yes, sorry, I am. On the team. I'm on the football team. And you're looking for Nate?"

She's wasted on Nate. While he's a great guy and my closest friend on the team, we all know he's hung up on some girl in his class. I could warn her, but—

"See my friend standing over by the trophy cabinet?" she asks and looks away, presumably toward her friend. I nod, even though my eyes don't leave her. When she turns back to me, her nose adorably scrunches up before she adds, "I know; she's hot, right?"

Whatever she's seen on my face must have given her the idea that I thought that, but my eyes have remained firmly in place, on her. I smile at the hint of annoyance in her tone and finally look at her friend. I agree, her friend is cute—beautiful even—but she has nothing on the girl in front of me. The girl I've realized is still holding my arm. I'm trying not to focus on the warmth of her touch, trying to pull my thoughts away from her, when her voice once again cuts through my mind.

"Anyway, she's interested in Nate. Can you introduce them?"

What? Her friend? "Your friend is interested in Nate?" I repeat each word slowly to allow my brain to catch up.

"Yes." She huffs, obviously annoyed at my questions.

So, she doesn't want him? "What about you?" I reply, not entirely sure what I'm asking, but it comes out of my mouth anyway.

"Me?" she questions. "No, I'm not interested in Nate. Just Cory," she laughs and the sound runs right through me.

"Who the f... Who's Cory?" I say, putting a stop to the unwelcome venom leaking into my voice. For some reason I need to know who Cory is. Is it her boyfriend? A crush? *Why the hell do I sound jealous? Get a grip.*

The girl lets out another laugh and points to her friend. "That's Cory."

Ah shit. "Okay...and why do you need me again?" *And why do I sound like a jerk? Really, what is wrong with me?* This entire conversation has me in knots, and I don't understand why.

"I need you to introduce them, because I don't know him." She gives me attitude, like that's an obvious answer. Which would make sense, except...

"You don't know me either..." *Yeah, take that.* Finally, I'm holding my own.

"Correct. I don't know you, but I wanted to...know you. Two birds, one stone." She shrugs but smiles, and it lights up her entire face. Her insecurities are now buried deep, proving her to be even more dangerous. And I'm a goner. Absolutely screwed.

Gemma, Gemma, Gemma. I repeat her name so that I snap out of whatever the fuck is going on inside me. *Shit, no wonder no one believes I'm not a player.* I have never once thought about someone else while in a relationship, because that's not me—before today, at least. I'm not that guy. I care about Gemma. I do. *Gemma.* Ignoring the war going on with my inner thoughts, I shake my head clear and introduce myself.

"I'm Dylan," I say, offering my hand. She shakes it while tilting her head toward an approaching Nate, only then releasing my arm.

"So..." she says and raises her eyebrows in silent question. I turn and grab Nate, eager to get this over with so I can keep talking to her.

"Hey, man, I've got a girl I want you to meet," I say, walking him over to Cory.

His eyes widen in surprise, but I don't give him time to explain as I push him in her direction. They say their hellos and start a conversation while I turn back to the girl.

"Hey, I didn't get your n—" My words fall flat when I see she's walking away through the crowd. *Damn.* She doesn't even look back. Shaking my head, I can't help but release a twisted laugh as I glance back at Nate. It's only then that I remember the name of the girl he's been hung up on and smile...*Cory.*

I spot the mesmerizing girl again when I'm heading back to my friends, and I'm still staring when I reach them.

"Something caught your eye, Mathers?" Luke asks smugly.

"What? No. Ah, who is that?" I ask, knowing he's busted me staring and fully aware that I sound like a dick.

"Dude, have you been living under a rock?" Luke laughs. "Wait, I can answer that. You've been living under, and on top of, a Jess rock, a Nicole rock, a Gemma—"

"I get it. So, who is she?" *And why do I feel like I know her?*

"What's it matter? *You* have a girlfriend," he teases.

Touché. "Just answer the question, asshole."

"That's Summer."

Summer? I stare at him blankly.

"Sum-mer." He says her name as two drawn-out syllables for extra emphasis.

I shrug and hold back a smile because it's fun to frustrate Luke. *Summer, Summer?* My smile finally breaks through. *Oh, Summer, as in...*

"Before you even go there in your mind, stop," Luke interrupts my thoughts. "It's Thomas's little sister, Summer." He stares at me, waiting for my recognition.

I know who she is, douchebag.

"Summer Kelly," he tries again.

"Yep, got that, thanks," I say, rolling my eyes.

Now, I understand why I recognize her. I can sort of see the resemblance. I may not have seen her before, but I've definitely heard a bit about her over the years. Thomas and his sister have a complicated relationship. From the whispers, I've pieced together that they're estranged, even though they're still living in the same town. Something big happened, and her parents had either kicked her out or she'd left. Both rumors circulated.

Thomas didn't like anyone mentioning her, but if she ever came up in conversation, he definitely insinuated that she'd wronged their family. I have no idea what's true and what's not, but one thing I know for sure is that I've never seen her at any of our college parties.

"So why is this the first time I'm seeing her here?" I ask Luke, my eyes focused straight ahead. On her.

"Thomas asked her to stay away from the team, and she respected his wishes. I guess now that—"

"He's graduated," I finish for him.

"Exactly." He raises his eyebrows, and we both look her way.

"Plus, the Cory thing," I add more to myself.

"What?" Luke asks.

"Never mind."

Luke stares at me for a moment, trying to figure me out, before speaking. "She's still off-limits, for Thomas's sake, and to be honest, you don't stand a chance. For one, you have a 'girlfriend.'" He misuses quote hands and pauses for dramatic effect. "And even though we all know Gemma won't last..."

What the hell does that mean? I intend to protest, but he raises a hand. "Regardless, Summer doesn't do relationships, and that seems to be *all* you do. God only knows why."

I roll my eyes and huff out a laugh before shoving him in the shoulder. He stumbles but rights himself, pushing me back. Our antics gain laughs from those around us. Yep, these guys are my family. Thomas included. End of story. My eyes follow Summer for one last look as she walks out the front door. I know who she is now, so it's time to move on.

Chapter Two

Summer

D*ylan Mathers.* I honestly never intended to approach him. Ever. But the opportunity presented itself and...here we are. I knew who he was when I grabbed his arm. Hell, I think everyone does. But did I think I'd actually talk to him one day? No, it had never even crossed my mind.

I somehow manage not to look back as I walk out the door and smile at my freedom. Cory's with Nate. *Finally.* Everything's the way it should be. I'll do the good friend thing and hang around a little longer, just to be sure, and then I'm done.

A little part of me still can't believe that I'm here, at the one place I never thought I'd enter. Huntington House, a.k.a. the Ball House, home to some of the football players.

The very house my dear brother previously lived in.

I'd held my breath as I stepped over the threshold, half expecting him to jump out of the shadows, grab me by the arm, and rip me outside. But I made it through the door unscathed. I was here for Cory, and nothing was going to stop that.

We've been best friends since the moment we met on her thirteenth birthday and have lived together since our junior year of high school. I love her like a sister. I mean, she is the closest thing to family that I've got. Being here is the least I can do after all she's done for me.

I'm searching for a place to sit when I hear Cory call my name from behind me. *Shit! This can't be good.*

When I turn toward her voice, I see her and Nate exiting the front door. Nate heads to a car in the driveway as Cory walks to me. She's already explaining as she approaches.

"Nate's one of the designated drivers for the team tonight. He said he wants to spend more time with me but has one more drop-off and then he'll hand it over to someone else."

What? I stare at her for a few seconds, shocked at what she just said. Not the part about wanting to spend more time with Cory, but designated driver? Who knew the football team was that responsible?

"What if it was an excuse? Maybe they all use that as a way to get rid of girls they don't want?" Cory says breathlessly. "Maybe—"

I race forward and grab Cory by the shoulders, looking her dead in the eye. "Stop. It's not an excuse. You're a catch. A major babe. But that aside, you may not have noticed because you were in the moment, but I saw the way he looked at you. He *wants* you."

She sighs, and her shoulders relax a little, but I can tell she's not entirely convinced. "I promise," I add, giving her a reassuring smile.

"Okay, okay," she says and pulls me into a hug. "Thank you. I love you."

"I love you too. Now, what are we going to do to pass the time?"

We chat outside for a bit longer until Cory decides it might look like she's desperately waiting for Nate if we're here when he gets back.

Cory still looks nervous as we reenter the house, but she shouldn't be. She looks amazing in an olive-green romper that perfectly complements her skin tone and copper-brown hair. Any boy would be crazy not to love her. She's cute as a button and can totally rock a pair of ridiculously high stilettos with her height. Lucky for me, I'm taller with long legs so I can get away with flats.

Today I've paired white Keds with a tight black miniskirt and a loosely fitted pink silk tank tucked in. Cory's long hair is styled into an intricate braid that hangs down over her left shoulder, while my blonde locks hang loose in curls that I quickly put together after napping instead of getting ready for our night out, otherwise known as the "didn't get time to style" look. Ah, *who am I kidding? I had time but chose not to do anything. And I still look pretty good.*

The house feels more packed than it did when I was here fifteen minutes ago, and I have to stop myself from turning around and walking back out again. *I'm doing this for Cory. God, please tell me Nate's on a short drive.*

We've just found ourselves a quietish spot to wait when Cory's whole demeanor changes and she smiles brightly. She's looking at her phone so it doesn't take a genius to realize why.

"Nate just texted." Yes! "He's back and asked if I could meet him in the yard." Cory squeals quietly, and I can't help but laugh. "Will you come with me?"

She grabs my hand without waiting for a response, and we push through the crowd, looking for the exit. When we near the back door, she hesitates again. Giving her a reassuring smile, I walk ahead and lead her outside. It takes all of two seconds to spot Nate, and his eyes are already on us. *Yeah, he wants her.* I pull her toward him, and he breaks away from his friends to join us. He acknowledges me with a smile before his eyes move to Cory's. Cory waves and bounces on her toes as Nate's responding smile tells me everything I need to know. He's already smitten. It's like watching kids with their first crush. Neither of them speaks, so I do.

"Hi, I'm Summer. Nice to meet you, Nate."

Nate's gaze leaves Cory and meets mine. "Summer, hi...hi. How are you?"

Aww, these two. "I'm great, but I need a drink. Point me in the kitchen's direction?" I say, waving my hand back toward the house.

"Of course, want me to show you both—"

"Nah, Cory's good for now. I'm a big girl."

He lets out a quick laugh and tells me where to go before turning back to Cory, eyes drawn to hers, a small smile playing on his lips.

"Look after my girl," I say to the side of his face.

"Always," he replies, his eyes never returning to mine.

Surprised by how easily I believe him, I give Cory a quick hug and whisper, "I'm here if you need me, but this guy's a good one."

She smiles and waves as I depart.

I follow the directions Nate gave me and search for a familiar face. Any familiar face will do. I figure I've got at least an hour before Cory gives me the all-clear to leave, and I'd prefer some company.

When I reach the bar, *yes, they have a bar*, I immediately abandon my plans to seek familiarity and instead choose the stranger in front of me. It's impossible not to. He's leaning back on the bar as he faces the mass of bodies on the makeshift dance floor. With his elbows resting on the counter, he's giving off an "I'm gorgeous and I know it" vibe, but I can't fault him for that because he is.

He has dark brown, almost black eyes that match his equally dark brown buzz-cut hair. A style that I rarely go for, but with his short stylish beard, it's really—and I mean *really*— working for him. He's tall, even for me, and he's wearing a fitted black tee that shows off his arms, highlighting that he definitely frequents a gym. He's very easy on the eyes. But the most intriguing thing about him is that he's not on the football team. Trust me, I know them all. I order a beer and then mirror his stance, our elbows almost touching.

"Come here often?" I ease into conversation with the worst pickup line ever, hoping he'll know it's a joke. He turns to me with a smirk.

"I do, but I've never seen such beauty within these walls."

"Wow, just wow," I deadpan and shake my head before smiling.

"I know, and to think I came up with that on the spot." He winks and then offers his hand. "I'm Joel."

"Summer."

"What brings you here tonight, Summer? I may have been playing along with your corny pickup line, but I meant what I said, I've never seen you here before, *and* you're beautiful."

"Thank you; flattery will get you everywhere," I joke, "and I'm here to support a friend." I wave my beer in Cory's direction through the window as they walk toward the gardens.

"You're Cory's friend?" he asks.

"That's me." I smile. "Do you know Cory?"

"We haven't met, but Nate mentioned her when I saw him out front."

Great, he's connected to the football team. I can't escape it. *You're at the Ball House!* I remind myself.

"How do you two know each other? You're not on the team, right?" Yep, I dropped that into the conversation just to be sure.

"Nah, they thought I was too good and didn't want me to overshadow them, so, voted me out."

And he's funny. "Ah, that's a shame. Bunch of pussies...all of 'em," I deadpan.

Joel cracks up laughing. "A girl who doesn't worship the football team. I love it," he says and clinks my drink with his.

After talking for a few more minutes, we quickly fall into a comfortable banter, moving away from the bar to continue our chat. Joel's funny and easygoing, so the conversation flows effortlessly. We've been talking for almost an hour when I notice his gaze momentarily drifts back to the bar a few times.

"Should I be offended that you keep looking toward the bar?"

He lets out a small laugh before answering. "Definitely not. Like you, I'm keeping an eye on my friend. He keeps getting himself into awkward situations."

"What's going on there?" I ask, genuinely confused.

"Women keep throwing themselves at him, one after another." He rolls his eyes like this is a bad thing.

"How unfortunate for him." My voice drips with sarcasm. I try getting a glimpse of his friend, but someone's blocking my view. I can see the girl, though, and she's gorgeous. Joel's laughter brings my eyes back to his.

"I probably should have mentioned that he has a girlfriend."

"Then why?"

"It doesn't seem to matter to them; they still think they have a shot."

"That must get annoying," I say, not entirely convinced that his friend isn't actually loving the attention.

"I know." He rolls his eyes again, clearly over it.

We both watch on in fascination as one girl leaves and the next instantly approaches. When she's gone and another one moves in, I've *also* had enough. I feel for both him *and* his girlfriend.

"I'm going in," I say confidently but not really sure how this will play out.

Joel throws his head back in laughter, before turning toward me. The second he sees that I'm serious, he pauses and then gives me an appreciative grin. "Good luck and be warned. Girls can be vicious."

I scowl at him jokingly and then laugh. "You're not wrong. But this needs to stop. Plus, I need a new drink." I shrug and move in their direction.

The man's back is to me so I maneuver around him and put my hands on his chest, my back to the woman trying to claim him, like I don't even register her existence.

"Geez, what's taking so long?" I ask as my gaze travels from where my hands are positioned on rock-hard pecs, up along the tight-fitted shirt until I reach a strong, incredibly sexy jawline complete with a five o'clock shadow. Raising my eyes higher, I pass tempting lips that shine as though they've just had a tongue pass over them.

I want to linger there for a while but stop myself, instead moving up to a pair of piercing crystal-blue eyes. Eyes that are sparkling with amusement and intrigue. When our gaze connects, recognition hits us both in an instant, and I feel an undeniable warmth spread through me. *Dylan.* I hold back a wistful sigh. *This is a welcome surprise.*

I vaguely hear the woman bark from behind me, breaking the spell. "Excuse me, we were talking."

"Oh, I'm sorry, but Dylan's mine tonight, and he promised me he'd be straight back with my drink. I don't like to be kept waiting." I smile innocently and take the drink that's in Dylan's hand, glad that it's a beer I like. I'm in this now. All I have to do is pretend I'm his hookup for the night, and when all is well, I'll be on my way.

"You're not Gemma!" the woman accuses, and I almost spit out the sip I just took.

Is this girl for real? "You know he has a girlfriend and yet you're still throwing yourself at him?" This absolutely baffles me. I wanted to give her the benefit of the doubt and not believe what Joel said, but...I mean, what happened to girl code? I'm pretty sure we have one. *Don't we?*

"You can't talk," she snaps back.

Dylan's eyes bounce back and forth between the two of us, a small alluring smile on his face. *Hmm. If I can't be the girlfriend, I'll have to be the next best thing.*

"Actually, I *can* talk. Dylan and I are friends. *Best* friends, in fact. Have been since we were kids. And I adore Gemma." *What? Just saying we are friends would have sufficed. Or not. The bitch just stares at me. There is no way she's going to believe the rubbish I'm spilling. Did I even get his girlfriend's name right?*

Dylan grabs my waist with both hands and jabs, causing me to flinch from the tickling sensation. I'm about to slap him when he jumps on board with my role playing. "Summer's right. I promised my bestie here that she'd have me all to herself tonight. It's been too long. Nice chatting with you, though," he says, barely looking her way. Linking his fingers with mine, Dylan pulls me away from the bar, straight to Joel. We both burst into laughter as we reach him.

"Well, that didn't go how I thought it would," I tell Joel.

"It looked like she was going to slap you. Please fill me in?" A mischievous smile lights up his face.

Dylan looks between us in confusion, his hand running through his short brown hair, messing up his previously styled quiff, making it even sexier. "Do you two know each other?" he asks accusingly.

Do I detect jealousy? Interesting...

"As of tonight, we do. Been chatting with this lovely lady for the last hour. Are you going to tell me what happened, or can Summer and I get back to it?" A subtle exchange happens between the two men, like they're having a silent conversation. It's weird; I don't like it.

Joel raises an eyebrow, silently asking for a response. Dylan puts his arm around me and fills him in. I can't take my eyes away from his lips as he talks, the way he smirks when he mentions my hands on his chest, the way his tongue darts out to lick his bottom lip when he adds that he loved how possessive I acted, something I hadn't realized I'd done. I'm still staring when he finishes his story, and my eyes rise to see his already on me. Busted. Thankfully, Joel seems oblivious.

"I've also known Dyl since we were kids, so are we best friends too?" Joel asks, bringing my eyes back to his deep and amused ones. *Joel, focus on Joel.* That's where my attention should be.

Should be.

And yet, even now my traitorous gaze flits back to Dylan. "Of course, but Dylan was and will always be my main man," I joke but take a much-needed step in Joel's direction.

To my surprise, Dylan pulls me back into his chest, wraps his arms around my waist, and leans his chin on my shoulder, his eyes focused on Joel. "So many memories." He sighs with fake content, giving me an idea.

I pull away and look back at him. "Remember when we went rappelling—"

"And you took one look over the edge and chickened out. How could I forget?" Dylan cuts me off with a killer smile that I'm not prepared for, sending my pulse into overdrive.

Somehow, I manage to appear unfazed. "Okay, well remember when we used to play hide-and-seek in the dark, and you cried when we couldn't find you?" I ask with a serious expression.

Without missing a beat, he throws his hands in the air and exclaims, "We were five! Who plays outside in the dark at five?"

I can't help but laugh. "What about the time I helped you sneak out of detention—"

"By flashing the gym teacher?" Dylan interjects, comically bouncing his eyebrows.

"Pretty sure you're thinking of the movie 10 *Things I Hate About You* there, buddy. Let's try and focus on actual memories."

Dylan cracks up but then shakes it off and returns to character. "My mistake." He shrugs.

I smile as we joke back and forth, happy to have found these two guys to keep me entertained.

"You. Are. Hilarious," Joel deadpans after we've been at it for a while. "Please continue for my amusement."

"Do I hear sarcasm? It couldn't possibly be, because hilarious we are," I reply.

Laughing, I turn to Dylan, wrapping an arm around his waist and winking at Joel. "I believe it's your turn, Dyl," I say, using the nickname Joel used. *See, we're friends.*

He rubs his knuckles through my hair and then puts his arm around my shoulders again. "Hmmm, there was the time we went skinny-dipping..."

Here we go; of course, his male mind goes there.

"Dylan?" A soft voice comes from behind us, causing us to turn. Dylan's arm drops and he steps toward the beautiful girl that's joined us.

"Gemma, you came. I didn't think you wanted to." He smiles, and it's easy to see that he really likes her.

23

"Yeah, well, someone mentioned I should be here," Gemma says, looking at me in confusion.

Her short red hair falls in waves to her chin, and her unblemished porcelain skin makes me instantly jealous. She's a lot smaller than Dylan but looks like she'd fit perfectly in his arms. *Why am I thinking about that, when I should think about...shit, shit. This looks bad. She's going to think I was hitting on her man when I was actually trying to help.*

"Hi, I'm Summer...I'm...Joel's girlfriend," I say at the same time Dylan says, "Summer and I go way back."

I want to facepalm. *Really, Summer?* I wrap my arms around Joel's waist and feel him stiffen slightly. Looking up into his eyes, I find he's kept the shock off his face. *Impressive.* Dylan, on the other hand, looks a bit thrown by the direction I've taken things. *Wait, what did Dylan say? Ugh, what a mess.*

Chapter Three

Summer

"You're Joel's...Oh...I'm sorry." Gemma turns to Dylan, confusion masking her face. "I thought you said Joel was single."

"I did, didn't I? Well..."

Dylan flashes me a panicked look while Gemma looks between me and Joel. I raise an eyebrow, wondering if he's going to come clean, but then Joel says, "He's right; I was single for a few weeks when this one had a temporary lapse in sanity." Wrapping his arms around me, he pulls me close and adds, "But as you can see, she came crawling back, and we've never been better."

Great, now Joel's in on the lies. I've never felt the need to roll my eyes so badly in my life.

"Oh, lovely, that's good," Gemma stammers before turning to Dylan with questioning eyes. "You've never mentioned—"

"How about we go for a walk and catch up?" he says and reaches for Gemma's hands, pulling her toward the backyard.

Joel and I stand silently for a few minutes, a little awkwardly, until he finally speaks. "So, I have to ask...?" He looks over toward Gemma and Dylan, his unspoken question loud and clear. I sigh.

"I honestly have no idea what that was. I was trying to help your friend and his girlfriend. I mean, come on, girls, he's taken. Why don't they respect that? Sure, he's hot and...not the point. Anyway, I was trying to help, then it turned into a bit of fun to pass time, and now..." I sigh again.

"You think he's hot." Joel raises an eyebrow. "Should I be worried my gal's gonna stray?"

"That's what you took away from that?" I laugh. "Don't worry. You and I, we're end game." I nudge him playfully, and we both laugh. Joel's one of the good ones, and even if I hadn't been sidetracked by Dylan, I know I wouldn't have gone home with him, despite my early intentions. He deserves better than a night with a screwup like me.

Before I can put any more thought into that, Gemma and Dylan return. They look happy and relaxed.

"Best friends, huh?" Gemma questions.

What? Are we still doing this? Keeping my face impassive, I look at Dylan. He shoots me a look to say, "just go with it," then smiles. *Okay then.*

"We all know how this is going to end. We've read the books, seen the movies," Gemma continues, her tone playful. It's obvious she's not threatened anymore, and I don't know if that should offend me.

I laugh and hope that it doesn't come across as awkward because that is definitely how I feel. "Oh, don't worry, there's no chance of that happening. I was around during Dylan's mohawk stage. You can never unsee something like that."

Gemma laughs and looks up at Dylan affectionately, but his eyes are on mine.

"And I was there when a young Summer used to raise her dresses over her head in public," he adds, playfully punching my arm, "or maybe she still does that?"

I shove him away, and when my eyes find his, I see he's a little flustered. He just might be regretting the hole he's dug for himself. I'm sure I can fix this. "There's also the fact that we kissed in high school, and there was zero chemistry." Hoping to further ease her mind, I add, "It was like kissing my brother. No thanks."

Dylan wraps his arms around Gemma. "Zero chemistry," he repeats, and she smiles as they stare into each other's eyes.

I quickly snap my gaze away to avoid intruding on their moment. I wish I believed my own words, zero chemistry. From the second I grabbed his arm earlier, I felt this tingle race through my body. I've never felt anything like it. My body felt warm, yet uncomfortable at the same time. The feeling may have been unfamiliar to me, but I knew enough to understand how dangerous it was. Especially when I felt it again at the bar. Looking into his eyes was like staring into his soul.

Like those bright-blue windows held all the answers I'd ever need, even though I had no plans to ask questions.

The four of us move on to light, easy conversation but I grow anxious, and the dance floor is calling my name. It's my element. Grabbing Joel's hand, I lead him through the crowd, hopeful that Dylan and Gemma will get the hint and cash in on the alone time. No such luck. They don't; instead they follow.

The music flows as I sway to the beat, my back to Joel's solid chest, one arm wrapped around his neck. His arms hug my waist, fingers brushing my skin and pulling me into him, barely a millimeter separating us. I try to keep my focus on my dance partner, I mean "boyfriend," but I can't help but steal glances at Dylan and Gemma.

While Joel and I look like we're ready to rip each other's clothes off, Dylan and Gemma look like a couple getting to know each other, and perhaps they are. They're facing each other and swaying to the music, eyes locked, smiles in place, subtle touches here and there. When a slow song comes on, he pulls her closer to him, and I cringe for a second before pushing my thoughts into the back of my mind.

Joel pulls back from me when the slow music begins. "I'm heading to the bar; you all up for another round?" he yells, and surprisingly, we hear him. He's breathing heavily and looks a little disheveled. Maybe I'm being too flirty. *Oops.* Everyone gives him the thumbs-up for drinks, and he heads off.

"I'm going to go to the restroom," Gemma announces and follows Joel off the dance floor, leaving Dylan and me alone. Well, not exactly alone; it's so crowded in here that three girls bump into me before the others have even left the room.

"So, best friends, huh?" Dylan asks, repeating Gemma's earlier question while bumping his shoulder into mine. It's the first time we've been alone since I started this never-ending lie, and I'm not at all comfortable with it.

"Ugh, I'm sorry; that wasn't supposed to spiral like that." I cringe. "But in fairness, you could have stopped it with Gemma. That one's on you."

"I know." He holds his hands up in defense. "It seemed easier to just go with it, and then I wanted to tell her, but her friend came over, and I guess I didn't think it would become such a big deal. Plus, I'm sure we would have been awesome friends." He laughs but shakes his head at the craziness of it all.

"The best." I laugh too and step back. "I'm just going to..." I signal behind me with my thumb and turn to leave.

"Summer, wait." Dylan's fingers curl around my wrist, pulling me to a stop. When I turn back to meet him, he's closer than I thought he'd be. His intense stare bores into me, filled with uncertainty. "I'm sorry I didn't come clean. I'm sorry you have to lie. I didn't mean—"

"Oh, it's totally fine; no bother at all. It's just a night, right?" *And then we're strangers again.* I don't add the latter, but it hangs in the air.

"Right. Well, thank you...for going along with it."

"Anytime."

"Are they always that touchy-feely?" Gemma yells to Joel, causing me to flinch in surprise. Her words draw my attention to Dylan's hand still lightly around my wrist and his other hand on my upper arm. *When did that get there?*

"Ever since they became best friends," Joel replies.

I'd laugh if I wasn't terrified of what I was about to see on Gemma's face. The last thing I wanted was to cause problems for them. Relief sets in when I find her laughing. Joel looks between the two of us and smirks while I move to his side and snuggle in to him, needing the distance from Dylan.

"He knows it's all fun and games; don't you, babe?" I bat my eyelids.

"Of course, I know you love me." At that, he surprises me by lifting my chin gently with two fingers and placing a light kiss on my lips.

Interesting. I don't know him well enough to decide if he's playing along or if he genuinely wants to kiss me. I do, however, know that kissing him is a bad idea, yet I go with it anyway because bad choices are the story of my life. I lift to my toes and wrap my arms around his neck to deepen the kiss slightly before pulling away. *Hmm, I could happily continue that, but something is niggling at me to stop.*

"You are the cutest couple," Gemma coos, and a little part of me feels bad for lying to her. I'll have to fake break up with Joel soon. *Ooh, the possibilities... Do I catch him in bed with his ex, do I have a secret crush on my gym instructor, are we incompatible in bed... Nah, that won't work.* I'm lost in my thoughts when I notice three sets of eyes on me.

"Thanks, we get that all the time," I say, looking back at Joel with a small smile.

"It's nauseating," Dylan notes, rolling his eyes with a tone that is nowhere near jovial. It's time for me to split.

Ignoring the rest of the conversation happening around me, I look in Cory's direction and realize she hasn't needed me at all. We make eye contact, and she smiles, then with a quick wave, she signals that I'm free to go.

"I'm going to head off, babe, but you can stay. Walk me out?" I say to Joel, grabbing his hand. As fun as it's been, he's too good to be just another man I'll forget by morning. I'm hoping my words made that clear. Emotion, even of the friendly variety, is generally not something I allow in the bedroom.

"I'm done too; let's go," he says, and I freeze. *Guess it wasn't clear at all.* I really shouldn't have kissed him. Aside from not being good for him, on some level I know, deep down, that I'm also concerned about how Dylan would react. *God, how do I let him down after flirting with him all night? Good one, Summer.*

As if sensing my unease, Joel squeezes my hand and pulls me close, pressing a kiss to my hair before whispering, "It's just a cab, Summer. Nothing more." His words bring me instant calm as we turn back to Dylan and Gemma to say our goodbyes.

"Don't do anything I wouldn't do," I say, giving them each a kiss on the cheek and turning to leave.

Don't look back at Dylan. Don't look back at Dylan. I try, I really try, but at the last second, before walking through the door, I look back. His eyes meet mine, watching us. He has a furrowed brow and a confused look on his face. When he notices me looking, he shakes his head and looks back at Gemma before pulling her close and giving her a kiss on the temple.

I walk away, laughing to myself, and shake off the thoughts that shouldn't be lingering. *I'm glad that's over.*

I wake early the next morning to my phone alerts going crazy and a thumping in my head. Deciding to tackle the headache first, I venture into the kitchen for painkillers and water. Glancing at the time on my way back to bed, I freeze–5:30 a.m. What the actual...? I'm going to kill whoever's texting me at this ungodly hour on a Sunday.

Unknown: Yo! How are you on this bright and sunny morning?

Unknown: Shit! It's still dark.

Unknown: Bestie you there?

Bestie? Dylan? Did I give him my number? And is he drunk? I save his contact in my phone as another text comes through.

Dylan: You and Joel huh?

Huh? Why is he still texting? And what?

Dylan: Fuck it's early.

A laugh escapes me at that. Yep, he's definitely drunk. For some stupid reason, I reply.

Me: No kidding; you woke me up. Are you still out drinking?

His reply comes through immediately, followed by the three little dots, saying there's more to come.

Dylan: Yes

Party animal, huh? He's typing some more, so I just stare down at the phone. Too tired to do anything else. *What could he possibly be writing for this long?*

Dylan: Wait, no I'm home... Saw the sock. Wink Wink.

I laugh out loud and roll my eyes, even though he can't see me. God, I'm tired. And yes, he actually wrote the words wink wink. I have no idea what he's talking about.

Me: Okay...

Dylan: Do you want sweet or savory for breakfast?

What the hell? I don't even know what to say to that. It's too early for this shit.

Me: I'm going back to bed.

I wait a few minutes for a reply, but nothing comes through, so I roll over. I'm finally drifting off when my phone dings again.
"Oh, come on!" I yell into my pillow.

Dylan: Good idea. Don't want to wake Joely boy.

Joely boy? Oh, sock on the door... He thinks I'm there. Wow! Joel hooked up after dropping me home. Good for him. Guess I was wrong about him. Maybe he is a casual hookup type of guy.

Me: I'm at home, Dylan.

Dylan: Already calling it home I see.

Dylan: ...

Me: Joel must be with someone else.

The three dots appear and disappear for a minute before Dylan responds. *God, please tell me he didn't check.*

Dylan: Okay.

I huff out a laugh at the short response, and shake my head. It's time to end this.

Me: Good night, Dylan.

Switching my phone to silent, I shove it under my pillow and bury my face. No more drunk conversations, even when I'm sober. When I wake again at 10 a.m., a much more respectable hour, I see his reply.

Dylan: Sweet dreams.

Without my consent, a small smile graces my lips, and a flutter occurs in my chest. Don't worry, though; I shut that shit down straight away. *Nope. No. Uh-uh. Not happening. He's a good guy, Sum, too good for you. And taken. Moving on.*

The apartment is silent when I finally force myself to get out of bed. I heard Cory come in about an hour after me. Alone. But I expected that. She's not one to sleep with a guy unless she really trusts him, and one night's not enough to know that.

Considering she's not normally such a night owl, I wonder if she's sleeping or if she still got up bright and early to start her day.

Cory and I share a decent-sized apartment, compared to some student accommodations. It boasts a full-size kitchen, separate living area, and two bedrooms each with their own en suite. It's rare to find something this big on our budget, so we were beyond excited when we secured this lease. The excitement was short-lived. Sure, the apartment itself is great. It's a converted warehouse with oak floorboards, modern appliances, plush carpets in the bedrooms, and a red brick feature wall. But what we didn't know was that the entire building next door was about to be renovated and would take years to complete. The noise alone is enough to annoy anyone in our building, but we have the bonus of a lovely view of the construction from every window. You win some, you lose some.

I drag myself to the kitchen in search of breakfast. When I've finished pouring my cereal and contemplating how to cope with no coffee, I hear the keys jingle in the lock. *Guess that answers my question.*

"Good morning," Cory practically sings as she opens the front door and enters the kitchen, coffees in hand. "Or is it already afternoon? I don't know. Anyway, here is your coffee."

"God, I need that." I greedily take the cup she holds out. "Thank you, angel woman."

"You are welcome." Cory smiles and waits patiently for me to take my first sip, knowing she'll get more conversation from me once I'm caffeinated.

"Ah, that's the stuff." I exhale. "Now, I need all the details."

"Oh Sum, he's perfect. Charming, attentive, fun. And his eyes! Summer, have you seen them?"

"I have looked at him. Yes."

"God, they are the most amazing hazel color and..." She sighs.

She's right. He has nice eyes. That's not a lie, but I haven't really thought about them much. Instead, icy-blue ones flash through my mind. *Dammit.*

"I had the best night, and he wants to take me on a date," Cory continues to gush.

"Ahh! I'm so excited for you. Where is he taking you?"

"It's a surprise."

"Very romantic." *Or he has nothing planned.* God, I'm cynical.

"I know." She smiles giddily.

"If he was so perfect, tell me—did he bring you home?"

"Yes, Mom." She rolls her eyes but smiles. "He even walked me to the door and kissed me good night."

"Swoon," I say and flutter my eyelashes.

"Shut up. It *was* swoon worthy," she counters, clearly thinking I'm being sarcastic.

Maybe a small part of me is, but I've never had the feeling Cory has right now. That new romance, will-he-won't-he, what's going to happen, giddy feeling. I've known exactly what to expect from every guy I've been with. No questions, no exciting buildup, and definitely no feelings. In, out, and done. *Ew, that wasn't meant to sound so literal.*

But it's the truth. So, while I don't get it, I am extremely happy for my friend, the beautiful soul standing before me.

"I can't wait to get to know him," I say.

"I can't wait for that too. We spoke about you."

What?

"And Thomas."

Shit.

"It seems they're all pretty close to your brother. They think he's a pretty good guy. And they know who you are. I'm sorry, Sum."

I guess I shouldn't be surprised at this information. Come to think about it, I don't remember actually telling Dylan my name, and yet he knew it. Thomas probably had a "do not touch this girl" poster in the house somewhere. With my eyes focused on my coffee cup, it takes me a second to realize Cory's are glassy.

"Oh, Cory. He's allowed to be a good guy," I say, truly meaning that. I actually never thought otherwise. My brother was one of the best people I knew when we were growing up. I'd always looked up to him. He'd been good to me. Until he wasn't...

"Then why is he such an ass to you? I had to bite my tongue so many times."

"Don't. You don't need to defend me. It's all in the past. He's no longer here, so let's just pretend he never was."

Cory offers a half-assed smile and changes the subject, knowing I'm done with this conversation.

"Are you up for a greasy breakfast, instead of that crap?" She points to my pathetic bowl of extremely unhealthy cereal.

"Absolutely; let's go."

When the night rolls around and the dreaded first day of the semester nerves kick in, I suddenly regret signing up for summer classes. I'm in my sophomore year, and I'd love to say it was because I had grand plans to graduate early or because I was interested in extra learning, but the truth is, I couldn't bear to stay home, and I didn't want to get a job in town. Doing that increased the chances of running into my family.

I know it's strange that a girl who wants nothing to do with her family stays in her hometown and attends the same college as her brother, but I had a good reason. From the moment we met, Cory and I had plans to attend college together. We applied to NYU and Columbia with the dream of moving to New York. When we were both accepted to NYU, we celebrated for days, high on excitement. Nothing could bring us down. Until something did. It brought us so far down, we almost didn't get back up.

Cory's mom was diagnosed with breast cancer. Stage three. She needed a lot of treatment and care, and Cory stayed home to be with her. Actually, that's not right. We both stayed home to be with her. When I'd moved out of my parents' house at sixteen, I'd moved straight into Cory's. I loved her mom. I *love* her mom. Her diagnosis devastated me. No matter how uncomfortable staying in this town made me, I wanted to be here for them. Now, as we head into our second year of college, Cory's mom is thankfully on the mend. Treatments are working and she's currently in remission. We could have moved to New York this year, but neither of us wanted to. We'd settled in, had a comfortable apartment, and now, it looks like Cory may have a new boyfriend. Things were good—as long as I avoided run-ins with other members of the Kelly family. So, that's why I'm here, getting ready for my summer classes. Bring it on.

Chapter Four

Dylan

I spent Sunday in a hangover haze, and come Monday, I'm still recovering from the weekend when my alarm goes off. I fight the tiredness and haul my ass out of bed at some ridiculous hour to go for a run.

Today, it all starts again. More classes, more homework, more training. So much less time. I get why Coach expects us to take classes over summer. Doesn't mean I enjoy it. Having said that, it's nice to have a quieter campus, and if I'm here anyway for training, I may as well get ahead. The hardest thing about it is that Gemma isn't taking any classes and is already complaining about how little time we'll have for each other. I completely understand why she's upset, and I feel the same, but there's nothing I can do about it, so it's a pointless argument.

As soon as my feet hit the pavement and the fresh air hits my lungs, I feel somewhat normal again. Some might think it's crazy to run on days I have training, but I need it to clear my mind and get my head back in the game. As I hit the three-mile mark on my extended route, I can't help but frown. I hadn't even realized I'd come this way. It's been a while since I've run in this direction. It's a beautiful area and a very popular run route, with tall tree-lined streets that lead toward a river trail with mountain views in the distance. But for me, the reminders of *him* cause the views to fade away.

We traveled along these exact roads, took in the same unchanging sights every weekend that he was home. Mostly, it's getting easier to think about the good memories, but there are also times when it still feels raw, no matter how much time has passed.

I'm constantly reminded of how lucky I am to have grown up here in Heartwood Falls, California, in such a picturesque and welcoming town with great schools, a college—Heartwood University—and access to different sporting clubs, theaters, and shops. I know it's true. But sometimes I wonder if I should have left or if I should consider leaving straight after college. As much as I love it here, it's hard to live up to the legend that was my father—Dean Mathers.

In my younger years, I was a quarterback and loved it. But after...when I changed to wide receiver, I'd made it clear that it was the position I wanted, even though deep down that was a lie. Don't get me wrong, I'm a pretty decent WR. My speed is one of my strongest qualities, and I love what I do, but I would have also loved to have been a quarterback like Dad.

I just couldn't live in his shadow. I didn't want to be compared to him. And make no mistake, that's exactly what would have happened because they do it now, even though I'm not the quarterback. It would be ten times worse if I were. So, I made the change after he died and never looked back. Everyone believes I'm happy, and I am, mostly.

I pass by parents with strollers on their morning walk, looking like they've been up for hours, PJ-wearing kids and adults as they take their dogs out for a quick bathroom break, while others rush to their cars, some with breakfast in hand to begin their morning commute to work. Every one of them waves or acknowledges my existence. By the time I knock out seven miles in my tired state, I'm wrecked.

As soon as I walk in the door, the smell of fresh coffee permeates the air, but I bypass the kitchen and instead head toward the living room and flop down on the couch next to Joel. *Much better.* He has a textbook open in front of him and his headphones in. I can clearly hear the music he's blasting, so I don't know how he can study, or why he's studying for that matter considering today's the first day, but the concentration on his face and the rapid note writing would suggest that he is.

Joel's smart—insanely smart—so he probably doesn't even need to study, although I guess some might argue that he's smart *because* he studies so much. Either way, it's not my concern. In my worn-out state, I stare at his pen drifting across the page. The way it moves and the slight scratching sound it makes almost feels therapeutic. When Joel looks up from his page and notices me staring, he pulls the earpiece from his ear.

"How is it we live together and yet I didn't see you at all yesterday?" he asks, ignoring my blank expression.

"Probably because you slept all day."

"That's almost true. I slept sixty percent of the day away." He pauses, then adds, "You were home much later than I was. How did you recover?"

"Slept for ninety percent of the day." I snort, still not quite believing my antics.

"Nice one." Joel laughs because he also knows it's not like me. I am not the guy that gets blind drunk. I'm also not sure I *recovered* at all yesterday; it was a total blur. Leaning my head on the backrest of the couch, I close my eyes. If only I could sleep today away too.

"Did Gemma come over?" he questions, and I hate that I have to say *no* again. "I still can't believe she showed up at the party," he adds, and I open my eyes without lifting my head.

Do we really have to go there? I ask with my look. On top of never coming out with me, Saturday night being the exception, Gemma also never spends the night at my place. Says she doesn't like the thought of someone else being there, and since she rooms alone on campus, it makes sense to stay at her place. I guess she's right, but I love living and sleeping here. Our place isn't much, but it's ours.

We have everything we need—a big, comfortable, grey couch, a huge-ass TV, a fridge big enough for food *and* beer, and two bedrooms. I'd given the en suite to Joel to secure the room with direct access to the back porch. Despite my previous complaints about waking up early, I'm actually a morning person and love a quick stretch and fresh air the moment I wake up.

My room itself is also slightly bigger than Joel's, so that's a bonus, and I have the main bathroom to myself, unless we have visitors, which is rare. What more could we want? Oh, I know! A decent-sized bed, something I *have* that Gemma does not. But alas, we spend nights together at her place because, and I quote, "I'm not a sock on the door kind of girl." And I wouldn't want her to be... *Wait. Sock on the door?* Why does that ring a bell?

I can feel Joel's eyes on me, but I'm lost in my thoughts. When I don't respond out loud, he moves back to his studying. I sit silently for a bit longer until I suddenly remember. *Shit! I texted Summer.* I'd completely forgotten. I remember asking Nate to get me Summer's number but had blanked on the rest. I'll need to go back through my messages later. Anyway, the sock is a running joke we have because it's actually pointless. We'd never barge into each other's rooms. It's more of a heads-up that we'll have company in the morning.

I wave my hand at Joel to get his attention. "Who was the lucky lady on Saturday night? Did you head out again after you took Summer home?"

"Huh?" He looks up from his notes, confused for a second and maybe even a little annoyed, then his eyes light up and he laughs to himself.

"What?" I'm obviously not in on the joke.

"You're talking about the sock, right?"

I nod.

He sits back on the couch with an amused expression and links his fingers behind his head. "How do you know it wasn't Summer?" he asks, smirking.

I answer before thinking, "I asked her."

Joel laughs again and shakes his head.

"What?" I repeat, annoyed that he's not filling me in on whatever he thinks is so funny.

"I must have done that in my drunkenness. I was alone. I noticed the sock when I got up in the morning."

I narrow my eyes. His story reeks of lies. He hadn't looked that drunk when he left.

"Speaking of Summer..." He hesitates, but smiles. I hold my breath, knowing this is the moment he tells me he wants to ask her out.

"What about her?" I huff, frustrated that it bothers me.

"You were very flirty. Or touchy-feely, as Gemma put it."

What? "I'm always flirty." I'm lying, but Joel doesn't call me out.

"Okay, let me reword it. You couldn't take your eyes off her, at least until Gemma arrived. Then it was just the occasional glance."

"What? That's not true." *Shit, is that true?* Picking up Joel's pen, I roll it between my fingers to avoid looking back at him. God, I hope he's wrong. But what if he's not?

"Don't worry, I'm sure I'm the only one who noticed."

"Or maybe it didn't happen," I mutter under my breath.

"If you say so."

I frown and internally groan. He's wrong. He has to be. Have I thought about her since Saturday night? Yes, I thought about her as a friend. *Just a friend.* I mean, I've never had to think about someone being a friend before. They either are or they aren't, but something about Summer makes it hard to just move on as though she's just some random girl I chatted with at a party. Maybe I couldn't take my eyes off her because I wanted to be friends? I'm with Gemma. I enjoy staring at Gemma... *God, what's she going to say? Did she notice?*

"Where did you go just now?" Joel smirks, and I punch him in the arm.

I'm about to respond, probably with another lie, when my phone rings, saving the day. *Gemma.* I jump up, thankful to have an out of this conversation.

"It's Gemma; I'm gonna take this in my room." I gesture toward the hallway.

"You do that," Joel says, waggling his eyebrows and then rolling his eyes. I laugh before throwing the pen back at his head.

When I reach my room, I shut the door and answer the call. "Hey, babe."

We've been talking for about ten minutes when Gemma finally broaches the subject I've been waiting for. I lie back on my pillow, cross my ankles together, and take a deep breath, my eyes closing as I release it.

"Why didn't you tell me about Summer?"

Here's my chance to come clean. Tell her it was all just a joke. That Summer was actually defending her honor. We can laugh about it and move on. Never to speak of it again.

"I was worried about how you'd react to me having a female best friend. It's been an issue in the past. Gotta say I'm relieved that you were so good about it when you met her."

What the fuck, Dylan? Where did that come from?

"I think she's great and obviously in love with Joel, so why would I worry?" Gemma pauses and then adds, "Should I be worried?"

I can hear her trying to hide the panic in her voice. *Why am I putting her through this when it's not really an issue?*

"Of course not; like you said, she's in love with Joel."

She's silent for too long, and I realize my mistake. *Shit, wrong answer. Try again.*

"But more importantly, I don't look at her that way." *But, according to Joel...nope, I don't.* "She's like a sister." *She's definitely NOT like a sister.*

Gemma breathes a sigh of relief as I inwardly curse myself. I have issues. I had an easy opening to correct a simple lapse in judgment, and instead, I dug a massive hole. *Good one, Dylan.* I'm being stupid. I have a great girl who likes me, who I like. I shouldn't, *couldn't*, screw it up because someone else suddenly piqued my interest. It was a fun night, but that's it.

Gemma moves our discussion to other topics, helping me to remember how easy it is between us. When we eventually make plans to see each other the following day, I know that forgetting Summer is the best and *only* option for me.

Chapter Five

Dylan

T raining is brutal over the next few weeks, and with studying on top of it, I'm a walking zombie. For some stupid reason, I decided to load myself up with subjects this summer term, and boy am I feeling it now. I want to enjoy some free time and sunshine, and that's not happening enough at the moment.

My frustration carries over, unfortunately, and I'm slow in the locker room today, making me the last one on the field. In my rush to catch up, I don't notice the familiar face in the crowd until I'm hot, sweaty, and ready to pass out.

"You missed an easy catch out there," Lucy yells from the stands. "You suck, Mathers."

I laugh, jumping the fence to meet my sister and engulf her in the biggest, sweatiest hug I can. "Ew, gross. Get off me," she shrieks and pushes me away, running her fingers through the long, thick, dark-brown hair that she got from our mom. It's the only thing that differentiates us; our eyes and skin tone are the same.

"Luce, we've missed you," Luke yells up from the grass. "Please tell me you've dumped that grumpy bastard, and you're single?"

"Never going to happen for you, Luke!" I yell back, not waiting for Lucy to respond. In truth, though, Luke is actually a much better option than her boyfriend, and that's saying a lot. And he isn't wrong; her man is grumpy. If I ever find out he's even so much as raised his voice to Lucy I'll...I don't know, I'm not a fighter. But I'll do something. No one messes with my big sis.

"Listen to Dylan, Luke. Even if I was single, I'm too good for you," Lucy jokes. She's actually telling the truth, but it's all in good fun. And if we were to sit and assess all of Lucy's past boyfriends, I'd say that "not good enough" is exactly her type.

Lucy waits for me as I change, and then we head out for brunch before I have to get back for my afternoon class.

We're sitting in a candy-striped booth at our favorite diner. I don't even bother picking up a menu, already knowing what I'll order. Pancakes and bacon, an after-training treat. I normally don't eat anything that unhealthy, but the smell of bacon wafting from the kitchen is too good to resist.

"What brings you to campus?" I ask, not that I'm unhappy to see her, but she usually lets me know before she visits.

"Can't a gal just visit her little bro because she misses him?"

"Sure, a gal can do that, but you don't," I call her on her bullshit.

"You got me there. I'm too busy for that shit."

"That shit being to visit because you miss me?" I deadpan, making sure she knows I'm joking. She's not lying about being busy. I shouldn't be giving her a rough time, but what can I say—I'm her brother; it's what I do.

"Exactly," she says, making me laugh. "But the real reason I'm here is because we need to plan Mom's birthday. She's the big five-oh this year." She smiles apologetically when I cringe at her words, and my smile drops from my face.

I love my mom. I do. We've just had less of a relationship since Dad died. I completely understand why; I look exactly like him, I play football, and I'm a part of the reason he died, so...I'd hate me too. In fact, we have that in common. But Luce tells me that her relationship with Mom isn't all sunshine and roses either, so maybe I'm wrong. Whatever the case may be, I am not looking forward to planning her party.

The waitress arrives then, interrupting my internal whine, and once we've ordered, Lucy fills me in on all of my duties for the party, which thankfully isn't much.

"How's Nicole?" she suddenly asks, shifting the conversation, and I almost spit out the drink I'd just sipped.

What the fuck? I stare at her in horror until she bursts out laughing at my expression.

"I'm kidding. Come on, you're too easy to tease. How's Gemma?" she asks, her focus on me as she rests her elbow on the table, her chin poised on the palm of her hand. Lucy is the picture of casual as she dives into my personal life like it's nothing.

God, I wish we were still kids so I could give her a noogie or wet willy or something.

"First, ouch! Nicole cheated on me, so that's still raw." I pretend I'm hurt and offended. "And second, Gemma's great. You'll love her. She's great, really great, and she's good company."

Lucy opens her mouth slightly and her eyebrows pull together, the expression telling me to brace myself for what she's about to say.

"It's just"—she pauses—"good to hear that she's *great.*"

Wow! "That's not what you were going to say," I accuse.

"Sure it is." She shrugs, obviously forgetting for a moment that I'm her brother, and I know her. "Do you love her?" she asks, catching me off guard.

"Ah, not yet," I answer, then hesitate, "but it's still fairly new."

"Are you falling in love?"

"Jesus. What's with the Spanish Inquisition?"

Gripping the back of my neck, I'm genuinely perplexed as to where she's taking this conversation. My sister is nosy—always has been—but she's not usually this direct. Her style is to drop subtle leading questions until I eventually spill everything. What's going on with her today?

"I'm just worried that you're going for the wrong people."

"Pot meet Kettle." I can't help but add my own jab. She kicks my shin under the table, and damn, it hurts. I bite my knuckle to distract from the pain and shoot a glare her way.

"Shut up," Lucy snaps. "This isn't about me. Just promise me that if you don't see a future with someone, you'll break free. Don't stay in a relationship if you're not *one hundred* percent sure, because you'll risk missing something amazing that passes you by."

My face scrunches in confusion. *Is she talking about me? Or is it actually about her, only she doesn't realize it?*

Maybe she needs someone to give her the same advice. That someone being anyone but me. There is no way she's taking dating advice from her little brother. Lucy looks at me questioningly. She actually wants an answer. This entire conversation has been very un-Lucy-like.

"I promise," I say, though I'm not sure it's true.

Gemma calls on my drive home. "Is Summer okay?" she asks before I've even said hello. *Ah, what?* The question is so out of the blue that I tap the brake, causing my body to jolt in response and the car behind me to screech to a halt, horn blaring. *Okay, maybe it was more than a tap.*

A little flustered, I wave out the window before I respond. "What do you mean?" I say into the phone, hesitantly. Until now, I've been doing really well at keeping my mind off Summer. I'm not going to say I've been able to stop thinking about her completely because that would be a lie. But I have at least reduced my, *always platonic* thoughts to a respectable number and never around my girlfriend. *Until now.*

"Well, I just saw Joel kissing someone on your doorstep when I stopped by. Someone who was not Summer. And calling it kissing is putting it lightly. What happened?"

Goddammit. I should have seen this coming. I should have prepared for this. Joel's been a bit of a... How do I put this without offending anyone? I can't; he's been a man whore. It's a fairly new thing for him, ever since Delilah.

In hindsight, I really should have been honest with Gemma about Summer from the start. *Or even now? Yeah, great advice.* Instead, I blurt. "She cheated on him." What? The already large hole of my lies is fast becoming a crater. "I'm kidding. Summer wouldn't do that." I quickly backtrack. *Again, what?* "They realized they wanted different things." *That's better.*

"Who broke up with who?" Gemma questions, sounding suspicious.

"It was mutual."

"It's never mutual," she supplies with attitude, and I hate that we are having this conversation, but I'm in too deep. Why stop now?

"Well, they said it was, so maybe they didn't want me to pick sides. That's all the information I know," I counter, praying we can move on. Nope.

"Okay…" Gemma says slowly. "So, back to my original question. How's Summer? And Joel, I guess. Although, he looks fine," she adds a little bitterly.

"We all grieve differently," I defend, not wanting her to judge my best friend for something he didn't actually do. "They're both as good as they can be, considering."

It's a few minutes and several questions later before the conversation is finally over, and I'm exhausted from the lies. I haven't even seen Summer since that night. Surely this has to be the end of the mess.

Arriving home, I'm just about to end the call when I remember something. "Did you get that weekend off work?" I ask, crossing my fingers and clenching my teeth in anticipation.

"I did, and I'm really looking forward to spending extra time together. Although I'd prefer if the accommodation was a higher star." She laughs, but it's obvious she's not joking. She's definitely a bit off from our earlier conversation.

"Next time, I promise we'll go to a hotel," I say, trying not to sound disappointed.

"I'll hold you to that. I better go, I'm about to get in the elevator."

"Okay, bye, Gem."

It's a pity she'd prefer a hotel, because I definitely prefer our current plans.

I'm inside my room by the time I hang up the phone, and I drop my bags in the corner in slight frustration because until a few minutes ago, I'd say things were going well with Gemma and me, and I'd rather things not start going off the rails with the whole Summer mess. Usually, the only thing Gemma and I struggle with is conflicting schedules. If I'm not attending classes, studying, or training, she's working, and when we finally catch a break, something always comes up. We're definitely not as close as I thought we'd be by now, but we're trying.

I'm still reflecting over our upcoming trip when Joel peers through the open door. "How's Gem? She seemed a little flustered when I saw her earlier. You two good?" he asks, breaking into my thoughts as he wanders in and sinks into my swivel chair, putting his feet up on the desk.

I scoff, ignoring his question, and say, "So, you broke up with Summer?"

He looks momentarily confused until it hits him, and he laughs. "Well, shit."

I can't help but laugh too, even though the situation is anything but funny.

Joel grins. "I'm guessing you had to come clean about the whole thing?"

"You would think so, wouldn't you?"

"You're not serious? You haven't spoken to Summer in weeks. It would have been a simple conversation."

"I know. I know! But she'll be mad that I lied."

"And continuing to lie is better in the long run?"

"No. Maybe? I don't know." I run my hand down my face as I contemplate my next words. "In all honesty, I assumed it would all be over. We'd never see Summer, and it would all go away." I wish I was lying because it actually makes me look really stupid, but I genuinely believed the issue had gone from our lives. *But not your mind... Oh, shut up, brain.*

"Something tells me that's never going to happen." Joel laughs. "Good luck with it," he adds as he disappears out of my room.

"Yeah, thanks. You truly are the best friend," I say sarcastically before lying back on my bed to contemplate the mess I've made.

"Isn't that Summer's title?" Joel yells with another quip from the hallway, and I don't know whether to laugh or punch myself in the nuts.

"I can feel the jealousy from here!" I yell back, hearing Joel's laughter fade as he walks away. *Could this get any worse?* Hmmm, it's best I don't answer that.

Chapter Six

Summer

I stroll across campus in no mood to start this day. The sun is beaming down on me, warming my exposed skin, but there's a cool breeze to counter it, making it optimal beach road trip weather. Unfortunately, it's a Friday, so I have class. *Ugh.* You'd think I'd be used to it after four weeks of summer classes, but I've gotta say, I'm not loving it.

When I walk into the auditorium a couple of minutes late, I notice Joel sitting in the second to last row and freeze, doing a double take. *Was he always in this class?* I guess I don't normally notice anyone in class, opting to focus on my studies, but I can't exactly ignore Joel now I know he's here. And it's not like I want to anyway.

Heading over to his row, I drop into the seat next to him. "Don't take this the wrong way, but how have I never noticed you here before?"

His eyes meet mine in surprise before a smile lights his face, and he opens his arms for a hug. "Honey, I've missed you," he jokes. "And to be honest, I haven't noticed you either. This is the only summer class I'm taking. I usually arrive late and... Having said that, I'm going to take your question as a compliment. Obviously, you're saying that I'm worth noticing and that you're surprised you haven't noticed me." He laughs.

"Obviously." I laugh in return. "That's why we're together. And speaking of being together..." I start to question, curious about his late-night hookup.

"Yes?" he hedges.

I roll my eyes and continue. "A little birdie told me that you may have cheated on me after the Ball House party?"

Joel's eyes shoot to mine, and he grins, "Which time?"

I bark out a laugh and then school my expression. "How many times have you cheated, Joel?" I ask sternly.

He sucks his lips into his mouth, trying to unsuccessfully hide a smirk. "About that..."

"I'm listening." I turn and give him my full attention, my face alight with curiosity.

"We broke up." Joel states matter-of-factly, delivering the heartbreaking news.

I squint in confusion. "We did?"

"Yep, sorry to break that to you." He sighs and pats my shoulder in pretend comfort.

"You win some, you lose some." I shrug while Joel snickers, causing me to bite back my own laugh, remembering we are in class.

"Now that we have *that* awkward conversation out of the way," he says, "I'm curious. What exactly did the little bird tell you and when, and also, have you spoken since? Because the bird *claims* he hasn't spoken to you."

I bite my lip and grimace. "Ah..." *Am I about to throw Dylan under a bus?*

Joel raises his eyebrows, a teasing glint in his eye.

Sorry, Dylan, hope the bus doesn't hurt. "He saw the sock and assumed I was the one there with you."

Joel laughs and waves his hand for me to continue.

Scrunching my nose, I add, "He texted around five that morning. But we haven't spoken since."

A huge smile spreads across his face, and he cracks up laughing, shaking his head and interrupting the lecture. "Sorry," he tells the professor and then faces forward, pen in hand, ready to listen. *Conversation over?*

"Messaging a girl he thinks I'm sleeping with. Tsk, Dylan," Joel mumbles to himself. At least, I think it's to himself because he's still facing the front of the room.

"Do you get a break today, Summer?" he asks, a little louder but still acting the part of attentive learner.

"I sure do. Straight after this," I say.

He smirks. "Perfect, want to have lunch with me?"

Campus Coffee is bustling due to the lunch hour, but after weaving through tables, Joel and I secure the last booth. My phone dings with a text as we sit down.

Cory: Please tell me you're free to come out Saturday night. I miss you.

I cringe and put the phone away. I've been a horrible friend and need to rectify that, but not right now. When I look up from my bag, Joel's smiling at a girl sitting at the table beside us. When he feels my eyes on him, he looks my way. "So, Summer, any big plans for your Friday night?"

"Ugh, yes." I sigh.

Joel laughs. "Must be some exciting plans."

I roll my eyes and grin. "I've got drinks with a study group. Maybe it will be fun."

"I'm sure you can create your own fun. I mean, I barely know you, but you come across as a fun gal." He shrugs, and I smile in thanks. He's right, at least about our knowledge of each other. But I plan to change that; I have questions.

Leaning forward across the table, I cup my hand around my mouth, as though my next words are a secret. Joel leans forward, poised to listen intently. "Don't let this swell your head too much, but how are you single?" I ask.

He laughs out loud, the force of it propelling him into the backrest of the booth. "Because I enjoy playing the field," he says with a shrug. *Hmmm.*

"I don't doubt that; I'm sure you find playing the field *quite* enjoyable, but I'm not buying it." I raise an eyebrow in challenge, and Joel furrows his own eyebrows in response.

"Are you sure we haven't known each other since childhood?" he asks, and it's my turn to laugh.

I stare him down. "Who is she? Come on; spill."

He runs his hand through his short beard. "This is not where I thought our conversation would go. I'd much rather discuss Dylan." Leaning back, he crosses his arms over his chest protectively before he smirks.

"Dylan? Ah, so he's the reason you're single," I joke, trying to suppress my sassy grin.

"Well, he is 'hot,' in your own words, but not my type." He shrugs. "I was—"

I know what he means, so I cut him off. "Right, because your type is…" I pause, but don't expect him to answer considering he hasn't moved from his protective posture.

Joel sighs. "Her name is Delilah."

I knew it! I mentally pump my fist, but now is definitely not the time to gloat. They are obviously not together considering Joel's player status, but from his current pose and the tone of his voice, I'd say it's not a happy story and not something he's in the mood to share. Smiling, I offer him an escape. "So speaking of Dylan…"

He laughs and relaxes, immediately jumping into a story about Dylan from his childhood. There is so much love in his voice it's not hard to see they really are the best of friends. When the time comes to part ways, we agree to make this a regular catch-up and say our goodbyes.

Could this be the start of a new friendship? I think it might be.

I smile at the thought until another face pops into my mind, bringing forth a frown. And as I head off to my next class, I try not to think of that face—the face of the boy we spent the past hour discussing, the boy with the penetrating blue eyes and the playful, sexy smile.

The cab comes to a stop in front of my building later that night, pulling me from my micro sleep. I pick up my shoes and pay the driver before making my way inside. The sight of Nate in the kitchen startles me, but I recover before he notices. He's been like a third housemate lately, but this is the first time he's stayed over. Looking at the time, I see it's four thirty-six a.m. I sigh. *Why do I do this to myself?*

"Why are you up so late? Or early?" I ask accusingly, as though having Nate in my kitchen is a regular occurrence.

"Early," he laughs. "I've got training this morning and have to eat before I train."

"What time do you train?" I scoff. I would have thought the punishment wouldn't start until at least six, but I could be wrong. *Wait?* "Isn't today Saturday?" My brows crease in confusion.

He laughs. "It is. I'm meeting some of the guys at the field for a run at six," he says.

"Committed. But again, why are you up so early?" I drag out the word "early" for emphasis. We live pretty close to the field, so I really can't fathom why he'd be up and dressed voluntarily. He can walk there in fifteen minutes, and he has a car.

Nate rubs his shoulder nervously and then runs a hand quickly through his mousy brown hair. "Cory wants to"—he pauses in thought—"uh...cuddle? For a bit before I leave."

My jaw drops in pretend shock to give him a hard time about sharing her secrets.

Nate's eyes flick toward Cory's door. "Um, sorry, ah..."

"I'm kidding. You kids have fun." I wink, moving toward my room. It's sweet that he's up extra early to please her.

"Why are you up so late?" Nate calls behind me.

That's a good question. I *was* only supposed to be going out with that study group for celebratory drinks after our intense test. That led to dancing, which led to me in Jake's bed. Or was it Jack? *Not relevant.* Instead of sharing all that information, I simplify it for Nate. "Because I'm an idiot."

Nate's eyebrows furrow in question, but he laughs instead of prying for information.

"And, luckily, as you confirmed, today is Saturday," I add.

"Speaking of Saturday..." Nate starts.

Oh crap, I forgot to get back to Cory on that. "I'm sorry, I can't."

A spark of fight flashes across his eyes. I'm ready for him to lay into me, but he doesn't. "Ah, okay. Sure. I'll break the news to Cory, I guess," he says, his voice somewhat subdued.

Ugh, I'd prefer anger. "I know. I'm sorry." I sigh.

His features soften, and he offers a small smile. "She just wants to spend time with you. She misses you, which I know is my fault."

"No, it's not. At all. I've been busy." *And maybe avoiding them a little. Third wheels are not my thing.*

Nate straightens up, his usual casual demeanor back in place. "Plus, I kind of want to get to know the girl that Cory can't stop talking about. Even her mom raves about you," he says with a genuine smile.

"You've met Alison and Rob?" I say excitedly, until the meaning of that hits me. *Shit.* That's kind of a big deal and something I should know. I really need to spend time with Cory.

"Don't worry, it was only a few nights ago," Nate says, as if sensing my worry.

"I'm so happy you've met them, and I'm sorry I can't go out this weekend. But I promise to keep next weekend free for you both."

"Perfect. Looking forward to it." He smiles, relieved. "Sleep well," he adds, before rinsing his dishes and heading to Cory's room.

"Train hard," I yell, hearing both Nate and Cory laugh from her room. I huff out my own laugh and smile. As soon as I get to my room, I crash on the bed, fully clothed.

Chapter Seven

Summer

"Y ou know I love camping, but are you sure you don't want to go alone?" I ask as Cory lifts on her toes, balancing dangerously on a stool to reach for her camping chairs. I probably could have reached without the extra height, but she's a determined little thing. She throws one down at me, and I catch it, despite the awkward shape.

Nate says he knows of this great camping spot that's practically a secret and wants to get away for the weekend. I said yes before Cory finished asking me to go but suddenly realized it may have been a pity invite. Cory and I have always camped together. Maybe she felt bad leaving me out. I should have known better. We've never been the type of friends to do things we didn't want to do. If she didn't want me there, I'd like to think she would have told me.

"I've already told you it's not just the two of us. Two of Nate's friends are coming with their girlfriends and—"

"Great, so I'm the seventh wheel." I roll my eyes playfully, knowing Cory would never do that to me. She rolls her eyes right back at me as she tosses another chair.

"Really, Summer? I thought you knew me better than that."

I knew it. "Who is he?" I ask and laugh.

"You'll have to wait and see. He's my surprise for you." She smiles, and I beam back at her. She's never been happier. I can't say this enough; Nate is perfect for her. And they both light up when they see each other. It's sickening, really, but I'm glad she's happy.

"What are you grinning about?" Cory asks, interrupting my thoughts.

"Just how happy I am for you," I say honestly.

She jumps down from the chair and wraps her arms around me. "Thank you. I am happy. So happy." She pulls back from me and holds on to my shoulders, looking me dead in the eye. "You could have this too."

That will teach me for being nice. She knows how I feel about my love life. Or why I have a lack of one. "Cory..." my voice hints with warning.

"I know, I know. I'll shut up. Plus, I haven't met anyone good enough for you yet, so you're off the hook." She hugs me again and then moves away to pack her bags. "Are you ready yet?"

"No, I've got a few things to finish up," I say and head out of her room, knowing she'll take hours as it is without me distracting her.

A tent has already been erected when we arrive, and it's not surprising that they beat us here. Nate jumps out of his truck first, followed by Cory, both hurrying to see if there's anything left to help with since we ended up being hours late, thanks to Cory's desperate need to unpack and repack every time she realized she'd forgotten something. I hang back, taking my time as I view the surroundings.

Before me is the definition of picture perfect. A large body of crystal-blue water glistens in the sun, surrounded by mountains of lush greenery. Golden sand paves the way from the tent to the lake, and in the distance, the sound of water crashing against rock tells me there is so much more to explore. Nate was not wrong. This place is something else. How it's a secret, I'll never know. It's hard to believe nobody's shared this on social media.

Cory and Nate are already approaching the campsite when I finally exit the car.

"Yo! Dyl, are you decent?" Nate yells and shakes the side of the tent.

Ah crap, Dyl? Nate's friend is Dylan? Why didn't that possibility even cross my mind? My heart rate speeds thinking about how this is going to play out. Does Gemma know the truth? Considering we only pretended to be best friends for that one night and then never spoke again, I'm assuming he confessed it all. Especially since she caught Joel kissing someone else. If that wasn't the perfect time to come clean, then I don't know what is. *But what if he didn't?* I shrug and take a deep breath. *Well, this could be fun. Or a complete mess...*

Dylan's pulling a T-shirt over his head as he steps out of the tent. Behind him, a tiny redhead ducks her head out. Gemma.

"I'll be right out." She smiles shyly before moving back inside. Nate raises his eyebrows, and Dylan laughs before offering his hand to Cory.

"I know we've seen each other plenty, but I don't think we've officially met, at least while I'm sober. I'm Dylan," he says.

She smiles, already well aware of who he is. Besides the fact that we've talked about him and the best friend saga, she's also never missed a football game. "Cory. Nice to meet you, Dylan," she replies, shaking his hand.

"Need help with your tent?" Dylan asks, looking over toward the car, the very car I'm still stupidly standing behind. I slam the door shut and head over with a confident stride, watching Dylan's eyes widen for a second when he notices me.

"Dylan," I say, with a tilt of my head, trying to appear unaffected by seeing him.

"Summer. Hi...Hi, nice to see you," he stumbles over his words. *Let the awkwardness begin.*

At that moment, Gemma pops out of the tent bouncing with energy. "Sorry about that. Can you believe how beautiful this spot is? This is going to be so much fun. I wasn't convinced at first, but.... Oh, Summer, hi." She smiles, but it's not as bright as it was seconds earlier. "Sorry to hear you and Joel broke up," she adds.

All eyes are now on me. Nate's confused, while Cory's clearly amused, and Dylan looks a little embarrassed. My own eyes find Dylan's, and he shrugs. *So, the lies continue.*

"Thanks. It's still hard to talk about," I say, and for added effect, I look to the ground and wipe a nonexistent tear from my eye. A snicker comes from Cory's direction.

"I'm sorry to hear that; I won't mention it again," Gemma says and looks toward Dylan with an expression I can't read. Cory breaks the awkwardness by introducing herself to Gemma, and then we all get to work setting up the other two tents.

An hour passes, and we flop down onto chairs around the newly started campfire, since the weather's cool enough here near the water. Nate hands out drinks as he unpacks some bags.

"What happened to Reed and McKenzie? I thought they were coming," Dylan asks Nate as I take my first sip.

"The jackass got food poisoning from old meat in the back of the fridge."

"Of course he did." Dylan scoffs, his question making me wonder if he's uncomfortable here with the small group.

When Nate's finally settled, Cory asks the question that's been on my mind since that fateful night. "How long have you two been dating?" She looks between Dylan and Gemma.

"Only two months, but there was an instant, deep connection, so it feels longer." Gemma smiles, and Dylan chokes on his drink. He recovers quickly by sneezing, and I take pity and decide to help him out.

"Bless you," I say as I give him a knowing smile. He clearly thinks differently about things with Gemma. *Why does that make me happy?*

As the sun sets, I realize I'd forgotten that Cory had a surprise for me. I'm only now remembering because headlights of an approaching car light up our little camping retreat. I glance at Cory, and she smiles, clapping her hands together. Her reaction makes me confident that I will not be disappointed. The car pulls up, and Logan jumps out of the driver's seat. I stare in shock. I'm pretty sure my jaw may even drop. His eyes scan our group before he beelines straight for me.

"Hey, baby girl, have you missed me?" he yells, snapping me out of my daze. I leap up from my chair, running into his arms before he's even finished his greeting.

"You're here! How did I not know that?" I squeal.

I don't act like an excited teenager often, but Logan brings that out in me. This man right here has been in my life since I was in elementary school. Other than Cory, he's the closest person in the world to me. He's closer to my brother's age, but they never really hit it off. We haven't spent longer than a weekend together in years, since his parents moved away when I was fifteen. It's safe to say I'm pretty excited to have him here.

"I'm so glad you're here," I stress.

We hug again and walk back to the group arm in arm. Cory jumps up and hugs him, and Nate stands to shake his hand. "Logan, man, I've heard a lot about you. I'm Nate."

"Nate?" Logan looks at Cory. "So, you're the man who's stolen our girl's heart?" He smiles. Corny as ever.

"That's me. I'm the lucky man," Nate agrees as he smiles widely.

"That you are. It's good to hear you admit it, so I don't have to give you the talk." Logan laughs and pats Nate on the back while giving his best "tough" look.

Logan is best described as a "Hot Surfer Dude" with tattoos. I realize I'm generalizing here, but the long, dirty-blond hair, tan skin, and ripped body give him that look. And he actually surfs.

He's currently looking mighty fine wearing a tight olive-green tee, black cargo pants that are fitted at the ankle, and sneakers without socks. This look he's got going is a total turn-on for me, and he knows it. There's something about a man's ankle... *Maybe that's just me.* Point is, he's hot.

Dylan and Gemma stand when Logan makes his way over, and Cory tells them we've known Logan forever. Logan and Gemma introduce themselves first, but when it comes to Dylan, Logan pauses.

"You look familiar. Have we met?" he asks.

Dylan furrows his brow and looks at me for answers. *Not that I have any.* I don't know how they know each other. Surprisingly, it's Gemma that answers.

"Considering you both *claim* to have known Summer all her life, one would assume you know each other." She's a little snarky but does have a valid point.

Logan looks to me for help, and whatever is displayed on my face must communicate the right thing, because he comes to my rescue. "Of course, Dylan. Wow! Man, it's been a long time. Good to see you again."

"Yeah, you too, Logan. Looking forward to catching up," Dylan adds to the charade.

They both smile, and I have to say it's convincing, for me anyway. Gemma, on the other hand, looks annoyed about something, but I'm sick of feeling unsure and awkward. *So, we are pretending to be best friends again—big deal.*

"Cory, please tell me you packed the ingredients for s'mores. We've never camped without them," I say once everyone has returned to their seats.

"What kind of person do you take me for? Of course, I packed them."

"I think it's best if I cook them for you, Summer," Dylan says out of nowhere. I'm about to tell him I'm perfectly capable, when he adds, "Last time you burnt the shit out of the marshmallow." He winks.

Cory barks out a laugh because he's not wrong.

"Don't worry, I remember exactly how you like them," he says with a grin.

I raise an eyebrow in challenge and wave a hand toward the fire. "Be my guest."

When the first one is cooked, Dylan holds it up high in triumph. "Perfection!" he exclaims, and I've got to admit, it looks mouth-watering.

"I'll be the judge of that," I say, jumping to my feet. I walk straight over and, without thinking, take a bite while it's still in his hands. It's completely innocent. My lips don't touch his fingers. There's no longing looks into each other's eyes. It's just one friend feeding another.

Dylan laughs at my antics, and the sound distracts us from realizing that everyone else is quiet. When I look back at Logan, he's smirking at me. *Ah.* "You can do better," I say, trying to recover and tapping Dylan on the nose before walking back toward my seat.

Logan pulls me into his lap as I walk past and wraps his arms around me. "What's going on with you and Dylan? What did I miss? When did you actually meet?" He lowers his voice and raises an eyebrow. I roll my eyes.

"Nothing. There's nothing going on. We officially met a month ago, but he's been friends with Thomas for a while."

"Ah, so I've probably seen him with Thomas before."

"Makes sense." I shrug. It is the most obvious reason. Not sure why I didn't think of that before.

"Why does Gemma think you've known each other for years?"

"Long story short, we may have told a few people we've been best friends since we were kids, and now, it's hard to backtrack."

Logan laughs out loud, drawing attention our way.

"Shhh!" I slap him on the arm.

"Only you..." He shakes his head and smirks.

"I know, but I didn't think we'd really see each other that often, if ever. It was harmless."

"Seems to piss Gemma off."

"I noticed that. It's strange. She was totally fine with it." Her mood swing is truly perplexing. Unless Dylan said something that would cause this reaction. Nothing else has changed.

"She mentioned you broke up with your boyfriend. Joel, I think she said?" He raises his eyebrows.

Oh, that's changed. Logan knows without me saying that I was never in a relationship.

"Maybe that made her worry about you. You know, now that you're single and all."

"Maybe." I smile.

"Well, I for one am *thrilled* that you're single again." He wiggles his eyebrows suggestively and playfully kisses my neck, causing me to giggle. God, he brings out the worst in me.

I push him away. "Later."

"You bet."

When we look back at the group, Dylan and Gemma are both watching us. Gemma's smiling, but Dylan looks uncomfortable. "And there's nothing else going on with you two?" Logan asks, clearly noticing what I do.

"Nothing at all. We're not even really friends."

"He doesn't look like someone you'd want to befriend. Looks like someone you'd want to f—" I swat at his arm, and he laughs.

"I'm not going to lie; he's gorgeous and fun to be around, but I'm not going there. As I said before, he's a friend of Thomas's," I explain, and I know Logan understands completely. Well, not completely, completely.

Because even though he's asked many times over the years, I haven't told him the full extent of my family issues, but he knows that Thomas and I don't get along and that he told me to stay away from his friends.

"Say no more," Logan says and drops the subject. We're silent for a moment until Logan adds more fuel to the fire, *figuratively.*

"Dylan, I forgot there for a moment, but you were the kid who got to take Summer to junior prom, right? I offered to come back, but she said you'd volunteered. Bet she was breathtaking. I was lucky, though, and got her senior year," he says with a wink.

"What are you doing?" I whisper.

"Having some fun; stirring the pot."

Dylan dives right in. "Of course, she was breathtaking; it's Summer. But as I recall, her dress was hideous."

I have to give it to him; Dylan appears unaffected through all our exchanges. He has such a confident and casual demeanor. *I like it. Hang on...*

"Excuse me?" I look at him in horror. "Hideous? Hideous! You picked it, you moron. Made me try on several options before deciding on that floral number," I jab. I actually wore navy. It's a struggle to hold back the laugh as I watch Dylan's mind working for a comeback.

"I stand by my comment. I picked it on purpose."

Cory and I both burst out laughing. Even Nate has a chuckle despite being new to our banter. And that begins a back and forth of memories between Dylan and me.

"Cool it a little. Even I'm getting jealous of your relationship," Cory whispers after we've been playing this game for a while.

"What does that mean? Shit, does it look like I'm flirting?" I ask, genuinely worried.

"It does, and I know you mean nothing by it, but I know you. Gemma doesn't."

She's right; I need to tone it down. I turn my attention back to Logan who says, "Nothing going on, huh?" I'm about to argue when he changes the subject. "I think I need to meet this Joel and congratulate him on being the first to get you to settle down." I slap his arm and laugh.

"Shut up," I hiss quietly. "You know there's no Joel. Well, there is a Joel, but he was never my boyfriend." *Oh, the lies we weave.*

"I don't know what to believe anymore," he jokes.

"Stop it," I laugh. "You'll always be my one and only."

"Damn straight," he says, pulling me closer and pressing a kiss to my cheek. Seriously, if I was ever going to say someone was perfect for me, it would have been him, but neither of us wants that. *Those* feelings just aren't there.

I draw my eyes to Dylan just as Gemma grabs his hand and leads him to their tent. Before they realize anyone's watching, I see her bite her bottom lip suggestively and pull at his sweatshirt.

"We're done for the night," Dylan calls to the group, his eyes briefly meeting mine with an expression I can't quite decipher. A hint of tightness fills my chest. *Ugh.* Now I've got my own feelings to decipher about that exchange, at least until the remainder of our group breaks into laughter before covering their mouths.

Nate and Cory are the next to go, and Logan and I enjoy the peace, wrapped in each other's arms as the flames flicker in front of us.

"Thanks so much for coming this weekend, Logan. It means a lot to me."

"I've missed you. It might seem like I'm busy all the time, but I'm always thinking about you." It's something so typical for him to say, but something in his voice seems different.

"Going soft on me?" I laugh, hinting at his shift in mood.

"Nah, just thankful for a great friend." *Yep, something's definitely off.*

"Everything okay back home?" I ask, hoping that he's okay.

"It will be, Sum. It's nice to be here and just switch off for a bit."

I raise my head up from his shoulder and turn to look at him. He smiles, but it doesn't meet his eyes.

"Loge?"

"I promise, I'm okay. I'd rather not get into it here. Can we talk about it another time?" he begs, and although I don't want to drop the topic, I know I have to.

"Okay," I say but make a note to ask him about it at a later date. I change the subject and we fall into our usual comfortable banter until we're both too tired to talk.

When I wake up sometime later, we're lying together on a picnic blanket in front of the now dwindled fire. At some point I must have become hot because I've stripped off my jeans. Could be because someone has placed a blanket over us. *Cory.* At least, I hope it was Cory because anyone else would be creepy.

I try to lift Logan's arm off my chest without waking him, but he's deadweight. When I try a second time, I accidentally elbow him in the chin.

"Shit." He yells loud enough to wake the camp, and I grimace. "What are you doing?" he mumbles.

"Sorry," I whisper. "I need to pee, and we should get into the tent."

He nods and stands up, pulling me to my feet. "Want me to come with you? It's dark and scary out there." He tries to whisper, but he's still half-asleep, so it actually sounds like he's trying to get someone's attention across a room.

"No, thanks. I don't need anyone watching me go. I'm a big girl now." I smile. He ducks into the tent as I head off into the dark.

This is the one thing I hate about camping—no toilets. I can go without showers and mirrors and kitchens, but having no toilet sucks. I walk deeper and deeper into the trees so that it's harder for anyone to stumble upon me, and the experience is uneventful, just the way I like it to be.

Chapter Eight

Dylan

Summer's here. The one person I've been trying to forget is sitting right outside my tent, laughing. I'm genuinely shocked to see her here. I really shouldn't be, but I am. Why the hell hadn't Nate mentioned she was coming? Probably didn't think it mattered. It shouldn't matter, yet it does. I'd become even better at pushing her out of my mind of late. Things with Gemma were going well. It wasn't love yet, but that didn't mean we wouldn't get there. Things were moving forward, and I was happy. *Was? Why am I thinking in past tense? I am happy. And yet... Nope, I'm happy.*

Do I think maybe it was easier when Summer was out of sight, out of mind? Sure. But until she'd pulled away today, I was having a fun time reminiscing with her. *Well, making shit up anyway.*

Why did she pull back? Did she think I wouldn't notice? That question has been driving me mad. I know Gemma was a little quiet. I'm not an idiot, but every time I looked her way, she was smiling. But was that the reason? Or was it because of Logan? Could that be it?

So many things run through my mind at once, but the biggest question is who the fuck is Logan? Yes, we pretended to know each other, but I honestly have no clue. She actually squealed like a schoolgirl at a boy band concert when she saw him. It wasn't fun to watch. *Shit! The real question I should ask is why do I care?*

Gemma isn't at all subtle with what she desires, and I know I played along when she pulled me in here, but my mind isn't in it. The second we got into the tent her hands began to wander, but because I'm an asshole, I pretended I was too tired and then proceeded to "pass out" asleep, hoping she'd give up.

Luckily, it worked, because I'm not that guy. I can't sleep with one person and think of another. And unfortunately, I am thinking of another. I need to keep a little distance from Gemma until I sort through my thoughts.

God, I wish Nate had mentioned Summer was coming. Maybe I wouldn't have come if I'd known.

Or maybe I would have.

We'll never know.

In the silence, I can hear movement and sounds from outside. Nate and Cory seem to have gone to bed, while Summer and Logan are still up. Without Nate and Cory, they're quieter, but I can still hear talking. Talking I can handle. I'm not sure how I'd feel about more happening between them, and I'm also not sure why I feel that way, but I can't seem to stop it.

Were Summer and Logan more than friends? It'd been impossible to miss their flirting, and I'd definitely seen him kissing her neck. *Stop thinking about it.*

When the whispers finally taper to an end and silence takes over, I check the time. Two a.m. Time to switch off. Now. And...go. Why can't I switch off? *Are they sleeping now? Is silence a good thing? Can I seriously lie here and pretend that I'm sure they've fallen asleep, and they are not, in fact, two people who hold a world record in silent lovemaking?*

Clearly, I'm going crazy, but it's too late to rein in my thoughts. I strain my ears and try to listen for any foreign sounds, any hint that they are more than just friends. *Get a grip, you pervert.*

I look over at the wonderful girl beside me. Gemma really is gorgeous; maybe I should wake her. Hearing her scream my name into the silence could be exactly what I need.

Nope, not happening. I am not that much of an asshole. Even though I'm acting like one right now. I stare at the roof of the tent and try to remember the words to a kids' nursery rhyme that I once loved. Why? I have no freaking idea, but it can't hurt, right?

I must have finally fallen asleep because a loud noise startles me awake. I'm disoriented at first, and my eyes bounce around to get my bearings. I'd been dreaming about Dad. Something I do a lot. This one wasn't anything specific, but fuck, it felt real. A pain grips my chest, like a fist is squeezing my heart, as the guilt of his death plagues me once again. The size of the tent suddenly becomes too small, and I need air. I need to walk off my thoughts before the darkness takes over.

Stepping out of the tent, I immediately notice a flaw in my plan; I can't see shit. Shaking off the tension, I pull a sweatshirt over my head and move toward the trees. No matter how blind I am, I need to do this.

I'm on my way down to the lake when I hear a rustling behind me. My eyes adjust to the darkness, and I turn in time to see Summer walking toward me. She's unaware of my presence, allowing me the advantage of watching her. My eyes rake from her shoes to her face. She's wearing boots that hit the middle of her shin, and her long legs are bare. *Bare! Shit!*

Oblivious to my existence, she moves closer in nothing but a tank top, cotton panties and a knee-length cardigan that falls loosely off one shoulder. *Fuck!*

Under the glow of the moon, she's breathtaking, and I'm finding it difficult to look away. She's playing with the ends of her long hair as it blows around her, stopping occasionally when a rustling sound moves through the air, loud enough that I hear it too. She doesn't seem concerned, more intrigued as to what it could be. When she finally notices me, she jumps, her hand racing to her heart.

"You scared the shit out of me. We're in the woods, for God's sake."

I cringe. "Sorry, I was taking a walk when I saw you. Thought I'd see if you want to join me, or I could walk you back." I shrug.

"Okay," she replies hesitantly, still frozen on the spot. "Nate said that the lake's beautiful in the moonlight. Want to walk that way?" she says with a soft smile, taking the first step toward me.

Now that my eyes have completely adjusted, it's easier to see in the distance. We make our way to the lake in silence, but it's not uncomfortable. It's cool out, and there's a slight breeze. Even though Summer's not close to me, I feel her shiver, and the need to wrap an arm around her is strong. You know, because I'm a nice guy. *Bullshit.*

I break the silence to redirect my thoughts. "Sorry about earlier. I know I should have told Gemma by now, but I just...I have no excuse." I shrug and run a hand through my mussed hair.

"At least you can see the error of your ways." She laughs. "I've actually enjoyed our role play to be honest."

"Your boyfriend doesn't mind?" I say and immediately cringe. *What the hell was that?* Summer laughs off my comment. We both know Logan's not her boyfriend, so it was a stupid thing to say. If I had to guess, I'd say my brain thought that was a good way of finding out what they mean to each other. *So, so wrong.*

"Cory and Nate seem to be going well," I say, not subtle in my need to move on.

"They're perfect for each other!" she gushes, stunning me for a second and causing me to pause and look her way. I may not actually know Summer as well as I joke I do, but she's no gusher. Before I can respond, she crinkles her perfectly formed nose, and the look can only be described as adorable.

"Does that face mean you don't really mean what you just said?" I ask.

"No, I mean it. I'm just not sure where that reaction came from." She swings her arms and moves ahead of me so I can no longer see her face.

"You're happy for them?" I take a guess. She stops and turns back to me, a warm smile brightening her features.

"I am. Some people deserve all the happiness in the world."

Interesting choice of words. "And some don't?" I ask cautiously.

"Some don't," she confirms in a whisper, turning away. I want to ask more, but I don't.

When we hit the sand, I follow Summer's lead and remove my shoes. The gritty sand moves between my toes, and I immediately regret it, hating the feeling. *Why did I agree to this walk again?*

After removing what has to be the pointiest stick from under my foot, I look up to see the second reason I agreed to walk this way. Summer's comment about the lake being beautiful did not do it justice. The clear night allows the stars to light up the sky, showcasing a spectacular view of the waterfall as it takes on the blue glow from the moonlight. The water splashing from the rocks causes the moon's bright reflection to ripple with the waves, holding my attention.

When I look back to catch Summer's reaction to the view, I'm rendered momentarily speechless. Her eyes are focused on the waterfall as she slowly removes her cardigan, leaving her in only a tank top and panties. With my mouth suddenly dry and my body frozen, I work hard to keep my thoughts from going where they shouldn't. Because of this, it takes me longer than it should to realize her intentions. *Shit!*

"You're insane; you're going to freeze," I rush to say. My words must break her spell because her eyes snap to mine before she takes off.

"Oh, don't be such a pussy," she yells, running toward the lake.

Double shit! If something happens to her because I'm a "pussy" as she put it, I'll never forgive myself. I quickly strip my sweats off and run after her. Thankfully, I'm a lot faster and manage to catch up to her as her feet break the water.

Wrapping my arms around her waist from behind, I lift her up and swing her back toward the sand. She screams but laughs uncontrollably while thrashing against me.

"Ah, come on. We've skinny-dipped before, remember?" she jokes, but I hold firm.

"You're no fun." She laughs, wriggling as much as possible in the hope I'll release my grip. *Not happening.* I grip tighter and walk farther from the shoreline. "Okay, fine. You win. I'll stop."

I turn her away from the lake and stand so that I'm between her and the water, in case she makes a run for it, and only then loosen my hold. She looks down at my briefs and raises an eyebrow, while holding back a smile. I'm lucky it's dark because I'm sure they hide nothing.

Summer finally stands still for a moment, her chest rising and falling, windswept hair blowing across her face, and I'm mesmerized. She must sense my trance because she runs again. *Shit!* I laugh.

Jumping in front of her at the last second, I pull her into me, and we crash together. Our bodies connect from knee to chest, and it's my turn to lose my breath.

I take a second to realize she's no longer laughing. She's so close that her breath warms my chin every time she exhales, which is more often than normal because of the energy she just expelled. Or maybe it's our proximity, because my breaths are equally quick and shallow.

Looking down into her eyes, I see that she's already looking up at me. It may be dark, but I can still make out flecks of blue mixed within her green eyes. The shining orbs make me think of sunshine over a grassy meadow, a new day or...summer. *Huh, fitting.* When did I even notice her eye color to begin with?

In a romantic comedy, this would be the moment we share our first kiss. It's the perfect setting—magical. But that's not what either of us wants. Or what we *should* want. I lean forward to touch my nose to hers instead and reduce the intensity of the moment, but it backfires when her breath hitches. *Ah!* I control my breathing, nuzzling her nose with my own before pulling away and bopping the same spot with my finger. She giggles, actually giggles, and it's a truly beautiful sound. Something I fear I'll never forget.

Yep, that might have been our moment. Our one chance to take it further, and I'm not disappointed that we didn't. Despite my obvious and completely inappropriate attraction to her, there is something about her that makes me want to be her friend. Something tells me she needs more of them.

"We better get back to the group, or someone will think we disappeared to have sex," she says, and I laugh.

"That would suck. All the accusations without the pleasure." She returns my laugh, and I relax.

We quickly dress and walk back in silence before each slipping into our tents. I'm a little thrown by what just happened. *I didn't kiss her. I decided to be her friend.* I don't really have girls who are friends. Maybe I'm growing? *Or maybe I just need her around?*

Gemma rolls over, pulling me from my thoughts of the girl that isn't her, and I hate myself a little for what happened tonight. But I can't regret it.

Once again, I find myself wide awake, and it has nothing to do with the uncomfortable blow-up mattress I'm lying on. *What did I do last time? That's right—nursery rhymes. I wonder if that will work again. Twinkle, twinkle...*

A groan interrupts my song.

What the fuck? You've got to be kidding me. Why the fuck did we set up the tents so close together? We have this entire place to ourselves.

The moans get a little louder but are slightly muffled. I'm hoping that means Nate bit down on something to keep himself quiet so that I don't have to cover my ears. Not waiting to find out, I move to cover them just in case and rush to lift the pillow out from under my head, but it's too late. I can't take back what I hear next.

"God, Summer."

Some part of me sinks. *Not Nate and Cory then.*

"Shh!" Summer giggles, and they both fall silent. I shove the pillow hard over my face and crush my head into the mattress. At least that answers any question from earlier—they are definitely not silent lovers, and I'm not at all happy about it. *I'm screwed.*

Chapter Nine

Dylan

I'm dragging my feet at training Monday morning. After spending the weekend camping, I would have preferred a sleep-in, but here we are. The guys are all discussing their recent hookups as we walk toward the locker room. My eyes find Nate's and we both shake our heads, neither of us interested in the team's version of gossip. Keeping my head down, I hold my breath until I reach the locker room, praying that no one will try and bring me into the chat. Pushing open the door, I beeline for my stuff. Resting both palms on the bench seat in front of me, I lean forward and stare into space with a sigh. I love these guys, but it seems like they have the same routine over and over. Another weekend, another Ball House party. I'm happy to have a few guys interested in other things, like camping.

The guys are still talking in the hall so I relax a little with the peace, my mind going to Summer. We spent the rest of the weekend acting like nothing had happened, but something had definitely changed between us. I felt it, and I know she did too, but we both ignored it, each for our own reasons. When it was time to depart the campsite, we exchanged a wave and a smile. And as Nate's car pulled away, a lump had formed in the pit of my stomach at the thought of that being our goodbye.

A phone buzzing on the bench near my hand causes me to abandon my thoughts. A picture of Cory lights up the screen. *Nate's phone then.* Without hesitation, I answer. Holding the phone in front of my face, I'm greeted with a very shocked Cory.

"Dylan?" She gasps and moves the phone closer to her face. "What if I was naked?"

"Hello to you too. Are you naked?" I ask and pretend to peer down at her body through the phone. She's not naked. I can see the top on her shoulders, but the straps *do* look lacy. *Natey, Natey. Good for you.* A pink tinge floods Cory's cheeks, and I regret my comment. I save her from further embarrassment and move on. "Nate's still coming in, shouldn't be long." The door opens and I spot him through the gap. Getting his attention, I wave him in.

"Thanks, Dylan," Cory breathes out. Her shoulders drop slightly at my change of subject, but she's still not completely comfortable. I really enjoyed getting to know her over the weekend. She's a lot of fun but can be a little shy at times. And that's definitely present now.

Offering her a warm smile, I ask the first thing that pops into my head to pass the time as we wait for Nate. "Where's my bestie today?" I laugh at my joke, but the joke's about to be on me.

Her eyebrows rise in question. "Don't you mean *my* bestie?" she asks.

"Nope, I meant what I said." I shrug, and she laughs, visibly relaxing.

"If *you* were really her bestie, *you'd* know she's still asleep after a big night," she sasses and laughs again, completely unaware of the unpleasant feelings her words have just conjured. I try hard not to react, but a slight cringe escapes me. *Does that mean what I think it means?* Luckily, Nate arrives so I don't have to respond.

"Ah, here he is," I say with a fake smile and pass the phone to Nate. No longer on screen, I close my eyes and take a deep breath, my reaction confirming exactly what I need to do. When I look up, I see Nate eyeing me curiously. *Guess I didn't hide that as well as I thought.* My lips pull into a half smile as I turn back to my locker without giving him a chance to question me. My mind drifts back to Summer and the serious decision I have to make. It's then I realize I've already made my decision. I just need to go through with it.

On Tuesday evening, Joel and I are sitting in the living room in the same positions we've been in for hours. Joel is slouched back on the couch with his arms behind his head, and I'm in our giant beanbag, feet crossed, kicking back. It's been an easy day after a hellish night. Yesterday, I did the right thing and broke up with Gemma. I've been debating when to tell Joel, because I know the second I do that he's going to analyze the situation. But I can't hold off forever. We both had classes this morning but spent the rest of the day flicking between different sports, chatting about useless shit, and playing video games. I've had so many opportunities to bring this up, and yet I wait until this very moment, when his precious San Francisco Giants are on the screen. *He's going to love me.*

"Gemma and I broke up," I say as he watches the game. His eyes move to mine briefly in acknowledgment and then he turns back to the screen.

"Okay. Why?" he asks but he's not really focused on me.

"A few reasons. One being that she gave me an ultimatum..."

I tell him most of the story, and by the time I pause, he's staring at me in shock.

"I think I'm confused," he says, now giving me his full attention. "Gemma *told* you to choose between her and Summer, and you chose Summer." His brows furrow in complete confusion.

"Kind of," I lie. We broke up after having that exact conversation, but I'd driven to her door ready to break things off *before* she hit me with the ultimatum. Turns out, Summer and I weren't the only ones that felt the change in our relationship. When those words had left her mouth, I felt sick. Gemma didn't deserve any of this. Taking a deep breath, I'd remained calm despite Gemma being obviously pissed at me. She has every right to be annoyed that I broke up with her, but telling me to choose? Come on, that's not right. I shake off my thoughts and look back at Joel.

"Okay, so you chose Summer. Why?" Joel prods for information.

"I didn't exactly choose Summer; I was already planning to break up with her when she threw that at me," I try to explain without actually being honest.

Joel squints at me in thought. "But you would have, right? You know Summer isn't actually your best friend," he states, and while it's valid, it's not the point.

"I know that, but Gemma doesn't. Even though I was going to end it, it's a pretty shit ultimatum," I huff, getting myself worked up for no reason.

"You're not wrong there," Joel agrees while studying me closely. Here it is; here's the analysis. He's studying to be a child psychologist and can't help but use me as a test subject, because yes, I can be a bit childish at times. A small smile plays on his lips when he says, "You have a thing for Summer." It's not a question. He thinks he's stating a fact.

I fight back a cringe. "Nope," I reply evenly, clasping my hands against my side so I don't make any gestures that would suggest otherwise.

"Nope?" he repeats, skepticism written all over his expression.

Possibly. "That's what I said." I shrug.

"Okaay," he drags out and then pauses. I wait for him to push the issue some more. He's never been one to shy away from a conversation. I raise an eyebrow in question. *Come at me, Joel...*

"Can't say I'm surprised you broke up. We are in the sweet spot," he quips.

What the fuck? "What's that supposed to mean?" My voice rises, back straightens, and I glare, ready to argue my defense.

Joel is unfazed. "All your relationships last between two and six months." He shrugs, like that piece of information means nothing.

"That's not true," I argue, but a quick calculation in my mind proves otherwise. I deflate back into the beanbag. "Well, it's not on purpose, anyway."

Joel laughs. "Of course it's not, it's just your thing."

"My thing?" I question and make myself comfortable, resigned to the fact that he could be right and he's about to tell me why.

Joel spends the next few minutes diagnosing me as a serial dater. Telling me some people are players, some find the *one* early on, and some ignore it all completely. But me? Apparently, I love to date. I guess it makes sense. But man, I didn't think it was a thing. I'm just trying to find my person, and once I realize the girl I'm with isn't the one for me, I move on. That's not a bad thing, is it? Better not to waste everyone's time. I tell Joel as much, in defense, but it backfires.

He sighs, exasperated. "Except you are purposely self-sabotaging any chance you might have by always going for the wrong people."

My brows furrow. "How do you figure that?" I ask, genuinely confused.

"Shall I list examples?" He rolls his eyes.

I laugh and shake my head. "Please do." *This should be good.*

"Senior year. Viv. You started dating right before prom, knowing she was going away for college and that you had no interest in dating long distance." He looks at me pointedly, his lips pulling into a thin line.

He's got me there, but that's only one...

"Freshman year of college. Amy. Everything was traveling along smoothly until you decided it wouldn't work out because she wanted to live overseas and you didn't. Even though we all knew this about her before you got together," he continues.

Okay, two...

"Sophomore year. Emily—" he starts, but I cut him off.

"Alright, I get—"

Joel continues as though I haven't spoken, "Also, sophomore year. Britney—"

Jesus. I cringe. I've heard enough. "Okay, well, Nicole and Jess cheated on me. How does that fit your mold?" I blurt, trying to turn this around. Because let's face it, it's not playing out well for me.

"Why'd they cheat?" he asks, leaning back in his seat.

Shit! "Not relevant. There's no excuse for cheating," I say.

Head tilted to the side, eyebrows pinched, Joel gives me a look that calls bullshit, and he's right. Jess claims she cheated because she felt like I already had one foot out the door. At the time, I thought it was absolute crap. I spent all my time with her. My friends said I abandoned them; my grades slipped. We stayed at each other's places most nights. What more could I do? But on reflection, emotionally, I wasn't as invested as she was. She told me she loved me, and I didn't say it back, because I hadn't felt it. So maybe to her I did have one foot out the door. *I mean I had been planning to break up with her... Ah crap.* But Nicole? She was just a bitch; I'm not taking the blame for that one. Even though she tried to blame me. She was cheating from day one. Well, seeing two guys at once is more like it. And neither of us knew. We've actually bonded about it since; he's a great guy and... *I digress.* Point is, Nicole cheating is not on me, but Jess, well...

All I do is shrug in response. I've got no comeback.

Joel laughs and shakes his head at me. "Okay, those two aside, I have pretty compelling evidence," he says.

I scratch the back of my neck and look down because he's not wrong. It really is undeniable. So, the big question is, "Who should I be going for?" I ask, and Joel facepalms. Literally smacks the palm of his hand into his forehead. I'm going to go out on a limb and say that's not the right question to have asked.

"Dude, really?" he replies, looking completely appalled.

I can't help but laugh at the direction this conversation has taken because of Joel's switch to psychologist mode. "Is that how you're going to speak to all your patients?" I ask.

"Probably,"—he shrugs—"since I'm hoping they'll mostly be kids and teenagers and you're acting the same age."

I take a deep breath. *Remember, he's your best friend. You've been through so much together that it's probably best if you don't punch him in the nuts.* Joel's shoulders shake in laughter as he covers his crotch. Sometimes I wonder if he's a mind reader.

"Why don't you stay single for a while?" he throws out there, like that's an easy answer to all my problems.

"Um, how long is a while?"

"I'm serious. You might miss your shot with the right girl because you're always in a relationship with the wrong one."

My brows pull together. *Has he been talking to Lucy?*

"Okay," I agree, defeated.

Joel's eyes flash to mine in shock. "Yeah? Wasn't expecting that, to be honest."

"Don't get a gigantic head about it, but you're right." I roll my eyes.

He narrows his eyes, waiting for the catch. He knows I value his opinion and that I often take his advice, but I usually give him a hard time about it and rarely tell him he's right. That's not how we roll. Since there isn't a catch, I say, "Are we done?" I'm ready to move on from having my life dissected.

Joel stares me down for a few more seconds and then laughs. "Yep, session over; that'll be three hundred and fifty."

"You wish," I scoff. "Consider me your pro bono case," I add, causing Joel to laugh.

We both turn back to the TV, but I'm staring at it rather than watching, my mind on Joel's words. *Serial dater? Is that really what I* am? I mean, sure, I've had a lot of girlfriends over the past few years, but isn't that better than sleeping around? Guess it depends on how you look at it. Have I ever started a relationship with someone and honestly thought they could be the one? Ah shit, it's best if I don't answer that out loud. It doesn't paint me in a good light. I shake my head, annoyed at myself. Maybe being single for a while, a small while, is the way to go. It can't hurt.

"I'm thinking we should make these appointments weekly," Joel interrupts my thoughts. "You clearly have a lot to work through," he says, without taking his eyes off the screen, a small smirk playing on his lips. *Yep, definitely a mind reader.*

I'm lying in bed later that night, staring at the ceiling, when my phone lights up the room. I lazily reach for it and raise it in front of my face without lifting my head off the pillow. *This better be important.* My head jerks in surprise, and my heart rate spikes at the sight of her name on the display.

Summer: Interesting fact. Nate tells me you hate making s'mores.

I laugh out loud. *Busted!* I do, I hate it.

Me: If that's true, consider yourself lucky.

Summer: The luckiest, they were delicious. I will never settle for burnt s'mores again.

We continue to message back and forth a few more times, the smile never leaving my face. And when my head finally hits the pillow again, I huff out a laugh. *Maybe our wave at the campsite wasn't goodbye after all.*

Chapter Ten

Summer

C ory laughs as Nate replays their eventful date from the night before. We're having a long lunch in the college cafeteria, and while I've heard the details from Cory, it's actually funnier to hear it from Nate. It's been a little over a week since our camping trip, and I'll admit, I should have started third wheeling it with these two earlier. Really getting to know Nate by the campfire made a world of difference, and I'm not even sure why I hesitated to begin with. I can't keep the smile from my face as I watch the two of them from across the table. Cory's gaze meets mine, and she smiles back with hearts in her eyes, until her gaze travels to above my head, and a sassy grin replaces the smile.

I feel a presence behind me, just as two powerful hands grip my shoulders. In the past, my response would have been to stiffen and move away, but Cory's reaction tells me exactly who it is, and the gesture feels oddly comforting. I don't even flinch. Another bonus to come out of the camping trip was the start of a genuine friendship with Dylan. We've been texting most days and even hung out together at Reilly's Place, a popular local bar for Heartwood University's students. It's a surprise, but I'm enjoying his company and friendship.

Now, if I could just get one little image out of my head, I'd feel much better, but the night at the lake is hard to let go of. The visual of Dylan's eyes focused on mine, the slight flicker of heat that crossed them, the conflicted expression that followed, and the warmth that finally settled there is running on repeat through my mind. I'm not used to seeing that kind of warmth directed my way. It's almost like his internal monologue was playing out in front of me, and he wasn't even aware he was doing it. We both felt the attraction between us. It was impossible to ignore.

But, the second his nose brushed mine, I knew he'd made a decision. A decision to be friends. To be honest, my chest felt lighter at that revelation. I can't shake this strange feeling that I need him in my life, and *friends* is a great place for him to be.

So what if he has a body like a Greek god and piercing eyes that make you want to divulge all your secrets? He's a relationship guy, *in a relationship*, and I want nothing more than a night. He's off-limits. I know this. I rarely obsess over men. Although I've never been in a situation where I've wanted someone but held back, so maybe I'm succumbing to the "want what you can't have" philosophy. In theory, that would mean that as soon as I had *it* I wouldn't want *it* anymore. *Nope, Summer, get that thought out of your head right now.* I shake off my thoughts and bring myself back to the present.

Without acknowledging me, Dylan joins the conversation. "You're not still talking about that disaster, are you?" he asks Nate.

Nate laughs and shakes his head. "Can't tell the grandkids, but it's one we'll be talking about for the rest of our lives, that's for sure."

Cory gasps and her eyes shoot to me before quickly looking at Nate in a mix of awe and panic. Nate and Dylan continue on in conversation, oblivious to Cory's reaction. She remains a little doe-eyed until I change the subject.

"I ran into Lisa at Campus Coffee yesterday," I say, bringing Cory back down to earth. "She asked how you were considering your favorite childhood band broke up."

"Oh! I'd actually forgotten about that." She laughs and visibly relaxes into her seat.

"Seems you've got more important things to focus on," I say with a smile.

"What band?" Nate asks, jumping from his conversation into ours. If he had noticed Cory's reaction earlier, he wasn't drawing attention to it. Dylan sits down in the empty seat beside me and bumps his shoulder into mine affectionately, looking at me for the first time since he wandered over. My heart rate increases at his genuine smile, and I inwardly curse myself. *Pick another guy.*

Dylan's eyebrows pull in, and he twists his mouth to the side in thought. *God, what is my face telling him right now?* He opens his mouth to speak, just as my phone vibrates loudly in front of us. Private number. I raise my finger to his lips. "Hold that thought." I smile and answer my phone. "Hello."

"Is this Summer Kelly?" the caller blurts in a rush.

Dylan bites the finger I still have pressed to his lips, and a tingle shoots through me. Is he flirting? This is going to complicate things. Trying not to laugh, I respond to my mystery caller. "Sorry, who is this?" I'm completely distracted trying to pull my finger away. Dylan grabs my wrist, keeping me in place, and opens his mouth with a mischievous grin. I stifle another laugh until the caller's next words freeze me in place.

"I just have a few questions about your brother, Thomas."

Dylan's smile drops, a look of concern replacing it. "Summer, what's happened?"

I feel the gaze of Cory and Nate without having to look their way. For a few minutes, or maybe just a few long-feeling seconds, nobody speaks, until Cory breaks the silence. "Summer, you're scaring me."

At the same time, the caller says, "Are you there? Is there any truth to the rumor that you stole from your family?"

My chair crashes to the floor as I jump from the table and run outside, phone still clutched to my ear. The door opens again behind me, and I pray that it's Cory. A quick glance over my shoulder confirms that, so I relax before yelling into my phone. "I don't know what you heard, but it's absolute bullshit. Lose my number. I have nothing to say to you." With that, I hang up and turn to Cory, her sheer panic strangely warming my heart.

"What's going on? Who was that?" she asks.

My eyes dart back toward the door, knowing that Dylan is likely to walk out any second.

"I told them both to stay there." Cory answers my thoughts, then grabs my hand and pulls me farther away, just in case. "Summer, please?" Cory begs, and it's only then that I realize I don't exactly know what just happened, but I can guess.

"I'm pretty sure it was a reporter. He asked about my family and mentioned Thomas."

"Thomas? Why?"

As much as I like to pretend that I don't know or care about Thomas's life, I do. I've looked into him. Couldn't help it. I might hate him for turning his back on me, but I still *love* him.

I blow out a breath. "He's creating a buzz in Seattle. Guess supporters want to know everything about him now that he's gone pro," I say, and Cory's face softens a little.

"You keep track?"

"Can't help myself." I shrug.

"So, what exactly did they ask?"

"That's the scary bit." I pause, knowing that as soon as I say it out loud, it's officially the start of the Kelly family rumor mill all over again. Cory waits patiently, but I see her gaze flit toward the door. Looks like not everyone has the same patience. I predict I have about thirty seconds before Dylan reaches me, so I rush out my words. "He asked if I stole from my family. Why would he say that? Do you think Thomas is saying that?"

"Let's talk later." Cory pats my arm and smiles just as Dylan steps in front of me, grabbing my shoulders in a comforting gesture.

"I tried. I really did. But Summer, I've never seen you so freaked out," he says apologetically and then laughs shyly. "You know...in all the years I've known you." He smiles and shrugs, obviously trying to cheer me up. I smile back because it actually works.

"Just an ex-boyfriend; nothing to worry about," I say, expecting it to ease his mind. *Boy, was I wrong.*

"Who? What the fuck did he say?" he yells, looking between Cory and me. "Tell me his name. Is he harassing you?"

I flinch at my lie and his reaction. "Jesus, no, calm down. He was just reaching out," I lie again, unconvincingly.

"Bullshit. You ran out of there in a panic. You—"

I cut him off before he can continue. "I wanted privacy. I wasn't panicked."

Dylan looks at Cory and me again. Cory shrugs and smiles, refusing to give anything away.

"If you say so. But you know I'm here for you? If you ever need me."

It's a statement and a question. *Do I know that?* There are few people in my life who are genuinely there for me, but the word yes springs into my mind. Despite our short, *minute* friendship, I know he's sincere. "Thanks, Dylan." I smile. "Now where's my dessert?" *Conversation over.*

For some stupid reason, the thought of our family's business being exposed hadn't even crossed my mind. Why didn't I prepare myself for that, considering Thomas's position on the Seattle football team? The thought of having to relive it now, to think about my family, makes my chest ache. To say it had shocked me when they hadn't taken my side was an understatement. It devastated me. I cried for days, until I had nothing left. No tears, no family, no trust. I wish things could have been different. Thomas had been one of my best friends, my biggest supporter, before it all went down. Maybe I should have confronted him and Mom and asked them why? Instead, I ran away and never looked back, terrified that if I *had* asked them, there was a strong possibility I wouldn't like the response. I mentally curse myself for letting this get to me again, but outwardly, my smile never wavers.

When we've finished eating, Dylan insists on walking me to class. You know, in case my big bad ex-boyfriend gets me. I feel a little bad considering I've never had a boyfriend to have an ex.

"Are you sure you're okay?" he asks when we reach the building my class is in.

I smile at his protectiveness. It's kind of nice. There's no doubt he's a caring boyfriend. Gemma's a lucky girl. "Positive; thank you for the escort," I say, bumping my shoulder into his.

"Pinkie promise," he says with a straight face.

I burst out laughing. "Are you six?"

His mouth drops into a pout. "It's our thing. How could you forget?"

I suppress my smile and school my features into the most serious expression I can muster. "You're right. I'm sorry." I hold out my pinkie, and he links it with his own. "Pinkie promise," I say and then let my smile free.

Chapter Eleven

Dylan

I stare at the page, but the words blur together. I can't focus. I massage my temples, but it doesn't help. Two things are consuming my thoughts and both involve Summer. Okay, if I'm being honest, there are more than two things, but let's start there. First, the look on her face when she received that call. Something was definitely wrong. And that ex-boyfriend crap. Did she actually think I'd buy that? Second, I'm wondering if I should have told her that I'm now single. I held off because something told me that everything would change again if she knew, and we only just got into a comfortable rhythm. Plus, we're *just* friends so I have no reason to tell her, right? I may as well enjoy our friendship, as it is, for as long as I can. And since there's no hope in hell I'm getting through this today, I'm going to start enjoying it now. Leaning back in my chair, I grab my phone and text the girl who's invading my mind.

Me: Remember the night you made me drive two hours for ice cream, because the one near us was closed?

I throw the first serve in my new favorite sport—memory tennis with Summer.

Her reply comes within a couple of minutes.

Summer: As I recall it was YOU that needed ice cream. Your beloved football team hadn't made the playoffs.

I laugh out loud before remembering where I am and cutting myself off. I notice a few glares directed my way and cringe. *My bad.* Before I can reply, three little dots appear on my phone.

She's returning serve.

Summer: Do you remember when my dog knocked you off your bike, and you cried because you got a hole in your jeans?

Summer: P.S. What are you up to?

Me: I'm in the library, NOT studying like I should be.

Me: AND... They were my favorite pair.

I imagine Summer smiling at that and wish I could see her face.

Summer: Remember the night we went swimming in Brian's pool, even though it was freezing out?

I snicker quietly, because fuck, she's funny. Do we have fake mutual friends now?
Point to Summer. Love-Fifteen.
Time for my comeback shot.

Me: You insisted on wearing a pink bikini that barely covered your ass, just to impress him.

Okay, so I'm flirting a little. Sue me.

Summer: Ew! Brian was 40. It wasn't him I wanted to impress...

A laugh bursts from within me before I can stop it.
"Shhh!" someone whispers loudly—actually several someones. It's echoing all around me.
I cover my mouth to shut myself up but fail to suppress it all. *She's good. So good.* I bet she knows exactly what she's doing.

Love-Thirty.

Rereading her message as I think up a reply, I... *Hang on! Is she talking about me?*

My heart jumps and then resumes its normal rhythm.

I'll go with yes.

Me: He was definitely impressed.

I have no doubt that's how I'd feel if I ever got the chance to see her in a bikini. *Hmmm, Summer in a bikini, Summer lifting her wet body out of the water, Summer...Shit, I need a new visual. I'm in a library!*

Me: Remember that boy Justin that always used to follow you around? The kid with the snotty nose.

Yep, that did the trick. Good old snotty-nosed Justin. If you exist, I thank you. Raising my water bottle in the air, I salute fake Justin and take a sip.

Summer: Of course! He was my first kiss.

At that, I lose it, and the water I'd just taken in flies out of my mouth. I try to recover, but it's too late. Ms. Librarian storms over and stops in front of me, her arms crossed over her chest. It's safe to say she is not happy. She doesn't say a word, but I know the deal. "I'm just leaving." I smile, but she continues to scowl. Packing up my books, I quickly send Summer a text before hanging my head in shame and walking out the door.

Me: Well, it's official. You got me kicked out of the library. No more studying for me.

Game. Set. Match.

I only have twenty minutes before practice, anyway, so the chance of me actually studying was pretty slim. Still, it doesn't hurt to make Summer feel a little bad. *Or not...*

Summer: Took longer than I thought.

Ha! I knew it. She'd been trying to get me kicked out. I can picture a wicked smile on her face, and I'm happy that I may have helped put it there. For the first time, I'm not second-guessing a girl. Summer and I are friends. She doesn't have an ulterior motive, and she isn't being friendly just to sleep with me, like most of the girls here. Sure, in this instance, that wouldn't be a bad thing, but it's actually good to have a girl to talk to with no expectations. *Even if I maybe, possibly want more.*

Me: I think you owe me.

I walk to the stadium as I wait for her no doubt witty reply.

Summer: That's fair. Worth it.

Dammit, why do I have practice? I really want to see her right now. But, then again, when do I not want to see her?

Me: I'll need time to come up with the appropriate retribution. Training starts soon, gotta get my head in the game.

Summer: I'll be waiting. Don't work too hard.

I'll be waiting. That gives me more joy than it should. And as I arrive at the locker room, I have to force myself to wipe the smile from my face and focus.

Training is once again brutal, but I make it through.

Before I can hit the showers, my name rings out above the chatter. "Mathers?" Coach yells.

"Yup, Coach."

"My office when you're clean. And, it's yes, Coach."

"Yes, Coach." I smile and head toward our locker room. A quick shower, deodorant, and a change of clothes, and I'm out the door in record time. The sooner I see Coach, the sooner I can get to my hot date with the TV.

"What's up, Coach?" I ask before leaping over the armrest and settling into the chair. He shakes his head at my casual behavior but doesn't hide his smirk. We get along well. I've never been nervous when called into his office, and today's no different. Relaxing back in the chair, I stop short of putting my feet up on the desk and smile.

"We've got a big game coming up after the opener, and I've just been told we'll be hosting a few scouts."

"Nice! The boys will be pretty happy about that. Most anyway. Any ideas who they're here to see?" I ask, knowing instantly why he wanted to see me. I may not be the captain, but I know every one of my teammates like the back of my hand. He knows I can tell him who'd benefit from this information in advance and who'd play better without the pressure. I have a rough idea in my mind of who they'd want to see. Edwards, Jones, Davis, Hamilton...

"You." *Okay, that was not on my list.*

"For real?" I ask. I haven't expressed any interest in the draft or going pro. In fact, I've done the opposite, so this is unexpected.

"For real." He smirks again, and I'm about to respond when he goes off on a spiel. "Before you say anything. You've been a huge asset to this team. You're an outstanding leader and an even better player. You know I'd play you at quarterback if you'd let me. With Kelly gone, we could sure use you. But I'm respecting your wishes. In that case, anyway. Plus, it doesn't hurt that you're a phenomenal receiver. Point is, I'm not letting you miss an opportunity you might regret in the future. I can't think of anyone else I'd rather recommend to any NFL teams."

I can't hear anymore. The guilt is already too much. My hand rubs over my face in an attempt to hide my anguish. "Ah, thanks, Coach. I appreciate that, but—"

"No buts yet. They're coming to the game to watch, not propose marriage. You don't need to declare anything at this stage. Assuming that's what you were about to say."

It *was*. That's exactly what I was about to say. While I love everything about the game, I've made peace with my decision not to play professionally. I couldn't, *wouldn't*, let this moment change that. "I don't want them to waste their time—"

Coach raises his hand to silence me. "I know you've always kept your head down when talk of an NFL career occurs, and I am not here to change your mind, but I think you should keep your options open. At least until the deadline has passed."

"Okay, Coach. Thank you," I say, standing from my chair.

"Oh, and Dylan, they want to see Bennett too. I'll leave it up to you to decide whether you tell him or not. That guy's head is big enough already."

Luke Bennett. I know the answer to that straightaway. "Sorry, Coach, did you say something?" I joke.

"Nothing at all," he replies with a knowing grin.

I can't help but laugh as I move toward the door. I'm about to leave when Coach calls me back.

"Just think about it, Dylan. For you, I mean."

I pause for a second. "I will, thanks." Really, what else was I going to say? Coach has always been good to me, always helped with extra training when I'd asked for it. He's been a mentor. Telling him I don't see football in my future would be a slap in his face. He lives and breathes football. The least I can do is appear to be considering it until the very last second. I don't want to disappoint him, but I decided long ago that I wouldn't follow the path of my father. He was, *still is*, the greatest man I've ever known, but football kept him away from us. I want a family one day, and I want that family to be my number one priority.

Pushing open the door to the parking lot, Summer's face comes to mind. Not because I was thinking about family. *We're friends*. She came to mind because I feel like I could talk to her about all this if I wanted to. She's someone I believe will really stop and listen. Someone I actually want to share things with. She's not like anyone I've ever met. On the outside she comes across as funny, easygoing, and confident, and she is all that, but underneath...I feel that she's sometimes putting on a front, and I want to know everything about her. *Need to* know everything about her. You know, as friends. *God, who am I kidding?*

Joel's in the kitchen when I arrive home. He's making a sandwich and has his book open on the counter next to a packet of sticky notes. Most people believe Joel to be the antithesis of a genius and yet that is exactly what he is. With his rugged good looks—yes, I can appreciate the male form—playboy ways, and chilled nature, people overlook that they are in the presence of a brilliant mind. I almost don't want to interrupt, *almost*, but instead rap my knuckles against the counter to get his attention.

"What's up?" he asks casually, without even looking at me.

I cut straight to the chase. "Coach says a scout is coming to see me at the Tigers game."

He pauses and abandons his books completely, giving me his full attention. "No shit? That's great!"

"Well..."

Joel shakes his head as soon as the word is out of my mouth. "Nope, stop right there. I know what you're going to say, and before you do, just hear me out."

"Okay." I wave my hand to gesture for him to begin.

"You've had a couple of shitty relationships, and now you're single."

"Thanks for the recap," I reply.

"You're welcome." Joel grins. "Anyway, my point is that maybe you shouldn't rule out the NFL just yet. I know your reasons." *Most of them.* "And you said yourself that you're going to try staying single for once, so all your concerns could be nonissues."

"For now." I laugh, and Joel shrugs.

He has a point, sort of. But it's still not going to help in the long run. It's better if I...

"Just keep your options open," he says, reading my mind like always. "It can't hurt," he adds to really drive his opinion home. Again, he's right. What's the harm in keeping my options open? Who knows what tomorrow will bring?

Chapter Twelve

Summer

I'm not paying attention as I walk across campus the day after texting with Dylan. I'm smiling at the thought of him being escorted out of the library, and so completely lost in the visual my mind creates that I startle when a group of girls call my name. They're waving frantically with big smiles on their faces. I offer a polite wave but otherwise ignore it and continue on. *That was weird.* When I approach the door to my building, a petite, bright-eyed and bubbly young girl runs in front of me and opens it before I can. "I've got it," she chirps with a smile and then moves to the side, allowing me to pass through.

"Thank you?" I say, because, again, it's the polite thing to do, but it comes out as a question because...I don't even know why? I mean, sure, most people I've met here at Heartwood U have been nice enough, but this is next level.

In the hall, another two girls smile at me and a third tells me to have a nice day. *Am I dreaming? What is happening here?* Taking my usual seat in literature, I wait for Cory to join me as she stayed at Nate's last night. It's the only class we have together, probably because it's her *only* summer class full stop. I somehow convinced her to take it *now* rather than later. I almost bounce in my seat, dying to tell her about the strange female attention I'm getting, knowing she'll get a kick out of it. When she finally walks through the door at the bottom of the lecture hall, she gives me a questioning look and raises an eyebrow, looking a little to my left. I follow her gaze and internally groan. Three girls are heading toward me with coffee and huge smiles on their overly made-up faces. I cringe when I recognize them. We've been in a few classes together, so I know them well enough to have secretly given them nicknames, but we are not friends.

I'm not religious at all, but at this moment, I find myself praying they'll walk past me. I do *not* need this right now. *My prayers are not answered.*

"I can't believe we didn't know you were in this class," Beach Barbie says before sitting down beside me.

I can't believe you even know who I am. I'm not usually one to judge others, especially women, and I don't generally have anything against anyone, but these women *scream* fake. I smile and keep looking at my phone, hoping they'll disappear. *No such luck, again.*

"How was your weekend?" Blonde Barbie asks as she squeezes her orange tanned body past me to sit on my other side.

It's Thursday, but I let that slide and answer. "I had a great weekend, and almost feel ready for the next one."

"You. Are. So. Funny. Isn't she, girls?"

Someone please get me a bucket. I need to puke. What is going on? If they think I'm tutoring their tiny, perfect looking asses, they can think again.

"I bet you and Dylan laugh *all* the time," says Bouncy Barbie. And *that's my final nickname. Unoriginal, I know.* The girls all sigh like Bouncy Barbie's comment is the cutest thing they've ever heard. Me? I'm completely confused.

"Come again?"

"You and Dylan must laugh together. You know, because you are both so funny."

Say what? "Huh?" I stare blankly, my eyes shifting between the two girls on my left, hoping one of them will give me more information. The Barbie on my right answers my question with her swooning.

"I wish he was *my* best friend," she whispers.

A laugh escapes me before I can stop it, so I cough to hide it. *I walked right into this. That will teach me for having a little fun. I wonder why this is coming up now?*

"Since you know him so well, which of us do you think has a better chance with him?"

I check the time on my phone. Class should have started, but no, today he's going to be late. I turn back to the girls. "Good question, Lilly."

"It's Lolly."

"Oh, apologies. I'm sorry, but he has a girlfriend," I say and then wave my phone in the air. "Excuse me for a second. I just received a text message," I lie and start a text to Cory even though she is in the room.

"No, he doesn't," one girl says after a minute of me ignoring them.

Keeping my eyes on the phone, I'm only half paying attention. "Doesn't what?" I ask. *God, why am I entertaining this?*

"He doesn't have a girlfriend," one of them says.

What? I freeze at her words, my heart beating so hard that I'm pretty sure I could feel it against my hand if I held it to my chest. *That can't be right? Can it?*

"Shouldn't you know that? Considering—"

Ah... "Of course, I know that. I just didn't know it was common knowledge yet," I quickly blurt, cutting her off. They smile in unison, and it's a little creepy.

"So...who has the best shot?"

What? Oh right. That's where this started. I wish this wasn't happening. I need to process this new information, but three sets of eyes are staring at me, waiting for a response. I shake off my thoughts, calm my breathing, and sigh. If they want an answer, I may as well enjoy it. Eyes down to my phone again, I quickly send Dylan a text.

Me: Are you a boob, ass, or legs man?

Lucky for me, the girls surrounding me each fit into a different one of these categories. While they're all equally fine, they know their best features and flaunt them. Beach Barbie has on Daisy Dukes, Blondie's in a low-cut top that's most definitely one size too small, and Bouncy Barbie is in a miniskirt. It doesn't take much to figure out who matches with each asset. And because I need answers, I shoot off another text straight after.

Me: Also, Gemma???

Dylan's reply is instant.

Dylan: Ummm, what?

Dylan: We broke up.

So it's true. My heart rate picks up again, but I ignore it. I got my answer, and it changes nothing, so...back to my initial query.

Me: Boobs, ass, or legs. Which is it? It's a simple question and one I need answered... right now.

Dylan: I feel like this is a trick.

I let out a very unattractive snort laugh, his words working to keep my thoughts on our easy friendship. The three Barbies were right. We laugh together all the time.

Me: Oh my god. Just answer me.

Dylan: ...

I smile in anticipation and then snort again at his response.

Dylan: Smile, definitely smile.

What a dork. I have to admit, being friends with Dylan is definitely entertaining.

Dylan: Personality?

Okay, that's a little cute

Dylan: Intelligence?

This guy...
My smile now firmly plastered on my face, I can't help but laugh again. When I look up from my phone, the three girls are staring at me. *Shit, they're still here and waiting for my answer. Where is the professor?*

"Sorry, I just need to respond to this important message." I shrug, somewhat apologetically, but it's insincere.

Summer: How very noble of you, but they weren't options. I'm waiting...

His reply comes before I've even had the chance to look away from my phone. He obviously has a favorite.

Dylan: Legs.

I look down at my long, toned legs and bite my lip with a smirk. I'm pretty happy with most of my body, but my legs are something I'm proud of. I like to keep fit, and as a result, I can definitely say that my legs are an asset. I like his answer. A lot. I don't give him the satisfaction of knowing that, though.

Me: Legs it is!

I turn back to the girls. "I think S...Simone is the best fit." I stumble a little over her name, hoping it is actually Simone. She beams at me and cheers, drawing attention to our little group. The professor, who finally graced us with his presence, ignores us and begins discussing topics for our upcoming

reports. The Barbie Trio start their own conversation about how lucky Simone is. They talk as though she already has a date with Dylan, completely oblivious to the fact that they forgot to ask me to put in a good word, which I would have very much enjoyed doing. If I've learned anything from my time with Dylan, it's that he enjoys decent conversation. I don't think he's going to get that from Simone, and that thought is very amusing.

A vibration in my hand alerts me to a new message.

Dylan: ???

Ignoring Dylan, I text Cory, who's been relegated to sitting at the other end of our row.

Me: Lunch?

Cory: Only if you invite your new friends.

I look her way and smile, shaking my head.

Me: Not a chance. Let's go off campus.

Cory: Sounds good. I just need to get my purse from Nate. He's meeting me out front.

When class finishes, Nate greets us as expected. What's not expected is a smiling Dylan standing beside him. Before he realizes I've noticed him, his eyes roam my legs like he's in some kind of trance. After a moment, he shakes his head and looks away. I bite my lip to suppress my smile. *So, he has noticed my legs?* An unwelcome flutter runs through me. I'm not sure how I feel about his new status. Ignoring my inner chaos, I smile with a raised eyebrow when I reach his side.

He doesn't waste any time in mentioning our texts. "So, want to tell me what that was all about?" he asks.

The unmistakable laugh of my new friends interrupts my response, and I roll my eyes. I actually had no intention of ever inflicting Simone onto Dylan, but since he decided to stalk me and she's here, well...I have no choice. He'll have to endure it. "Dylan, I'd like you to meet"—I grab Simone's hand and pull her closer to me—"Simone."

A flash of disappointment crosses his face, but I ignore it.

"Simone, this is Dylan."

"Your best friend, Dylan? The guy you mentioned in class?" she says, pretending she doesn't know him. *Huh, so maybe she's smarter than I thought. Nice move, Simone.*

Dylan looks between the two of us, his eyes questioning me as I say, "The one and only."

Nate and Cory flash me identical confused expressions, and I gotta say, I'm right there with them. I actually have no idea what I'm doing. Knowing he's now single is throwing me off balance. It's easier to push him toward other girls than to let my mind go places it shouldn't.

As soon as her number is programmed in Dylan's phone, Simone walks away with a bounce in her step. I glance in his direction and see he's already looking at me, eyes narrowed in question. I scrunch my nose and shrug apologetically, before Cory drags me away.

Chapter Thirteen

Dylan

For once, the guys decide to have a somewhat quiet boys' night instead of a party, and I'm relieved. Turns out, trying to stay single is not as easy as you might think. Girls literally throw themselves at me, and while I'm not interested in the desperate types, I have come across a few genuine girls on my nights out. Girls that I probably would have tried to get to know in the past. So yeah, I'm *not* complaining about the change of company tonight; a boys' night is exactly what I need. The only downside being that I have a faint headache I can't seem to shake. Not big enough to do anything about it, but enough to be annoying.

I spend an hour chatting with my teammates and playing pool, finally getting to unwind, and I'm relaxing in the living room when the energy in the room shifts. It shouldn't surprise me when Cory and Summer arrive, but it does. Nate's been sneaking glances at his phone since I arrived, so it's on me for not seeing this coming. I raise my eyebrows at him, and he shrugs with a goofy smile, not at all ashamed. And I get it. I really do. He may not have admitted it yet, or maybe he has, but either way, he is definitely in love.

Summer catches my eye when she enters the room. She makes a beeline for me, without bothering to take in the surrounding scene, and for some reason, I straighten in my seat. Before saying a word, she grabs the beer from my hand, knocking half of it back in one go. "Thanks, I needed that." She smiles and then sits on the armrest of the couch beside me. "So, what does one do on a boys' night? Should I belch, drink straight from a bottle of bourbon, bust out my best video game moves, smoke a cigar?" I snort out a laugh as she raises an eyebrow in question. She's holding back her smile, but I can see the corners of her lips itching to rise.

Wiping the smile off my face, I play along. "All of those things, *obviously*, but so much more. You'll need to talk a lot of shit about nothing, watch sports, and play poker. Oh, and you should be naked," I deadpan and wait for her laugh.

She maintains her facade, and with a shrug of her shoulders, like it's no big deal, says, "I'm down with all that."

Then comes the laughter I was waiting for; it's loud and obnoxious and it's *mine*.

A sassy smile crosses Summer's face, and she winks. *How have I not been friends with this girl my entire life?* I befriended the wrong Kelly. Thomas isn't this cool and definitely not as hot. Summer is fun and fresh, she's easy to talk to, smart, and she's so goddamn beautiful it's hard to look away sometimes, not to mention the way her eyes...*What the fuck, Dylan. Stop. She's just a friend.*

Something must show on my face, as the thoughts drift through my mind, because Summer gives me a curious look before grabbing my beer again and chugging the rest of it down. "I'll get another," she announces and walks toward the bar without looking back. *Good one, Dylan.*

When she returns, smile in place and curiosity gone, we quickly fall back into our easy banter, and I relax. *Maybe it's not so bad having girls here after all.*

We've just finished watching one of the guys do the worm across the room, when Summer turns to me with a furrowed brow. "How come these guys are your closest friends—" I raise an eyebrow, silently asking where she's going with this. She pauses and laughs, and it's a beautiful sound. A sound I wouldn't mind hearing more often. "Let me finish," she says, playfully shoving my chest. "What I mean is, why don't you live at the 'Ball House' if you're so close to these guys?" She uses quote fingers and crinkles her nose when she says "Ball House," like the very thought of it disgusts her.

I smile at her adorable expression. "Never even thought about it, to be honest. Joel and I always had plans to live together, so that's what we did." I shrug.

"Well, I think you made a good decision."

"Phew, that's lucky. I was worried for a minute," I say while pretending to wipe sweat off my forehead.

Summer laughs and playfully shoves my chest again, but this time she runs a finger down my abs before pulling away. Both our eyes follow the movement, and when we look up at each other, I'm disappointed to see she's not nearly as affected as I am. *Damn.* Cory arrives at that moment and joins our conversation, saving me from giving it any more thought.

With drinks flowing, the noise level gets louder as the night goes on, and my headache gets significantly worse. I should have taken something for it hours ago, but no, I'm an idiot. I'm leaning against a wall in the living room, taking a moment for myself, my eyes never straying away from Summer for too long. I rub my temples and pinch the bridge of my nose to try and dull the pain, briefly closing my eyes. When I open them again, I'm met with Cory's concerned gaze. "Are you okay?" she asks in a sympathetic tone. In the weeks since the camping trip, she's become like a mother hen to the boys.

"Pounding headache, but I'll be all right." I smile.

A hint of amusement crosses her face and then disappears. *Not the response I expected.* Before I have the chance to question it, she gets Summer's attention from where she's now talking to Luke. "Summer gives the best head and neck massages," she says, trying to act all innocent, like a sneaky idea didn't just pop into her mind. "They've helped my headaches in the past," she continues, and when Summer's mouth drops open midsip of her drink, I hide my smile. *What's Cory up to?* I mean, I can think of worse things than a head massage from a beautiful girl, but I have to wonder what Cory's thinking as she sets this up. Still, I'm not going to pass up this opportunity. All in the name of making Summer uncomfortable, of course.

"Does she now?" I ask.

"Summer, he's struggling over here. Look at him," Cory says.

I rub my temples again, for show, and groan. Eyes squinted, nose wrinkled, and teeth clenched, a look of fake and overexaggerated agony crosses my face.

"Drop the act and sit down," Summer snaps as she walks my way and rolls her eyes.

I give her a salute and drop to the loveseat.

"The loveseat. Really? And how I am supposed to...Never mind." She sighs and steps up onto the two-seater.

I instantly realize my mistake. She needs access to my head and neck, and the loveseat is up against a wall and low to the ground. I move to stand, but she pushes me back down and signals for me to slide forward in the seat. I do as asked, and she slips in behind me. On her knees, she parts her legs and pulls me back slightly into her. *Shit, I thought this was supposed to make* her *uncomfortable.*

We are both dead silent and still at first, but then I hear an intake of breath, and soft fingertips make their way through my hair, pressing down into my scalp. Summer moves her fingers in and out, focusing on different areas, increasing the pressure as she does. I lean back into her a little more, and her legs clench around my sides. It takes a lot of willpower to stop myself from grabbing her thighs and pulling her even closer as she works my shoulders and neck, finding knots I didn't even realize I had. When she moves back to my head and rakes her nails through my hair, my eyes close involuntarily and my body sags. Even with the noise in the room, I can hear Summer's breathing, so I focus on that and relax even more.

When her nails scratch my head a second time, a soft moan escapes my mouth. Summer's breath hitches and she clenches her legs again. If this isn't the sexiest, nonsexual thing that's ever happened to me, then...I don't even know. I'm not even sure I could tell you the date or year right now.

After a few minutes, Summer's strokes become softer, like she's exploring my head and shoulders rather than massaging them. This new sensation sends a tingle down my spine, and I can't stop myself from shivering. *Fuck!*

She stops suddenly, as though my movement broke her from a trance. When I finally open my eyes, I see that we're alone. *Hmm, when did that happen?*

"Better?" Summer whispers. I'm still lost in thought so I don't answer, too busy wondering if the others felt the same sexual tension I did and had to get away. I can hear voices in the backyard. *God, what is wrong with me?*

"They left as soon as you closed your eyes." Summer answers my unspoken question. Her usually confident voice is softer and breathy. "Don't worry, they didn't hear your moans," she jokes, but her voice does nothing to hide the fact that she's equally affected. She jumps up off the couch and attempts to pull her short shorts down her legs.

"I'm going to get another drink," she blurts out and rushes away. I listen as she moves about the kitchen, then the back door opens and closes with a loud clang. She's gone. I take a much-needed moment, readjusting myself, before I join the group. *What the hell just happened?* I didn't even speak or thank her. I couldn't. *Again, what the hell is wrong with me?*

When I step outside about ten minutes later, Summer is raising a shot of something black to her lips.

"Three down, two to go," Luke yells and passes another. *What is she doing?* She's going to be out cold after five. Cory shouldn't be letting this happen. *Where's mother hen?* My eyes search through the crowd of men, but no luck. She must be hiding away with Nate somewhere. Cheers ring out behind me.

"Who's next?" Summer asks and smiles while searching for the next victim. When her eyes find me, her smile grows and my body moves toward her without asking my mind for permission. She wraps her arms around my neck and presses her body into mine, the shots already affecting her judgment. Stepping up on her toes, she pulls my head down and moves her mouth to my ear. My mouth goes dry. *Please say you want to get out of here.* I wrap my arms around her, the palms of my hands gently pressing on her back, bringing her closer to me. It's like the head massage has destroyed all my brain cells and I'm no longer in control. I know I shouldn't be doing this, but when she takes a quick sharp breath, I lose all reasoning.

I'm just about to tell her to screw our friendship, when she whispers. "You're up. Five. Or. Dive?" Pulling her head back, she looks me dead in the eyes. Any effect I had on her has gone. She's once again cool, calm, and collected. She raises an eyebrow, and I remember she asked a question. *Five or what? Oh, the stupid game.* I can't help but smile.

Releasing my hold on her, I step away. There is no way I'm jumping in that pool fully clothed, so... "Five" I reply and my promise to limit alcohol during the season goes straight out the window along with my insane belief that I'd be happy with Summer in the friend zone. I knock back the five shots with barely a breath in between. *Stupid, stupid idea.*

Summer laughs and leans in to me. "Impressive," she says, her teeth pulling at her bottom lip. I inwardly groan, and it takes all my self-control not to lean forward and take my own bite.

"Who's up for beer pong?" someone yells, and I roll my eyes. *Ain't gonna be me.* I don't really care for drinking games and have avoided them all these years until—

"Dylan and I are in," Summer yells, grabbing my hand and pulling me toward the table. "We're going to kick ass." *Of course, that was going to happen.*

Two rounds later and only three drinks in, we *are* kicking ass. I have no idea how, considering Summer spends most of the time swaying, and I spend most of my time watching her hips move, but here we are on the last shot.

"You can do this, babe," I say, and her eyes spring up to mine. *Fuck, why did I say that?*

She winks and smiles. "You bet your ass I can." *We really need to cool it on the ass talk, because Summer's looks amazing in those tiny shorts, and I'm already struggling to focus.*

She's still swaying as she lines up for her shot, even worse than before, so I grab her hips to steady her. Expecting her to freeze or push me away, I'm shocked when I hear a quick thank you leave her mouth. Her arms rise and I feel the release of the ball. I say *feel* because my eyes may be looking in that direction, but with my hands splayed across Summer's hips and my fingertips resting just under the top of her shorts, I'm not seeing anything. I only realize we've won when her hands shoot up in the air and she turns around, breaking my hold. I take a step back and snap out of it, just in time for her to leap into my arms and wrap her legs around me. Her forest-green eyes lock with mine, and I freeze. *What I wouldn't give to push her up against a wall right now.* Heat flashes in her gaze, and I know it matches mine. She rubs her nose against mine, taking me back to the night by the lake, then smiles before screaming "woo hoo" at the top of her lungs and raising her fist in the air. If only she was always this uninhibited around me. She tries to jump down, but when her feet hit the ground, she stumbles and falls into my arms.

"I think I need to lie down," she whispers and smiles.

"I'll get you home," I say, walking her back inside to collect her things.

"You live right around the corner, right, yes, correct?" she mumbles, and it's adorable. I try not to laugh.

"Yes, but I don't mind going past your place first. I want to make sure you get home safely."

"Aww, that's sweet. But since your place is closer, we'll just go there." The words leave her mouth like it's no big deal. *We'll just go there. What does she even mean?* She's drunk, so I'm obviously not going to take advantage, but does this mean she wants to? I book a cab, and we say our goodbyes. When I wave to Luke, he raises an eyebrow and gives me a disapproving head shake. I know he's referring to Thomas, but right now, I couldn't care less.

Summer rests her head on my shoulder and hums, something I've noticed her doing before, and a minute after the cab starts moving, she falls asleep. Her soft blonde hair tickles my cheek, but I can't bear to move her. I don't want to. What I want to do is grab her hand and curl our fingers together while resting my head on hers, but instead, I stay still and spend the entire trip trying not to wake her. Despite my earlier concerns, I'm pretty stoked that the girls crashed our boys' night.

After paying the driver, I gently lift her into my arms and carry her inside and straight to my room. Laying her on my bed, I remove her shoes and pull the blankets up, tucking them just under her shoulders. She looks so beautiful and innocent with her soft curls fanning my pillow and her hand resting against her forehead. I could stare at her all night, but I won't.

Trying to be as quiet as possible, I grab a pair of boxer briefs and move to leave the room, resigned to a night on the couch. Just before the door shuts behind me, Summer calls my name. When I look back, she's moved to one side of the bed and has flipped the comforter open. All she has to say is "stay" and I'm stripping down and moving across the room to the bed before she changes her mind.

I slip in next to her and roll her over so that her back is to me, pulling her close. When I wrap my arm around her, she connects her fingers with mine and stills. Within seconds, her breathing evens out and she's once again out cold. Unable to resist, I gently press a kiss to her head and then it's not long before I join her in sleep.

Chapter Fourteen

Summer

My head is throbbing when I wake, and it feels like my body's being pressed into the mattress. *Dammit, Brutus.* That mutt has broken into my room for the last...*hang on.* I quiet my thoughts to allow my brain to catch up with the times. *Summer, you no longer live at home, and you haven't seen the family dog since you left.* And I'm back in the present. I barely have time to be saddened by the memory before it occurs to me that if the weight isn't a dog, then it must be...*Shit!* I open my eyes and bite my lip before slowly turning my head to look over my shoulder. Sure enough, Dylan is sleeping behind me, arms and legs pinning me down. His long, perfect lashes rest against his cheek, and his lips are parted slightly and dangerously close to my skin. Add to that his messy bed hair and you have a sight that's difficult to look away from.

There's nothing comfortable about this situation. Okay, that's a lie, there is *plenty* comfortable about this situation. The feel of his hand splayed over my waist, his face buried in my hair, the way his body aligns perfectly with mine...*Ugh, stop.* I need out, and fast. Slowly and gently, I try to pull my limbs free from his clutches, but it doesn't take long to figure out that's not a workable option. Attempt two, roll onto my tummy and slide...

"Keep wriggling like that and you're going to have to finish what you've started," Dylan whispers, humor lacing his raspy, just woken voice. The sound of it instantly turns me on, and I shake my head to clear my mind.

Sneaking another peek over my shoulder, I see his eyes are still closed. "I thought you were asleep," I say, trying harder to move out from under him, since he's now awake, but he doesn't budge.

"I am still asleep. So, *stop* moving." He doesn't open his eyes, but the sexiest smile I've ever received lights up his face, and it takes everything I have to ignore it and calm my breathing.

"I can't, you're on top of me," I say, with my lip between my teeth to suppress the nervous laugh trying to escape. I wriggle one more time just for the fun of it, making sure that my body presses back into his. *I bet that makes him move.*

Quick as a flash, Dylan releases his hold on me, but before I have the chance to move, he pushes me onto my back and hovers over me, his hands braced on the bed, one on each side of my face. "You're wrong," he says, and I look at him in shock, but furrow my brows in question. He lowers his body toward me and stops right before we touch. I try to hide my sharp intake of breath, but he notices and smiles. This playful yet assertive side of Dylan is new, and I can't decide how I feel about it. My eyes hold his, waiting for him to continue.

"*This* is me on top of you," he says. His gaze intensifies, as though he's searching for something in my eyes. I'm about to look away when he shakes his head then laughs, moving back to his side of the bed. He relaxes into the pillow, arms locked behind his head. "It's nice to wake up next to you again. It's been too long," he says casually, moving this conversation in another direction and confusing the hell out of me.

"Um, we've never—"

"It brings me back to the days we had sleepovers in my tree house," he continues, ignoring my question but answering it at the same time. He's reminiscing about our make-believe childhood together. A game I have come to love.

I lie back on the pillow beside Dylan, my body position mimicking his. The tips of our elbows touch with our proximity, and I will myself to focus. "God, that feels like it was only yesterday. As I recall, you were a bed hog then too," I play along.

"At least I didn't talk in my sleep." He knocks my elbow with his.

"Oh, because snoring is so much better." I return the gesture.

He laughs. "And remember that god-awful music you used to make me listen to? You were obsessed with the nineties as I recall." His eyes flash to mine, and when I raise an eyebrow, he smirks. "I'm going to guess you still are," he teases. "Faking aside, let me see. You have an unhealthy number of boy bands on your playlists." He scans my face for a reaction. "Or hard rock and grunge?"

He's right, and I wish I didn't feel the need to acknowledge it. "All three actually—rock, grunge, and a tiny bit of boy band music on there." I hold my thumb and finger an inch apart, though it's actually more like eighty percent boy bands.

"Okay, I'll give you hard rock and grunge, but boy bands, really?"

I sit up in a flash, a look of shock on my face. "Hold up, hold up. Pause for a second. I'm happy to play along with this little game of ours," I say, motioning my hand back and forth between us. "But don't you dare say a bad word about my taste in music," I scoff.

Dylan stares at me for seconds and then breaks into laughter. It's so infectious that I join him.

"Okay then, what's your favorite song of all time?" I ask, eyebrows raised, hoping I can return the tease.

He pauses for a second and then closes his eyes. "Metallica, 'Nothing Else Matters,'" he says with melancholy in his voice. There's definitely a story there, but he doesn't explain it; instead, he says, "You?"

I almost don't want to tell him. He's never going to believe me, and I certainly don't have the same feelings toward it as he does, but I confess, anyway. "Metallica, 'Nothing Else Matters.'"

Crystal-blue eyes flash to mine, and he squints, no doubt looking for signs of mockery. I offer a soft smile and a shrug in confirmation, and his slightly hardened gaze softens.

"Okay, now that's out of the way, remember when..." and just like that, we've moved on without Dylan offering any explanation. We continue our game, back and forth, teasing and laughing, until Dylan pauses and once again turns to look at me.

"You know, Mom always said we'd end up together," he jokes, but I feel the air shift a little.

"That's because she always wanted a daughter." I laugh, a little uncomfortably, but hopefully he doesn't notice. He scoffs and pulls my attention from my thoughts. *Did I say something wrong?*

"Ah, I don't think Lucy would appreciate that comment," he replies.

Shit, he has a sister? "Then maybe it's because I was the *only* girl, other than Lucy, who'd put up with you." I wink and am instantly rewarded with a sexy smile.

"You're probably right." He laughs until his smile morphs into a cocky grin. "Another thing I'll always remember is that you have a ticklish spot right about..." his voice trails off.

Jumping to his knees, he places himself near the middle of my body. "Here," he says, starting his pursuit behind my knees. He pokes his fingers into the flesh but gets nothing in return, not even a flinch. Next, he moves his fingers up to under my arms, a confident smile in place, but gets the same result—nothing. I bite back a smile at his failure, as his brows furrow in concentration. I see the moment an idea pops into his head, before he slowly drags his fingers across my skin, his eyes following the same path. I resist the urge to swallow when he moves over the ridge of my collarbone and stops at the base of my neck, but I can't stop the shiver that takes over me. Thankfully, Dylan's unwavering in his mission to figure out my weak spot, so he doesn't notice the effect he's having on me. Either that or he's equally affected. *This is no longer funny.*

When his next attempt, once again, gives him nothing, he pulls back and looks at me for a minute, studying my face. I recover from my internal moment and raise an eyebrow, slightly impressed that I seem to have thwarted his plans so far. That is until a devilish look crosses his face. He positions himself up on one hand and places the other on my waist, just above my hips. *Oh shit!* The second his fingers touch my skin, my body jumps on pure reflex.

It's Dylan's turn to raise his eyebrows in question, but his look is pure gloating. Before I can get him off me, he starts using several fingers to tickle me to tears. My body thrashes around as I laugh uncontrollably and scream at him to stop.

Dylan laughs along, putting every effort into making me squirm, until I'm basically jelly, then stops. "Just like old times," he smirks. "Except I'm pretty sure we also made out," he states matter-of-factly.

"Ha, that never happened." I mean, none of this has actually ever happened, but I feel the need to argue with this one. It's one line we are better off *not* crossing, as fake as it may be.

"Sure, it did. I remember it vividly; you were terrible, but I wanted the practice."

What? He didn't. "I was terrible? Me? I think you have that backwards."

"Ah, so you're admitting we made out. I knew it!"

Shit. So much for that. "Maybe a couple of times before we decided, rightfully so, that friends shouldn't make out." I'm no longer sure if I'm talking about our pretend childhood or trying to make a point about right now.

Dylan lets out a small laugh, and I know he's thinking the same thing. Breaking the awkwardness or perhaps adding more, he straddles my legs and grips my waist, tickling me once again. This time with a little more force.

We both laugh as I wriggle around unnaturally beneath him. "Stop, Dylan. I'm dying here." I snort and cringe at the sound.

He laughs again and gives me one last jab in that little spot, now known as the forbidden zone. My hips bounce off the bed, straight into his groin, while my arms involuntarily reach out and grab his back, pulling him down into me. The movement stills us both.

Dylan pulls back slightly to look into my eyes, his face only a few inches from mine. I can feel his chest moving up and down, as his heavy breathing matches mine. We stare at each other, for how long, I don't know, until he slowly lowers his face to mine. I scream *don't do it* in my mind, but do nothing to actually stop him. He closes his eyes and then lowers slowly until his soft lips meet mine with the faintest pressure. He pulls my lower lip between his own, sucking gently, before moving to the top, once, twice, and then repeating the movement a few more times. It feels good, so good. The whole thing lasts only a few seconds, but it's enough. The butterflies inside me flutter at an alarming speed, and I feel like my heart is going to break through my chest. This is too much. Don't get me wrong; I enjoy being physical with men, *love* it. But this is something else, something *deeper. Something I don't want. Shit! I can't be here. I can't do this.* My body stiffens, and my breathing becomes shallow for an entirely new reason, as I consider the mess I've made. I'm no longer kissing Dylan back, and he notices. His lips gently caress mine one last time before he pulls back, scanning my face again with a small smile. And that smile breaks me.

I don't know how to express the feelings I have about what just happened. Yes, I enjoyed it, but nothing more can come of it. It shouldn't have happened. I'm at a loss for words. *What does Dylan think this means? God, why did I kiss him back? Did I just completely screw up this friendship, before it really had a chance?*

Breaking the silence, I speak before I've even formed the right words to say. "Dylan, I-"

"Yep, I was right," he interrupts, shaking his head, a little lost in thought. "You're a terrible kisser." He laughs and rises off the bed, completely relaxed. "Come on, time to get up and start the day. I'm thinking...a greasy breakfast at Reilly's."

Just like that. I'd love to say he's put my mind at ease, but while his words are reassuring, I can't help but worry that one kiss changed everything.

Since ignoring my feelings *is* what I do best, I shrug my shoulders, take a deep breath, and jump out of bed. "Breakfast sounds great," I say with a smile, and after smoothing down my clothes, I follow him out the door.

Chapter Fifteen

Summer

Over the next few days, our friendship returns to normal following the kiss. To say I'm relieved is an understatement. It was a brief detour from our friendship, but it's over now, and no matter what I do or don't feel, we've moved on.

If only that was all I had going on in my life, but the situation with Dylan has actually been the least of my worries. Calls from that stupid reporter have increased and started to jam up my phone on a daily basis, and I'm almost at my breaking point. I'm too nervous to listen to the voicemails but have kept a few saved on my phone in case I change my mind. Cory and Dylan can sense something's up and both ask me about it regularly. *Well, Dylan asks if my dickhead ex is still harassing me, but it's still concern.* I lie *every single time.*

"Nope, must have been a one-off," I'd say, with a shrug of my shoulders. Until now, it *had* only been the one guy, so I thought I could handle it, but whatever information they thought they had must have been good because more people were becoming interested in it. It's getting out of control. Ignoring it is no longer an option. I should have expected this since it's almost fall and the football season is gearing up. But I didn't. And now, even turning my phone off just leads to a mild heart attack when I turn it back on. A million thoughts consume me. If they have any actual facts, I could, *would*, lose everything. The shame of what I've done rises to the surface, no longer contained in the box I'd locked it in. I have to do something before it is too late. *But what?*

It's a casual Wednesday when it all comes to a head. Already late for class, I make a dash across campus to the west buildings. The west wing of Heartwood U is host to the original buildings erected when the college first opened, and the gothic-like structures are beyond stunning. Pointed arches grace the stone structures with large windows and intricate detailing across the doorways and roofline. I can't help but get caught up in the beauty almost every time I walk by. But not today.

My walk quickens as I near the building, but comes to a halt when my phone vibrates in my pocket for the sixth time since arriving on campus. Curiosity gets the better of me, and I pull it out to check. *Big mistake.* What started as daily calls now looks like six missed calls and nine text messages in a matter of minutes. All different phone numbers. I'm sure all reporters. My heart races as the panic sets in. I'm frozen. In the open. With nowhere to hide. *This isn't happening. This can't be happening. I need air. Why can't I get air?*

Dropping to my knees, I jam the palms of my hands into my eyes to stop the tears and try to recall anything that might rid me of this panic attack. *What is it I'm supposed to do? Count five things I can smell? Five I can see? Or hear? Or all of those? God, this isn't helping. Breathe, Summer. Breathe. It will be okay. It has to be okay.* I'm rocking slightly, but can't control it. Nothing's working. *Breathe. Breathe. Breathe.*

"Come on, Summer, breathe."

Yes, breathe, Sum... Wait, what? A voice comes from above, entering my subconscious and making me more aware of my surroundings. There's a hand on my shoulder, and another stroking my back.

"You're okay. I've got you," the voice says, and while calm, it holds an edge almost bordering on its own panic.

I try to focus, but I still can't quite break free. "Breathe," the voice whispers again, and this time, I recognize it. *Dylan.*

A second voice laced with urgency breaks through. "I'm going to get help."

I *don't* need help. *I can do this.* I will myself to focus and clear the fog. I don't need any more witnesses.

"No, wait! I'm pretty sure she's having a panic attack," Dylan says, and I listen intently to his words. "Mom used to have them after Dad died, when the reporters wouldn't leave her alone."

Dammit. The mention of reporters pulls me down into the darkness once again. I don't even know if they keep talking or if Dylan's still rubbing my back. My mind drifts to other things. Back to that night.

They can't possibly know, can they? Am I actually going to relive it? Start over again? It's bad enough that the rumors, as false as they are, were still floating around but...

Jesus!

A loud crack breaks my thoughts, and pain sears across the side of my face. *Did Dylan just slap me? What in the world?* Finally looking up from the ground, I find Cory staring down at me.

"You told me to slap you if that ever happened again." She shrugs and smiles like it's no big deal, like it didn't kill her to do that. Cory's a lover, not a fighter. When I'd told her to slap me after the last panic attack years ago, I never actually thought she'd do it. Props to her.

"Thank you," I say, standing, as my breathing slowly returns to normal. Embarrassed, I quickly scan the area to see how much attention I've gathered, but we're alone, Dylan and his friend no longer in sight.

"Where did Dylan go? I could have sworn—"

"They stayed until I arrived and then went to run interference on anyone heading this way. Class is still in session so traffic has been minimal."

I release a sigh of relief. "I must have been out of it for a while, huh? If you made it here from home."

"While I'd love to pretend I sprinted all the way here, in a desperate rush to be by your side, I was actually meeting Nate in that building." She points behind her, and I laugh and then groan. *Nate was the other voice.*

"Nate knows too, then?" I sigh.

"Sorry." She scrunches her nose, feeling my embarrassment.

"Thank you, again." I smile. I'm still looking toward the building Cory had pointed to when I see Dylan peek from behind a wall. "It's safe," I yell and wait for him to run over. Nate arrives at the same time from the other direction.

"Please don't ask questions," I say. "But thank you for being there for me," I add, forcing a smile.

Dylan stares at me, concern and question darkening his eyes. I tense up, waiting for the words to leave his mouth, but he surprises me. "Well, we missed class; let's go eat," he says with a comforting smile, and I'm quickly realizing food is his answer for every awkward moment. Without waiting for a response, he walks off toward the parking lot, letting me off the hook. *For now.*

❧   ❧   ❧

I'm anything but comfortable as we eat, yet I'm the picture of confidence to anyone looking my way. Hiding my feelings is a strength I'm proud of. My phone vibrates again in my pocket, and I tense until I realize it's been an hour since the last call. Looking at the screen, I relax when I see it's a news alert rather than a call or text, but can't hide my gasp when I see the headline. *Thomas Kelly's statement on those rumors.* Several sets of eyes stare at me suspiciously, so I smile and pocket my phone.

When I'm home and alone in my room, an hour later, I pull up the alert, clench my fist in nervous anticipation, and finally read the statement.

"There is no truth to the rumors surrounding my family. Anything you may have heard or read about my relationship with my family, in particular my sister, is fallacious and should be ignored. I am fortunate enough to be surrounded by a loving and supportive community, and I'd appreciate it if we did not subject them to harassment and lies simply because I'm in the public eye. I will be making no further comments on this matter. Thank you."

My whole body lightens with relief, and I shake out my hands, cringing at the pain caused by my nails digging into my palms. Although I know that part of his statement is a lie, I finally relax. Only a handful of people know the truth, so if Thomas is presenting a united front, then I'm pretty confident it will all blow over and morph into nothing but hearsay.

Taking a deep breath, I sink back into my bed and fight to keep my eyes open, the toll of the last couple of weeks taking over me.

Chapter Sixteen

Dylan

Cheers ring out as we enter the Ball House after our first game. My teammates lap up the attention, hands raised high in the air, proud smiles on their faces. The single guys have a girl—or two—by their side within seconds of our arrival, while the guys with girlfriends open their arms for the affection they're about to receive. I'm one of the last to enter and immediately turn for the bar. Not because I want to get drunk, but because I need a distraction from the madness surrounding me. The house speakers come to life as "We Are the Champions" blasts through the rooms. The team all sing along in their loudest, most obnoxious voices, and I want to be there with them. I *do*. But not tonight.

Out of the corner of my eye, I notice a girl approaching me with fierce determination, and I inwardly cringe. I can tell from a distance that she's beautiful with her long blonde hair and curves in all the right places. But she's not the blonde I want right now. The one I *need* right now. When she's about ten steps away, her smile grows and she bites her lip. My eyebrows crease, and I try to hold off a frown as I prepare to reject her. At the last second, she's intercepted by Joel, and I sigh in relief. He gently grabs ahold of her elbow to get her attention and pulls out his best smile when she looks his way. She's a goner on impact. Joel is definitely better looking than I am and a *thousand* times more likely to give her what she wants. I don't feel sorry for her at all. Instead, I grab a beer, lean back against the bar, and take a deep breath. *I can do this.*

Joel returns from a *bathroom break* a little while later and attempts to cheer me up. I've met Nate's curious gaze several times, and I know he suspects something's up, but he's keeping it to himself. The other guys are completely clueless. If my absence would go unnoticed, I'd disappear, but since it was our first game *and* we're celebrating a big win, I'm expected to party. My mind, however, is elsewhere. It's been nine years, but it still hurts like a fresh wound. I can still remember it like it was yesterday. The police officers arriving at the door. My mom falling to the floor. The media outside our house barely twenty-four hours later.

The great Dean Mathers had died tragically just shy of twelve months after his retirement. The story was in the news for weeks. In the first few days, we couldn't escape it, and I stupidly assumed it would be easier if it all went away. I was wrong. As the story died down and his face no longer flashed across the papers and TV screens, I missed him even more than I thought I could.

This morning, like every year, Mom, Luce, and I headed to the cemetery at the crack of dawn to avoid the diehard fans who also visited. The well-maintained headstone sat high on a green hill at the back of the cemetery, an empty plot sitting beside it. I stood against a tree as Mom filled Dad in on the happenings of the past year, even though she visited monthly. Now that I think about it, she was most likely updating Lucy and me on her life, not Dad, because a lot of what she was saying was new to me. While Lucy and I were close to each other, we'd both drifted a little from Mom, or maybe she'd drifted from us. I couldn't say. Today Mom spoke of her new small business, of Lucy's impressive internship, and of my achievements in football. How she knew anything about my football is anyone's guess. When she mentioned her recent vacation with her current partner, I cringed. Did Dad really need to know that? Sure, Sam was nice and supportive and he was great to Mom, but I didn't think she needed to mention him here. Today.

Lucy was next and kept it light, as always. Crouching down in front of the grave, she spoke with a smile on her face. "Mom filled you in on all the good bits, so I'll just add that I love you, Paps." He hated that name. "I miss you. And remember, if you are watching over me, please, please, leave when I'm with a man. I can't stress that enough. I would like to remain your perfect little angel for all eternity." At that, she stood and brushed out her dress, clasping her hands together in front of her and standing tall with a glint in her eyes. Acting the part of daddy's little girl.

"Lucy!" Mom scolded.

I rolled my eyes and bit back a laugh. Trust Lucy to try to pull me out of my bad mood.

Once again, I'd remained silent. I never spoke when we visited, never told him about my life, never even read the words on the stone. After all this time, I still couldn't face my dad.

Lucy put her arm around my waist and pulled me close as we walked back to our cars. "You need to let go of this misplaced guilt."

It wasn't the first time she's said something like that to me, and just like last time, I ignored her. "Coming to the game today?" I asked.

She offered an understanding smile and allowed the change of subject. "Wouldn't miss it, little bro," she said, lifting on her toes to scruff my hair, emphasizing how not so little I was.

Shouts from a nearby drinking game bring me back to the present and the party going on around me.

"You should go home; I'll cover for you," Joel says at my side.

I turn to him with a raised eyebrow. "You can't cover for me. No one would ever believe you were a wide receiver. You're not fast enough," I say and we both laugh when Joel shoves me into the wall. The relief is clear in his eyes now that I've finally started joking around.

"I'll have you know I received best on field, *twice* during my career," he points to his chest, before holding two fingers in the air and nodding his head.

I shake mine in return. "Joel, I've known you since we were kids. Did that really happen? You only played two seasons with our junior team."

"Oh, it happened. I got one each year."

"Ah, that's right." I click my fingers and point at him with recognition. "That was back when they made sure *everyone* was a winner." I laugh and push him away before he shoves me again. He crashes into someone entering the room, and I cringe. *Damn.* I'd normally apologize profusely to the poor girl, and I'm about to, until she lifts her head and I see her face. *Could this night get any worse?* Unfortunately, the girl now glaring at Joel isn't *just* someone. It's my ex, Nicole. The only person other than Joel who might know what today is. Our eyes lock, but I remain stoic as I wait to see her reaction. She was never good at hiding her emotions. One look will confirm if she's sympathetic or still holding on to the anger toward me. She holds my stare for a moment, trying to appear nonchalant, before her eyebrows pull in, her eyes flash with darkness, and she walks away. *The latter then.*

"*Great.* This will be fun," Joel says, turning back to me. My best friend and Nicole had been friendly before I dated her but hadn't exchanged two words with each other since we'd broken up. Even now, the always courteous Joel hadn't even bothered to say sorry for bumping her. He's team Dylan all the way.

For the next couple of hours, I'm forced to endure Nicole's open and excessive flirting with every single guy on my team, and even some that are *not*, in fact, single. I'm not jealous of her actions, more pissed off that it had to be today, of all days, and when she flicks her hair and unabashedly giggles at horrible jokes, I want to puke more than anything. I try as best I can to ignore her. She's free to do whatever she pleases, and I have every intention of minding my business until I overhear her next conversation and *lose my shit.*

"I really appreciate your support," she says, her tone laced with false innocence. "I know he's your teammate, but it's just so hard to be around him, after what he did to me. I didn't think he'd be here considering—"

"Enough!" I yell, pushing my way past the brick wall that is one of our linebackers and making it known that I'd been standing behind her. I'm fine with her trash talking me, but I'm *not* fine with her airing my personal issues. And that's exactly what she was about to do.

"What? Did I say something wrong? You hurt me, Dylan. Broke my—"

"You have got to be fuckin' kidding me. *You* cheated on *me.* No, that's too trivial for what you did. You were a two-timing bitch, and in hindsight, a shitty girlfriend. I dodged a bullet when we broke up."

Despite the loud music, we garner a lot of attention, and shocked eyes pierce me from every direction. The Dylan they all know does *not* behave the way they just witnessed.

One face, however, is unperturbed—Joel. In fact, he has the smallest of smirks on his lips. "Drop it. It's over," he says to Nicole with his eyebrow raised in challenge.

She pouts and walks away in a huff, dragging my teammate with her. He looks back over his shoulder with an apologetic gaze. I ignore him.

Standing still, I calm my anger and take a deep breath. Movement catches my eye, and I look over in time to see Nate throw his keys my way and point up the stairs. "My room is locked, but you are welcome to use it," he yells, sympathy in his eyes.

I mouth a quick, *"Thank you,"* and make my way upstairs, before shutting myself inside, away from the noise.

The room is not at all what I expected of Nate, the obvious reason being the mess. The grey and black comforter and matching sheet are hanging off the end of the bed. Books and papers litter the floor, and his desk chair is unusable with clothes strewn all over. It looks like he's been ransacked. That's the best way to describe it. A small smile pulls at my lips at having finally discovered Nate's flaw. This is information I can use. *Maybe tonight won't be a complete bust.*

When my phone starts buzzing with texts from the boys, I throw it across the room, before finding a clean spot and sinking to the floor. Leaning back against Nate's bed, I will this day to end. I'm not interested in being a part of anyone's games. I know that I've never previously bothered to correct the rumor that I cheated on *her*, but I never expected Nicole to give the rumor legs with blatant lies. *God, I'm bad at choosing women.*

After finding a tennis ball among the chaos of Nate's floor, I play catch with the wall and try to break out of my funk. The thud of the ball hitting the floor and wall is actually working, and I find my mood increasing with each catch. The door swings open just as the ball rebounds, and the distraction sends it crashing into the lamp beside the bed. I offer Nate an apologetic glance, but he laughs and waves it off. "Beer?" he says, holding one out to me in question.

I shake my head and thank him, this time smiling to reassure him I'm fine. Nate seems to understand because he grabs another ball from his desk and tosses it my way, before shutting the door and leaving me to my pity party for one.

Hours, or maybe minutes, pass with nothing but the reverberating bass from downstairs and the thump of the tennis ball, so when my phone rings, I jump at the new sound. It takes too long to find where I threw it, so I miss the call. When I finally get to it, it pings with a text. *Summer.* The first contact I've received in days. *Damn.*

Summer: I need a friend. Are you still at the Ball House? I'm coming over.

She needs a friend? *Join the club.* Does this mean she's finally going to open up about her panic attack? Probably not. But I'll take anything I can get. And who knows, maybe helping her through her own shit *could* help me forget mine. *Maybe.*

Me: Yep. Door's open. I'm in Nate's room.

It's not a warm message, but it's the best I can do.

I once thought that kissing Summer might cause her to avoid me, but no, all was fine in the wake of that moment. Witnessing her panic attack, though? *That* apparently warranted my ghosting. Phone calls unanswered, texts unread. She was obviously embarrassed, *for no reason*, and the best way to deal was to cut me off. I wish she'd talked to me instead, but until now, I'd heard nothing. Maybe I had ruined everything with that kiss.

That kiss. God, that kiss. While it was only brief and gentle, I felt a connection I've never felt before. It gave me a sense of clarity, and yet...it was a complete mind fuck. I could have sworn she felt the connection I did, that she felt the same force pulling us together, but I sensed the moment she regretted it. I'd been ready to tell her I wanted more. How *much* more, I didn't know, just something more, *anything* more. But the second I pulled back and saw her face, I *knew*. She didn't feel the same. We'd be nothing more than friends. She'd been adamant that's all we were, and yet, I'd kissed her. I'd *screwed* up. So, instead of telling her how I felt, I sucked it up and tried to maintain control of the situation. I was not prepared to lose her from my life. I'd give her whatever she wanted. With a quick shake of my head and an innocent smile, I played the kiss off as a joke and all was well. At least, until the panic attack took her from me, anyway.

I'm sitting on the bed staring at the wall when I hear the soft tap on the door. Taking a deep breath, I try to snap out of my shit. Summer needs a friend. She knocks again, louder this time, because I haven't moved. I'm clearly still affected. *Answer the fucking door.* I shake out my entire body and jump off the bed. Surprisingly, it helps. Running my hand over my face, as though it will erase the shitty feelings displayed there, I put on a smile and open the door.

"Hey, Sum. Are you okay?" I ask before taking in her appearance and swallowing a lump in my throat. She's an absolute knockout in black yoga pants and a loose-fitting army green T-shirt that's slipping off one shoulder, revealing the strap of her black lace bra. Her hair's pulled up into one of those birds' nest looking, messy things on top of her head. I can see a bit of makeup on her, but she's mostly au naturel. Damn, she looks good. My focus pulls to her eyes, and I'm relieved to see they're clear, not a hint of redness. Her reason for needing me hasn't brought her to tears.

As I scan the rest of her face, looking for clues, I notice she's doing the same to me. *What can she see?*

"I'm fine," she answers with a shrug of her shoulders, her eyes still holding a questioning gaze. "I just needed cheering up and you're always good for a laugh." She relaxes and smiles, and I feel the darkness leaving my body. The anguish and guilt that's been festering for hours slowly lifts with that one smile.

"Want to talk about it?" I ask, bringing my thoughts back to the conversation.

"Nah, let's get ice cream," she says, pulling me to my feet and out of the room. I'm not at all surprised that she doesn't want to talk about it, but the fact that she's here, with me, when she needs someone...It makes my heart swell, and I feel this fierce need to protect her. To pull her into my arms and tell her it will all be okay. Instead, I relish the feel of my hand in hers as she leads us through the house and out the front door.

Chapter Seventeen

Dylan

T he air is warm outside, but there's a welcoming cool breeze. The music mutes to a dull roar as the door shuts behind us, and a feeling of relief washes over me. My watch tells me it's close to midnight, signaling the end of my hellish day. Letting go of my hand, Summer jogs over to an old, beat-up looking Honda Civic that's double parked on the road. I ignore the empty feeling the loss of her hand gives me, and raise my eyebrows, staring at the car.

She jumps into the driver's side and reaches over to unlock the passenger door. "Hurry, Frozen Goodness will be closed soon." Starting the ignition, she puts her hands at ten and two, ready to go, and looks out the window. The frustrated glare tells me she's fully prepared to go without me. I laugh as I enter the car, *only the third laugh of the day,* and already know things are about to turn around for the better.

Armed with two tubs of ice cream—cookies and cream for me and triple berry for Summer—we come to a stop in a gravel parking lot. I'm confused to see it's the local high school, but I follow her lead. I watch her and smile, as she hums another nineties hit, NSYNC this time, and rummages around in the trunk of her car, before producing an outdoor rug, a bag, and a blanket. Without speaking, she grabs my hand again and pulls me through the parking lot toward a wire fence, and behind that...a football field. *Shit! I'm stupid.* It's taken far too long to realize *she* doesn't need a friend. She's here for *me.* I stop in my tracks, pulling Summer back toward me.

"I promise I won't get you arrested." She laughs and gives my arm a gentle tug, nodding her head in the direction of the field. The place I feel most at home.

"You really are something, Summer," I whisper, mostly to myself, but secretly hoping she'll hear me. Her breath hitches, and I know she has.

We continue in silence until we reach the fence, and I'm not entirely convinced that her promise to keep me out of jail holds true. Summer easily slides her body through the hole in the wire, as though she's done this a million times, and then holds her hands out for me, to pass her our things. She waits patiently for me to join her, as I assess the likelihood of making it through unharmed. It doesn't take long to conclude that the size of the hole versus the size of my body will not end well. It'll be hole one, Dylan zero.

Instead of risking it, I scale the fence and jump to the ground, landing with a thud beside Summer.

"Shh! If we get caught, it's on you," she whispers loudly, with a laugh.

We sneak through the gap in the stands and step out onto the field. I move forward toward the grass, but Summer turns and heads in the opposite direction.

"The bleachers?" I'd assumed we'd be sitting on the field, but alas, here we are, making our way up the stands, toward the gods.

"I thought you should see how the other half live. You know, those of us who aren't lucky enough to be down there." She points to the field as I balk at her words.

"Luck? Don't you mean talent? Skill? Determination? Hard work?"

"Nope, I meant what I said." She smiles, and I know at that moment I would be an idiot to do anything to mess up this friendship. She's right, I'm lucky. Lucky to have someone who wants to cheer me up and help me through my problems, without even asking me what they are.

"Your high opinion of me is humbling," I say sarcastically but can't stop the laugh that escapes me.

"Just shut up and follow me." She smirks, and I bite my cheek, stopping myself from saying I'd follow her anywhere.

We've been talking for hours, and everything about it feels natural. The conversation flows from one thing to the next. Sometimes playful, sometimes serious, sometimes mundane, but never forced or uncomfortable. As we sit on the cold bleachers, with a blanket across our legs, knees touching, I decide I never want to stop talking to her. I'm pulled out of the moment as the realization hits me.

In my eyes, Summer is a goddess. She has a wicked sense of humor that matches my own, she's crazy smart but doesn't like to make a show of it, she's beautiful inside and out, and has a body I'd do anything to touch. She's also hiding some deep issues that I assume revolve around her family. She doesn't need another guy wanting to get under her skirt; she needs a friend. And right now, I could use one too. Would I like to pull her into my lap, frame her face with my hands and kiss her until she's breathless? Absolutely. Will I? No. The last thing I want is for Summer to be another one of my dating disasters, and I definitely don't want to be just another notch on her bedpost.

We've both been silent for a few minutes, and when I look over at Summer, she's also lost in thought. The urge to discover everything about her takes over, and I break our peace. "At the risk of having you ghost me again, I need to ask…"

She cringes at my words—whether it's because she knows what's coming or because she feels bad for ghosting me, I'm not sure. I continue anyway. "The panic attack—"

"It was stupid. I'd rather not talk about it." She cuts me off, dropping her face in her hands briefly, before straightening up. The move tells me it's anything *but* stupid.

I turn to face her, needing to look her in the eyes. She remains focused on the field in front of us, even as my eyes bore into her. "There's nothing stupid about a panic attack, Summer. Something caused that. I know they can come on for no logical reason. I know they're beyond your control, but—"

Her eyes flash to mine, and her hand shoots out and grabs my thigh. "Oh God, I'm sorry. I remember you said your mom gets them. I didn't mean to downplay the seriousness of—"

"Summer, stop," I cut in, placing my hand over hers. "This has nothing to do with my mom. That's not what I was going to say at all."

She looks down at our hands before pulling hers away. "I'm sorry," she whispers.

"Please look at me, and stop apologizing."

She turns slowly, and when her eyes meet mine, I see a flash of heartache before a blank stare replaces it, her mask secured firmly back in place. "It doesn't matter anymore, Dylan. It happened, it's over now, and it won't happen again."

"How do you know? You should talk about it. Does Cory, at least, know what's going on?"

"There's nothing more to talk about. It's sorted." She pulls her phone from her pocket and stares at the locked screen, avoiding my gaze, like she avoids my questions. I'm ninety-nine percent sure that her panic attack has everything to do with whatever baggage she's carrying around. And it's baggage she has no intention of offloading. I can't seem to take my eyes off her, so I don't miss when she suddenly straightens her shoulders, takes a deep but silent breath, and turns back to face me, a new casual demeanor in place.

"If you want to go all deep and meaningful tonight, why don't we talk about why we're really here?" She raises an eyebrow, the smallest hint of a sneer on her face, as if to say "how do *you* like it?"

She has a point. I had no intention of sharing, but I should. I lean forward and rest my elbows on my knees, release a deep breath, and tell her what's wrong. Most of it, anyway. I tell her about my father's death, my distant relationship with my mother, and my public outburst at Nicole. What I don't tell her, what I still can't face, is my part in my father's death and the dark thoughts I have because of that.

Summer sits quietly and listens to my every word. When I talk about being a twelve-year-old without a dad, she squeezes my hand in comfort. When I mention Lucy's unwavering support, her face lights up, mimicking my own. And at the mention of my outburst, she bites her lip to hold back a laugh, bringing a smile to my face.

I haven't vented like that in...well, ever. Lucy and Joel know almost everything about my life, but I've always delivered the information in pieces. There's something to be said about verbally spewing up all your thoughts at once. It feels good.

"Enough with the heavy and the bleachers. It's time we move down to where the magic happens," I say after a moment of silence. "Don't think I didn't notice the football in your bag."

Her nose crinkles, and she sighs. "Ah, you caught that?"

"I did."

"I brought it for extreme circumstances only. Just in case my wit and charm weren't enough to cheer you up."

"You brought it for me? Here I was thinking you secretly played." I smirk.

She playfully shoves my shoulder. "Shut up; you know it's for you."

"Have you ever played?"

Her smile drops ever so slightly. "Yep." If I wasn't so focused on her, I never would have noticed the change in expression.

"Want to play now?" Based on her reaction to my last question, I'm expecting a no, but we are definitely playing.

"Ugh, are you going to let me say no?"

Ha, it's like she knows me so well already. "Definitely not," I say with a smile.

She rolls her eyes and waves her hand toward the field. "Well, lead the way."

"No fair," she yells, as I throw the ball down for the sixth time. She's right. It's not at all fair, but I'm letting her get a few wins. At least, I *was* letting her get some wins, until she started playing dirty.

She catches up and grabs ahold of my arm, leaning over to catch her breath. "I thought we agreed you'd run at half speed?"

"That was before you stripped."

"What? That wasn't...I didn't *strip*. I *changed* into a tank top. It's hot." She backs away from me with her hands in the air.

"You were trying to distract me."

"What? Never," she says innocently, but she can't hide the small smirk adorning her face.

"Okay. My mistake. Your turn," I say, kicking the ball along the ground in her direction.

She eyes me suspiciously, for good reason, but then picks it up and moves into place. I sit on the grass and cross my legs, dutifully complying to the starting position Summer assigned me.

I see her grin before I close my eyes and say, "Okay, I'm ready."

"Mickey twenty-two, Donald, hut," she yells, and I hear her take off running. I can't help but laugh at her ridiculous but inventive attempts at calling the play.

Leaping from the ground, I sprint after her. There's no half speed this time, not with what I have planned.

She's almost at our designated end zone, her bag, when I dart in front of her and slam my shoulders into her waist. The impact catches her off guard, allowing me to lift her off the ground and over my shoulder in one quick motion.

The ball drops to the turf, just shy of its mark.

"Mathers does it! He wins the game," I yell and run around, holding Summer in the firefighter's hold.

She slaps my ass like a drum, while trying to kick her legs. "Put me down, you dirty cheat," she yells in between laughter.

My grip on her thighs tightens as I stop and readjust her position. "Nope, I think I'll celebrate once more," I say and take off running again, whipping Summer around as I do.

Her glorious laughter increases as she abandons her escape and joins me in celebration. "Woo hoo! Dylan Mathers, you rock!" She whistles through her fingers and then slaps my ass again.

When I finally stop, we're both out of breath. Bending over, I carefully lower Summer down, resting her back on the grass, and then drop beside her. Tucking my hands under my head, I look at the stars and relish in the comfortable silence that ensues.

When my breathing returns to normal, I peer at Summer and am stunned by how peaceful she looks. I don't think I've ever seen anyone so serenely beautiful. Her lashes brush against her cheekbones, and her lips are slightly parted, with the hint of a smile. She has one hand resting near her shoulder, while the other lays across her stomach. After a deep breath, her smile widens, and she opens her eyes, not yet noticing my attention. When she stifles a yawn, I take it as our cue to wrap up our night.

"Thanks for tonight, Sum. It means a lot," I say, rising up on my elbows.

She mimics my position, and her eyes find mine. "Anytime," she says, and I believe it.

Jumping to my feet, I grip her hand and pull her up, before collecting our things and heading to the car.

We pull up in my drive with the sun in the sky, and Summer sighs before shutting off the engine. "I had fun tonight. Can I walk you to your door?" she jokes, wiggling her eyebrows.

"I'm not going to sleep with you, Summer," I deadpan and then laugh at her wide-eyed expression.

She recovers quickly and smiles. "I know that. You're not the guy who has one-night stands; you're a relationship guy."

My eyebrows pull together in confusion as Summer shoots me a challenging look in return. Begging me to say otherwise, so she can prove me wrong. Why does everyone keep mentioning the relationship thing? Is it my defining feature? And why does it sound like a bad thing when she says it? When *anybody* says it?

Summer eyes me curiously before reaching out and clasping my arm. "Hey, it's not a negative thing. You're lucky to have been in love so many times."

In love? "Ah..."

"How many times have you said I love you, anyway?" she questions. She sounds so unaffected by that notion that it stings a little. "I'm not mocking you either; it's a serious question."

"Never," I admit, completely shocking her.

"What?"

Running a hand through my hair, I grip the back of my neck and grimace. "Never. I've never said that."

She stares at me incredulously. "But you've felt it? I mean, surely you've felt it, at least once, in all your relationships."

I cringe at how bad this conversation is making me look, but answer honestly. "I've never said it, because I've never felt it."

"I don't believe you."

I shrug, because what can I really say to that? "No way I can prove it."

"I guess not."

"Whether or not it's my *thing*, it's not working," I say with another shrug before opening the door and jumping out of the car. "Goodnight, Summer."

"You *will* find that special someone. I know it. You're a great guy, Dylan," Summer calls out as I'm shutting the door. I acknowledge her comment with a wave and a smile, before walking away.

"And you're by far the most special someone I know," I whisper, only turning back when I hear Summer's car pulling out of the drive.

Taking a deep breath, I shake off my thoughts and sigh.

Chapter Eighteen

Summer

O ver the next month or so, Dylan and I give being best friends a red-hot go. Something changed between us on that football field, and while I'm not entirely sure what elicited that change, I'm grateful. I didn't think I needed anyone else in my life, with Cory being there for me day to day and Logan only a phone call away. But I thought wrong. I needed Dylan. I just hadn't known it.

Everything about our friendship is easy. Through late-night chats, we discovered our shared love of true crime television shows, Elton John—specifically his song "I'm Still Standing"—and peanut M&M's. Through movie nights spent at theaters or curled up on the couch, we discovered our love of psychological thrillers. And through our continuous fake reminiscing, I learned that Dylan can *bake*, like actually bake, and it's edible. I made him prove it one Sunday afternoon, and he did *not* disappoint. To compensate for his secret revelation, I let slip that I learned to dance as a kid. Big mistake. Gone was the lazy Sunday afternoon, instead...*Dance-off!*

Our communication increased from a few texts, to a catch-up here and there, to seeing or talking to each other daily. We were both taking our new roles as best friends *very* seriously. Now, here we are, almost two months later, and I'm happy. Well, I was happy until this very moment. Now I'm happy *and* a little apprehensive.

After Cory's insistent begging, I'm finally attending one of Dylan and Nate's football games. I'd love to say that I'm completely fine, but I'm not. I haven't attended a game since the last time I watched Thomas play, the same day my life turned to shit. I can still remember the buzz of excitement at finally being at a college football game—Thomas's first college game as starting quarterback in his sophomore year. I remember bouncing in my seat the entire drive to the field, decked out in his school colors, the same school colors I'm wearing now. I was ready to scream his name at the top of my lungs. And I did. I jumped, I cheered, I sat on the edge of my seat. I'd never experienced anything like it. The crowd, the atmosphere, the support for my own flesh and blood. I was so proud of him. Deep down, I still am. It hadn't taken long for Thomas to make friends at college. He's charismatic, easygoing, and loyal to a fault. At least, he *was*. So, despite it being unusual for a sophomore to host the opening game party, that's exactly what he did. I've always wondered if things would be different if that party had been somewhere else, but I guess I'll never know.

I'm lost in thought as Cory and I scan our tickets and enter the stadium. With a quick shake of my head and a deep breath, I plaster a smile on my face and rid myself of the negativity. My family isn't here; Thomas isn't here. This is for Dylan, Nate, and Cory. It's time for a new start.

"I hope you realize how much you owe me for this," I say to Cory as we push through the crowd. Okay, not quite a new start, but I couldn't resist a small tease.

She stops and pulls me to the side, out of the way of the stampede. A look of motherly concern graces her face. "Believe me, I know, and I really appreciate it, Sum. But if you can't do this—"

"I'm messing with you, Cory. Thomas is thousands of miles away, focused on his own team. He won't be here and neither will my family," I smile, and it's genuine this time.

"I know that, but I can still understand if you'd prefer—"

"Hey now. I didn't paint my cheeks for no reason," I say with a laugh, waving my hand in front of the Heartwood U logo and colors currently taking up real estate on my face.

"Good point, *aaaand* why did you do that again?" She looks at me with a knowing smile, eyebrows raised in question.

"For Nate. *Obviously*."

"Right, Nate. *Obviously*." Cory laughs, mocking me with an eye roll.

"Well, if I say it's for Dylan, he'll never let me live it down. Neither will you," I say with a shrug, causing Cory's laughter to build as she drags me back into the sea of people heading to their seats.

We're seated for a few minutes when Joel drops down next to me, arms loaded with snacks, a nervous expression on his face. "By the way, I may have lied to Dylan about who the extra ticket was for," he says, not even offering a hello.

His words make the unease I'm trying to bury rise again. Not because I'm worried Dylan won't be happy I'm here, but because I failed to tell him myself. If roles were reversed, I'd hate the surprise. *But he isn't you.* I should have known Joel would try to mess with his head. "Who does he think is sitting in this seat?" I ask.

"Lucy."

"Lucy?! Why didn't you tell him it was me?" *Shit! Of all people...* He's not going to be happy that it's not actually Lucy. He said last week that he misses her.

"Thought It would be more fun this way. Why didn't *you* tell him?" He smirks, eyes on the field.

"Nate knew," Cory adds, her eyes glued to the tunnel, waiting for Nate, completely unaware of my concern.

"Yeah, I told him to keep his mouth shut," Joel says with a shrug.

My lips pull into a thin line as I consider his words. I hadn't mentioned the game to Dylan in case I changed my mind, but I'd never asked Joel to keep it a secret. "I know why I kept it a secret, but why did you?" I ask. He's definitely up to something.

"You'll see." He bounces his eyebrows, holding back a grin. I shake my head and huff out a laugh, because what else can I say?

"Here they come," Cory squeals excitedly, causing Joel and me to laugh and my worry to be long forgotten.

I scan the field looking for Dylan, and find him doing the same thing, but searching the crowd. When he looks in our direction, he freezes, still as a post, not even a twitch, until a teammate whacks him on the back, drawing his attention. He moves to follow, but not before looking back over his shoulder and offering a half wave. It's difficult to make eye contact with his helmet on, so I don't wave back. You know, in case it was directed at someone else. *It was definitely me.*

Joel chuckles beside me. "That *was* fun; may have even thrown him off his game."

I smack him in the arm but can't stop a snigger from escaping. "You better hope not."

"Hey! It's your fault. Did you or did you not tell him there was absolutely *no* chance you would ever attend a game?"

"I said that, yes."

"Yet, here you are," he says with a grin.

"Here I am." I return it.

The game is intense, and thankfully Dylan seems in top form. At least, I assume he's playing his best, because he's pretty *freaking* impressive. I hold my breath as I watch the quarterback release the ball, sending it sailing in Dylan's direction. He has two men on him and little chance of making the catch, but I'm still gripped by the action. The ball overshoots its mark, passing over the heads of the pack. There's a collective sigh among the crowd, until at the last second, Dylan's arm shoots out backwards, catching the ball with one hand. The other players are too stunned to react quickly enough, as he breaks away and makes a run for the end zone, slamming the ball down over the line.

I scream and jump to my feet to cheer him on, my heart racing when he throws his hand up in celebration and turns my way. *Our way, Summer, our way.* He rips off his helmet and pumps his fist in the air, in a "this is for you" gesture. I return the gesture, no longer caring if it's aimed at me or someone else. The adrenaline coursing through my veins is dictating my every move. The roar of the crowd is deafening and they're all yelling the same thing... Mathers! Mathers! *Dylan Mathers.* His name runs on repeat through my mind as the celebrations die down. If I thought he was attractive *before*, it's nothing compared to now. Seeing him play is really messing with my mind. There's something to be said about witnessing someone in their element. Day to day, Dylan's not a shy person; he has confidence, but he doesn't really project it on others. On the field, he's a completely different person. He's cocky and in control. Muscles that I never noticed flex with every catch, every sprint, every jump. And the way his body moves, uhh, it's...it's something else.

I'm tracking his every move, unable to take my eyes off him, when a throat clears beside me.

"I said, did you want a bite?"

My eyes flash to Cory's. *What is she talking about? I don't...* She waves a Twizzler in my face. Oh! That is not where my mind went with her question, and by the look on her face, she knows it. I grab the deliciously red goodness from her hand and take an over-the-top bite, pulling at it, with my teeth bared.

Cory laughs. "Bet he tastes better," she says with grin.

"What?" I ask, pretending I don't know what she's talking about. My body heats with embarrassment, and I know if I look in the mirror, I'll see a pinkish tinge on my face and chest.

"Nah, he's too chewy," Joel adds beside me, and I burst out laughing. He remains focused on the game and I'm thankful for his distraction until I turn in time to see the smirk on his face. Ugh!

At halftime, I rush off for a much-needed bathroom break. Cory received a phone call and disappeared not long after my drool session, so I'm on my own. I'm on my way back, shaking water from my hands, when I hear my name.

"Summer!"

I scan the crowd, a little on edge, until my eyes meet with the warm gaze of Cory's dad, Rob. Every part of me relaxes as I walk toward this wonderful man, who's like a father figure to me.

"Hey, sweetheart," he says, engulfing me in a welcome hug. It's been a little while since I've seen him, so I grip tight and enjoy the feeling of a parent's love, even if he's not *my* parent.

"What are you doing here?" I ask when I finally release him. "It's so good to see you."

"It's good to see you too, kiddo. I came to check out if Nate's football skills live up to Cory's constant gushing," he says, and I know he's only half joking. "I'm actually glad I ran into you. You can fill me in on all the gossip." He chuckles at his use of the term gossip. It's not a word that I'd usually hear coming out of his mouth.

"If you are referring to Nate, I can put your mind at ease, right now. He's wonderful and treats Cory well. You know I wouldn't let just any guy date our girl?"

"That I do." He smiles. "It really is good to see you, Summer. It's been too long since you've been home."

Home. It always catches me off guard when Cory's family refer to their home as mine. I lived there for two years before college, so it makes sense, but I feel a pinch in my gut all the same. I'm in awe that a friend's parents would take me in, provide food and shelter, and even love without questions. They blindly trusted me, and I will forever be grateful to them.

"And you know we'd call, but..."

I wince at the sadness on his face. He thinks he's let me down, when in actuality, it's the opposite. "You've always let me set the pace. I know. I'm sorry. I should have called *you.*"

Cory appears at my side, snacks in hand and a giddy smile still plastered on her face. Rob pulls her into an embrace, tucking her tightly under his arm. "No need for apologies, Sum. This one only calls me when she wants something."

"Hey, that's not true," Cory says, shaking her head until Rob gives her a disbelieving look. "Okay, it's a little true," she adds sheepishly.

"How about Cory, Nate, and I come for dinner next week?" I say, the prospect actually exciting me. I really miss my unofficial adopted family.

"That would be lovely. I'll have our playlist ready to go," Rob says, referring to the nineties rock we bonded over. To say I was bitter when I first moved into Cory's house, at sixteen, is an understatement. I was pretty convinced that all adults were assholes. Even the ones that had treated me well my entire life. Rob discovered my weakness for nineties hits and exploited it. We spent hours on the back deck, listening to Pearl Jam, Guns N' Roses, and Metallica, to name a few. In the beginning, we sat silently, engrossed in the music. We then graduated to discussing the music and popular television series of the era. Eventually, I opened up and Rob became my confidant. I honestly don't know what I'd do without him and Alison. Thankfully, I'll never have to find out.

When I finally return to our seats, a girl I don't recognize has taken my spot next to Joel. She's giving him her full attention, and he looks more than comfortable in her presence. *Hmmm, appears as though Joel's getting lucky tonight.* I sit down in Cory's seat, wave at Joel, and wait for the glare that's bound to come my way as soon as the girl notices me. Only it doesn't come.

As soon as she's aware of my presence, she turns around excitedly, her big smile beaming at me. "I'm so happy to meet you, Summer. Joel was just telling me about you," she says, reaching over and squeezing my leg.

My eyes shoot to Joel's, but he doesn't even look apologetic for discussing me behind my back. In fact, he's barely taken his eyes off the woman in front of me. *Who is she?* I'm about to ask just that when Joel introduces us.

"Summer, this is Delilah."

Delilah! Finally, I can put a face to the name. Joel may have only shared crumbs when it comes to Delilah, but it's easy to see, from the look on his face as he introduced us, that she holds his heart in her hands.

With her porcelain skin and deep red hair cascading in thick waves to the middle of her back, she's absolutely stunning in an understated way. She has olive-green doe eyes that are hard to look away from and a sweet voice that makes her sound innocent and young, and yet something about her tells me she's been through something tough.

"Delilah, it's nice to meet you," I say, and I genuinely mean it. "Are you joining us for the rest of the game?"

"Oh no. I was just passing by and saw Joel. It's been a while so..." she fades off.

"Would you like some alone time?" I ask, realizing too late that I am probably interrupting something.

"No, please stay," she says, and shifts away from Joel a little with a shy smile.

Despite her insistence that she isn't joining us, it's fifteen minutes into the second half before she leaves. Cory is perched on my lap as we both cheer along with the crowd. I learned a lot about the person I'm now calling "the love of Joel's life" during her visit. Turns out she's as beautiful on the inside as she is out. I'm dying to know the backstory of these two, because from that brief conversation, it's obvious they share some pretty strong feelings.

As soon as Delilah exits our row, Cory and I both turn to Joel. "Wow!" is all I can say.

"I know." He smiles, but it's not his usual playful grin.

"Why are you *not* together?" I ask, not even concerned with how that question might sound. It's Joel. He's not one to beat around the bush.

"It's a long story." He sighs, and my heart breaks a little for him.

"We have time," Cory adds, and I can't help but laugh. She's already focused back on the game and has once again failed to pick up on the mood.

"Maybe after the game?" I scrunch my nose because he looks so uncomfortable.

"Maybe," he mumbles with a shrug and turns back to the game. *That's definitely a no.*

"She's lovely, Joel. I hope you work things out," I say, and I truly mean it.

"Thanks, Summer." He smiles and this time I'm happy to see it reaches his eyes.

When Nate makes a play, Cory wriggles with excitement on my lap, drawing my attention to the fact that she's still sitting on me unnecessarily. I toss her onto the seat beside me and turn back to the game as though nothing happened. Cory and Joel both chuckle, and I relax at the sound of Joel's laughter.

When the game ends, I follow Cory to meet the players. I'm bouncing on my toes, like a giddy fan girl, waiting for Dylan to finish in the locker room. *What the hell is wrong with me?* As soon as I see him, I can't stop myself as I leap into his arms, wrapping my legs around his waist. "You were incredible, Dylan. I knew you were fast, but damn, and God, that one-handed grab...No wonder you've got scouts on the lookout. Bet you're thrilled." I'm talking a million miles a minute, the high of the game still in full effect. I don't mention how good he *looks* out on the field, even though I know he'd get a kick out of it, because I'm completely over that. *Mostly.*

Instinctively, Dylan grips under my thighs, holding me in place, but then stills at my ambush. Our faces are only inches apart, so I can see every thought and emotion play out on his features. His eyes bounce between mine, as though he's trying to process that I'm really there. After a second or two, he huffs out a small laugh, shaking his head. "You're here?" he says, with a look of adoration, completely ignoring everything I've said.

The attention makes me blush uncomfortably. I'm about to pull out of his hold when a look of confusion flashes across his face. "Wait, what did you say? How did you know about the scouts?" he asks, sounding almost taut as he lowers me to the ground and takes a step back.

Shit! Did I say the wrong thing? "Joel let it slip during the game. Was it supposed to be a secret?" I ask.

"No, sorry." He grabs the back of his neck and gives me a stressed look. "Sorry, it's just...I think I'm still in shock that you came." He reaches out and prods my face, checking that I'm real.

I laugh and push him away, happy to be back in playful mode. Things got a little tense for a second. "Of course, I did. We're best friends," I say, further trying to lighten the mood.

"Well, thank you. I appreciate it," he says softly, his eyes conveying how true those words are.

I lean in close and look around conspiratorially, before whispering in his ear. "So, any teams watching today? Who's going to steal you away from us?"

"Um, I don't think... I—" He cuts himself off and runs a hand through his hair, clearly holding something back.

"Come on, don't tell me you're going to pretend to be modest," I say, keeping things light, though I'm not stupid. Something's definitely going through his head.

"That's me, modest," he jokes, but it's a little forced. "Are you ready to party?" he adds, changing the subject.

I let it go but make a mental note to ask him about it later. "Sure, as long as there's dancing," I say with a wink and then pull him toward the exit.

Chapter Nineteen

Dylan

Summer came to my game. After seeing her sad expression when she told me she'd never attend one, I had given up hope and stopped looking for her. Then she came. Not only did she make the effort to attend, but she looked incredibly adorable with her face paint and team colors. The only thing that could have topped her look was if she was wearing my name on her back. *Fuck, would I love to see that.*

As expected, she played it down on the drive over to the party, acting like it was no big deal that she'd been there in the stands cheering me on. She even mentioned that Cory had begged her to go. While that might be the case, deep down, we both knew she was there for me, and that means *everything*.

The last couple of months with Summer have really cemented our friendship. I've seen her almost as much as I've seen the guys and wanted to see her even more. Does my mind sometimes drift where it shouldn't and conjure up images of us as more than just friends? Yes. But would I ever do anything about it? I doubt it. I respect Summer and I respect our friendship too much for that. I'd rather have her in my life as a friend than not at all.

As we push through the doors of the bar, our night plays out the same as those we've shared before this. Summer and I arrive together. She heads to the bar and then makes her presence known on the dance floor before she's even had her first sip; meanwhile, I get stopped every few steps from the moment I enter the building. By the time I make it all the way into the room, Summer is usually in her element, bumping and grinding with some guy. And today is no different. I know that we'll catch each other at different stages throughout the night. We'll flirt, and we may even dance. But when the night ends, we never leave together, and only one of us goes home alone. *Me.*

Leaning back on the bar, I take in the scene around me, trying hard to avert my gaze from the dance floor. Not only am I unsuccessful, but I also have the worst timing. My eyes find Summer at the exact moment she turns and presses her ass into the guy dancing behind her, gliding her hands up her body before locking them behind his neck. I want to look away, *need* to look away, but instead my eyes scan her body, only stopping when I see two hands grip her waist and then move up her sides, almost mimicking the path she took. I swallow a lump in my throat and attempt to ignore the heavy feeling in the pit of my stomach. I've seen Summer with guys before, but this is different. She's different. *Why?*

I need a distraction, and fast. A few of my teammates have gathered about a table and are knocking back shots. While I don't want the shots, I decide to join them to keep my mind—and eyes—off the dance floor. Time passes slowly, without so much as a hi from Summer. Something is definitely different tonight. *Is it her or me that's changed?* Has she sensed that something has changed in me so is keeping her distance? *Has something changed in me?* Either way, it's like she's ignoring me. No, worse, it's like we're strangers. She hasn't even looked my way. I know this, because I've looked her way plenty. I'm doing it right now.

"You expect me to believe there's nothing going on with you and Summer?" Luke says, taking the spare seat at our table and interrupting my thoughts.

"I honestly don't care what you believe, but yep, that's the truth." Luke loves to push my buttons most days, and right now he's looking at me with mischief in his eyes.

"All right then. Let's do this." He sneers and rises from the seat again, before he's even warmed it. I send out a silent prayer that he doesn't mean what I think he means, but of course, he does.

"We are getting you laid," he announces proudly, like he's doing me a favor. Like I couldn't walk up to any girl in this room and make her mine, if I wanted to. *What the fuck am I saying? Cocky much? I can't get anyone I want. I can't get Summer.* Saying I want to be single and actually playing the field are very different, and Luke doesn't seem to get that. I'm actually enjoying the single life. It's nice to only have to worry about myself for a change, with no

one to answer to. *Or maybe it's nice because it means more time to spend with Summer. Shit!*

I seek out Summer again, without meaning to, and am once again hit with a scene I have no interest in witnessing. Only this time, I recognize her suitor. Their bodies are flush together, and her arms are around his neck, while his hands rest on her ass. The guy she's with is pretty decent. We've always gotten along fine, but right now I have the strongest urge to break his nose. *Fuck!* Summer comes to one game, and I'm acting like she offered me a rose and it's time to win her heart. *What is this woman doing to me?*

"Mother fucker." I hear Luke curse behind me and turn to see what's pissed him off, only to discover he's glaring at me. He pulls me to the side, but then, not so quietly, says, "You're not single because you *want* to be. You're just biding your time, hoping Summer will change her ways."

He's wrong. Right? I roll my eyes at him and take a sip of my water. "Summer and I are—"

"Friends. I know that's the line you keep spinning, but we all know you want to fuck her." I cringe at his words. "I hate to break it to you, man, but she ain't changing for you. If she was going to, she would have done it by now." I open my mouth to speak, but he cuts me off. "I feel ya; she's hot and fun to be around. I get it. But look at all the other hot and fun chicks out there. Go grab yourself one of them for the night. 'Cause that one ain't for you."

I'm about to tell him he's got it all wrong when he adds, "And fuck you for making me sound like a girl in a chick flick."

I laugh, even though his words are far from script worthy.

"Luke, you don't have to worry. I know exactly where I stand with Summer. Where we both stand." *Sadly, that's the truth.*

"Okay then, let's get out there. That chick can't take her eyes off you, and she's looking mighty fine tonight."

He's right. The girl staring at me is stunning and definitely mine for the taking, but I'm still not interested. In her, or anyone else. So when a familiar face comes into view, a plan forms in my mind.

Luke notices at the same time I do. "Ah, man. Of course, Kylie is heading your way. I've changed my mind. Pine for Summer," Luke grumbles to me before yelling to the room, "Stop throwing yourselves at him. He's got a small c—"

"Shut the fuck up," I say, elbowing him in the ribs before he can finish his comment. "Jealous much?" I add as Kylie approaches, raising my beer with a smirk.

Simply put, Kylie is a ten—no, eleven. But there is nothing simple about her. She graduated last year with plans to attend Yale Law school but is putting her studies on hold for a year to become the face of some new celebrity makeup line. She's smart and hot and knows what she wants. And she also knows exactly what I want, or rather what I don't. That's why I let this play out.

"They say it's not about size but how you use it," Kylie says, gesturing to my crotch, clearly bullshitting.

"You wouldn't say that if you'd been with me," Luke adds, mouthing the word "huge" and winking at Kylie before leaving us alone. Kylie laughs as I roll my eyes. I know how much he wants her, so this must be driving him crazy.

"Kylie Jenkins. How are you?" I greet her with a kiss on the cheek.

"Never better, Mathers. I'm glad I ran into you." She calls me by my last name, something only the team does.

"Oh yeah, and why's that?" I ask, knowing the answer before the words leave her mouth. She winks before she speaks.

"It's late, and I'm flying to London tomorrow, so I'm about to head off..." She pauses before nodding toward the door. "Want to join me?"

I release a breath and smile. When I look back to where Summer was dancing, I notice she's gone. Not even a goodbye. So yes, I want to join her. I'm officially done with this party. "Yes, I really do."

"Meet you out front in ten?"

I smile and nod, watching Kylie head toward her friends as Joel joins my side, raising his eyebrows.

"I'm going home with Kylie," I say, raising my eyebrows as my lips pull up in a half smile.

"Ha, you're funny," he says sarcastically, elbowing me in the ribs.

"What's that supposed to mean?" I ask, despite knowing he can see right through my charade.

"Well, for one, you won't admit it, but you're hung up on Summer," he says and I scoff, but he ignores me. "And another thing...cut the crap. You forget I know you. *And* I briefly dated your sister. I know who Kylie is. They were best friends."

"Dude, you can't call it 'dating.' You and Lucy were kids!" I exclaim.

Joel wraps an arm around my shoulder, smirking. "And yet it still pisses you off."

I shove him away, but the truth is, I love Joel like a brother, so while dating my sister would be weird, if anyone was going to do it... Actually, no, none of my friends may go there. Luckily, I know he's joking.

"On that note, I'm off."

"Okay, I'll meet you at home in thirty." He winks like a douche. *Smart-ass.* I give him the finger and walk away.

Across the room, I meet Luke's eye, and he holds up a fresh beer to ask if I want another. We both know he's not really asking me about the drink. I shake my head and grin. He rolls his eyes in response, but as he turns away, I see his smile. He would never say it outright, but I know he would prefer to see the player Dylan over the committed one. Too bad I can't say the same. I can't explain why I feel the need to make him believe I'm going home with Kylie, for reasons other than a lift home, but it's a "no questions asked" escape and I'm taking it. I'll tell the truth later. Maybe.

Kylie is leaning against the hood of a classic Ford Mustang convertible as I approach. Damn, she's hot. Her position on the car has her dress rising slightly, showing off her long, toned legs. My eyes scan up from her stilettos, taking her all in, until I reach her face. She smirks when our eyes meet. Little Kylie Jenkins... Well, she's not so little anymore, and yet will always be the little girl in pretty pink dresses to me. Growing up, she was my sister's best friend. They were inseparable but have since drifted apart. We don't advertise it, but we know each other well, and she's doing me a solid here.

"You owe me big time. I could have hooked up for real," she says, but it's obvious she doesn't mean it. Ignoring her comment, I walk closer. She smiles and stands, planting a kiss on my cheek.

"Thanks for that? How did you know Luke was on my back?"

"Why are you thanking me? Maybe I actually want to take you home," she says as she runs her fingers through my hair.

I smile big at that. If that were true, I think it would have happened years ago. She's a great catch, but...

"Have you changed teams since we last spoke? Because I'm up for it if—"

She slaps my arm and moves to jump in the car. She hasn't come out publicly, so most guys at college still try their luck with her, but those that know her well have known the truth for years. And it's not changing any time soon.

"Should I move into acting or stick to modeling?" she asks, peering at me over the open door while batting her eyelashes.

"Acting seems to be your calling." I laugh, and then look at her seriously and add "thank you."

I love my boys, but they don't get it. They don't understand that I'm not interested in one-night stands like they are. Letting them believe I'm out hooking up when I'm not is a shit thing to do, but sadly, it will keep them quiet for a while.

"Come on; jump in. Are you heading home?"

"Yes, home, thanks," I say as I pull out my cell and check for anything from Summer. It's a little concerning that two people called me out for having feelings for her. Joel, I get, he sees everything, but Luke? Do I act like I have feelings for her? Because I've been working really hard to suppress that. Seeing her with other guys wasn't great, but surely that's just because my head's messed up since she came to the game. *Right?* I rub my hands down my face in frustration. God, I thought I was past this. I thought I was doing fine as her friend. I shake my head to rid my thoughts and jump in the passenger seat next to Kylie, waving to a few of my teammates hanging around outside.

As we drive past a few parked cars, I notice Summer standing next to a black Escalade, staring straight at me. I recognize the car, and another pang of jealousy hits me. The jealous feeling doesn't surprise me, because I'm obviously not over her. What does surprise me is that Summer has the same jealous look aimed at me.

Chapter Twenty

Summer

T he second we enter the bar, I secure myself a drink and a dance partner. My goal is to forget the last few hours and focus on the present. At some point between our movie night midweek and this moment, something changed between Dylan and me, and I'm not entirely sure how to deal with it. Jumping into his arms had been an impulsive decision and one I hadn't given a second thought at the time. But as soon as he looked into my eyes and stared at me like I hung the moon, I knew something was different. I was different. I suddenly had the strongest pull toward him, more specifically, toward his lips. I've never wanted to kiss someone so badly in my entire life. And that scared the hell out of me, which is probably why I did what I did next.

For the rest of the night, I avoid Dylan at all costs, only allowing myself glances out of the corner of my eyes. I'm not naive. I know Dylan feels something for me. It's not his feelings I'm concerned about. It's mine. I spent my childhood and early teens being told over and over again that I'm not good enough. That no man will ever want me.

Keeping Dylan in the friend zone is the safest option for my heart and his. Developing feelings is out of the question. My dad may have been wrong about guys not wanting me. I'm definitely wanted. I've proven that many times over. Most of the guys even come back for more. But none have ever come close to showing me that there's something out there worth opening myself up for. *Until now.*

I'm not even sure I trust myself enough to follow my instincts. If I've learned anything from my family, it's that loving someone unconditionally, or otherwise, is giving them the power to completely destroy you. I've experienced that firsthand, and I'm not prepared to go through it again.

So instead, I protect my heart and ignore the one person who brings me so much happiness while unknowingly causing so much pain.

I'm dancing with a different guy for the fourth time tonight. *Or is it fifth? I don't know.* Point is, I'm moving through men as fast as I'm knocking back drinks, because none of them—no matter how attractive or flirty—not a single one holds my attention. That attention was reserved earlier tonight, and despite him having no knowledge of it, it's going to remain with him.

When I chance a quick look his way, Dylan's talking with Luke, both of their eyes on a group of cheerleaders sitting nearby. An uncomfortable feeling swarms in my chest as I watch a smile light up his face. I have no right to feel this way, but I recognize it for what it is—jealousy.

I spin around in my dance partner's arms, after briefly forgetting he was there. His hands are on my waist, gripping tightly, and the fact that I couldn't even feel them scares me. But there's no processing that issue right now. I need to escape these feelings.

"I think I need a break. Can we go outside?" I ask and manage to bring a smile to my face. I could just leave him here and go outside alone, but I need something to take my mind off Dylan.

"Of course. Lead the way," he says, gesturing toward the exit. We walk in single file through the room, and once we're outside, I feel instantly calmer.

The guy starts talking about the latest must-see horror movie, and I tune him out and think about the last thriller I watched with Dylan instead. *Dammit!* So much for forgetting about Dylan.

Why am I being so stupid, anyway? He hasn't done anything wrong. I'm the one who has issues, not him. Ignoring him won't solve anything. I need to talk to him and apologize for my shitty behavior. I'm actually shocked he hasn't called me out on it. I turn and offer an apologetic smile. "I need to—"

"I know," he says with a genuine, albeit shy smile. "You've been sneaking glances at Dylan all night. I'm not sure what's going on between the two of you, but there's something. I'm pretty sure at one point he wanted to knock me out."

I laugh, though I feel pretty bad for ditching him. "I'm sorry," I say, crinkling my nose in apology.

"Don't be," he says, and I think he actually means it. "Dylan's a good guy." *That he is.*

I feel the need to set him straight about Dylan and me, even though I don't owe him anything. "Nothing's going on with us," I say, but don't quite believe it myself. "I just need to talk to him. Clear the air about something."

"Gotcha," he says, leaning back against his car, waiting for me to depart.

I smile and move to head back inside, just as a familiar figure walks out the door. I can't help but smile. *Maybe he came looking for me.* I'm about to call out when he walks over to a beautiful woman and stops in front of her and her car. She leans forward and kisses his cheek, bringing about a fresh wave of jealousy.

God, I need this to stop.

They talk for a moment, with big smiles, before Dylan joins her in the car. *Well, this is a familiar scene.* Only difference is that I'm usually the one looking at it from his point of view.

When the car moves toward me, I try to look away, but for the life of me I can't break my stare. Something in me needs to watch this play out until the very end.

They're both still smiling at each other as they approach. When the car is level with us, Dylan's eyes suddenly lock on mine with a look I can't decipher. He doesn't look happy to see me with the guy next to me, even though he's the one leaving the party with someone else.

"Ah, shit. That sucks," the guy says from behind me, but I ignore him. As soon as the car is out of sight, I walk back inside, leaving him alone in the parking lot.

He went home with someone? Dylan went home with someone. I mean, of course he did. He's single. We've talked a lot about the fact that he's taking a different approach to his love life. This was inevitable, and yet, I did not see it coming. Nor did I ever stop to think about how I'd feel when it happened. Dylan and I can never be more than friends. I know this. I'm the one who set that boundary. I placed him securely in a friendship box, locked it up tight, and threw away the key. Watching him leave just now made me want to find that metaphorical key, pick it up, and place it in my back pocket for safekeeping. Just in case I want more. In other words, I'm screwed.

I told myself that going to a game was a bad idea, only I never predicted Dylan would be the reason. Or rather, my feelings toward Dylan. The electricity I felt between us when I jumped into his arms was hard to ignore, but something I wanted to forget. Fast. I practically pushed him into that girl's arms, walked him into her room, turned back her sheets and said "have at it." I deserve the sting of jealousy I'm feeling.

No matter how much we both try to pretend, things have definitely changed between us. I know it seems I'm keeping Dylan in the friend zone because he deserves better than a one-night stand. That's right, but it's so much more complicated than that. I should have kept my distance from the start. I never should have pretended to be his best friend. And I definitely shouldn't have let him into my heart, even platonically. I should have left him alone. *Should have, but didn't.* And now, I have no idea what to do with the situation I've gotten myself in. But I can't seem to bring myself to walk away.

After tossing and turning all night, I decide the only way to move forward is to apologize to Dylan for avoiding him at the bar and then try and focus on our friendship. We've got the football team fundraiser this weekend, so the last thing I want to do is make things awkward between us. I take a deep breath and pick up my phone to text him just as someone bangs on the door.

"I'm coming," I yell, jumping out of bed wearing only my panties and tank top. Whoever is at the door is going to get an eye full for knocking this early in the morning. *I'm kidding.* When I reach the door, I barely open it wide enough to peek through. No one needs to see my pajamas, or lack thereof. I internally laugh at my own thoughts until I see the figure waiting to greet me. Dylan is standing in the doorway with his arms locked onto the frame above his head.

He's wearing different clothes from last night and smells freshly showered, so I allow myself to pretend he went home alone last night. Why he's here now, though, is anyone's guess. He looks confident and determined and...hot.

"Dylan, what—" I don't get to finish my sentence before he flings the door all the way open, pushes me against it, and slams his lips to mine, like this moment is completely out of his control. I still for a second, shocked, before my brain fires and I match his intensity.

Dylan holds my shoulder in one hand and pushes the other into my hair, gripping tightly before palming my neck and deepening our kiss. My own hands travel up along the ridges of his strong back until I reach his shoulders and pull him tighter against me. The movement causes Dylan to press into me, eliminating all space between us. As soon as our bodies touch, he expels a guttural groan, and if it isn't the sexiest sound I've ever heard... *Mmm.* My own moan escapes this time.

The pressure of his warm lips feels amazing, and when he purposely bites my bottom lip, an electric current shoots through my entire body, causing my skin to pebble with goose bumps. As cliché as this might be, I have *never* felt like this before.

One of my hands moves to his hair, and with our bodies flush and Dylan's hand gripping the back of my neck possessively, I'm completely lost in the moment. I moan into his lips as he pulls away, and I feel the loss of him all over. Our gazes lock, and neither of us release our grip on the other. It's an intense moment that I'd usually shy away from, but I'm still stunned over what just transpired.

Dylan searches my eyes for something as my pulse slowly returns to normal. "I think we both needed that. To get it out of our systems," he says, completely shocking me. He steps back, creating some breathing room between us, and his eyes scan over my body, lingering on my panties longer than everywhere else. "*Fuck!* Where are your clothes?" he groans and runs his hand up through his hair, further tangling the mess I just made.

I let out a giggle. I can't help it. I'm nervous, confused, and completely turned on by this new "take control" version of Dylan.

He shoots me a panty-melting smile which causes my heart rate to pick up again barely seconds after it settled from the kiss. Dylan takes

151

another step back, bringing him to the doorway, then points over his shoulder. "I'm going to go before I do something stupid. Something *else* stupid." He shrugs and then walks away, leaving me frozen in place, completely unfazed that I'm in my underwear.

I run a hand through my knotted hair before pressing my fingers to my lips. *Who was that? And more importantly, where did he go?*

Chapter Twenty-One

Summer

I f you'd have told me a few months ago that I'd not only have made friends with some of the football team, but that I'd be attending their yearly fundraiser, I would have laughed in your face. But, here I am. Standing on the threshold, waiting to enter.

After Dylan attacked me with one hell of a kiss last week, we've barely spoken. Our communication has consisted of one phone call and a bunch of texts. Dylan's words still run through my head on repeat, *to get it out of our systems.* It might have worked for him, but for me it had the opposite effect. Nothing has changed when it comes to my feelings on starting something with Dylan, but one thing has definitely changed in me. Kissing Dylan Mathers now consumes my every thought. But it can't happen. It will ruin both of us.

Taking a deep breath, my eyes wander over the many beautiful women prancing around the football team as they make their way inside. I'm definitely underdressed, actually maybe overdressed is the right word, judging by all the scantily clad girls. I mean, sure, I'm wearing a dress, but it's not so short that it reveals my ass, and doesn't have pieces missing in random places. I'm wearing a simple black wrap dress with capped sleeves that's fitted to my curves but still allows movement. It hits me a few inches above the knee, and the neckline dips just enough to see a hint of cleavage. It's nothing special but I feel confident when I'm wearing it. Rather than sky-high stilettos, I've paired it with little black ankle boots. I probably should have worn something strappy when it came to shoes, but I didn't. So, sue me.

Joel sees me in the entry when I step through the doors and rushes to my side to usher me to our seats. The room is beautifully decorated with flower arrangements, white tablecloths, and candelabra centerpieces. Not to mention polished silver and plush looking chairs. It's classy. I like it. It's not at all what you'd expect from a football function, or based on the attire of some of the female attendees. Nonetheless, my judgment of this event is off to a good start.

I'm attending tonight as Joel's date, much to Dylan's displeasure. It's not that I didn't want to go with Dylan. Joel just asked me first. Dylan argued I should support my *football player* best friend, since it was a football team event, which made complete sense, but Joel won me over with, and I quote, "please, Sum, I know I'm going to get messy drunk. I always do at these things, and I can't afford to do anything stupid." I couldn't say no, especially with his puppy dog eyes and soft husky voice. When I'd explained that to Dylan, his expression softened, and he immediately agreed with me. There was definitely a story there. The list of things I wanted to know about Joel was increasing. For someone who had the uncanny ability to pull secrets from everyone he met, he sure kept his own locked up. All I can say now is, thank God for Joel, because I'm not sure I could have been Dylan's date tonight with my head so messed up.

Dylan stands as we reach the table, and I don't miss the way his gaze sweeps over my body before landing on my face. His Adam's apple bobs before his eyes meet mine. Our eyes lock, and his intense stare is full of heat, a heat that I'm feeling but desperately trying not to project. This blatant lust is not typical Dylan behavior, but not at all unwelcome, even though it should be. I bite my lip and take a deep breath to control my breathing. Dylan's face scrunches in agony, and he shakes his head before running a hand through his hair, breaking our connection.

It's only been a matter of seconds since I arrived, but enough time for Dylan to completely rattle me. We've settled into such a comfortable friendship, one I rely on. I've never once thought about taking things in another direction since our friendship became real. *Okay, maybe once.* But now, it's all so confusing. I don't want a relationship—full stop—and definitely don't want to start something with Dylan when I know it's going to end badly. It will ruin him. I will ruin him. Why did things have to change?

A throat clears beside me, and my face reddens at being busted, lost in thought. I mutter a quick apology and sit down. When I look back at Dylan, the heat has diminished, a sympathetic smile in its place.

I relax after that and vow to enjoy the night. Drinks flow, conversation moves easily, and the formalities are actually not the borefest I was expecting. At one point, I even scan the silent auction items, feigning interest, with no intention of bidding. I might be a supportive presence here, but I can't afford to help in any other way. The ticket cost was all I could manage, though a signed Led Zeppelin record has caught my eye. *Rob would kill for this.*

"I knew that one would gain your interest," a deep voice says from behind me. I can practically feel Dylan's touch, but when I turn around, he's not as close as I thought.

"If I could afford it, I'd definitely be interested. Only not for me—for Cory's dad. I kind of owe him, big time."

Dylan shakes his head and takes a step closer to me. My body heats at our proximity. "For taking you in?" he asks, but doesn't wait for a reply. Instead, he leans forward to speak directly into my ear. "Summer, I'd bet my life savings on him *not* thinking you owe him a dime, and I've never met him. You seem to mistakenly think it's a hardship to care for you. Trust me, it's not."

I can't stop the blush from coating my skin. Unsure how to answer that, I take the coward's way out. "Either way, I can't afford it. But it was nice to see what's on offer. I'm going to head back."

I move to walk away until Dylan speaks. "I could always steal it for you, like the candy bar you made me pinch in middle school."

He's offering me an out. An opening to walk through. A free ride back to our friendship. I take it and run. Shrugging my shoulders, I give him my best "what can you do" look and say, "You chose dare. Would you rather I asked you to kiss Joel?"

"Definitely," he replies with a straight face. "At least then I wouldn't have been grounded for a month."

I shake my head and laugh.

"Wish I'd known you felt that way, Dyl," Joel says, coming to a stop at my side. "Would have been a huge ego boost back in the day." He winks.

I roll my eyes and laugh at the two guys who have so deeply penetrated my life. "Thank you both for always keeping me entertained," I say, linking my arms through theirs and walking us back to the table.

I'm having a great night until, to my horror, they announce that the last part of the fundraiser is karaoke. *How did I not know this beforehand?* Makes sense to wait until they have an intoxicated crowd, but it's still not enough for me. I glare at Cory, and she shrugs. I do not sing in public, ever. I'm not a terrible singer, but I don't enjoy the spotlight, despite often projecting that image. In order to raise extra money, each table must volunteer five of the ten seated to sing. If they don't, the table has to donate a thousand dollars from their own pockets. If five people volunteer, the coaching team donates the money instead. *Lovely idea, but geez. Warn a girl.*

As soon as the announcements conclude, Dylan speaks. "I'm out. Sorry team, but I'm not drunk enough for this. I'd rather pay the cash."

"That's because you're tone deaf," his teammate jokes. Dylan shrugs in response.

Another three people follow suit and refuse. Cory and Nate both agree to sing. Cory may be shy, but she is one hell of a performer. I'm excited to see her and Nate duet. Luke says he's in, and the boys on the table all snicker, joking about his terrible voice that still miraculously gets him the ladies. Their words, not mine. He mumbles something about singing "Pony" by Ginuwine, and I bark out a laugh, picturing him dancing the moves.

I'm still laughing when I feel Joel watching me, his eyebrows raised in question. "I'm game if you are?" He smiles, and I freeze.

This can't be happening. How do I say no? I can't afford the money, but the thought of standing up there? The only other person left is one of the guy's dates. I turn to look at her as she sits down. Her date must have asked because I see her frantically shaking her head. *Shit!* I'm the only one left. My hands begin to sweat as I look back at Joel's excited face. He can see my hesitancy, because he smiles with encouragement, but he obviously doesn't realize how terrified I am. *Dammit, Joel, I thought you had the power to read people.*

"Come on, it'll be fun." He tries to play it down, but the thought of this is really freaking me out. I can feel Cory moving behind me, no doubt trying to get Joel's attention, but he ignores her.

Clenching my fists, I look to the floor, then to my hands, then around the room. Anywhere I can, before looking back at Joel. I have no choice. "I—"

"I've changed my mind," Dylan suddenly announces to the table, and I let out a very obvious sigh of relief. "I feel like getting my sing on tonight."

He stands and raises his glass in the air. "Let's do this," he yells and knocks back the rest of his drink. I'm momentarily caught off guard that he's drinking until his eyes meet mine, and he smiles shyly. Understanding dawns on me. He's doing this for me.

My beautiful savior. My heart rate picks up as I'm caught in yet another moment of lust. I subtly clench my fist and dig my nails into my palm to focus on something else. This isn't the first time Dylan has done something nice for me, but it's the first time it's elicited this intense reaction.

I mouth a *thank you* while he shakes his head like it's nothing. If only he knew that couldn't be further from the truth. It means the world to me.

The singers all move to the stage to discuss song choices and what not. Since I'm left at the table with people I rarely interact with, it's difficult to avoid my thoughts. A dangerous situation to be in. I can't afford to be lost in Dylan right now. *He did a nice thing; move on.* If only it were that easy. My traitorous eyes seek him out, and when I find him, he's looking back at me with a gleam in his eyes. With a devilish smile that could melt hearts, he winks and then focuses back on his task, completely unaware of the fire he's igniting inside me.

As I predicted, Cory and Nate are superstars, receiving a standing ovation for their rendition of "Don't Go Breaking My Heart."

Dylan walks onto the stage next, and I cringe for him as Cory takes her seat beside me. "Ah, I'd hate to be Dylan right now. You two were amazing."

"We were, weren't we?" Nate replies, even though I was talking to Cory. We both laugh.

"Have you ever heard Dylan sing?" I ask Nate, desperate to know what he's putting himself through. For me.

Cory spins in her chair to face him and bounces excitedly. "Ooh, is he as bad as they say?" she asks.

Instead of responding, he simply smirks and looks back to the stage. *Well, that was strange.* Cory and I raise our eyebrows in confusion.

All thoughts flee my mind the second I hear a familiar guitar riff start. My heart leaps in my chest, and my breath hitches. Metallica's "Nothing Else Matters" fills the space as the room becomes silent. Seems I'm not the only one waiting to hear Dylan's voice. Leaning forward, I rest my elbows on the table and unashamedly give Dylan my undivided attention. When he finally sings, everything stills, and I have to remind myself to keep breathing.

His voice has the same deep powerful quality as the lead singer, but there is something uniquely Dylan about it. He can sing. *God, can he sing.* He kept that piece of information quiet. I'm completely lost in his voice. I feel his words and the notes of the song in the depth of my soul. I can't take my eyes off him. Dylan Mathers is a very attractive guy, Dylan the football player is mouthwateringly hot, but Dylan the singer...ugh, he's the sexiest thing I've ever seen.

He's casually sitting on a bar stool, with one foot resting on the footrest and the other touching the floor, the hand not holding the mic resting between his legs, briefly drawing my eyes there. *What would it be like to see him naked? Thank God we're not alone right now, because I don't think I could stop myself from finding out.* Biting my lip to suppress a moan from the image my mind just conjured, I lean back in my seat and try to calm my breathing, but don't look away.

I know the lights are blinding him on stage, but I feel his eyes bore into mine, like he's singing to me, for me, maybe even about me. I have to pinch my leg to snap out of the stupid notion. *It's his favorite song. It has nothing to do with me. Get a grip!* It's hard to focus as his voice cuts me to the core. He's incredible. Why isn't he openly sharing this part of himself with the world?

My pulse speeds up along with the song, and his eyes never waver. I feel naked under his gaze, like he's looking at all my layers and assessing what he finds. Like he wants to dig deep until he discovers every part of me. But the killer, the hardest thing to process, is that as he sings, he's looking at me like he actually *wants* to know every piece of me. Like he'll die if he doesn't. And no one has ever looked at me like that.

I'm frozen in time until someone stands in front of me, saving me from my inner torment. My foolish notion. I must have it all wrong. He probably can't even see me, let alone *see* me.

"Is he singing to you?" Cory asks, pulling my attention from my thoughts. My gaze flits to her.

"What? No," I answer quickly, not at all playing it cool. And really, why should I when I can tell by her raised eyebrow and confident expression that she's been watching us both.

"He's looking right at you, Sum," she states matter-of-factly.

My eyes drift back to the stage. "The audience is dark; he's just looking straight ahead."

"If you say so."

I take my eyes off Dylan again and look at her wicked grin. "Friends, my ass," she mumbles to herself, and I choose to let it pass.

Standing, I walk toward the bar as Dylan finishes the song. I need a distraction.

When the music stops, I look back at him. Sure enough, his eyes are still on me, even though I'm halfway across the room. A few seconds pass before he breaks the connection, laughs, and takes a bow. The audience stands, and cheer and whistles fill the room. He's a crowd pleaser, that's for sure. Girls around me are screaming his name and clapping. When the lights come back on for the next singer, Dylan's eyes catch mine, and he smiles, once again unleashing his devilish grin. *What's that about?* He calls out to Luke, Nate, and Joel to join him on stage, before whispering to them in a huddle. Joel's eyes light up as they meet mine before they all disappear off stage. *God, what is happening?*

The lights go out again, and the audience goes quiet as other singers grace the stage. Cory joins me at the bar, clearly as confused as I am, and we drink while we wait for the boys to return. Thankfully, this is not a dry event, and by some miracle we're not carded. Three shots and a cocktail later, the crowd erupts in sudden applause. It's the loudest they've been all night. The opening chords to NSYNC's "Bye Bye Bye" begin, pulling my interest toward the stage. Cory and I both look at the same time and freeze in shock before simultaneously bursting out with laughter. The boys are standing side by side, mics in hand, ready to sing. I have no words.

We head back to our seats for a better view as the boys sing and dance, with Dylan and Nate taking the lead. They clearly had a quick choreography session backstage because they're attempting a few synchronized dance moves. Attempting being the key word here. Laughter and joy rings out around me, and while I've got a huge smile plastered on my face, deep down, my mind is spinning. *He is going to ruin me.*

I can only hope that he chose this song simply because he knows I love it. Not as a subtle way of telling me he's done with us.

When the song finishes and the bright lights come on, Dylan's eyes lock with mine again and he winks, before they all link arms and take a bow. I bite my lip to suppress the size of my smile and shake my head. When Dylan beams back at me, I can't stop the laughter that escapes.

I am so screwed. With that in mind, I jump up from my seat and power walk to the bar. *I need a drink.*

Chapter Twenty-Two

Dylan

How much time do I give Summer before I approach? We've been dancing around each other all night, and even though she's tried to hide it, it's impossible to miss the heat reflected in her beautiful green eyes. Especially when that heat is directed at me. When I made the decision to kiss her last week, I knew there was a strong chance I'd ruined everything. Despite saying it was to get her out of my system, I actually hoped it might spark something in her, and it absolutely did. I felt it the second she kissed me back. Now I just need to convince her to embrace it. She hasn't left the bar since we finished our song, a fact that doesn't bode well for me. She's like a wild animal, always seconds away from activating her fight-or-flight response. Never completely trusting those around her, always on guard. I guarantee my overt desire for her since I kissed her has thrown her off her game. I need to proceed with caution.

Gathering all the confidence I can muster, I square my shoulders, take a deep breath, and make my way across the room. "Be honest, we were better than NSYNC, right?" I ask, dropping into the empty seat beside Summer.

She tenses slightly but then relaxes as she clasps a shot glass between her hands. "Too close to call." She smiles. "You are a talented bunch, that's for sure. Is there anything you can't do?"

I laugh. "Oh, there is so much I can't do." *I can't figure you out for one.* "But I'm always willing to give something a go." My eyes lock on her hands as she rolls the glass along her fingers.

She releases it suddenly and turns in her seat to face me. "Thank you again for taking my place. I know you didn't want to sing, so it means a lot to me. And thanks for singing 'Bye Bye Bye.' I got a lot of joy out of watching you sing a song that I know you can't stand. I'm assuming that song was for me."

"They were both for you. It was a toss-up between 'Nothing Else Matters' and 'Shimmer' by Fuel, but since I've sung Metallica before, it was a no-brainer." I don't comment on her thanks for taking her place because she looks a little embarrassed by it. She's right. I hadn't wanted to sing, but with one look at Summer's face, I knew I had to. She's so good at maintaining a facade that no one else could see the signs, but I've made it my mission to break through her walls, so I'm learning. And tonight, I'm thankful that I could see through her mask and help her.

"They had 'Shimmer'?" she asks with a skeptical glare.

"They did not," I say, and she bursts out laughing.

"Okay, next question. You've sung before!?" she asks, gripping my thigh and squeezing. "How did I not know this? Here I was thinking you were hiding this amazing part of yourself from the world. But only from me apparently." Her brow furrows, but it's playful.

"It was before your time," I reply, trying not to look down at her hand on my leg. I don't sing often, but I have been known to break into song when drunk. It's been a while, though, and the thought of telling Summer I can sing never even crossed my mind.

"So, when you were a toddler?" she says and then laughs hysterically at her joke about our fake friendship, slapping my arm with her free hand, the other still on my leg.

I laugh a little with her, because her response is funny, but it's not "laugh out loud, slap the person next to you" funny. I'm going to go out on a limb and say she's drunk, or at the very least extremely tipsy.

When her laughter dies down, she removes her hand from my leg and straightens, running her hands over her legs as though she's fixing her dress. "So, apparently that last drink has entered my bloodstream. I need to dance it off. Please tell me I can dance somewhere?" She giggles, and fuck, I love that sound.

"There's an after party," I say, and it's the truth, but I would have found her a place to dance, no matter what. I would have organized an after party at my place if I had to. I'd just about make anything happen for her right now. Standing, I pull her to her feet and link my fingers through hers.

Wordlessly, we collect our things and head for the exit. The warmth of her hand in mine has my mind going places it shouldn't. I'm surprised she's allowing this contact but keep that to myself, aware that sudden movement could rock this already shaky boat.

Our hands are still linked when we settle in a cab. She taps her fingers to the beat of the music as we speed along, never once looking my way. I'm unsure if the movement results from nerves or a drunken characteristic, but I enjoy it, nonetheless. We have to break apart when it comes time to pay the driver, but the second she steps out of the car, Summer entwines our fingers again, playfully swinging our arms as we make our way inside.

I try not to read too much into the sudden PDA, because she's definitely drunk, but I can't stop the hope from rising and making an appearance. I'm not stupid. I've noticed the shift in our relationship. I felt it the second she jumped into my arms after the football game. And even though it cooled off a bit after that, I felt it again when we kissed and even more so tonight when she walked into the room, looking like sex on legs, in that tight dress and short boots. Her legs were so tantalizing, that I couldn't stop my eyes from raking over them. Better my eyes than my hands or lips, either of which would have been my preference. In the split second before I met her gaze, I decided I was going to own my feelings. Tonight, I wasn't holding anything back. And fuck am I happy I did, because it's led us to this moment.

I've almost convinced myself that tonight is going to change everything, when Summer stops and releases my hand. "In the wise words of my good friend Dylan, 'let's get our drink on,'" she yells, elbowing me in the stomach and bouncing her shoulders. Her entire demeanor changes as she not so subtly reminds me where I stand. She may as well be shouting it from the rooftop, "friends, Dylan, nothing else." *Fuck, I'm getting whiplash.*

The whiskey no longer burns on the way down my throat. I know I shouldn't be drinking this much, but there's no game this week, and it's something I need to do to survive the night. We've been at the club for hours. At least, I hope it's been hours, because if not, I've consumed a lot of alcohol in a brief space of time. I've just passed the point of no return. I've officially drunk enough to kill all feelings, and the weightlessness of my mind feels good. *Is that even a word? Weightlessness...weightless...ness. It's kind of funny, but it works.* I'm laughing at myself when Joel's arm wraps around Summer as he hands her another drink, some pink shit with a straw. I stand tall and puff out my chest, ready to stake my claim. And even though I know he's not interested in her, because we've discussed it, I still can't help the possessive feeling taking over.

Summer and I have been back and forth, friendly one minute and *very* friendly the next, if you catch my drift. So when she walks my way, I'm unsure of where we currently stand, until she walks her fingers up my chest and then uses her pointer to pull down my lip, her eyes focused on her action. When my lip slips free, I lick it, before biting down to suppress a groan.

"Are you going to dance with me, Dyl? They're playing our song," she says in a sultry tone. They're not playing our song; we don't have a song, but I play along.

Following her to the dance floor, I grip her hips, keeping her close as we walk. When we blend ourselves into the sea of bodies, I whip her around and pull her into me so our bodies align. We move in time to the beat of the song. A song I can't even name. If I had to choose a song for us, it would be "Crocodile Rock" by Elton John. It was our dance-off song that lazy Sunday afternoon when I discovered that Summer had dance lessons as a child. I also would have accepted "Nothing Else Matters," *for obvious reasons*, or Sir Mix-a-Lot's "Baby Got Back." I got my groove on to that stellar hit too.

Summer unashamedly rubs her body against mine, occasionally leaning back to give me a perfect view of her perky tits, her hands in constant exploration of my body. Talk about mixed signals. I try to be a gentleman. I do. But it's impossible with someone so beautiful practically dry humping me as we dance. Thank God for the packed dance floor, because no one is paying us any mind. I hike one of her legs up to wrap around me and grind into her, making sure she knows exactly what she's doing to me. The little minx doesn't even react. She just continues in her quest to turn me on.

Summer spins around at the exact moment Cory waves to get her attention. I expect her to disappear without a word, but she surprises me by placing a soft kiss on the edge of my lips before whispering in my ear. "I'm not done with this yet. Come with me?" Then, without waiting for an answer, she links our fingers and pulls me along with her. Who am I to argue?

I promised myself I wouldn't sleep with her, because that's a one-way ticket to a Summer-free life. Something I am *not* ready for. Keeping that promise is testing me tonight. There have definitely been moments where it's felt like I'm the man Summer has set her sights on. She's been running hot and cold, but for the last hour, the "hot" has taken the reins. Especially after she just pressed her lips to mine, albeit briefly. No one could deny the shift in the air surrounding us. She wants me; that I know. But only for tonight. She couldn't have been clearer about that. For every touch of the hand, for every flirty look, there's an accompanying comment about how much our friendship means to her, how special our friendship is. She's drunk and has either lost her reasoning or is choosing to ignore it. Either way, there's no doubt in my mind that I could have her tonight. And despite acting to the contrary, I'm the idiot who's going to reject her.

Cory ends up needing Summer for longer than we both thought, so I spend some time with the team and even get talked into a dance by a cheerleader. She's gorgeous in a tight little number that leaves nothing to the imagination, but my eyes seem to roam of their own accord to seek the beautiful woman I wish was in her place.

I'm at the bar—fuck if I know why, considering I'm way beyond my limit—but I'm here, drink in hand, when I next see Summer.

"I think you've got a definite chance with the cheerleader. She hasn't taken her eyes off you. I mean, she's not as hot as the beauty you took home last time, but she's still a solid nine, maybe even nine and a half," she rambles, something I've noticed she does when she's drunk.

I bop her on the nose, because she's so adorable, and then study her face to verify if she's back on the friends' bandwagon and wants me to hook up, or if she's jealous. She raises her eyebrows in question, and

I'm happy to see there's still a trace of heat in her eyes and a hint of jealousy that she's trying to hide. It would probably be easier to resist her if it wasn't there, but I'm definitely glad that it is.

For the next hour, I remain on my best behavior, and it sucks big time. Every time I look at Summer, I imagine my lips on her neck, biting down as she moans my name. I picture her legs wrapped around my waist as I press her down onto a bed. Specifically, my bed. My mind won't stop whirring. Lucky for me, Summer's also managed to keep this platonic, and judging by the time and the tired looks on our friends' faces, I'd say the night is almost over.

I'm making my way back from the toilet when I see Summer walking toward me. She doesn't stop, but as she walks past, she runs her hand across my upper thigh and over my groin, making my member twitch. Last, she brushes her fingers over my abs and then she, and her inquisitive hand, disappears. The whole encounter took only a couple of seconds, but it was enough to turn me on beyond belief.

And I snap.

All resolve evaporates. Turning quickly, I grab her by the wrist and pull her back toward me. Ignoring her startled look, I push her against the wall. Her shocked expression quickly makes way for her lust-filled stare as I possessively cup her neck and move forward until our noses are almost touching.

Her eyes bounce between mine, waiting for my next move. She's so close I can feel her chest rising and falling with her rapid breathing. I want to take her against this wall. I want to say fuck it to all the reasons we shouldn't be here. But I can't stop it running through my head.

This will change everything...

This is my last shot...

Is another kiss worth ruining the friendship?

Time stands still as I stare down at the heavenly creature trapped in front of me. I need her more than I need air right now. I'm about to make my move when she pushes me back, perhaps sensing my hesitation and using it to escape. I open my mouth to apologize when she secures her arms around my neck and jumps, wrapping her legs around my waist. *Thank fuck!* Her dress rides up her thighs, and I force back a groan as my hands grip her ass to hold her up. She's with me. This is happening, and she's not running in the opposite direction. Wasting no more time, I crash my lips against hers and push her back against the wall.

The alcohol may have previously numbed my senses, but I feel everything in this kiss, even more than our first one. The way her soft lips fit perfectly with mine. The way our tongues move in sync, exploring, needy. The way her legs clench a little when I tighten my hold on her. And no matter how drunk I am, I can still sense that there's something inherently different about this kiss. I feel a pull I've never experienced before. There's no coming back from this for me, and yet Summer only wants friendship. It's safe to say that I'm fucked. May as well make the most of it while I can.

Using one hand to support her, I push my other into her hair and tighten my hold. I shouldn't be doing this, but fuck, there's no chance I can stop this now. I don't want to. When I increase the pressure of our kiss, something changes in Summer, and in the next second, she's pulling me into her and matching the fervor of the kiss. A groan rips from within me, and I need more. God, this feels like heaven. *She* feels like heaven.

Without breaking our kiss, I move us toward the restrooms and reach to open the door with one hand. It's not my first choice of location, or my second or tenth, but nothing is going to stop this moment. Summer reaches between us, impatiently trying to unbutton my pants, before I've even got the door open. "Fuck," I groan. I've never been more desperate or craved someone as much as I do at this moment. Jiggling the door handle a few times, I pray that it's vacant. I'm about to give up and move on to the next one, when it clicks and opens. *Thank fuck.*

As soon as we're inside, I slow down a bit and gently place Summer on her feet, my hands moving toward the hem of her dress. *This is happening.* After spinning us around, I blindly kick out my foot to close the door behind us, when a force slams it open again, causing us both to stumble from the movement. I grip Summer's shoulders to steady her, and turn just in time to see a woman bend over and vomit next to our feet. *Wow!* Turns out I was wrong. Something could, in fact, kill the moment.

There's nothing to do but laugh, and laugh we do, until realization hits, and a hint of redness crosses Summer's face. Though we may never speak of what happened here, ever again, I take solace in a vital piece of information I discovered tonight. Summer wants this too, and *that* changes everything.

With that in mind, I laugh again, then help Summer clean up her shoes and hold her hand as we head back to the group. As predicted, we immediately revert to being friends, as though we hadn't been seconds from ripping each other's clothes off, as though nothing even happened. But, I'm actually okay with that. For now.

Chapter Twenty-Three

Summer

I 'm not ready to face Dylan again after our public mauling session, but I made a promise, and I'm sticking to it. We sobered up pretty quickly after witnessing a poor girl expel the contents of her stomach, and Dylan apologized, alluding to the fact that it never would have happened if he'd been sober. An uncomfortable tightness had gripped my chest with his words, and I wished I could confidently say the same, but I couldn't. I'm just not sure I would have resisted his advance, sober or otherwise. That being said, at least our friendship remains intact. Even if I feel a little awkward right now.

Taking a deep breath, I knock on the front door of Dylan and Joel's and pray that Joel answers. Cory should be here too, but she canceled this morning, something to do with Nate's parents. A couple of minutes go by without a response, so I knock again, louder and more forcefully. Still nothing. *The assholes invited me here and didn't even bother listening for the door.* I give them one last chance to answer, and when I get crickets, I turn to leave. I've barely taken a step when I hear movement approaching, and the door flies open.

"Sorry, I was in the show...Sum...Summer?" Dylan says, stumbling over his words, one hand holding the door frame, the other gripping the back of his neck.

I freeze. He's standing before me, dripping wet, with nothing but a towel wrapped around his waist. My eyes rake over his body, taking him in. I've felt his abs. I knew they were there, but my mind did not give them justice. I have a powerful urge to lick my lips but somehow refrain. I can't, however, bring myself to look away. *And God, he smells amazing. Is that his body wash, or is that just how he smells?* My eyes flash to his neck as a drop of water falls from his hair. I watch as it

169

moves down his chest, over his glorious abs, before disappearing into his belly button. I bite my tongue and lock my fingers together in front of me, not wanting to follow the water path with either of them.

I'm vaguely aware that Dylan's talking to me, but I can't focus on that right now. It's not important. What is important is figuring out how to get Dylan to remove that towel. What I wouldn't give for a peek. *Stop! Come on, Summer, you've seen naked men before. Snap out of it.*

"Summer?" Dylan questions again, and this time I hear him loud and clear. He's asking me something, but what?

I snap out of my daze and try to formulate an answer. "Joel," is all I can say. *What kind of response is that?* Dylan smiles, and I swear for a second, I turn into a giddy schoolgirl. *Geez, get your shit together, Summer.* "Sorry. I'm here for the movie," I say and hold up a bag of popcorn, waving it in front of him, like it's the answer to life's biggest questions.

He stares at me, his expression blank.

"Joel's trying to impress someone and invited her and her friends over for a movie," I say slowly, so he understands. "Ring any bells?" I ask.

Dylan nods but eyes me strangely, like he's trying to process some new information. "Are you the someone or her friend?" he finally asks.

What the hell? "I'm neither. Why would you... Actually, never mind. Where's Joel?" I'm baffled why he'd ask me that after last night. "Her name is Julia, I think?" I hadn't asked Joel questions about this mystery woman, even though I was more than curious about her. Did this mean Delilah was a thing of the past?

"Shit, yep. Now I remember. Is that tonight?" Dylan asks, stepping aside and signaling for me to come in. I hadn't even realized I was still hovering in the doorway.

"Sooo, where is he?" I ignore Dylan's question. Of course it's tonight or I wouldn't be here.

"Who?"

Ugh! Well, this isn't awkward at all. Maybe I should just leave. "Joel. Where is Joel?" I ask, making sure it's clear as day. I *really* should leave. His mind is clearly elsewhere. Shit, maybe he wasn't alone in the shower. Dylan runs a hand through his wet hair and avoids eye contact.

His eyes flit down the hall toward the bathroom before returning to me. *Yep, he definitely has a girl here.*

"He left about fifteen minutes ago, but if he's having people over, I guess he'll be back soon." He shrugs.

"Okay." *Shit.* "I might head off for now. Tell him to call me, and I'll stop by a bit later, if he still needs me to."

I turn to leave, but Dylan grabs my arm and pulls me back to face him. "No, wait...I mean, you're welcome to wait." I stare at him for a moment until he speaks again. "Please wait. I'll only be a minute." He gestures toward the couch and then jogs back down the hall.

I drop into my usual spot on the couch and pull my legs up under me, while wondering why the hell I'm here. Do I really want to be here when Dylan and a woman walk out? Am I jumping to conclusions? Hell, yes. But who has a shower at five in the afternoon if they're just staying in for a movie night? Unless he has a date tonight. He said he forgot about the movie. *Shit! Stop thinking. Just leave.* As if things aren't awkward enough.

True to his word, Dylan returns in just over a minute, leaving me with no time to sneak out. He's alone and dressed in a pair of grey sweats and a tee. He has mussed hair, like he just ran his hands through it. He's definitely *not* dressed for a date but still looking as sexy as sin. *What is wrong with me?* I know Dylan well enough to know there was never going to be a girl here, and he was never going on a date. I'm acting delusional. He's making me delusional.

As if sensing the tension in the air, Dylan cuts through my thoughts. "Sorry, that was weird. I wasn't expecting you or anyone, really." He flops down on the couch next to me, just like always.

He runs his hand through his hair and smiles brightly. "Can I get you a drink?" he asks. It's a pretty simple question, but can I answer it? No, because my mind's stuck on his half-naked body. Dylan raises an eyebrow in question, and when I still don't answer, he grips my thigh and gives me a gentle squeeze. "Everything okay?"

No, everything is not okay. You came out of the shower looking all wet and sexy, when I hadn't even gotten over us having one of the hottest make-out sessions I've ever experienced. I can't stop thinking about it. Despite being drunk out of my mind, my brain is screwing with me by having the insane ability to recall every second of our kiss, and yet, I can't even remember what club we were at. And the worst thing, the absolute kicker, is that sleeping with you will ruin our friendship, but not sleeping with you seems to mess with me all the same. I don't know how to move forward. The sexual chemistry is killing me, and I have this niggling feeling...nope, not thinking about that. Anyway, I know one night won't be enough for you, and that's all I can offer. So no, I'm not okay.

"Yep. Sorry. My head was on other things. I'd love a water, thanks," I say and grin. "Want to watch a movie while we wait for Joel?"

I lean back into the chair and pick up the remote from the armrest, not even waiting for Dylan's reply.

"You better choose a good one." He laughs at his own joke, knowing I *always* choose good ones. It's his choices that are questionable. Jumping up from the seat, he does a slow jog into the kitchen to get my water and our movie snacks. We are nothing, if not predictable.

I take this opportunity to chastise myself and pull my shit together. *Enough is enough. You and Dylan are friends. Start acting like it.* Massaging my temples, I breathe—inhale, one, two, three, exhale, one, two, three—and then relax. I'm the queen of suppressed feelings. This will be a piece of cake.

"You waited until halfway through the movie to tell me that?" I shriek in utter shock. "We've bonded over thrillers. I told you this was my favorite. You could have owned up to it then or maybe even watched it alone to see what the big deal was." Biting my lip, I try to suppress my smile. I'm shocked, but I'm also messing with him a little. I don't really care that he hasn't seen this film. In fact, I'm looking forward to seeing his reaction to the ending, even if I still think, as a thriller fan, he should have watched it.

"I honestly have no excuse. And it's really fucking good so far. I'm actually a little ashamed of myself," he says softly, shaking his head and furrowing his brow. I can't stop the smile from breaking free.

"I'm jealous you get to experience it for the first time. I'd go as far as to say it's Edward Norton's best work."

"Ah, what about *Fight Club*?"

"Hmmm." I grip my chin and bite my cheek in thought. That's a good question. *Fight Club* is amazing, but *Primal Fear*? "Let's revisit this conversation at the end of the movie," I say, not willing to decide on my own.

Dylan laughs and resumes the movie. He leans back in his seat and kicks his legs up onto the coffee table, something he never does when Joel's here. Sometimes those two act like an old married couple. In his relaxed state, he looks over and smiles, eliciting another smile from me. "Bring it on," he says before we sit in silence for the rest of the film.

"What the fuck just happened?" Dylan yells when the credits roll. He looks completely perplexed, and I'm so pleased I'm here to witness this moment. His face contorts before he rubs a hand over his features and shakes his head.

When he finally looks at me with a crestfallen expression, I burst out with laughter and then quickly cover my mouth to control myself. "I'm sorry; you just look so sad."

"And that's something to laugh about."

"Well, no, not usually, but..."

"But what? I have so many things running through my head right now. One. How is it possible that I've never seen this film?"

I open my mouth to give him a smartass answer, but he presses his finger to my lip and shushes me.

"Two. While I'm still a little in shock, I think that might be one of the greatest endings I've ever seen. And three. There is no way I'm deciding between this and *Fight Club*. Can we just agree that Edward Norton is a fucking legend?"

I laugh at the seriousness of his tone. Like my answer to his question will solve world peace. "That's the smartest thing to ever come out of your mouth," I joke. "Agreed."

"Thank fuck," he sighs, running a hand down his face again. This is really messing with him, and I love it. I can't stop myself from laughing.

"Stop laughing. I'm really not coping here. I think I need you to hold me," he says, staring me down with puppy dog eyes.

"Shut up; no, you don't."

"I really do. I think you owe me."

Rolling my eyes, I move up onto my knees to offer him a consolation pat on the back. "I don't see your logic, so here is my offer of comfort." I pat him twice, thinking that will suffice, before moving back to my cushion. Dylan doesn't accept my generous support, and instead, grips my hand and pulls me across the couch until I'm awkwardly sitting on his lap. Before I can protest, he wraps his arms around me and buries his face in my neck, hugging me tightly to his chest. The shock of it stalls my reaction, and when my mind catches up, I burst into laughter again and pat his head. "There, there."

"I'm so overwhelmed," he says solemnly, but I can hear the smile in his voice.

I shake my head at his antics and pull back to look in his beautiful piercing blue eyes. We both stare at each other for a moment before Dylan's hand reaches to my face and pushes a lock of hair behind my ear. When he looks down at my lips and then back up to my eyes, I desperately want him to kiss me. More than I need anything else. I move my lips closer to his, hoping he'll take the hint, but the front door flies open with a bang, causing us both to jump. "Fuuck!" Dylan curses under his breath as I jump off his lap faster than light, then stand awkwardly in front of him.

Joel takes in the scene and raises an eyebrow in question. Before I can answer him, he speaks. "Oh fuck, I forgot to text you. Delilah canceled again. What's happening here?"

I ignore his question because I don't have an answer. Instead, I throw the awkward questioning back on him. "Delilah? Your ex? I thought you said something about Julia?"

"Julia's her friend. They were both supposed to come." He shrugs.

I'm confused and embarrassed, but also a little concerned at the heartbroken look on his face. I put my issues aside and offer comfort. Walking forward, I place my hands on his shoulder and squeeze. "I'm sorry, Joel. One day she'll realize how amazing you are, but don't wait around. Anyone would be lucky to have you." I kiss him on the cheek and head for the door.

"Where are you going?" Joel and Dylan ask at the same time, and I realize that's the first thing Dylan's said since Joel arrived.

I scrunch up my nose and shrug apologetically. "Sorry, I've got to go. I have tons of studying to do. So, if you no longer need me..." I don't bother finishing my sentence or letting either of them respond. I give them a quick wave and depart, completely aware that I just made a mountain out of a molehill. I just had to get away.

Chapter Twenty-Four

Dylan

First, I'm thrown by Summer turning up when I'd just been thinking about her in the shower. *Lucky she wasn't a minute earlier.* Then there was Joel's bullshit timing. I swear someone's out to mess with me. I hadn't planned for my joke hug to turn into anything, but when Summer's eyes locked with mine, I saw some of the heat return. And that, paired with her reaction to seeing me in a towel, confirmed things for me. *She feels the same.*

I'm going to woo her. As corny as that sounds, it's the truth. I'm going to take my time and win her over. I'm going to do everything properly, and I'm not going to stop until she's mine. Being friends is not enough. Not after our last kiss. The flirting I could handle. I'd even been able to force myself back into the friend zone after the time I kissed her in her doorway. But after *that* kiss in the bar, with her body pressed against mine and her moans forever ingrained in my mind—not possible. Not now that I know she wants me. She just needs a little help to realize it.

With that in mind, I send her a text before she's even left our front yard.

Me: Sorry you had to rush off. Want to take a drive with me tomorrow, after class?

I sit by my phone like a lovesick puppy for too long before I realize she's not replying. Finally moving from the couch, I find Joel in the kitchen and grab my keys from the bench. "I'm heading out for a beer. You in?"

Since Delilah didn't show, there's a good chance he'll want to drown his sorrows. Joel empties the contents of his glass down the sink and grabs his wallet. "Let's go," he says and walks to the front door. As he crosses the threshold, he looks back and shakes his head at me, laughing. Damn, looks like we'll be talking about me, not him.

Two hours and five beers later, I'm over my self-imposed limit again. We haven't spoken about Summer or Delilah, but I feel it coming. Joel is absolutely going to ask about Summer. I knew it the second he laughed at me when we were leaving. I mean, Summer practically sprinted from the house without warning. He knows something happened. It was pretty obvious.

As though my thoughts have mixed with hers, Summer chooses this moment to reply.

Summer: Where to?

That's not a no. I'm off to a good start.

Me: There's a film festival running in the city. I thought we could grab dinner and check out a thriller.

Okay, so today may have been the first time I've actually tried to woo her, but the truth is, I've been thinking of cool places to take Summer since I met her. This is just the first time I've proceeded with a plan.

Summer: Oh, so a lengthy drive? It sounds like a lot of fun, but I've got a few assignments due back. I'm going to have my head in the books all week. I'm sorry, Dyl.

Damn. Maybe I shouldn't have mentioned dinner. That probably made it sound like a date. Well, *if it walks like a duck and sounds like a duck...*

Me: No stress, another time.

Summer: How about you take someone else? I can set you up? (Wink emoji)

I laugh and groan at the same time. No way is that happening.

"Is that Summer?" Joel asks, bringing me back to the bar. Shit, I'd completely forgotten I wasn't alone. He can't possibly see my screen, can he? "Ask her if she wants to have lunch on Friday?" he adds. *What the fuck?* I look down at my phone and back up at him.

"It's not Summer," I say, with no clue why I'm lying.

"It's not Summer?" he repeats, his eyebrows practically hitting the ceiling by how much he's not buying it. "So, you've got yourself another girl then?"

"What, no!? There's no one else," I'm quick to respond. He smirks and I realize my mistake. "No one in *general*," I correct. *Not even Summer.*

"Okay, well, if you happen to text Summer, ask her about lunch." He laughs and takes a swig of his beer. Why does he want to have lunch with her? Is there something going on? I'm too curious for my own good, so I ignore her question about a date for me and instead ask about Joel.

Me: Joel asked if you want to have lunch with him on Friday???

Dammit. What's with the three question marks? One will suffice.

Summer: Tell him I'd love to.

Great. That makes me feel worse. That was so easy, but I got a no.

"She says she'd love to," I state without looking up from my phone. My tone is so bitter I can taste it. I feel Joel's smirk without having to witness it.

"Great! Thanks," he replies nonchalantly.

My gaze shoots to his, and I stare him down. *Don't ask, don't ask.* "Why are you having lunch?" *I ask.*

"We have lunch together every Friday. Ever since we had the class together at the beginning of summer," he says with a shrug, like it's no big deal.

"How did I not know this?" I accuse.

He shrugs again. *Asshole.*

And why would he get me to ask her if they always have lunch? Does he want to annoy me? What an ass. I want to tell him to stay away from her. I want to punch the little smirk off his face. I want to...*Shit!* I see what he did, and I stupidly fell for it.

He's watching the emotions play out on my face and starts laughing out loud. "Man, you have it so bad."

"Fuck off." *He's not wrong.*

"So, you like her. It's no big deal," he continues, really pushing my buttons.

"She's just a friend. She isn't interested in that."

"Are you sure about that? After what I witnessed the other night..."

Fuck! "You saw that?"

"Everybody saw that. I may have been drunk, but it was hard to miss the back and forth between you all night. And then the kiss. Good on you. It was so full on, I don't even think you can call it a kiss. Kiss is too PG for what I witnessed. And don't think I didn't see you disappear into the restroom."

I cringe as I remember how that panned out. "If that was true, you would have also seen us come straight back out."

"Oh yeah, I saw that." He chuckles to himself. "You may not have succeeded, but the intent was there. Not like you at all, really."

"What does that mean?" I ask, though I can guess the answer. I don't have sex in bathrooms, or in clubs, or parties, or...basically anywhere public.

"It means you like her, and you're hooked." He stares me down.

I grip the back of my neck and sigh. He knows me too well to avoid this. "Fine, I'm hooked." Now that's out of the way, I bring our conversation full circle and ask about their lunches. "So, you have weekly lunches. Does she...uh..."

"Talk about you?"

"Yeah?" I run my hand up through my hair. *Did it get hot in here?*

"Honestly?"

"No, dickwad. I want you to lie." God, sometimes Joel makes it hard not to smack him across the head.

"Then she never shuts up about you. You are all we talk about," he deadpans, and man, do his words hit me like a sucker punch to the gut.

"Fuck, that's a no, then?"

"Afraid so," he says, playfulness gone. He sits in front of me, hands under his chin, with a sympathetic grimace on his face, and I have to change the subject.

"Okay, now we've discussed my love life—"

"Nope, not discussing her." He's shaking his head vigorously while crossing his arms over his chest. I'm guessing he really doesn't want to talk about it. I thought he would definitely want to vent.

"I know I usually take her side, but I have to say I'm not loving her at the moment."

"Dylan," he warns, but I ignore him.

"It was one mistake. One!" I say for the millionth time. I love Delilah, and I completely understand how hurt she must be, but she's been messing with Joel's head a little lately. "Do you think she'll ever get past it? I mean, it wasn't your fault."

"Not the point." He's right; it's not the point, but it still needs to be considered. Although, he's not exactly helping his case.

"You could ease up on the man whoring. That might increase your odds."

"Don't start. I know I'm a fuckup." Joel is most definitely *not* a fuckup, but he never listens when I tell him otherwise and instead continues to dig himself further into his pit of pain.

Reaching forward, I grip his arm and look him in the eye just as my phone buzzes, causing Joel to shake himself off and plaster on a smile. Ready to move on.

I look down at the screen, and my heart jumps in my chest. I hadn't replied to her last message or the one about setting me up, but she's clearly been thinking about it.

Summer: How about the weekend?

Fuck, I can't. But Summer's attempt to reschedule is good news. She wants to spend time with me.

"There's that grin again."

God, I really need to learn to keep my emotions off my face. I lean back in my chair so he can't see my screen and text Summer back, ignoring Joel's comment.

Me: We have an away game this weekend. What about Tuesday after class?

I know she finishes early Tuesdays and doesn't start until late Wednesday, so I hope that plays in my favor. It takes a few minutes for her to reply, so I waste time playing around on my phone. When I look up to take in the room, Joel's staring at me, his drink halfway to his mouth.

"You're fucked," he says, and it's surprisingly sympathetic.

I run a hand down my face. He's right; I have it bad. "I know."

Joel leans forward in his chair, placing both palms on the table. "No, I don't think you do. I've never seen you like this with a girl and...fuck, how do I say this without hurting you?"

"She doesn't feel the same," I answer for him, even though I've seen something more between us. *God, he's probably right; I have no shot with her. Why am I even entertaining the idea?*

"Oh, she definitely feels something; maybe not the same, but she has *some* feelings for you."

Come again? That's not what I expected him to say. A small smile pulls at my lips. But Joel's next words stop it in its tracks.

"Only, I don't think she's going to change for you."

Fuck! Luke said the same thing, but it went in one ear and out the other, because I didn't want to believe him and, well...it's Luke. But if Joel's saying it, after all the time he's spent with Summer and me, then I should probably pay attention. There's just something stopping me.

"You might be right, but I need to know for sure."

"What are you going to do?"

"I don't know, man. Try to woo her, and if that doesn't work, I'll be there for her in any way I can. If that's only friendship, so be it. But I need to take a shot first."

Joel sits back and thinks about that for a minute, a contemplative look on his face. "Aren't you worried taking the shot might backfire, and then you'll lose the friendship too?"

"Terrified," I say, running a hand through my hair again. God, it must look awful right now, but I'm beyond caring. "The thing is, I think there's something real between us, and I know she feels it."

"Well, I hope it works out. I love having Summer around, and she deserves a great guy like you."

"Thanks, man."

"I mean it. She's been through so much crap already, and I'm worried we don't even know the half of it." His lips pull into a frown and mine follows.

"Of that, I'm sure. But since she's not likely to tell us, all I can do is be there for her and make sure the bad in her life is a thing of the past."

My phone vibrates again, and I almost drop it in surprise. Joel and I laugh. Thankfully, something broke the seriousness of our conversation. We need something uplifting after that.

Summer: Tuesday sounds great.

And there it is. I don't bother hiding the smile on my face now that the cat's out of the bag. Instead, I pass my phone over so Joel can read our exchange and sit back for his response.

"I'm team Dylan and Summer all the way," he says with a genuine smile, big enough to rival my own.

The weekend arrives quickly, and before I know it, we're at our away game. True to her word, Summer spent the week at home studying, so I haven't seen her, but we have at least spoken on the phone.

Seconds remain on the clock. It's a close game and tensions are high. We've already had two on-field brawls, and we're all skating on thin ice. Our quarterback launches the ball into the air toward our other receiver. I watch, on guard, as it plays out in slow motion. Their defense is good, probably the best of any side, but today, our offense is better. Peters secures the ball in his hands, fakes left and then runs right, sprinting to the end zone.

The crowd roars. Despite being an away game, we still have lots of support. Luke jumps on my back, seconds before we're flattened to the ground in celebration. We beat our biggest rivals. It's been a long time coming, and honestly, something I didn't think would happen during my time on the team. Even Coach is smiling. He's always happy when we win, but he usually waits until the locker room to show any emotion.

A hand appears in my face, and I grip it to pull myself up. Nate slaps me on the back in a hug. "We did it, man," he says.

"Feels like a championship." I laugh.

"That it does. We deserve several days of celebrations."

"You can have tomorrow. Then it's back to training," Coach interrupts sternly, but his smirk gives him away. He's wanted this as much as we have, probably even more.

After another celebration in the locker room and a speech from the coaches, we're on the bus headed home. Spirits are high; there's talk of championships. We all feel invincible. *I feel invincible.*

Bouncing in my seat, I sing along to our pump-up playlist as it blares through the bus. My smile's big, my heart's full, life is good.

And then I get the call I've always feared would come.

Chapter Twenty-Five

Summer

I'm in a rush to get ready for the night when my phone buzzes on the nightstand. *Shit! This better not be Joel saying he's early.* Joel, Cory, and I, and a few of Joel's friends, are heading to Reilly's to watch Dylan's game. I'm willing to admit he's got me hooked on football again, and I'm not complaining.

I crawl across the bed and reach for my phone to see it's Rob calling. I don't have time to answer, but since I still haven't called him after seeing him at the game, and Cory and I postponed our planned dinner, I can't let it go to voicemail.

"Hi, Rob."

"Hi, sweetheart; how are you?" he says, his voice full of warmth.

I sit back into the pillows on my bed, getting comfortable, in case this is a long call. "I'm good. Just getting ready for a night out. How are you and Alison?"

"Good, good. Listen, I don't want to interrupt your night. I just wanted to say thank you for the Led Zeppelin record. I don't know where you found it, and I definitely don't want to know how much you spent, because any amount is too much, but it means a lot to me. I only wish you'd dropped it off in person."

Uh, what? Record? I'm so confused until...

I shake my head, cursing inwardly. I'm not going to outright lie, so instead I say, "When I saw it, I knew you would love it. You'll be happy to know that the money spent on it went to a good cause. It was an item at a charity fundraiser." I should tell him it wasn't me, but that will open a whole new can of worms regarding who Dylan is and why he'd do this for Rob, or me. In fact, I'm curious as to why myself. And yes, it doesn't take a genius to figure out this is Dylan's doing. *Ugh, I'm so angry at him for doing it, but...God, Rob sounds so happy.* My chest tightens, and I feel a crack in my armor. It's not the first, if I'm being completely honest, and it terrifies me to think it may not be the last. Sure, we're friends, but why does he have to be so freaking good to me?

"Well, thank you. It was really thoughtful, and I appreciate it. I love you, kid," Rob says, his voice breaking on the last words, making me feel guilty for taking the credit. I know the intention was there. I wanted to get it for him, but it wasn't actually me who bought it. And, although it's not the first time Rob's said I love you, it still doesn't feel right.

I swallow down my emotions and change the subject. As usual, I don't say I love you back, but he never seems to mind. After a few more minutes of talking, Rob ends the call, and I sag into the bed.

Thoughts of Dylan drift through my mind, and I find myself wishing he were here. *Dammit!* That's definitely not supposed to happen. *Get it together. It's only been a few days.* It's actually a good thing that he's away this weekend. We need the space; I need the space. My head's been all over the place lately. It's time I sorted my shit out. Taking a deep breath, I jump from the bed, adjusting my outfit for the night, mini skirt and silk top, before rushing to fix my makeup so I will be ready as soon as Joel gets here. I need to get this night started.

The bar is already pumping when we arrive. The sound of background music is being drowned out by the excited tones of the patrons, ready for the big game, which I've been told is almost as big as a championship game. Rivalry at its best. Since everyone's here for the same thing, the tables closest to the screens are all full. Luckily a few of our group beat us here, so we have a table secured in prime position.

The score is close, but our boys win in the end. Dylan played another killer game and should be extremely proud of himself. Hell, I'm proud of him, my friend, that I was definitely *not* checking out.

There's no doubt in my mind that Dylan's going to be picked up by an NFL team next year and end up somewhere on the other side of the country, living out his dream. Away from here, away from his friends,

185

away from me. I feel a faint pang in my chest and have to consciously stop myself from raising my hand to the site. *Shit! So much for getting him out of my head.*

I drag Cory to the dance floor as soon as the interviews wrap up, and this is where we spend the rest of the night. Joel and his friends join us occasionally, but, other than them, I reject all guys that approach. For some reason, I'm not feeling it tonight. *Okay, maybe I know the reason.*

It's a little after midnight when Cory's had enough. I know I should go home with her, but I'm not ready. So instead, I make eye contact with Joel and signal him over. Pulling him into my arms for a dance, I send out a silent prayer that he wants to stay for a bit longer, since he's my ride home. "Got it in you to keep me company for another hour or so?" I ask.

"Of course," he agrees with a smirk. "But I'm not driving any drunk guys home with you." He laughs.

"Have you seen me with anyone tonight?" I sass.

He eyes me curiously, and I fear he's trying to read something into my words. "Now that you mention it, I haven't," he says, sounding a little shocked.

Geez, I don't go home with someone every night. Actually it's been a while.

I roll my eyes as a new song begins, and we both get wrapped up in the music.

I'm hot and sweaty from another hour of dancing and need some air. I scan the room, looking for Joel or any of the group, but can't see anyone in the first few seconds, so I shrug and head outside.

The cool October night air is refreshing and very welcome. Pulling the hair away from my neck, I allow the breeze to cool me and take a deep breath. I definitely needed this break.

The creak of the door pulls my gaze in that direction, and I tense as a guy walks out with a cigarette in hand. Just when I think it's safe to relax—he only wants a hit of his vice—his eyes catch mine, and he gives me a sly leer. "Hey, baby, are you leaving already? We didn't get to dance," he drawls, taking a step closer to me, forcing me to step back. He's clearly drunk.

"Not interested, but thanks," I say with a fake smile. *I just want some peace.*

"You give it up for everyone else; why not me?" he whines.

Do I know this guy? "I'm not going to 'give it up' for you because that statement is false. I may sleep with different guys, but I have standards." I move to go inside, but he pulls me back by my hair and slams me to the ground. The move evokes memories and freezes me in place. While this isn't the first time a guy has tried something without my permission, it's the first time a guy's been violent. Flashes of the past run through my mind, and in my moment of weakness, the creep straddles my legs and uses his full weight to keep me down while he presses my hands into the dirt above my head.

I try to fight back, but my drunken state slows my reactions. With one hand still on mine, he moves the other up my thighs until he reaches my panties. I struggle and thrash my body around, trying to buck him off.

"The fight only makes this more fun," he says while getting his fingers under the waistband of the delicate silk. I finally come to my senses and snap. *He will not be hurting me tonight.*

Before I even get the chance to fight back again, his weight disappears, and my arms move along with him as he's ripped off me. When he struggles to maintain his grip on me, I fall back onto the ground. It takes a second to get my balance, but when I finally look up, it's just in time to see another woman punch my attacker square in the nose. *Impressive.* As much as I'm enjoying his takedown, I don't want her to get hurt, so I scream out for help. I'm shocked when the guy pushes the woman down and scrambles to his feet, running away like a coward.

The woman jumps up and runs over to where I'm lying on the ground. "Jesus, are you okay? Did he hurt you?"

"I'm okay. Thanks to you. You are one badass chick. Did he hurt *you?*" I reply, trying to turn this back on her. That's how I'll get past this.

A small smile plays on her lips at my "badass" comment, before she turns serious again. "What can I do to help?"

Pulling myself up off the ground, I dust off my clothes, as the door flies open and Joel looks at me in question. Ignoring him for now, I turn to my savior. "You've done more than enough; my friend can take over." I motion to Joel but keep my eyes focused on the raven-haired girl in front of me. I called her a woman before, but now that I'm really looking at her, I'd say she's actually around the same age as me. "Thank you again. I'm Summer, by the way." I offer her my hand to shake.

"Lainey," she replies and pulls me into a hug. "Are you sure you're okay? If I hadn't come, I don't know what he—"

"I'm fine. I promise," I quickly say, cutting her off before she alerts Joel to what happened.

Joel walks over to meet us when I finally make eye contact. "Are you going to tell me what's going on, or do I need to ask Lainey here?"

He knows Lainey. How do I not know her? Now is not the time to worry about that. "Take me home?" I say and give him my best smile and puppy dog eyes. He rolls his eyes in return and turns to move away. *Phew, that was close. Much better if he doesn't know what happened.*

"We should call the police."

Dammit, Lainey.

I shake my head and smile. "They won't do anything. Never do. I promise I'm fine." I look over at Joel and cringe as I say the next words. "Plus, he's gone."

"Who's gone, and why the fuck do you need the police?" he yells, but it sounds more panicky than angry.

Lainey cringes beside me. "Shit. I'm sorry. You weren't going to tell Joel, were you?"

"Nope, but it's actually not him I'm worried about." I bite a nail at the thought of Dylan finding out. Lainey looks at me with concern, so I add, "I'm fine. You and your badass moves saved me. That guy will think twice before trying it on anyone again; that's for sure."

Lainey smiles, but it doesn't quite reach her eyes. "Can I get your number? I'd feel better if I could check on you tomorrow, when the adrenaline has worn off." Her face reddens slightly. She can beat a guy up without batting an eyelid but struggles to make new friends. I already know I'll love her. We exchange numbers, and she heads inside.

Joel grips my hand and walks me toward his car. "Come on, let's get out of here."

"Can I stay with you? I don't want to worry Cory tonight, if she's still up talking to Nate."

"Of course. But I'm going to have to give Dyl a heads-up."

A lump sticks in my throat. He won't be happy if he learns what happened tonight. "Maybe lie? Tell him I lost my keys."

"Let's just focus on getting you home," he says, and I don't miss the fact he didn't answer my question.

Chapter Twenty-Six

Summer

W hen we arrive back at Joel and Dylan's, Joel immediately disappears into his room with the phone to his ear, no doubt calling Dylan. I make myself at home, feeling oddly calm, considering. I told Joel the entire story on the way home and could see the concern and pity written all over his face. I didn't need any of it. Nothing happened. Lainey, who I discovered is a sister of one of the football players, got there before he'd done anything. I've experienced much worse. Not that I told either of them that.

Only a few minutes pass before Joel returns and flops onto the couch beside me. "Summer, I don't know what to say. I can't even imagine…" he trails off.

"Don't imagine anything, because *nothing* happened. He tried and failed. End of story."

"You should talk about it. I'm not saying I'm the right person. In fact, I can guarantee I'm not, but you can't just pretend it didn't happen."

I pull my legs underneath me on the couch and give Joel the eye. Raising an eyebrow, I say, "Why wouldn't you be the right person? Isn't this situation exactly what you're studying for?"

He laughs and shakes his head. "I know you're trying to distract me. I mean that I think someone already qualified would be more beneficial. You can't keep this bottled up."

"I can, and I will," I say with a smile, hoping to ease his mind. "Plus, it wouldn't be the first time," I mumble, but instantly regret it.

"What does that mean?!"

"You said you weren't the right person to talk to, so can we please just watch a movie or something?" I beg. He agrees without further question and heads into the kitchen, hopefully for snacks.

When he sits back down on the couch, snacks in hand, I pull him into a quick hug. "Thank you," I whisper before turning back to the TV.

I must fall asleep because the next thing I know, I'm awakened by a crash that resembles a door slamming open. *Oh no.*

"Where is she?" Dylan yells, and I hear the loud thud of his football bag dropping to the floor.

Joel rises from beside me and kisses me on the head. "In here, Dyl. Calm down; she's okay," he says as he tries to intercept Dylan at the door.

I glimpse Dylan before Joel pushes him back into the hallway. He lowers his voice to talk, but it's not enough. I can still hear them. "The last thing she needs is for you to make a big deal out of this."

I lean forward in my seat, so I don't miss anything.

"It is a big deal, if—"

"Dyl, stop. She's okay. She didn't even want me to tell you."

"How can she be okay? You said she..." Dylan's words drop off as he lets out a loud breath.

"Lainey found her. She kicked the guy's ass before he could..." He cuts off, and I'm glad. I'd rather not hear a reply.

"I need to see her." Dylan's voice breaks, and my heart shatters with it.

I'm met with silence. They've known each other long enough to speak without words. They do it often. I'm sure decisions are being made. I should say something. *I'm okay. I'm okay. I'm okay.* If I keep saying it, it will come true, right? I'm *mostly* okay, anyway.

"You can—" I begin, but before I can finish, Dylan rushes into the room and drops to his knees in front of me, gently placing his hands on mine—my hands that I've just realized have been gripping my legs tightly since I woke up.

Dylan pries my fingers off my skin and brings them to his mouth, kissing them softly. "I've been so worried," he whispers, his voice gravelly.

"I'm okay," I say, my own voice coming out raspy. Definitely not convincing anyone. Turns out I can only maintain a facade for so long.

"Did he hurt you?" Dylan asks, his eyes scanning my body for injury.

"No, I'm fine. Honestly, it was nothing."

"Summer, it wasn't nothing. Talk to me. I'm here for you." He looks up at me with so much sincerity that it freaks me out. I don't want this to be a thing I have to work through. I want to forget about it.

"Dylan, I said I'm fine. Can we drop it?"

"Why are you acting like it's no big deal?" Dylan asks with a terse tone.

"Because it's true," I lie, speaking louder than necessary, and pull my hands from his.

"You're lucky Lainey was there; you need to be more careful," Dylan says, standing to his feet, pacing.

"What?" *Am I being told off? How did we get here?* He came home worried about me, and now he's annoyed. "That wasn't my first time at a bar, Dylan. Remember, we've been to bars and clubs together. It—"

"I wasn't there to protect you," he yells, cutting me off, and stops his pacing. The anger in his voice freezes me momentarily, but it's the hurt I can hear that softens my own feelings.

"It's not your job to protect me. I've been on my own long enough."

He looks at me with a concerned frown, and his eyebrows furrow. "You obviously need someone to—"

"No, I can take care of myself. I don't need you to protect me. I don't need anyone to protect me. Stop trying to be a big brother."

"That's not what I'm doing. Do you really think that's what I'm doing?" He stares at me in shock and confusion.

"Feels like it." I shrug.

Dylan runs his hands over his face and shakes his head. "God, you are so clueless sometimes," he seethes. "No, not clueless. In denial."

Again, how did we get here? "We shouldn't be fighting about this," I say and then stare at him blankly, unsure what else to say.

His face morphs into one of regret. "Fuck, I'm sorry," he says, gripping the back of his neck. "I've just been so worried, I lost it."

I smile but this is all too much. He feels too much. "Maybe we just need a bit of space. We've been spending a lot—"

Dylan's eyes flash to me, full of pain, before he cuts me off. "Yep, I get it," he says, his voice now void of emotion. "I'll leave you be." And with that, he walks away.

I sink back into my seat as Joel walks into the room. His sympathetic expression tells me he heard everything. "Dylan really cares about you."

"I know." I don't blame him for leaving. I basically pushed him to leave.

"He shouldn't have spoken to you the way he did, but Summer...he was so concerned about you. I've never heard him as panicked as he was when I told him what had happened."

I stand to head home. "Joel, I appreciate—"

"No, please just hear me out," he pleads.

I nod and sit back down, giving him my full attention.

"Dylan's been through some family stuff. He will kill me for telling you this, but the reason he doesn't want to pursue an NFL career is because he doesn't want to be away from his family." *He doesn't? What?*

"But his sister's in—"

"No, his future family. Wife, kids..."

I scrunch up my nose. "Okaay." *I don't know what this has to do with me.*

"Now, imagine he learns that his BFF..."—he pauses, a small smile on his lips, that I can't help but return—"Imagine he discovers someone he cares about was attacked, and he's hours away and helpless. It's his fear coming to life." He pauses again, letting his words sink in.

I swallow a lump in my throat, and my pulse quickens. Trying to ignore the feelings that are stirring, I pull Joel toward me and hold him tight. "Thank you, Joel. For everything tonight." I stand to my feet and iron out my skirt with my hands.

"Don't even think about trying to head home."

"I'm not; I was going to see Dylan."

"Good to hear." He smiles, and I shove his shoulder before walking away.

I quietly open the door to Dylan's room. The light from the hall shows me he's asleep, or pretending to be, with his back to the door. When I step inside, the door closes behind me with a soft click, plunging the room into darkness. I pause for a second beside the bed and think about my next move. Deciding I don't care about the consequences, I pull back the covers and slip in behind Dylan, wrapping my arms around him. "I'm sorry, Dyl," I whisper and give him a gentle kiss on the shoulder, just like the kiss he placed on my head the last time we were here together.

Dylan doesn't stir for a moment, so I make myself comfortable to sleep. I've barely closed my eyes when he rolls over and pulls me into his arms, squeezing me tight. "God, Summer, you have nothing to be sorry about. *I'm* sorry. I was so scared. If something had happened…" He stops suddenly, but he's said enough for me to hear the emotion in his voice. My chest tightens at the thought of someone caring about me like he does.

"I'm here, Dylan. I'm here," I say, gripping his shoulders, trying to pull him closer, like it's possible. Dylan does the opposite and moves away from me slightly, taking my face in his hands. My eyes have adjusted to the darkness, so I can make out his face. He's staring down at me. His eyes are full of an emotion I've never seen before. No one has ever looked at me the way he's looking at me now. My heart races as my own emotions bubble. *I can't handle these feelings.*

Dylan takes a breath and speaks. "Summer, I—"

Nope. Not ready for whatever you're about to say. I don't let him finish; instead I grab his face in my hands, exactly like he has mine, and press my lips to his.

The kiss starts off gentle, tentative, with neither of us knowing where this is going. Sliding my hand around to the back of Dylan's neck, I pull on the short hairs, deepening our kiss. He reacts instantly, groaning before dropping a hand to my waist and squeezing me tightly. When he pulls me closer, I wrap one leg around his body and curl into him, bringing our bodies flush. I moan at the feeling, and Dylan uses that to his advantage, his tongue brushing with mine. He tastes like a mixture of berry sports drink and peppermint, flavors that wouldn't normally go together, but taste delicious on his tongue.

My grip on his hair tightens as the need for him increases. I wait patiently for him to make a move, but when he continues to keep his hands in the safe zone, I let mine roam instead. I run my hand down the grooves of his abs and feel him tense under my touch. He's shirtless, and the feel of his skin under my fingertips sends my pulse into overdrive as I picture his body dripping in water and my tongue licking a free-falling drop. The memory of the only time I've ever seen his ripped chest is clear in my mind. *What I wouldn't give for the lights to be on, so I can properly marvel in his beauty.* Removing my leg from around his hip, I push him onto his back and secure my knee right over his groin, continuing my exploration. Gliding my hand lower, I'm met with a dip that I know is the ridiculously hot V that's been haunting my dreams, pointing me toward my destination.

Dylan grows harder beneath my leg and takes in a sharp breath, grabbing my hand before I reach the waistband of his briefs. "Summer..." he warns, but I ignore him and pull my hand from his grasp, returning to my previous position. I keep my hand still, for now, but bite Dylan's lip, sucking it into my mouth to distract him. After another minute of making out, I slide my hand into his briefs and wrap my fingers around his length.

"Fuck!" Dylan groans and bucks into my hand. I once again hold still, giving him a chance to stop this. If he removes my hand a second time, I'm not going to force it. I'll play nice. But he doesn't do that. No, instead he pulls at my hair, to angle my head the way he wants me, and then punishes me with a bruising kiss. And it's the best punishment I've ever had. Taking this as permission to proceed, I squeeze him tight and pump my hand causing Dylan's hips to buck again, and a string of curse words leaves his mouth.

I bite back a laugh, loving the feeling of having him under my control until... "That's enough!" he roars and rips my hand away.

Before I even have time to ask what's wrong, he flips me onto my back and bites my nipple through my top and bra. "Oh God," I moan. Now it's my turn to curse. Dylan focuses on my breasts for a minute, massaging one while he bites the other, working me into a frenzy.

I'm writhing beneath him, desperate for something to relieve the pressure building inside me. As if hearing my prayers, Dylan rises to his knees and moves down the bed until he's positioned between my legs. Taking his time, he pushes my skirt slowly up my thighs, placing delicate kisses along the same path. The feel of the soft material and his lips against my already sensitive skin causes a shiver to run through me. He must notice because he releases a breath that I feel between my legs. *He's so close.* As my skirt moves higher, I stiffen slightly and move my hands into position, ready to stop his pursuit. He won't be seeing me naked tonight. Not a chance. *No one does.* Thankfully, he stops at my waist and I inwardly sigh.

I forget my small freak-out as soon as the tips of Dylan's fingers move across my hips to the apex of my thighs. Both of us take in a sharp breath when his fingers reach my core. He takes his time moving his finger in and out, while continuing to kiss my thighs and stomach. It feels amazing, but I can't take it anymore. The teasing I can handle, but the intimacy is too much. Gripping under his arms, I pull him up my body. I'm expecting a fight, but he complies, without even questioning my motives.

I need to get myself out of my head, and I need to do it now.

Chapter Twenty-Seven

Dylan

God, I could have stayed between her legs for hours. I wanted to, but I'm not going to argue if it's not what Summer wants. And I know exactly what she wants. Reaching into my drawer I pull out the foil packet, wasting no time in sheathing myself, ready to go. I wanted to worship Summer's entire body. Show her exactly how I feel about her, but now's not the time.

Ripping her underwear down her legs, I throw them across the room, before hitching one of her legs up over my elbow. A soft curse leaves her lips and I hold back a smile. *Yes, Summer. I can take control.* Spreading her wide, I line myself up with her core and sink inside.

"Fuuck," I curse, at the same time Summer moans my name, and I almost lose it. I've been dreaming of this moment, and God, it feels good. I lock my eyes on Summer's and rock back before pushing in again, deeper this time. Summer bites her lip and her head flops back into the pillow. It's a sight that will be ingrained in my memory for years to come.

I take a moment to control myself, so this isn't over in a few seconds, and wait for Summer to react. Her head rises from the pillow, her brow slightly furrowed. When she opens her eyes, I see her feelings written there, clear as day. *Don't worry, Sum, I got you.* I give her a small smirk, tighten my hold on her leg, and then pull out, before pounding into her, hard and fast, over and over.

"Oh, God. Yes!" she yells, and it's music to my ears. She's not ready for slow, but she will be, one day, and fuck, it will be amazing. But this, right now, is mind-blowingly good.

Sweat pools on my neck as I keep up the pace and try to hold off my finish. She feels too good; I'm not going to last much longer. When I feel Summer tighten around me, I release a breath of relief and slide my hand between us, to offer her a little more. Her breathing picks up, and she meets my intensity, desperate to fall over the edge. "Yes. God, yes, that's it," she rasps, and the sound alone almost pushes me over too.

I lean forward and press my lips to hers. The movement opens her up even more and this new angle rips a groan from deep within me. Summer screams my name as she finds her release, and I thank God before following her.

Expecting her to look away, I'm shocked when her eyes lock with mine as we both come down from our high. "Fuck, you're beautiful," I tell her as my eyes run across her flushed face, messy hair, and swollen lips. I take a mental picture of her lying breathless and sated beneath me, because I never want to forget this moment, and then drop down onto the bed beside her.

I can't stop the smile from gracing my lips as soon as I'm conscious. I'm still shocked at how my night panned out. My emotions had taken a beating, and when I shut the door to my room and lay on the bed, I was sure I'd just fucked up our friendship. I never expected Summer to come into my room and slip into my bed. It felt like a dream. In fact, it still feels like a dream, and I'm almost positive that when I open my eyes Summer won't be next to me, providing further proof that it's all in my head.

Choosing to live in the fantasy for a bit longer, I keep my eyes shut and remain still. To an outside observer I look peaceful, or asleep, but the truth is, my mind is whirring, busy replaying last night in vivid detail. The feel of her body merging with mine. The smell of her hair as I buried my face in her neck. The taste of her. The sound of her moans, my name on her breath, and the way it felt to finally be inside her. It was truly phenomenal.

Last night was anything but a one-night stand; I could see my feelings reflected back in Summer's eyes as we moved together as one.

The passion, the intensity, the euphoric feelings, could not have been meaningless, and yet... When I finally open my eyes, sure enough, I'm alone. *Damn.*

Throwing on a pair of sweatpants, I head into the kitchen, suddenly starving. I'm met by a very awake-looking Joel with a somber look on his face. *What happened to cause that?*

"How's Summer doing this morning?" he asks, his tone full of concern, answering my question. A feeling of guilt rises up my chest like bile. *What the fuck is wrong with me?* Of course Summer skipped out on me this morning. I'd taken advantage of her when she wasn't of sound mind. She'd almost been attacked and instead of being there for her, I fought with her and then slept with her when she came to make up.

"Fuck!" I yell, slamming my fist down onto the bench.

"Hey, it's all right, man. She's safe," Joel says, assuming I'm angry at what happened to Summer. If only that was the truth.

"I fucked up, Joel."

"Yeah you did, but she went to your room; she forgave you. After I—"

"No, I fucked up *after* that." I cut him off. "I slept with her. She was hurting and vulnerable, and I took advantage. I didn't even stop to think about her attack after she kissed me."

"There is nothing vulnerable about Summer. And she was definitely of sound mind when she left to see you. Plus, you said it, *she* kissed *you* first. Go talk to her. I'm sure you're beating yourself up for nothing."

Joel, a.k.a. "Mr. I always have something to say," try and answer this one...

"She left," I say, a smug look on my face when I'm met with silence. *Ha! Stumped you.* That is until Joel bursts into laughter.

"What the fuck is funny?" I spit angrily.

"So, that's why you look so sad?"

"No, I'm worried about Summer. She must think I'm an asshole after last night. I mean, she left." I blow out a breath and lean against the bench, looking out the window instead of at Joel.

"You look so defeated right now. Was this your first one-night stand?" he asks, even though he knows the answer. "And, of course she left.

That's what she does. Did you think you were going to change her after one romp?"

Ouch, that hurts, probably because it's true. "You can be such a dick when you're honest."

"But you love me." He smiles, because he knows he hit the nail on the head.

"Alright, enough about Summer and my problems. What are we doing today? I need a distraction."

"Ahh…" Joel cringes and then smiles apologetically as he sees recognition on my face.

"Shit!"

"Yep—lunch at Summer and Cory's place."

"Of course. I don't think she'll want me there. Maybe we should cancel." *God, when did I become such a pussy? I should be able to face her.*

"I hate to say this, but I think you are reading *way* too much into last night. My guess, she'll be acting like nothing even happened. Might be wise to do the same."

Ouch. "So I shouldn't even talk to her about it?"

"If it was me, I'd wait until she makes a move."

That doesn't sound like a good plan, but he's generally right. No matter her feelings, Summer will need to process what happened last night. Maybe giving her that time won't be such a bad thing.

After a quick run and a shower, Joel and I head over to the girls' place. Cory doesn't cook, ever, but said she wanted to cook for Nate, and Joel, Summer, and I invited ourselves along. Was that a little harsh of us, considering she's never cooked before? Probably, but too late.

As we approach their building, I start regretting my decision to come. I need time to process how I feel about last night, and Summer does too. I know I *want* Summer, but I want more than just sex. How can I expect her *not* to think of me as just another notch when I act like one? So much for wooing her first.

Joel waves his hand in front of my face when we reach Summer's door. "You ready?" he asks. His eyebrows are furrowed in concern, but there's also a hint of a smile on his face, like deep down, he finds my mess hilarious.

I shove him away and knock on the door. Within seconds, it flies open, and a frazzled looking Summer steps out. "Thank God. Cory is going out of her mind with worry because you're late. Wait..."

She looks from me to Joel and then behind us. We both turn to see what she's looking at, but I can't see anything.

"Where's Nate?" she asks in a panic.

"What?" I ask. "Isn't he inside?"

"Uh, no. Do you think I'd be out here, asking you, if he was? Shit! Can you call him?"

"Sure." I pull out my phone and dial. It's strange that he's not here, but I'm sure there's a perfectly good explanation. I mean, I hope there is. I do *not* want to be the one to have to break any news to anyone. I'll kill him if he's done something stupid to hurt Cory. But that can't be the case. On the plus side, this has caused quite the distraction from a potentially awkward encounter with Summer. Remind me to thank Nate when he gets here.

He doesn't answer on the first try, so I call again. Smiling at Summer, I pretend I'm not at all concerned, while out of the corner of my eye, I see Joel discreetly reach for his phone and start texting, obviously getting nervous like I am. When my third call goes unanswered, I flinch. Keeping my phone to my ear, I pretend it hasn't hit voicemail, to buy myself a few seconds to think of something to say. I need to give Nate the benefit of the doubt and try to keep him in their good graces, at least until I figure out what's happened. "He didn't answer but..." I pretend I'm reading a text. "I've just got a text that says—"

"I'm here. Shit! I'm here," Nate yells, running up the stairs.

"Thank God!" I mumble repeating Summer's earlier sentiment. I was not looking forward to the repercussions of lying for him.

"Family emergency," is all he says as he pushes past the three of us and runs through the door.

"We should probably give them a minute," Summer says with a smile. "He's about to get his balls busted."

Joel and I laugh and cringe at the same time. *God, what time was he supposed to be here?*

"So, Joely boy, you're still going to cash in on this celebratory lunch even though you don't play?"

"Sure am; just like you." He laughs, but then his expression becomes somber, for the second time today, and I know he's thinking about last night. "Are you—"

"It's a new day, Joel. I'm good," Summer answers, cutting him off at the pass, but then her voice softens, and she adds, "Thank you both. For caring so much."

I want to pull her into my arms and show her just how much I care, but I resist. Instead I do the one thing I know Summer wants; I change the subject. "Glad you're okay. Can we eat yet? I'm dying here," I joke, and her thankful smile beams at me, making me happy I did the *right* thing over what I really wanted to do.

Summer presses her ear to the door. "I can't hear any yelling. I think it's safe to go in." She pushes the door open, and we all freeze at the sight before us.

Cory and Nate are hugging, but it looks like he's comforting her, rather than a lovers' embrace. There's a food bowl on the floor, its contents spread throughout the kitchen, and a pitcher of water has tipped over on the counter, the liquid running over the edge like a waterfall. If I wasn't ninety percent sure something was wrong, the scene would be comical.

When Summer gasps, Nate and Cory jump apart. It's impossible to miss the tears in her eyes. "Sorry, I'm a mess," she says, wiping the tears away.

"Cory, what's wrong?" Summer asks, her eyes full of concern.

Cory laughs, but I'm not buying it. "I'm crying because I dropped the salad I'd just made. Nate was trying to calm me down."

Yeah, definitely not buying that. And by the look on Summer's face, neither is she. Even Joel's expression screams skepticism. Instead of voicing our concern, we act like we believe every word and move right on, but I can tell just by looking at her that Summer is definitely going to seek answers later.

After an eventful start to the lunch, the rest of the afternoon is quite tame and normal. So normal, that I'm both relieved and annoyed at the same time. On one hand, Joel was right. Summer is acting like nothing happened. She's still treating me the same as she did before we slept together. Meaning, she's treating me as a friend who she flirts with. *That's gotta be good, right?*

On the other hand, Joel was right, and Summer is acting like nothing happened. Like it meant nothing; it's already forgotten, and she's moved on. And that sucks. I mean, I'm not exactly looking for opportunities to bring it up, but I have been a little more handsy, just to gauge her reaction. A casual touch of her leg with mine, an arm around her when sharing a story. Innocent stuff. While she hasn't reacted negatively toward any of it, she hasn't reacted positively either. She's basically ignoring it.

"Oh Sum, I forgot to ask. Are you *trying* to replace me as the number one daughter?" Cory asks in a playful tone.

"Always," Summer replies, "But what did I specifically do? I'd like to know so I can repeat it."

"I don't think you'll be repeating it anytime soon. That record must have cost a fortune." *Shit!*

Summer's eyes slam shut, and her cheeks pinken. "It wasn't actually—"

"You won the bid? That's great. You mentioned he'd love it," I say, stopping her from admitting my involvement. That's not why I did it. I was going to donate that amount to the cause anyway. *Sort* of. I figured I may as well get something for it.

Summer eyes me suspiciously, so I wink and turn away. From the corner of my eye, I see a beautiful smile light up her face before she continues her conversation. And that's the only reason I did what I did. I'll do just about anything to see that smile.

When Joel and I say our goodbyes, after a surprisingly delicious meal, I want to punch something. I'm frustrated as hell with Summer's reaction to me today. We both know there's something between us, so pretending nothing happened is killing me.

Joel heads down the stairs, and I move to do the same, when a delicate hand grips my wrist, reminding me of the first time we met. When I turn back to Summer, her lips quickly and gently press into mine. "I'll see you on Tuesday. For the film festival," she says, before darting back inside without looking back. I don't move. I'm stuck in a trance, staring at the door that Summer just walked through. *What just happened?*

"Maybe there's hope for you yet," Joel says, laughing as he runs down the stairs.

I grip the back of my neck and smile at the door, as though she's still standing in front of it. *Maybe there is.*

Chapter Twenty-Eight

Summer

Dylan arrives at three on the dot to pick me up for our *outing*. I'm calling it an outing because I'm not entirely sure how to describe it, and that seems like a safe option. Bouncing down the steps of my building, I burst through the front door with a big smile and almost screech to a halt at the image in front of me. In a ridiculously tight long-sleeved black tee, sunglasses, and a cap, Dylan looks like he's ready for a double page photo shoot in a women's magazine. In other words, way hotter than I'd like him to look for our d—outing. *Oops. Almost said the wrong thing.*

With a smirk that tells me he knows exactly what I'm thinking, he's leaning against his mammoth truck, feet crossed over at the ankle, completely relaxed. There's definitely room for a penis size joke here, based on the aforementioned truck, but since I've now seen said penis, I can no longer joke about the size. Because it's definitely *not* small.

My mind offers me a thumbnail preview of our night together, and I realize too late that I'm biting my lip, lost in thought. When I meet Dylan's eyes, he huffs out a laugh and runs a hand down his face, most likely to hide the tortured expression that resides there. I take a deep breath and bridge the space between us. "Hi," I say and smile. He laughs again and offers a hi in return before opening the passenger door for me and helping me inside. When he settles beside me and shuts his door, I can feel the tension in the air. He's as nervous as I am but trying to hide it. If only I knew if his nervous energy was for the same reason as mine.

I shouldn't have slept with Dylan. It had the potential to ruin everything between us, and yet, I can't bring myself to regret it. I could try to tell myself it was meaningless, but there was an undeniable connection. Every kiss, every touch, every word spoken shot off a spark deep within me. It was more than I'd felt before, *and* the very reason I had to get the hell out of there. The second Dylan's breathing evened out, I ran. *Literally. Ran.* And in record time, I was tucked up in my own bed, ready for sleep. Sleep that didn't come.

I know it's wrong to pretend nothing happened. I'm completely aware of how unfair and selfish it is. I'm just not ready to talk about it. I'm not even ready to *think* about it. This entire mess is my fault, but rather than calling me out on my bullshit, Dylan seems to understand. He's giving me the space I need, and God, I love him for it. *Figuratively speaking.* So, while Dylan's plans for today sound very dateish, I'm hoping he's happy that we're here as friends.

The hour drive to San Francisco settled most of my nerves and allowed me to relax. Dylan hit play on a nineties rock playlist the second we got in the car and sang along for most of our trip. I tried to be subtle, but like a moth to a flame, I couldn't help but stare at him in awe as his incredible voice penetrated my soul, distracting me from the outside world passing us by.

"We're here," Dylan announces, as we pull into an overpriced parking lot near the center of town.

Breaking myself from my daydream, I turn to Dylan and match his beaming smile with my own. "Where to first, leader?" I ask, with a nod of my head, pretending to bow down to his greatness.

"That's for me to know, and you to find out." He taps my nose with his finger, something he's quite fond of doing, before reaching for the door handle. "Come on, milady. Your chariot awaits." He opens his door and jumps from the car.

"Shouldn't that line have come *before* we got in the car to drive here?" I yell from inside the car.

"Semantics," he says with a shrug, slamming the door and heading to the curb. I laugh before following him out.

The evening is flying by and going much smoother than I expected. The film festival was a blast, giving us plenty to talk about, and I even managed to convince Dylan to head over to Pier 39, despite not being part of his plans. There are so many beautiful spots in this city, but walking the pier is one of the few happy childhood memories I have. The breeze is cold, so I fasten my coat before linking my arm through Dylan's and pulling him close. "Remember walking along this very spot, during Christmas, with the fairy lights covering the buildings, and the carolers on every corner? It was so magical; it was like a dream," I say, wistfully.

Dylan laughs without looking my way. "Was that the time you won that ball toss competition they had near the carousel?"

"It sure was." I smile. "I'll never forget the look of defeat on your face."

"And *I'll* never forget you walking backwards while gloating, and falling flat on your ass. It was a sight to be seen." He laughs while patting my arm sympathetically.

I elbow him in the stomach and pull away. Walking ahead of him, my hands run along the brick of the building beside me. *Would my life have turned out differently, if I had known Dylan as a child?*

As if reading my mind, Dylan muses in a tone laced with melancholy. "If only we had some real childhood memories together."

Plastering on my trademark smile, even though he can't see my face, I think about his words. *Oh Dylan, we do. They're just not of the happy variety.* I shake out my thoughts and bring myself back to the present, continuing on with our game.

"My favorite memory from this pier is standing by the ocean, listening to the crashing waves with the wind in my hair, while watching the sunset...and eating the biggest bag of taffy you've ever seen," I joke and laugh at myself.

Dylan doesn't answer right away, and when I look back at him, he's leaning against a signpost, hands in his pockets, eyes locked on me. There's a soft smile playing on his lips and a look of pure contentment on his face.

"This right here, right now. *This* is my favorite memory. Or at least, it will be, the second after I drop you home," he says, briefly looking around before returning his eyes to mine.

I feel the blush spread across my skin as butterflies do acrobatics in my stomach. *Ugh, why does he have to be so freaking amazing all the time? Not to mention gorgeous. The way his eyes light up when he smiles, and the sexy way he...shit! I'm staring.*

With a small smile and shoulder shrug, I turn my back on him once again. I don't make it far before his arm wraps around my shoulders, and he pulls me close, tucking me into his side. With the warmth of his embrace, the feel of his body pressed to mine, and the smell of his familiar rich woodsy cologne, I suddenly feel protected like I haven't in a long time. Like no matter what happens, Dylan will be there for me. And that feeling is as wonderful as it is terrifying.

When we reach the end of the pier, I stare out into the darkness and listen to the waves. The breeze of the ocean hits me in the face, and I shiver involuntarily. Without missing a beat, Dylan pulls me close and presses a kiss to my hair before wrapping his other arm tightly around me. Comfortable in the moment, and perhaps a little caught up in unfamiliar feelings, I allow myself to burrow into his chest. As my mind stills I can't help but admit that Dylan was right...

This moment is going to be hard to forget.

An hour later, we find ourselves in our current location, Dumpling Way, for dinner. The place looks like a dive, considering its location, but the food... I've never had anything like it. The place is crowded, the tables are old wrought iron and not particularly comfortable, and the noise level is high due to the concrete walls, but the food definitely makes up for it.

They don't do table service, so I'm currently standing in line at the counter to order our dessert, even though we've already polished off an unmentionable number of dumplings between us. Dylan insists we try the dessert buns, and who am I to say no?

When I get back to the table, Dylan's staring out the window in a daze. "What's got that nostalgic look on your face?" I ask, clicking my fingers in front of his face to get his attention.

His eyes flash to mine, and he stares at me for a moment, as if trying to process that I'm standing in front of him. "Football?"

"Is that a question?" I laugh.

"No?"

I frown as he shakes his head and offers a small smile before rolling his eyes. "Sorry, my mind was elsewhere, but I was thinking about football—about a chat I had with the coach."

"About not wanting to go pro?" I ask, and I'm met with a look of pure shock. "Sorry. Am I way off base?"

Dylan's brows furrow, and his eyes look up to the left, as though he's trying to recall information. "No, I'm sorry," he says and then finally looks my way again. "Your question just caught me off guard. I didn't think I'd told you that. Sorry, I don't remember it."

Oh shit! "Oh. Uh, no, you didn't. You haven't. Shit. Joel told me," I say, as I nervously bite my lip. *Was it meant to be a secret?*

Dylan's expression softens, and he smiles. "No big deal. What exactly did he say?" He sounds nervous, and I'd bet my last penny it's because it's not something he likes to share.

I scrunch up my nose and answer, not wanting to lie since I've already dug a hole. "Just that you don't want to go pro because you want to be around for your future family." He cringes, all but confirming my suspicion. "Was he not supposed to tell me that?"

"It's not that I didn't want *you* to know. I just don't talk about it in general."

That's somewhat of a relief, but I don't understand why he'd keep it a secret. "Why?" I ask, trying to keep my voice void of emotion so he doesn't think I'm judging him for his decision.

"Why do I feel that way, or why don't I talk about it?"

"Both," I say, almost apologetically. I'm asking him to open up, even though I'd never do the same.

He sighs and runs his hand through his hair before gripping his neck. I see it the second he decides to confide in me. His gaze softens, and the smallest hint of relief flashes across his face. He's wanted to get this off his chest for a while. He closes his eyes tightly as if pained by a memory and then shakes his thoughts away. "Dad was away a lot during my childhood and missed some pretty big moments. I don't just mean

209

dance recitals, or sporting events. I mean Lucy fell off a horse and broke her arm, and he wasn't there when she was rushed to the hospital. He wasn't around when we got the news that my grandmother, his mother, had passed away. He missed anniversaries and birthdays. Sure, he was only ever gone a day or so at a time but that's not the point. He wasn't even there the day I was born."

He pauses to let that sink in. I'm hooked on his every word, flashes of a little lost Dylan playing through my mind.

"He was a wonderful dad. When he was present, *he was present*. He gave one hundred percent. But he still missed things. Important things. And when he finally retired, he promised us the world, only to die less than a year later. I don't want that for my family."

I flinch involuntarily at his words, but he doesn't notice. He's too lost in thought. I'm about to speak, attempt to offer him some sort of comfort, when he continues.

"When Joel called me the other night, to tell me about what happened to you,"—he pauses and runs a hand down his face—"Summer, it nearly killed me. All my fears... You were hurting, and I wasn't..." His voice wavers with emotion as he trails off.

My chest tightens, and my pulse races. I bite my cheek to stave off any other emotional reaction. This conversation is exactly what I was avoiding while lying in his bed. I'm not good with feelings, and mine are out of control.

"Anyway." Dylan clears his throat and continues, "I never apologized for how I acted that night. I'm sorry. I was just caught off guard."

"Apology accepted," I say and then quickly repeat the second part of my question to change the subject.

He huffs out a breath and then leans back in his chair, arms crossed over his chest. It's a defensive stance I've seen him use before. "It's easier not to talk about it because people tend to try and convince me to change my mind. Joel included. They don't get it."

"I do," I say and watch as his shoulders deflate in relief. I do get it; I'm not lying about that, but... "Doesn't mean I'm not going to try and convince you to change your mind. You have talent." Too much talent to throw it all away, especially when he doesn't even have the family he's so worried about protecting.

When my words register, Dylan's walls come back up. "That's not the point," he says bitterly, like he's said it a million times before, and he probably has. I should just leave it alone. God, if he tried to offer his opinion on my life, I wouldn't be happy about it. All the reasoning makes sense. And if he goes pro, he might find himself in some of the very situations he's concerned about. It's unavoidable. But I have a gut feeling that I need to say these words. I don't know why, but I do.

"I know. I understand what you are saying," I begin, easing my way into it. "From someone who's completely lost her family, I get why you'd want to spend all your time with yours." I pause, having just spoken about my family, out loud, for the first time. I hate the look of pity that crosses Dylan's face. I know he doesn't mean it. He wasn't expecting my honesty. But it still hurts to think people assume my life is less because my family isn't in it. I'm coping. I'm making do.

"Having said that," I continue, and bring the focus back to Dylan. "I don't think you should rule it out just yet. You don't know who you'll end up with. Maybe she'll be a football reporter who travels with you and brings the kids along. I mean, it's not like baseball or hockey where the travel schedule is insane, and if it was me, I'd want you..." *Shit! Where did that come from?* "Never mind, I don't know. Point is...don't rule it out."

Dylan's ocean-blue eyes penetrate mine as he stares me down for a second. He's looking for something, but what, I can't say. He finally releases a breath and runs a hand through his hair, huffing out a small laugh. "I'll think about it, okay?"

I release my own breath and smile. "That's all I ask."

We sit in silence, enjoying our dessert, until a puzzled expression crosses Dylan's face. He holds his hand up in a half wave and then shakes his head as a tight smile graces his face. I follow his gaze and spot a stunning woman beaming at him like he's the best person in the world. I'm surprised when a slight sting of jealousy hits me, even though it's not the first time I've felt this uncomfortable feeling. *Shit!* I need to get things under control.

When the girl reaches our table, her eyes find mine, and instead of looking smug, or annoyed, or jealous, her features brighten in surprise and maybe even a bit of excitement. *I'm so confused.*

"Is this Summer?" she asks, looking toward Dylan. He gives her a pissy look and then recovers.

"Yep...thanks," he huffs and shakes his head with an expression I can't decipher.

The woman laughs and sits down at our table, forcing Dylan to move his chair right next to mine. Without permission, that little niggle of jealousy rises again as she smiles his way. "God, Dylan was right. You really are gorgeous. I'm Lucy."

Lucy? I move my gaze between them, and it hits me. *How did I miss the resemblance?* This is Lucy. Dylan's sister. And now the hint of embarrassment makes sense. Dylan's "thanks" was sarcastic. He didn't want me to know he'd talked about me. *Why does that make me feel good?*

Lucy reaches over and grabs my hand, and I force myself to ignore the urge to pull away since I know she's trying to be nice. "I'm so happy to meet you."

"What are you doing here?" Dylan says through slightly clenched teeth.

"Collecting takeout. I *did* introduce you to this place. Anyway, I saw you here and..." She shrugs.

"So you thought you'd stop by and interrupt? Well, by all means, join us," Dylan says, his voice laced with teasing sarcasm.

Lucy just grins before looking at me. "Sorry, is that okay?"

"Of course," I reply, offering a warm smile that I hope she buys. It's a little awkward, but I must admit, it's fun to see Dylan a little off balance.

Spending time with Lucy and Dylan is not at all what I would have expected. They come across as friends more than siblings, and have a comfortable relationship that has my chest filling with jealousy once more. I had that. Their teasing banter reminds me so much of what mine and Thomas's was like that it hurts a little to witness. But, it's been nice getting to know Lucy and hearing *real* stories about Dylan's childhood, opposed to the ones we've been making up. God, can she talk. It's only been twenty minutes, and I have so much new information to process.

"I hear you're a big NSYNC fan as well," Lucy says, changing the subject. I'm a little uncomfortable with how much she knows about me, but hide my thoughts. "I'm so glad Dylan finally has someone around who understands good music; he could learn a thing or two," she continues, pointing to Dylan with a laugh. "Has he told you what he used to listen to in middle school? Aqua anyone?"

Dylan puts his arm around my shoulder and pulls me in tight. "Come on, you both know I have great taste in music. 'Barbie Girl' was a hit, and that singer was hot. This ganging up on me better be a one-off." It *definitely won't be.*

Lucy and I manage to talk about embarrassing Dylan stories for the next ten minutes while we wait for her order. Dylan grumbles beside me, alternating between squeezing my leg or poking my ribs whenever I can't stop laughing. He may appear annoyed, but he's not fooling anyone. I can see the small smile he's trying to hide.

My nerves seem so unwarranted now, and I actually feel comfortable in Lucy's presence. At least, until I excuse myself to use the restroom and hear Lucy tell Dylan to listen out for her food. She's coming with me. Girl code for "let's have a private chat." I run through the *talk* possibilities as we walk slowly toward the back of the café. Does she want to warn me to stay away from Dylan? She and Dylan are obviously close, and she kinda gives off a protective vibe, so that could be the case. Not knowing how much she knows about us leaves me at a disadvantage. Maybe she'll tell me I'm not good enough for him. It would definitely make sense.

When we enter the ladies' room, Lucy ducks into a stall. *Or maybe she actually just needed to pee. Here's hoping.* We dry our hands and are heading for the door when she says, "So…" *Dammit…almost in the clear. Here it comes.* "I don't mean to be so forward, but I think you need to drop the friends act you and Dylan have going on. Especially after what happened the other night." *Ugh…I inwardly groan. Turns out, she knows a lot.*

"I…I'm sorry." I stumble over my own words. "That's not. It was only once. I know he deserves someone better. I—"

"Wait. What?" she asks as her smile disappears.

God, this is awkward. "Um, the friend thing is not an act. The other won't happen again. He deserves…"

"I know what you said, but why? Summer, I meant that you should be *together*, not *friends*. I think it's obvious to everyone, *but you*, that you're perfect for each other."

"What?"

"Dylan is adamant in saying you're just friends, but it's clear that you two have something, and I've only been watching you for thirty minutes. You may not realize this, but he's different around you—more comfortable, more at home."

I clench my fists subtly, digging my nails into my palms as I try to figure out how to reply. *Was that really how we came off?*

As if sensing my unease, Lucy continues. "I'm sorry, it's just Dylan doesn't realize it, but he's always had a wall up when it comes to women. The wall is nonexistent with you. I can tell from the way he talks about you, looks at you, acts around you. I just want him to be happy."

I feel the heat rising from my chest to my face and give her a quick nod and what I hope is a smile.

She gives me a sympathetic smile in return as we make our way back to Dylan. He stands as we approach, holding Lucy's food order, and thankfully, he and Lucy walk ahead of me toward the exit, allowing me to take a few deep breaths to shake off my rising panic.

Chapter Twenty-Nine

Summer

There's silence on the drive home, and I'm ninety percent sure it's not just me who doesn't know what to say. It's obvious that Dylan knows something is up, and I have to wonder if he's nervous to ask. We're pulling up to a red light when I blurt, "You know you're free to date, right?" My chest tightens as the words leave my mouth, but I ignore it.

Dylan taps the brake accidentally, propelling us forward in our seats, and half laughs, looking at me like I'm being ridiculous. I rub my chest where the seat belt locked and meet his stare. Whatever he sees must convince him I'm serious because his brows furrow before he nods and starts driving again. "I do now."

I gulp as the pain in my chest intensifies. *Wow, the seat belt really did a number on me. Yep, that's what I'm telling myself.* When I hear the ding of a text, I almost drop the phone for how quickly I retrieve it from my bag.

"It's Cory. They're all at Reilly's. Want to go?" It's just hit eleven, still plenty of time to dance my troubles away, and God knows I need the distraction.

"Yeah, Joel mentioned it. That works for me." *Huh? When did Joel mention it? Dylan hasn't been on his phone for hours.* I shrug to myself and stare out the window, breathing in the thick awkward air I created, as we head toward our new destination.

We've been here for an hour, and I'm already significantly buzzed. The type of alcohol high that makes everything okay. This is my favorite place to be, but it's a sweet spot—hard to find and even harder to keep. A bead of sweat runs down my back from the amount of time I've spent squashed between bodies on the dance floor. Cory, who is equally buzzed, has been faithfully by my side. The only difference between the two of us is that she's been solo or with Nate, whereas I've had a revolving door of dance partners. My current partner, let's call him Hottie, is another perfect stranger. His dirty-blond hair looks like it was styled into that bedhead look, and his body feels toned beneath my fingers—not to mention he's very easy on the eyes in his ripped jeans and a tight tee.

For all intents and purposes, my mind should be on him. But I can't keep my eyes from seeking Dylan out. Until this very moment, whenever I've looked his way, I've found him looking back at me. But now his attention is elsewhere, or specifically on a cute little brunette with perky tits and a tight butt. She laughs hysterically at something he says and slaps him in the chest, shamelessly flirting. He smiles down at her, and I cringe before looking away. *I'm not jealous at all.*

I mean, I *am* the one who told him to find someone else. Yet, right now, I want to go over there and rip the beautiful girl away from him. Must be the sweet spot I was talking about. The one that makes me throw all reason out the window.

Closing my eyes, I turn around and press my back into Hottie's chest so that I'm no longer facing Dylan's direction. His hands instantly grip my waist, pulling me closer, as I lift mine up and wrap them around his neck. When I finally open my eyes, I'm faced with a smirking Joel.

"Mind if I cut in?" he asks, loud enough to hear over the music. My eyes move between Joel and Hottie, thinking it through. I've already made up my mind that I'm not going home with this guy, but he sure is fun to dance with...and look at. Seeing my indecisiveness, Joel leans in closer so that only I can hear his next words. "We both know he's not the guy you want."

Ugh, he's right, but I hate that he knows that. "Actually Joel, I'm good here," I say, hoping to put an end to his train of thought. I turn back around to ignore him, but Hottie has other ideas.

"It's okay, babe, I'm going to head to the bar. One dance and I'll be back. You're mine tonight." *Well, that's a turnoff.* I hate it when guys make assumptions like that. Just because we're dancing doesn't mean you get an automatic invite into my pants.

Left with no option, I turn back to Joel. "Fine, Joel, let's dance."

He spins me around so I'm forced to face Dylan again, and his lips pull into a grin. "So you're going home with that guy, then?"

God, no. "Yep," I say as my eyes move to Dylan without permission.

"And there's no one else you're interested in?"

"Nope." I pop the p and watch as the girl leans in to whisper something in Dylan's ear, her hand on his arm, her lips practically touching him. Joel says something else, but I don't hear what it is. "Huh?" I ask, shifting my eyes away.

"That's what I thought," he says and sniggers, leaving me thoroughly confused. My brows furrow as I try to guess what he said. I quickly smile again when I notice Hottie making his way over, until I catch movement out of the corner of my eye. I turn just in time to see Dylan head out the back door, the brunette following close behind him. *Shit.*

"I need air," I yell to Joel and Hottie when he settles beside me.

"I'll bet you do," Joel says as I walk away from them both, moving as quickly as I can without drawing attention.

Slamming the door open, I pause to get my bearings. *What the hell am I doing? Go back inside.*

I turn to do just that when Dylan speaks. "Summer? Are you okay?"

Shit! I squint in the darkness and follow the sound of his voice. He's standing beside a car I don't recognize. The girl he left with is leaning against the door with her finger in her mouth, obviously trying to draw attention to her lips. I stare without saying a word. *Am I okay?*

Dylan takes a step toward me, concern on his face. "Summer?"

"I'm fine," I say, snapping out of it. "Don't mind me." I reach for the door. *I need to get out of here. This is insane. I'm being insane. I just told him to see other people, and now, I'm acting like a jealous girlfriend. Cut the crap, Summer. Go inside.*

"Wait!" Dylan calls, and I stop with the door half-open.

"She said she's fine," the girl argues, prompting me to turn around. "Come on, like I said, you should come home with me," she continues, running her finger down his chest. *That little...*

Something inside me snaps, and before I can control it, I slam the door shut and move toward Dylan. His eyes widen in surprise, but there's a hint of something else—heat. It fuels me to move faster, and before I know it, I'm grabbing his face in my hands and slamming my lips to his.

"What the hell?" I hear beside me, but I ignore her. Dylan, however, has better manners. He pulls away, causing my chest to tighten. *What was I thinking?*

"Sorry, but—"

"Asshole," she yells and then jumps in her car. My gaze snaps back to Dylan's as her door bangs shut and she drives away.

"But?" I ask.

He links his fingers through mine and walks us back toward the building. *Ugh, is he taking us inside? Guess that was an epic fail.* But before we reach the door, Dylan spins me around, pressing my back into the brick. "But this," he says before his mouth crashes to mine in a powerful and all-consuming kiss.

I melt into him, as he grips my hip with one hand while the other slides along my neck to the back of my hair. I lift my leg to wrap around him, and he groans at our connection. And right there, in the parking lot of a bar, we make out like horny teenagers.

I'm not sure how much time has passed, but it's definitely been a little while. When the backdoor slams open again, we jump apart like we've been busted doing something wrong.

"Oh, good, you're already out here," Joel states, clearly not surprised. "It's time to go, and you're my driver," he tells Dylan as he moves toward us. Nate and a very drunk Cory follow behind, and I rush to help Nate get Cory in the car, a little concerned at the state she's in. She smiles up at me in thanks, and I try not to frown down at her. I've seen drunk Cory, but this is a lot. *When did that happen? She wasn't this bad when I left. That must have been some make-out session. No wonder I'm worked up. I need a release.*

I stare at Dylan longingly, in silent question, *how's this going to work?* As if reading my mind, Joel bursts out laughing. "Relax, you two. I was kidding. I'm not going home; you have the place to yourselves tonight. Have fun." He winks and then bounces his eyebrows.

I should be embarrassed that he easily figured out what's going on, but right now, I wouldn't care if the world knew. That's future Summer's problem. Dylan remains expressionless, trying to appear unfazed by what's happening, but I know he's worried about my reaction.

"Bye, guys," I say and walk to Dylan's truck, bringing a full smile to his face. I'm sure I'm sending the wrong message by going home with him tonight, but thanks to my sweet spot, I can't bring myself to care right now.

Dylan and I walk casually from the truck to his door. There's no touching or words. We look like two innocent people heading in the same direction, if you don't see the playful grins we're both trying to hide. The second we step inside, everything changes. Dylan pushes me against a wall and devours me, kissing my lips, my neck, that little spot below the ear. Every visible inch of skin.

I hitch one leg up and wrap it around his waist, mimicking our parking lot romp as my hands grip his tee and pull him closer. When our bodies connect, I moan, and Dylan slips his tongue into my mouth. He grinds into me a few times before grabbing my legs under my ass and lifting me up into his arms like I weigh nothing at all. Without breaking our kiss, he carries me into the kitchen and sets me down on the counter.

"This isn't how I wanted to do this, but fuck, I need you," he rasps in my ear and then bites down on my earlobe. I moan again and then pull his lips back to mine. I'm sure I should be reading something into his comment, but I'm too far gone to care.

Dylan pushes my dress up my legs and then lifts me slightly to pull it higher. When my butt lifts off the counter, I pull my leggings and panties down to create a distraction, stopping Dylan from undressing me. He groans when I drop them at his feet and then spread my legs wide enough for him to step between.

Within seconds, his pants are around his ankles, and he's sheathed and pressing inside me. Our foreplay started back at the bar, so there's no time for that now. I moan at the feel of him as he moves inside me.

The sex is hot and quick, just like the last time. It's like he knows what I want, without me having to voice it. He can read me like no one has before.

A feeling of increased pleasure hits me in my core as Dylan slides me to the edge and presses in deeper. "Oh, God," I scream, not even caring if the neighbors can hear me. *Did we even shut the front door?*

Dylan leans his forehead against mine and stares down at our connection. "Fuck. Fuck! Summer, you feel so good," he rasps as he slams into me. The euphoric sound of his voice, and the knowledge that he's watching us, pushes me over the edge. I scream for God and buck against him as I experience one of the most intoxicating climaxes I've ever had.

Dylan follows straight after me with a drawn-out groan and then drops down with his head resting on my stomach. Without giving it much thought, I wrap my arms around him and hold him close.

We lie like that, unmoving, until Dylan lifts his head from my chest and smiles. He looks sated and happy and...something else that I don't yet want to touch on.

I awkwardly begin to sit up as Dylan pulls out of me, and the feeling makes me moan, involuntarily, in pleasure. He grunts like he's in physical pain, and next thing I know, I'm being tossed over his shoulder as he runs down the hall toward his room. He gives my ass a slap just before we reach the door and then squeezes me tightly. I can't stop the giggled words from erupting out of me. "What are you doing?"

"Round two," he growls, playfully biting the side of my thigh, which does all sorts of things to my insides. He throws me onto the bed and then lowers himself on top of me, sealing our lips in a passionate kiss and inserting a finger inside me. My heart races, and my skin tingles with pleasure. *I think I like this take-charge version of Dylan, a lot.*

Chapter Thirty

Dylan

B rushing the hair away from her face, I kiss Summer once more and then hover above her. I never would have guessed we'd end up back here after our non date, especially after her telling me I should see other people, but fuck, am I glad we did. She smiles up at me with flushed cheeks and messy hair, relaxed, like she could stay in this moment forever.

"God, Summer. Today was perfect. Tonight was perfect. *You're* perfect," I whisper, leaning down and pressing a kiss to her forehead before slipping onto the bed beside her. She freezes beside me, and I instantly regret my words, even though I meant them.

She sits up, bringing her knees to her chest and pulling her top, *my top*, down over them, covering the lower half of her body. After we had sex for the third time without getting naked, Summer showered and changed into one of my shirts. I can't help but get the sense that it's not just circumstantial accidents that have stopped me from seeing her body, and it's actually a big deal for Summer. Something else I wish she'd talk to me about.

That aside, to say seeing her in my shirt does something to me is an understatement. I never thought I was a possessive guy, but with Summer, I want to brand her and tell the world that she's mine.

Getting sidetracked, I'm still trying to sort through my thoughts when she blurts, "I've got to go," and starts scanning the room, almost frantically. When she can't see what she wants, presumably her clothes, she huffs in annoyance before standing up and stepping over me to leave.

We need to talk about this. About us. And we can't do that if she leaves. Before thinking through my actions, I jump up and follow her into the kitchen, grabbing ahold of her wrist. She flinches before she looks at me. *Fuck!* "I'm not letting you run again," I say bluntly—possibly a little too bluntly, but call it frustration.

"That's not something you get to decide," she says, pulling her hand out of mine. *Fair point; she's right.*

Taking a deep breath, I calm myself and try to sound a bit more caring. "What are you afraid will happen if you stay?"

She sighs and looks up to the roof. "I'm not afraid of anything, it's just not something I want to do. It is what it is—a release. For both of us. Let's not try to make it something it's not."

"*Bullshit!* Anyone with eyes can see it's more than that. It's not just a release. You want this—me." I point to my chest.

She shrugs like she's completely unfazed, but I can see the nervousness reflected in her eyes. "It's the truth," she says, but she's shaking her head like she can't even look at me.

I stare at her silently until she finally looks my way. "I'll repeat...bullshit." There's no anger in my tone, no fight. It's just a statement, delivered with no emotion, because I've got nothing left.

Summer closes her eyes, and when she opens them again, the pain is unbearable to look at. "I think we should stop," she whispers, and God, I hope I heard her incorrectly. When I don't say anything right away, she repeats herself, a little louder this time. "We should stop."

Shit, that's not what I wanted to come from this talk. My chest aches at the thought of never touching her again. I should've just let her leave. What was there to complain about really? I had a good friend, we had good sex, and she didn't want to have anything more. A lot of men would kill to be in my shoes, and yet, here I was, screwing it up.

"It's getting a bit much, and I would hate for it to ruin our friendship somehow," Summer adds, not even realizing that she's tearing me up inside. She's thrown around the friendship card many times during our relationship, and I've let it slide, but this time wasn't going to be that easy. I don't think I can go back.

Her phone rings on the table beside me, and I look to see the name Logan flashing across the screen. *Why the fuck is he calling at four in the morning?* A flashback of me lying in the tent, listening to their moans, invades my mind, uninvited, and I cringe.

"Why is it so easy with you and Logan, then? Your friendship doesn't seem to be affected."

Summer's eyes widen as my words sink in, and she realizes I know there's more to them. *Yeah, that's right. I heard it all.* We've never discussed it. In fact, the name Logan has never come up between us, despite him being one of her best friends. She looks to the ground and bites the inside of her cheek before responding just above a whisper. "It's not the same."

Is she denying it? "It's exactly the same," I snap and then wince with regret. I soften my tone slightly and continue. "You and Logan are friends with benefits, right? How is what we're doing any different?" I wince again as my own words actually hit me. *Fuck, is that all we are?*

She doesn't answer right away, instead playing with the hem of my shirt. "Come on, Summer. What's. The. Difference?" I say, getting worked up over her avoidance. *God, Dylan. Calm down.* My emotions are clearly out of control.

"He doesn't want more," she yells before I've even finished the last word of my question.

"Neither do I!" I roar as panic that I'm about to lose her flares up inside. Is it a complete lie? Of course, it is. But if that's what it takes... She recoils like I've slapped her in the face and then looks away for a second.

When she turns back to face me, she looks utterly broken. "Good to know, but it doesn't change a thing," she says, and the words feel like they're dripping with poison.

"Then what's the problem?" I run my hands through my hair to keep them from clenching; I'm so frustrated that we keep ending up back here. I watch Summer as she looks everywhere but at me. Our chemistry is off the charts. We have an amazing physical and emotional connection. I wish she'd talk to me about what's really going on. I cover my face in my hands and sigh. If she truly believes I don't want more, why is she still freaked out? She said it works with Logan because he doesn't want more, so I don't... *Wait! Does she want more? Is that it?*

My eyes flash to Summer's and she's looking back at me with a vulnerable fear. I can feel her pulling away again and know she's about to run. *God, am I right? I need to tell her how I feel.*

"Summer, I—"

"I have to go," she says again, grabbing her phone and keys from the table and running out the door. I chase after her, unable to let her leave. Not even sure how she's planning to leave. It's drizzling when I get outside, and despite being half-naked and shoeless, I don't hesitate in running after her.

"Summer, wait. Please."

She stops and turns back to face me. "What, Dylan? What do you want?"

"This," I say, closing the distance between us and grabbing her face in my hands. Her eyes bounce between mine when I stop an inch from her lips. "I want you. All of you."

I'm not sure who makes the first move, but our lips meet, and it's nothing like our previous kisses. It's slow, it's explorative, it's perfect. Every feeling I have for Summer is being poured into it. Our bodies stay still, our hands don't roam. Nothing matters in this moment except for this kiss, and when I finally pull away, we're both breathless. I touch my nose to hers and then take a step back with a feeling of hope in my chest. I'm graced with the most beautifully shy smile I think I've ever witnessed. "Stay," I say and hope to God she's feeling the same as me.

She bites her lips and looks at me apologetically. I tense, preparing for her rejection. "I should go. I've got a lot happening this week, and I need sleep."

That's not an outright rejection. "Stay and sleep. I just want you here." I take a breath and hold it, waiting for her reply; her answer now could change everything between us.

She looks to the street, then the ground, and then finally settles her gaze on me. "Okay," she whispers, biting back a small smile.

"Thank you." I link my fingers through hers as we walk back into the house. To sleep.

When I wake the next morning, I'm surprised to feel her body still curled into mine, reminding me of the first night we slept in this bed.

She starts to stir beside me, so I run my hand along her arm and into her hair, pressing a kiss to her head. I can honestly say that nothing beats waking up with Summer in my arms, but I know better than to get comfortable. Even after everything that happened last night, I'd still guess I have three, two, one...

"I need to go for a run," she blurts, springing from the bed and stretching her arms above her head. The shirt she's wearing rises to give me a sneak peek of her perfect stomach. "Can you give me a ride home?"

I laugh at her obvious excuse to make a getaway as I sit up and rest back on my elbows. "Of course. Let me grab my things and I'll come with you," I say, pretending I don't know what she's doing. God, whatever she's been through really messed her up. She's scared shitless of any type of emotion.

"Hell no," she screeches, shaking her head. "I've seen you run, *and* you're the fastest on the football team. I'm more of a jogger."

"Keeping up with my achievements?" I smile and raise my eyebrows.

"Nah, Joel mentioned it at the game." She shrugs, but I don't miss the beautiful red blush that makes its way from her chest to her cheeks, and hell, does it get my heart racing. "Point is, you're not coming," she states and jumps out of bed, revealing her toned legs that have featured in many of my dreams. I need to get myself an invite on this run, because watching those legs work is high on my priority list.

"What about if I run at your pace?"

"No." *Well okay, then.*

"Run backwards while next to you?"

"No." She laughs.

"Run behind you?" *Oh, please say yes to this one.*

"Definitely not." *Damn.*

"What about—"

"No." She cuts me off.

"You actually can't stop me if we happen to be running in the same place, at the same time." I smirk, and she rolls her eyes.

"*True*," she says slowly and then delivers a punch with her next words. "But, I could kick you in the nuts and then make my getaway."

Ouch! My hands move to cover said nuts instinctively.

Summer laughs again but then scrunches her face up. "Ugh, fine."

Yes! That was easier than I thought. I wasn't above begging.

"I'll go to yoga instead. You are welcome to come to that."

Uh, what? My triumphant smile fades. "Come again?"

"You can join me at yoga. I'm sure Cory will come too," she says with a shrug, but I can see the smile she's trying to hold back.

Yeah, that's not happening. I mean, I've done yoga before; we sometimes do it during the off season, but I'm not good at it and don't feel like embarrassing myself while trying to win Summer over. Her wicked smile makes me crack one of my own before I accept defeat and give her what she wants. "Fine, you are free to exercise alone."

"Thank you for the permission," she teases.

"You're welcome." I wink. "Oh, I forgot...can we have lunch for your birthday this weekend? I've got a present for you."

Her smile drops instantly, but I'm not concerned about it. I know it's because she's worried that I'm reading too much into our relationship, but I'm not. It's definitely a best friend gift, not something you give to the girl you're sleeping with. If that's what we're doing.

I laugh off her concern and bop her on the nose. "It's nothing big. No need to worry your pretty little face."

"You think I'm pretty?" she jokes and bats her eyelashes.

"Incredibly beautiful, actually," I reply as I bend down to pick up my jeans from the floor.

Summer doesn't respond, but when I look back up at her, the gorgeous red hue is back gracing her skin, along with the smallest hint of a smile.

"It's alright. We can talk about it later." I finish dressing and make my way over to Summer. She seems to be waiting for me to leave before dressing, because she's standing still, clothes in hand. I press a kiss to her forehead and head out the door to give her some space and grab my keys. "I'll meet you in the kitchen."

When she pops out a few minutes later, her face is void of emotion. "Cory's almost here to pick me up." Right, okay. So I'm not taking her home?

I inwardly flinch. That could have gone better. I pretend I'm calm as I watch her wave and walk away. She just needs time to adjust to us.

I call out just as she reaches the door and hope that I'm right. "See you soon, Summer."

Famous. Last. Words.

Chapter Thirty-One

Summer

"So, has Summer filled you in on Dylan?" Cory asks Logan, clearly trying to see if I've told him more than I've told her. I haven't.

The mention of Dylan has my stomach in all kinds of knots. I feel guilty for the way I left things and for the fact I've been ghosting him since our non-date, but I also feel this spark whenever I hear his name. Waking up in his arms really messed with me. When he held my hand and walked me inside to "sleep," I honestly thought nothing of it, until he kissed my temple and pulled me in close, wrapping his arms around me. It suddenly occurred to me that I'd only ever done that with one person. Dylan. So not only did I break my never-see-a-guy-twice rule, but I also spent the night...twice. Sure, I sleep next to Logan regularly, but we do *not* cuddle, *at all*.

Logan looks at me and winks, and I swear he knows exactly what I'm thinking. Hell, they probably both do. He gives Cory a knowing look. "I've barely heard a thing about Dylan, so I'm going to assume there is more to the story," he says, and I laugh.

"She's keeping things quiet, but I see what's going on," Cory adds, like I'm not even in the room. *Oh, this I've got to hear.*

"What's going on, Cory? Perhaps you can enlighten me," I ask, leaning back on the counter and raising an eyebrow. We're hovering in the kitchen, waiting for Nate to pick Cory up. I've been noticing lately that something might be up with those two. I wish she'd tell me what's going on, but instead the topic of conversation remains on me. Logan's here visiting for my birthday tomorrow and staying for Thanksgiving. The three of us spent the day having a quiet catch-up, something we haven't done in years, but still, Cory remained locked tight when it came to her love life.

Looking at Cory expectantly, I wait for her reply.

"You both want each other," she says with a challenge in her expression. "But you're too scared to move past whatever you've got going on. Dylan, because he's nervous you'll run, and you because you're *you*."

Logan tries unsuccessfully to disguise a laugh under a cough while Cory just smiles smugly. I don't bother correcting her to say that Dylan's actually always made it clear that he wants more; this is a less is more situation.

"Or...we are both happy as friends because neither of us see a future?" I add, lying through my teeth.

"Nope, that's not it," Cory says matter-of-factly, and this time Logan doesn't bother to hide his laughter.

"Aren't you supposed to be leaving?" I sass with my best fake smile.

She looks at her watch and leaps up in a panic. "Ah, yes. I'm already late. Nate said he'd be downstairs by five. Couldn't resist ribbing you a little. Nate will understand. Are you sure you won't come?"

"Positive."

She pouts for a second, until her phone dings with a text. Her eyes flash over the screen before she waves and runs out the door.

I count down in my head waiting for Logan to press me for details. Five, four, three, two... "Are we having a movie night or heading out?" he asks while looking at his phone. *Huh. Didn't see that coming.*

"Movies," I say without having to think about it.

"You got it!" He leaps onto the couch and grabs the remote control, making himself comfortable. I'm just about to sit down when he adds, "I'd love a beer while you're up."

I laugh and walk back to the kitchen. "You're lucky I love you."

Logan's head pops up over the back of the couch, and I'm graced with his killer smile. "Don't I know it," he says, and my whole body relaxes with the feeling of comfort his presence brings. I don't add that I'm actually the lucky one. To have a pseudo boyfriend, who loves and cares for me but doesn't ever ask for or want commitment, is a pretty amazing thing. Our relationship is actually pretty perfect when he's around. At least, it used to be. Now it kind of feels wrong to be thinking like that. Either way, God, I miss him when he's not around.

We settle into our usual positions on the couch, but before we begin, I bring up something that's been on my mind. "I've tried to wait for you to talk about this, but you're clearly not going to, so here goes." Logan rolls his eyes at me but doesn't speak, so I continue. "Something's going on with you, and I want to, no, *need* to know what's wrong. I hate thinking that something's not right, *especially* when you live so far away and I can't be there for you."

"That sounds suspiciously like how I feel about you. *Especially* when I only know half of the story." He raises his eyebrows in a "tell me I'm wrong" expression. Unfortunately, I can't. Because he's one hundred percent right.

My eyes soften at his words, and I give him a quick hug before pulling away and once again giving him a serious look. "This isn't about me."

Shaking his head, Logan gives me a small smirk before he leans back into the couch and runs his hands through his already messy hair. "God, where do I even start?" he begins. "I don't even think you're going to believe me."

"Try me," I answer, moving closer to him and linking our hands.

"My dad had an affair," he says, then pauses at my intake of breath. When I don't speak, he continues. "And I don't mean a few hookups here and there. A full-blown affair. One that resulted in him moving his entire family to be closer to her."

Hearing that, I can't keep quiet. "You have got to be kidding me!" I yell. "What an asshole." It pains me to say that as it leaves my mouth. Even though what he did was awful, I don't actually mean those words. I love Logan's dad. He's always been there for me. He even offered for me to move in there if I wanted to go to college with Logan. It's hard to imagine that he'd do something like this. It's also shocking to discover he lied about moving his family away for work. "How's your mom?" I ask. I love her too. She doesn't deserve this. She's the most loyal and caring wife and mother. Not that anyone deserves this, but...

"She's shocked, but trying her hardest to forgive him and move forward."

"What? Why? How can she stay?" *God, I'd be divorcing his ass faster than—*

"He has a kid," Logan interrupts my questions with a huge bombshell. "He ended the affair years ago. The only reason we found out was because it turns out he has a three-year-old son, who is now in my father's care. Mom and Dad are going to raise him together."

I'm speechless. So many questions run through my mind, but I have no idea what to say to comfort my friend. Instead, I crawl onto his lap and pull him into a hug to try to show him how much I care and that I understand how gut-wrenching this must be.

Logan's still for a few seconds, but then he wraps his arms around me and pulls me closer, resting his chin on the top of my head. I breathe in his scent as I kiss his chest and then rest my ear over his heart.

We stay like that until Logan breaks the silence. "He's an amazing little boy. He's been through so much, in such a short amount of time, and yet, he's always smiling. I don't know how he does it."

Without pulling away, I ask a question that has me nervous for the answer. "Where's his mom?"

"She died in a car accident. Liam..." He pauses. "My brother,"—he pauses again, shaking his head like he still can't believe it—"he was in the car."

Oh, God. That breaks my heart. I can't even imagine what Liam or any of Logan's family are going through right now. Instead of focusing on the sadness of the situation, I lean back and look into Logan's eyes. "You have a brother," I say, genuinely excited for him.

"I know." His returning smile lights up his face. "When we were camping, I'd just found out, and it was hard to focus on the positives, but now..."

"Now, you have a brother," I finish for him. "I want to meet him."

"I want you to meet him too. You're going to love him."

"Oh, watch out; this new side of you might have me swooning." I laugh.

"Unlikely." He laughs with me, and I'm happy that there is lightness in this difficult situation. To lose your mother at such a young age—my heart aches for Liam. He will grow up without his mom, and here I am upset about mine, who is very much still alive. Makes me wonder if I should reach out.

"What brought on that frown?" Logan breaks my thoughts.

"Just thinking about Liam's mom." I offer him a half-truth.

"I know. It's sad to think that he'll grow up without her, but he will have my mom, and she's pretty awesome."

"Oh, I know; trust me. I was always jealous of you." I laugh. "He's a lucky boy, but he'll still be missing her."

"No doubt," he says, and his smile fades a little, most likely thinking about Liam's mom now too. "Alright, enough of that. It's time for the movie," he announces and pushes me off his lap onto the couch beside him.

"Hey! Dick move," I yell but can't hide my smile.

We get through a movie and a half, plus two pizzas, before Logan starts running his hand up and down my arm. It's his go-to move on me. I know exactly what it means. This scene would usually play out as follows... I'd let it go on until Logan's hand moved higher and began massaging my neck, then I'd turn my head, look into his eyes and *bam*, the kissing would begin. Only this time, something feels different. Not from Logan's end but from mine. Don't get me wrong, his hands feel amazing, and like always, I'm enjoying every second, but something feels wrong. The desire isn't there.

Logan's fingers reach my hairline, and I now have a split-second decision to make. For the first time, since our first time, I hesitate. It doesn't take him long to notice. His fingers stop their ministrations, and he uses his other hand to lift my chin, so our eyes meet. "Everything okay?"

"Of course. I'm just really tired tonight. It's been a long week."

Logan smirks at me. "You messing with me, Sum?"

"What? No." I stare in his eyes, not really sure what I'm hoping to convey.

"Ah, I get it; you want me to mix it up a little." Before I have a chance to answer, he flips me onto my back and moves between my legs. I open my mouth to speak, but I'm cut off as his lips meet mine in a bruising kiss. A kiss that feels all wrong. I can't do this. *Goddammit! Why can't I do this?*

One of Logan's hands moves to my cheek while the other travels down my side. When he reaches my thighs, I grab his hand. "Stop."

He does, instantly. "What's going on?"

"Nothing, I'm just not in the mood."

"I'm pretty confident I can change that." Logan moves down my body and presses his mouth to my inner thigh before kissing his way up. God, that feels good, but no.

"Logan," I warn.

"Tell me the truth, and I'll stop." He kisses me again, only an inch from my center.

"It's Dylan," I bark out frantically.

He pulls back completely and moves to the end of the couch. I wait for the anger, or the hurt. I'm definitely not expecting what comes next. "I know." He smiles.

I stare at him dumbfounded for a moment before I find my words. "What do you mean?"

"I had my suspicions that there was more to you and Dylan, and then when Cory said the same, and you argued, it confirmed it."

"Confirmed what?" I ask.

"It confirmed that maybe *you* don't realize that there's more to you and Dylan." I can't respond. I don't know what to say, what to think. Logan's expression softens, and he reaches over to pull me into a hug. "You deserve love, Summer. And I don't just mean the love that Cory and I have for you. I mean the love I think you have for Dylan. I don't really know him yet, but I plan to, because whether you realize it or not, he's clearly important to you.

"Summer, you mean the world to me," Logan adds when I still can't speak. "I'd say you're like a sister, but that's gross considering what we've done in the past." I laugh, finally breaking my silence. Logan continues. "You are the closest person to me. I wish I knew what happened to make you feel like you're not worthy of a proper relationship, because you deserve the world. I've always wished I could give you that, but—"

I press my fingers to his lips because neither of us should ever feel guilty for not having romantic feelings toward each other. "I know. And you do. You've always been my savior. It's why I don't need a relationship. I don't want—"

He sighs as his brows furrow. "If that's the case, then, I'm sorry. I've been holding you back."

233

"No, that's not what I mean. Logan, I'm not in love with Dylan. You're not holding me back."

"I'm not?" He raises his eyebrows, unconvinced.

"No. You're not."

"Great, then let's get back to it." He grabs my face and tries to press his lips to mine. I push back instantly, ready to argue, until he laughs again. "Come on, Summer. How can you not see it? You may not love him yet, but you have definitely caught the feels."

I laugh at that because it's not a Logan thing to say. He suddenly jumps to his feet. "I think it's time to call it a night. Do you want me to sleep out here?"

"No, of course not. I trust you to keep it in your pants."

"Good, because I would never want to come between you and someone else." He smiles and leans down to kiss my forehead, and I grin in return.

He glances at me with a look that tells me he's turned serious again. "Think about what I said." I'm about to answer when he adds, "No, Summer, really think about it. Don't risk missing out on something special. You've never had feelings for anyone before. Dylan's a lucky guy."

I smile as he walks away, but this time it's faked. Is he right? Do I have strong feelings for Dylan? God, who am I kidding? I like Dylan. I *like* Dylan. Now that I've admitted it, I realize how foreign this feeling is. Every little flicker in my chest, every spark I've tried to ignore... But now that it's out there, I'm not sure I can put it back.

I toss and turn beside Logan until he starts to stir. Worried I'm going to wake him completely, I quietly leave the room and settle on the couch. It's three in the morning. I've been lying awake for hours with one thing on my mind. Well, more specifically...one person. Before thinking it through, I pull out my phone and send off a text.

Me: I miss you.

It's not a very *me* thing to say, but it's the truth, and if I've learned anything during the time I've spent staring into space, listening to Logan's breathing, it's that I want to see Dylan, badly. I don't expect a reply tonight, so I make myself comfortable and attempt to sleep on the couch. As my head hits the pillow, my phone vibrates. The fact that I get excited and jump to read it should tell me everything I need to know about my feelings.

Dylan: Is this for real? I miss you too. I'm pretty sure this is a dream though.

Dork. I laugh at his response as my phone vibrates again.

Dylan: and Happy Birthday.

My smile grows, and I shake my head. Of course, he remembered. The physical response I'm getting in my chest is not something I'm used to. *Stupid heart.* I'm not ready to admit my feelings to him; I've stepped as far outside the lines as I can go tonight. But still, I owe him something.

Summer: You said it was my turn to plan our next date, so be ready at five. Wear comfortable shoes.

Dylan: I can't wait.

Dylan: P.S. I'm a guy, what kind of shoes did you think I'd wear?

I burst out laughing and then cover my mouth so as to not wake Logan.

Summer: Goodnight, Dylan.

Dylan: Goodnight, Summer.

I sigh and fall back into the cushions, excited to see what tomorrow brings but scared all the same. This is real. Our friendship, my feelings, all of it is *real*. And, God, that terrifies me.

Chapter Thirty-Two

Dylan

When I open the door to Summer, my jaw drops to the ground before I have a chance to stop it. She's standing before me in a pair of ripped black skinny jeans that look painted on her skin, with a pale pink top that's sheer in some strategic places across the front, providing a peep show to a black lace bra underneath. I feel my jeans tighten as I grow hard at the sight of her. *God, I want to kiss her.*

Summer's text said *date*, but I'm wary about making the first move. I'm still not sure where we stand, and the last thing I want to do is push her away again. So instead of a kiss, I pull her into me and wrap my arms around her. Date or no date, I'm not getting through the night without this. She gasps but pulls me closer, squeezing me a little and...is she smelling me? Definitely not complaining if she is. I pull away and take a step back, running a hand through my previously styled hair to stop myself from asking for more. "Shall we go?" I say and then make a move to Summer's car. I don't hear movement following me, and when I look over my shoulder, I find her staring at me curiously, with a small smile on her lips. *This is going to be a good night. I feel it.*

As soon as we're in the car, Summer pounces on me. Verbally, not physically, *unfortunately.* "So what did you get me for my birthday? Can I have it now? I can't see any presents."

I can't help but laugh. I didn't even think she'd remember.

"I told you it wasn't big, and I wasn't kidding." I lift up and reach into the pocket of my jeans. Summer stills with her hand raised to her mouth. *Jesus, does she think I'm holding an engagement ring in here?* These are pretty fitted jeans; they may not be skintight, but let's just say I am not fitting a ring box in here. I pull the piece of paper out, and Summer visibly relaxes.

Unfolding the paper I printed from the online store giftsforbesties.com, I hand it over, and almost instantly she's roaring in laughter. Which is exactly what I was going for. "Is this for real?" she asks, finally taking a breath before laughing again.

"Sure is." I smirk, leaning back in my chair with my arms behind my head.

"But how?" She shakes her head and laughs again, but this one's quieter and holds more emotion.

Before I can answer, she has her phone out and is typing the web address noted in front of her. I know as soon as the page has loaded because she laughs out loud again. She presses on the screen and Queen's "You're my Best Friend" begins to play, giving her a beautifully designed montage of our "seventeen years" of friendship, using random photos I found on the Internet.

Whoever made this montage must have been thoroughly confused at the fact that every image features a different male and female best friend duo. I even added in a young Ryan Gosling and Britney Spears from the Mickey Mouse Club for shits and giggles.

The only genuine photo of us is used on the first slide, along with the words, "Dylan and Summer—Best Friends Forever!"

Summer's laughter continues as the years go by until the music finally comes to an end. Her eyes meet mine, and I'm blessed with the most beautiful, heartfelt smile she's ever given me. Her whole face lights up, and her eyes bore into my soul, rendering me speechless at the realization that I've never seen her full smile before. *How much hurt is she hiding?*

That smile right there makes everything we are doing together worth it. Maybe I was wrong to want more from her because I will happily stay in this limbo state of being, until the end of my days, if I can continue to get smiles like that.

"You are one in a million," she says and shakes her head, laughing again. "This must have taken hours."

"Nah, I just found the photos. A company made it look pretty."

"The photos are the best bit." She giggles and looks back at her phone, pressing play again. "This one's my favorite," she says, pausing the montage and handing me the phone. It's a picture of "us" in fifty years' time sharing ice cream at the beach, wearing matching sweaters that say, "Ice cream: Keeping friends together since 1935."

"Ah, I remember that day like it was yesterday," I say, looking to the roof, appearing lost in thought.

Summer whacks me on the knee and laughs again. I actually don't remember her ever being so happy and relaxed. I decide then and there that I'm going to do everything in my power to ensure she has more moments, no, more *days*, like these.

She watches the video for a third time—*I'm going to go out on a limb and say the gift was successful*—then leans across the car and pulls me into another tight hug, surrounding me in warmth and her addictive mango and coconut scent. She presses her lips to my cheek before whispering in my ear, "Thank you. This means the world to me." When she pulls away her eyes drop to the floor, almost shyly, and I'm not sure what it means, except that it makes my heart jump. Before I can question it, she starts the ignition and pulls out of my drive.

"Best present ever," she exclaims and laughs again.

It's a short drive to the next town, our apparent destination, so Summer and I talk about mundane shit like the weather and classes. When she pulls into a full parking lot, I look around for some clue as to where we are. A worn-out billboard advertising live music covers the red brick wall of the building that faces the lot. I look at Summer in question, but all she does is smirk in response.

The closer we walk to the building, the louder the music gets, until it's so loud I recognize the song. All-4-One's "I Swear" floats through the open doors as a sea of people push their way through. *Uh, what am I walking into?*

A banner above the entrance grabs my attention. In large black font, the words "One Night Only—Boyz Rock the Music" are written, taking up most of the banner. Those words alone mean nothing to me; it's the smaller words below that have me stopping in my tracks and bursting out laughing. "Nineties pop cover band winner of the year," *but wait there's more...* "five years running." *Oh, this is so bad.*

"Please tell me we are walking right on by and heading into that creepy-looking used car lot instead." I point to the lot down the road. *Anything but this.*

Summer laughs and links her arm through mine. "Come on. Like Lucy said, you need some music education. Plus, it's my birthday, so you can't say no."

She's got me there.

I'm shocked but I'm actually enjoying the music. Good ole Boyz Rock the Music has played three sets so far, and despite what I'd normally call *poor song choices*, they're really good. Maybe even cover-band-of-the-year good.

Five's "If Ya Gettin' Down" begins, and Summer cheers in front of me like she has for almost every song. I laugh and pull her tight against me. She definitely loves boy bands *way* more than she was letting on. As she sways in front of me, I note the other reason I'm enjoying the music...*Summer*. She peers back at me over her shoulder, and a look of pure giddiness shines across her face. God, she's so beautiful I could spend a lifetime looking into her eyes and never get tired of it. A nervous feeling swirls within me at the thought. But I shake it off.

Still unsure of Summer's thoughts on us, I follow her lead when it comes to anything physical between us. While there's been no kissing, Summer's been very flirty and *coupley* all night. Not a real word, but it's exactly what I mean. Like now, for instance, she has her fingers linked through mine as she bounces to the music. Squeezing her hand tight, I sway along beside her, not quite matching her enthusiasm. I'm happy to be here, but not bouncing-and-cheering happy. When the song ends, the tempo changes to NSYNC's "Tearin' Up My Heart," and this time, I'm not ashamed to admit I know all the words. I may have listened to their albums a few times since Summer told me she loved them so much.

Moving Summer in front of me, I rest my hands on her hips and lean down so my lips are pressed to her ear. I sing along to every word of the song as we move slowly, as one, to the rhythm. Summer's arms come up around my neck, and her fingers run through the ends of my hair. This new position pushes her chest out, giving me the perfect view and prompting me to slowly move my hands up to under her breasts. When her head falls back to rest on my shoulder and she closes her eyes, I'm done for.

I know I should resist her—we're in public—but her neck is too close, and she smells fucking amazing. I press my lips to the base of her ear and then kiss my way down her neck, alternating between sucking and a light touch. I'm so close, I can both hear and feel her sharp intake of breath, and as I continue to kiss her, my thumb starts to subtly swipe across her breast of its own accord. Despite being involuntary, when I finally realize I'm doing it, I can't seem to stop.

I lower a hand to squeeze her hip bone, and she tightens her grip on my hair as a soft moan leaves her lips. *And that's enough.* I practically growl, "we're leaving," into her ear and then pull her from the dance floor, not even looking back to gauge her reaction. Summer lets me drag her behind me, without complaint, making me feel a little bad about my outburst. As soon as we get to the car, I turn to apologize. "Sorry, I—"

My words are cut off as Summer leaps into my arms and presses her lips to mine, sending us stumbling into the car. I catch her before we fall and dig my fingers into her ass, pulling her down onto me. We both groan in ecstasy as our bodies grind together, completely lost in the moment.

We continue making out like that until a car door slams in the distance. It's faint and far away, but it's enough to break me from the Summer-infused trance I'm in.

"Wait," I rasp against her lips. I'm constantly losing my mind when it comes to Summer, but tonight, I'm going to do the right thing.

She breaks away from the kiss and looks up at me through her lashes. Her chest heaves along with mine, and she's clearly flustered. I smile and am blessed with a beautiful smile in return.

I brush the hair from her face and press a kiss to her nose. "This feels like a date," I say with a cocky smile. Summer begins to say something, but I press a finger to her lips to stop her. "To me, it feels like a date. I want it to be a date. And I want it to end the right way. The way you deserve."

She gives me a puzzled expression but doesn't speak.

"We're going to go home, I'm going to kiss you good night, and then we are going to make plans to see each other again."

Summer's eyebrows rise in surprise. "Is that so?" she says with a smile.

"It's so. And you're going to love it."

She laughs at that and moves toward the driver's door. I grab her hand and pull her back toward me for one more kiss. "And I'm driving," I add before walking her to the passenger door and directing her inside. Thankfully, she doesn't protest. If I don't drive, my mind might get other ideas, and I want to see this through.

When we pull up at my place, I walk around to Summer's door and open it for her. She gives me a wry smile but continues to play along. Taking her hand, I guide her back to the driver's side and then stop her before she gets in, pushing her against the door. My hand moves into her hair, and I kiss her with everything I've got.

When I pull away, she's breathless.

"I had a great time tonight. I'll see you at our Friendsgiving, right?"

She nods her head with a smile. "I'll be there."

"Great. Goodnight, Summer." I kiss her again and then walk to my door. When I'm halfway, I look back over my shoulder to see her shaking her head with a smirk. She's so fucking adorable it's almost impossible to leave. But I will...after one more kiss.

I run back to her and sweep her into my arms before dipping her back and pressing my lips to hers in a scorching kiss. She giggles against my lips and then moans when my tongue brushes against hers. We stay like that for a minute until I pull away.

"I'll be seeing you," I say with a corny exaggerated wink.

"You will," Summer replies breathlessly with her bottom lip between her teeth.

I walk to my door for the second time tonight, and this time when I look back, she's leaning against her car with her fingers to her lips and the most beautiful smile on her face.

God, I hope I did the right thing.

Chapter Thirty-Three

Dylan

The days leading up to Thanksgiving were insanely busy with training, classes, and family, especially since we celebrated early when Mom and her boyfriend, Sam, decided to go away for the weekend. The plus side of that was our little group that had formed was able to use my family home for a Friendsgiving dinner we'd put together. The negative of being so busy meant I didn't have time to see Summer. We spoke every day, sometimes twice, but never about us or what was happening between us. As desperate as I was to know, I could definitely feel that something was different. Maybe, if I was lucky, it even meant she wouldn't run this time.

By Friendsgiving, I'm so anxious to see Summer, the morning feels like it's absolutely dragging. So when evening finally rolls around and she arrives with Logan, I can't stop the jealousy from rearing its ugly head. I do my best to keep it in check because I know things ended well between us after our date, but I can't help but wonder if something has happened between *them* since he's been at her place all week.

When I open the door, Summer's smile lights up her face, and she jumps into my arms, wrapping hers around my neck.

"Happy Friendsgiving, Dylan," she says as her lips connect with mine in a heated kiss. *This is new.*

When she pulls back, I look over her shoulder at Logan and silently ask, "who is this person?" He shrugs his shoulders with what I can only guess must be a knowing smile.

Summer drops back to the floor and steps aside so Logan can move forward. "Happy Thanksgiving," I greet him, holding a hand out for him to shake, but he surprises me by pulling me into a half hug. "Thanks for having me, man," he says as he pats my shoulder.

Summer laughs and walks away, leaving Logan and me alone. He stands tall, squaring his shoulders, and waits until she's out of earshot before he speaks. "I'm not going to read you the riot act, because both Summer and Cory think you're a decent guy, but don't hurt her, okay?" There's a desperate plea in his tone, showing me just how deeply he cares for her.

I swallow slowly and say, "Never," a little stunned to be having this conversation. *Does this mean Summer's told him she wants more between us?*

Logan smiles and pats my back once more before moving to Summer's side. I stare at them both for a moment and wonder what it all means. God, I'd love to talk to her. Alone. But do I think that will happen tonight? Not a chance.

Lucy greets Summer with a warm hug and smiles at Logan before introducing them to her douchebag boyfriend, Greg. I'm about to join them when the doorbell rings, and Nate, Cory, and Joel walk in, arms full of food and alcohol, plus a stack of board games. I welcome them in and then run a hand down my face to hide my frustration. *It's going to be a long night.*

During the gathering, Summer and I mingle with our friends. Sometimes together, sometimes apart, but always in each other's sights. She's currently standing next to Cory, deep in conversation, but stealing glances my way.

"And then he had the nerve to say it was my fault," Nate says beside me. I'm only half listening to his conversation as he tells Joel about the complete mess that was our training session yesterday. The boys are partying too much at the moment, and it shows.

"Dylan tells me the freshmen and sophomores are fucking around," Joel says, getting Nate started on another rant. One that I'd usually join in on if I wasn't so distracted.

I look back at Summer for the hundredth time to see her walking my way. She has a flirty look on her face with her sights set on me, so I raise an eyebrow in question.

I'm about to move toward her when Lucy announces loudly that it's time to set the table, causing me to jump in surprise at her close proximity. Summer smirks and shakes her head. I roll my eyes and move to the kitchen on autopilot, knowing that Lucy's words were meant for me. When Summer joins us to help, I abandon my job and stand against the wall, watching her flit around the room before she heads my way. There's a sassy smile playing on her lips that tells me she knows too well where my eyes have been glued.

"I really want to kiss you right now," she whispers in my ear as she walks past me. I freeze and my chest feels tight. God, I really want to kiss her too, but not just now, *always*. It's all I think about. Not knowing where we stand is killing me. Our friendship couldn't be better, and while I have loved being Summer's friend, I want more. I've never wanted anyone as much as I want her, and lately, I think she feels the same.

She peers over her shoulder before disappearing out of view, and her smile lights up the room, not to mention my world. I shake my head and laugh because at that moment, I know I'm going to make this girl mine.

As the night goes on, Logan easily becomes the life of the party, having discovered he remembers Lucy from before he moved away. He can't seem to shut up about "little Lucy Mathers," and I've got to say, it's nice to have the teasing thrown back at *her* for a change. Joel adds his own stories occasionally, allowing me to steal secret glances Summer's way.

She's in a constant state of happiness at my side as she listens to the boys' antics, and I swear, her smiles are something I'll never take for granted. They need to be savored, especially since I know she's hurting underneath it all. When she notices me staring, she winks and bites her lip, making me fight the urge to grab her face and kiss her in front of our closest friends. She's not ready for that yet. As if understanding my thoughts, she places her hand on my thigh and bumps her shoulder into mine. *Be patient, Dylan.*

I shake my head to get it back into party mode, which isn't hard because the drinks are flowing and conversation is getting louder. We barely pause when our final guest, one of Lucy's friends, arrives. "Sorry I'm late, everyone," she announces as she walks in.

When Lucy introduces her to everyone, I notice Logan's eyes following her around the room. *He's interested.* My own shoot to Summer, hoping I don't find jealousy in her expression, but there's only a playful grin as she looks at Logan from across the table. She raises an eyebrow, and he winks before turning away again.

Time passes in a blur, and before we know it, we're on to dessert. Since Logan's now coupled up, Joel's the only one going solo, but he doesn't seem to mind. I've seen him on his phone, a lot, and I'd bet my last dollar it's Delilah.

"Why is it that we never hooked up?" Logan asks Lucy, with raised eyebrow, clearly joking.

"Because, God only knows who you've been with, and diseases aren't really my thing," Lucy jokes, and I cringe when I feel Summer stiffen beside me. Logan, however, laughs.

"Hey! I'm clean, I'll have you know."

"Sounds like you dodged a bullet not sleeping with Luce," Greg adds. "Because now you get a shot at her fine-as-fuck friend."

What the fuck? I rise in my seat but feel a small hand grip my thigh, breaking my trance. "I'd love another drink while you're up, Dyl." Summer smiles at me, not hiding what she's doing. And dammit, it works, because as much as I want to pummel this guy, now is not the time.

Where does Lucy find these guys? I can't help but wonder as I go to get Summer's drink and try to calm down. *Doesn't she realize her worth?* I'll never understand girls who stay with guys that treat them badly. Actually, I'll never understand dating them in the first place. God, I hope he treats her like a princess when they're alone. Maybe he just acts like this when he's drunk?

When I return, I find Greg's eyes now on Summer and have to stop myself from reacting *again.* Summer meets my gaze with a smile before mouthing, "it's harmless," and gesturing for me to sit. I do as I'm told, and she takes my hand in hers, curling our fingers together out of sight.

Her electrifying touch distracts me from my anger, and conversation buzzes around me as I relish in the warmth of Summer's hand. Her fingers are bouncing on my knuckles as though she's keeping time with a tune, and I'm suddenly hit with a flash of déjà vu. I smile, lost for a moment in the memory, until I notice Greg's eyes bore into Summer once more before he winks. *What the actual...* "Get the fuck out of my house," I yell, slamming my fist on the table and scaring the shit out of everyone, including myself.

"Dylan!" Lucy exclaims, a flush of red staining her cheeks.

I'm about to defend my actions when Logan does it for me. "Dylan's right. Lucy, this guy's a dickwad. You deserve better. Hell, anyone would deserve better. What's the deal?"

"You don't have to answer that, Lucy," Summer interjects. "Let's go into the kitchen. I'll help you clean up."

"It's fine," Lucy says, turning back to me. "Dylan, you're out of line."

"What?" *Seriously, what? It wasn't just me.*

Lucy gives me a stern look, but before she can answer, Greg pushes his chair back and gets up. "Fuck this. I'm out of here," he says before moving over to Lucy and kissing her briefly on the lips. "Call me later, babe."

She smiles and nods before shooting a glare my way. *If looks could kill.*

As soon as the door shuts, Lucy and Summer start clearing our plates.

Before Summer walks away, she catches my eye and shakes her head with a grin before biting her lip. I raise an eyebrow in question, but she leaves without a response.

I feel a little guilty after witnessing Greg's gentle kiss and then watching him leave. He obviously respects Lucy enough to not cause a scene, but I couldn't just sit back and accept his behavior. This possessive feeling is new to me. We all know I've had girlfriends. I'm a serial dater. *Insert eye roll here.* But I've never felt this cut up over someone staring at my girl. *My girl? Fuck!* I can't even call her that, but God, do I want to.

No matter my reasons, I was an asshole and need to apologize. I move to the kitchen to find Lucy but stop when I hear her whispered voice.

"He's not the same when we're alone. I don't know why he acts that way. Anyway, it's not like he's the one or anything. It's just a bit of fun." *Well, that's lucky, since I can't see him asking me to be his best man anytime soon.* "Let's change the subject, you and my brother seem good tonight," Lucy says to Summer, unaware of my presence. I shouldn't listen, especially now the topic has turned to me. I should walk away now. Turn and head in the opposite direction, but I can see their reflections in a mirror and can't seem to get my legs to move. I'm stuck, watching Summer's reaction.

"He's a good guy, Luce. I don't need to tell you that." She smiles as Lucy nods, a sparkle of hope in her eyes. "He's different from other guys I've been with. I've never had someone be protective of me like he was out there. The feeling I got was unexpected."

Lucy smiles. "You liked it," she states.

"I usually wouldn't but..." She shrugs with a puzzled expression and then turns serious. "I think I like him, Luce," she adds, and my heart leaps into my chest. That's all I've wanted to hear from the very beginning, and God, I hope she says it to me too.

"Does he know that?"

"Not unless it's obvious." She sighs.

"Then tell him. I can pretty much guarantee he feels the same."

I grimace, but she's not wrong. I've been at the "like" stage for months.

I don't waste any time when the girls walk out of the kitchen a few minutes later, and before Summer has had a chance to acknowledge me, I grab her by the hand and drag her down the hall. "What's happening right now?" she asks with a nervous laugh as she follows behind me.

Instead of answering with words, I stop suddenly and pin her against the wall, crashing my lips to hers. One of my hands cups her face while the other grabs her hip, locking her in place.

It takes a moment for her to get her bearings, but when she does, she's with me one hundred percent. Her hands wrap around me, moving under my shirt and pulling me closer, bringing our bodies flush together.

As difficult as it is, I somehow manage to not get lost in the moment and pull away, taking a step back. Our heated breaths are in sync as we both stare at each other, trying to come back down to earth.

"Was that all you wanted?" Summer asks sweetly, looking up at me with eyelashes flickering as fast as my rapid heartbeat.

"Not even close," I reply and grab her hand once more, this time leading her straight to my childhood bedroom.

Chapter Thirty-Four

Summer

From the moment we enter the bedroom, the energy between us shifts. I want to take a moment to enjoy the fact that I'm standing in Dylan's old room, a place I dreamed about when I was younger, but my mind is too wound up to focus on that. Plus, he doesn't remember me so that would be weird.

Dylan takes a tentative step toward me and presses his lips to mine in a slow but passionate kiss. I gasp when he runs a hand up and over my breast, stopping when he reaches my neck, cupping it possessively.

I'm hesitant toward the change in our usual pace but remind myself that this is what I want. I want to take this slow. I want...I'm not even sure what I want yet, but this is definitely heading in the right direction.

Always sensing my moods, Dylan pulls back and smiles, setting me alight and grounding me at the same time. "I've got you. I'll always have you," he says, walking me slowly backwards toward his bed. "Maybe we should talk first," he adds as he links his pinkie with mine.

I shake my head and grip his shirt with my free hand, pulling him closer. We definitely need to talk. But talking first is no longer an option. I need him. I need this.

When he kisses me again, it's packed with emotion. I feel his lips all over my body, though in reality, they haven't left my mouth. My hands grip him tightly as his own roam my body, sending an electric current straight to my core. I softly moan at his touch and try hard not to speed things up.

Dylan kisses his way down my neck before looking into my eyes. "God, Summer. This is how I wanted our first time to be. This is how it should have been." He continues his exploration and groans when my hands make their way into his hair.

"I'm sorry it took me so long to realize that," I say honestly, ready to take a leap of faith. He pulls back suddenly and stares into my soul, stealing another piece of my heart.

"What...I mean, does—"

I stop his words with another kiss and then stand on my toes so that my lips meet his ear. "I want this. I want you. I want *us*. I don't think I've ever wanted anything more."

Dylan releases a sigh and then lifts me off the ground, burying his face in my neck. "About time," he jokes and then rests my feet back on the floor before pressing our foreheads together. "You make me so happy, Summer. I've never felt this way."

My breath hitches, and he stifles it with a kiss before dropping to his knees and removing my heels one at a time. He gently brushes his lips across the marks left by the straps and then kisses his way up my calf and thigh until he reaches my hips under my dress.

He hooks his fingers into the waistband of my lace panties and slides them down, groaning when he notices how skimpy they are. When he stands back up, he tucks my hair behind my ear and then presses a kiss to my jaw. I shiver at his touch when another bolt of electricity courses through me. This speed—this intimacy—is all new to me and has my heart begging to be released from my chest.

We continue to take our time, savoring every moment, until we're both almost naked, a place we've never been before. Dylan runs his hands down my sides until he reaches my hips and the hem of my dress. I knew this moment was coming. I planned for it, but now that it's here, I'm nervous. I somehow manage to control my breathing, and when I don't resist, Dylan slowly raises the material up along my body and over my head, dropping it to the floor. I shiver and inhale a sharp breath. *This is it.* Dylan pulls back, no doubt sensing my unease, and looks me in the eyes, silently questioning me without actually having to ask. I nervously shake my head and hide into his chest.

He tries to wrap his arms around me, but I don't allow it. I can do this. I don't need him to comfort me. This is Dylan. I trust him.

Taking a step back, I smile and lift his shirt up over his head, marveling at his beautiful body. I feather kisses across his chest and pecs, until the moment I feel Dylan start to relax. He kisses me on the forehead, making me sigh because I've never felt more loved in my life. *Loved? Is that what Dylan feels?* I wait for the panic to start, but when it doesn't, I realize the idea of that doesn't scare me anymore.

I'm so wrapped up in my thoughts that it takes me a moment to realize Dylan's stopped moving. "Stage fright?" I tease and look up at him with a playful smile. When he doesn't respond, I wave my hand in front of his eyes and laugh before turning around to see what's caught his gaze behind me. As soon as my eyes meet his in the mirror, I cringe and push him away as a sharp pain stabs at my chest. He snaps out of his daze, but his eyes flash back to my scars.

I try to breathe; I try not to react, but all rationality seems to go out the window when I see what looks like disgust on his face.

"I didn't think this would be an issue for you. I thought you were better than that," I snap and rush to put my clothes back on. "I never...never show this part of myself, but I thought..." I shake my head and start throwing his stuff around the room. "Dammit, where is my dress?" *It can't be far. Where did he throw it?*

On a deep, and I mean *deep* level, I know I'm being stupid. Dylan hasn't done anything wrong, but there's too much hurt inside for me to process that right now.

"Summer, please stop. Please. That's not what's happening here." He bends down to meet me and takes my face in my hands. "Please." He begs with so much sincerity in his eyes that I can't help but pause.

Dropping to the floor, I sit down and pull my knees up to my chest. We're both quiet for a minute until I do the right thing and break the silence. "I'm sorry. I just..." I pause, unsure what to say or how much to reveal.

"You have nothing to apologize for," Dylan says, dropping down beside me. "Something tells me you are not going to believe what I'm about to say, but Summer... You. Are. Beautiful. Every part of you is beautiful. I'm sorry. I shouldn't have frozen like that. I just..."

His words penetrate my mind like it's the first time they've ever been said. I've been called beautiful. Dylan has even called me beautiful. In

251

fact, I've had many compliments tossed my way, but there's something different about those words now. It could be in the sincerity in his voice, or the look in his eyes. It could even be the way he paused after each word, making sure I understood their importance. Hell, it could have been all three. Whatever the reason, three simple words just ignited my already blazing heart.

"I definitely didn't freeze because I'm no longer attracted to you," he continues. "You're...I mean I...God, I'm so attracted to you."

He's rambling and probably thinks he's completely fucking this up, especially when I laugh. It's a nervous giggle, but from the look on his face, it's what he needed to hear. His words are what I needed to hear.

Dylan takes a deep breath and reaches forward to link our pinkies together like he's making me a promise. "Summer, I really like you. I want us to be together. I've never...This feels different. I don't know how to describe it, but I know what I feel. There's nothing you could say or do or *show* me that could change that right now."

His inclusion of the words "right now" make all the difference. He once promised to never lie to me, and that's his way of showing me that he's keeping that promise. He doesn't know what the future holds, but right now...

Using our linked pinkies, I pull him closer and press a soft kiss to his cheek. "I...I like you too, and I..." I pause, not entirely sure what I want to say next. I like him. I want us to be together, but I need a moment. Dylan breathes a sigh of relief, obviously not expecting me to admit that, and then smiles. I'm about to ask him what we do next when his smile fades and is replaced with a look of apology.

"Before you continue, I have to ask...I'm sorry, but I have to know." I brace myself for what I know is coming. "What happened?"

"A car accident," I say without hesitation. It's a lie, but the truth is something I'm not sure I'll ever divulge. I know he's not going to believe it, and I honestly don't expect him to. But I need him to accept it as my answer. To see through my response and let it go.

He sighs and runs a hand through his hair. "A car accident?" he asks, giving me the chance to change my answer, but I can't. I'm not ready, and I certainly don't have a backup plan in case the truth gets out.

I nod because I don't want to lie to him again and then cover my face in my hands, ashamed of everything I've done until this point.

Dylan pulls my hands away, and I see the end of an angry frown before he changes his expression and leans down to look me in the eyes. "Please don't hide. You never have to hide. Especially from me." He rests his hand on my knee and gives me a gentle squeeze. "Why do you hide? I mean, people must know about the accident, so why...?" He trails off, shaking his head, and I know it's because he's realized that *if* it was an accident, I probably wouldn't hide it.

"Like your stuff with football and your dad, it's just something I keep to myself. So please, *please* don't talk to anyone about it. Promise me you won't," I say, not even trying to hide my panic.

Dylan flashes me a disbelieving look. "Do you really think I'd do that?"

I grimace at the hurt in his voice. I don't actually think he'd do that, but I can't take the risk of not saying anything. I need to protect myself at all costs. "I'm sorry..."

Dylan pulls me into a hug without letting me say another word and kisses my hair. When he runs his hands up and down my back in comfort, I realize I'm still naked and pull away self-consciously. There's another flash of anger on Dylan's face before he transforms it to a soft smile.

"So, what now?" he asks, letting me make the first move, something I'm grateful for. *What now? God, I wish I knew.*

"I think I'm going to go home," I say when I realize my head is too messed up to move forward right now. Dylan's face drops until I add, "but can I see you tomorrow?"

The smile I get in return is everything I'll need to get me through this mess. With that one tiny pull of the lips, I know he's got my back, and he'll always be there for me. I need tonight for me, so that I can give him my all. Tomorrow is a new day and a fresh start. Tomorrow I'll put all my fears aside and be strong for us.

Rising to my knees, I place my hands on Dylan's chest and press my lips to his. He smiles into the kiss and places his hands on my face, tenderly sucking my bottom lip before pulling back and looking deep into my eyes. "I..." My breath hitches as I wait for him to continue. "I'll always be here. I need you to trust in that," he finally finishes. I nod, though I can't help but feel like something is off, and he sighs. "I'll see you soon?"

I nod again. "Tomorrow."

Dylan hands me my dress, the one that's apparently been right in front of my eyes, and stands to get himself dressed.

When I'm decent, we kiss goodnight, and I leave, not even allowing him the chance to walk me out. I'm smiling, though, after tonight, and as I head to my car, I vow to myself that I'll figure out a way to tell Dylan what's going on. I'll work through my hang-ups, and tomorrow I'll be better. *We'll* be better.

Chapter Thirty-Five

Dylan

It's just after two in the morning by the time I get to the Ball House. I didn't stick around the house long after Summer left tonight. I had to get out of there. Most of the guys are drunk, or close to it, and since we've got a game on Saturday, only my teammates who live nearby are spending Thanksgiving with their families. I walk straight through to the kitchen needing a strong drink. The counter is littered with empty bottles and red cups, but I manage to find an unopened bottle of bourbon under the sink. Nate's hiding spot.

I want to hurt someone. I've never felt like this before. I'm not an angry man. Nicole was cheating on me for our entire relationship, and I didn't feel even a tenth of the hatred I feel for whoever did that to Summer. An accident? A *fucking* accident? Why is she covering for someone? Who is she covering for? As much as I wanted Summer to stay, it's definitely better that she left. I'm not sure I could have continued to hide the anger I had itching to come out.

Cup in hand, I've just stepped out of the room when Thomas enters my line of sight. I'd completely forgotten he'd be here, and he's the perfect outlet for this tense energy. My nostrils flare at the sight of him as my hands clench into fists.

"Hey, Dylan, my man," Thomas says, walking toward me without a care in the world. *Never mind that his sister has scars on her back, serious commitment issues, and no family.*

Without thinking, I shove him against the wall, pushing my hands into his shoulders to stop him from moving. "Was it you?" I yell. "Did you hurt her?"

"What the fuck, Dylan? What are you talking about? Who?" He tries to shove me back but fails. He's stronger than I am, but the adrenaline is keeping us more evenly matched.

I shove him again, and get up in his face. "Summer? Did you cause those scars?" I can't believe Summer thought I'd buy her car accident story. She's got to be kidding herself. There were a few scars, and from what I saw, they varied in color, and one was a lot more faded than the others. It can't have been one accident.

"What scars? What—"

I don't let him finish, and while I'm aware of our audience, I can't walk away. "Don't play dumb. The scars all over her back."

"Her back? Dylan, whatever she said is bullshit." He spits out his words and grips my forearms to try and release my hold.

"It's not bullshit, you asshole. I've seen them. I—"

"Wait..." He cuts me off. "You've fucked her, haven't you? Did she suck you in? Don't tell me you've fallen for her? I fucking warned you. I warned all of you!" he yells to no one in particular. *What the hell is wrong with this guy?*

I stare at Thomas in complete shock at the venom in his voice, my hands still locked firmly on his shoulders. How can someone be this callous toward their own flesh and blood? Whatever happened between them must have been seriously fucked-up. I need to know—I'm desperate to know—and Summer's not sharing. I pull Thomas back from the wall and loosen my grip without letting go, completely ignoring his rant. "You claim she did something to you. So, what happened?"

"I'd rather not—"

I slam him back against the wall and release him again. "What the fuck happened?"

"She stole from my parents and ran away from home." *What?* I stare at him with a raised eyebrow. He can't really expect me to believe that, right?

He takes a deep breath and huffs out a laugh. "Whatever, man, I don't care if you think that's bullshit. It's the truth. Dad said she used to sneak guys into her room and they'd fight about it. One day, actually it was the day I had the post-game party at my house, your freshman year, remember?"

I nod in acknowledgement, playing it cool while my heart begins to race. It was the only party he ever held at his place. I remember that party, but I don't remember Summer. *Is that why I thought I recognized her the first time I saw her? Have we met before?*

Thomas nods back at me and continues. "Well, something happened that day, and she left. She stole their entire life savings, and instead of disappearing like a normal runaway, she chose to live here and rub it in their faces. She's lucky they didn't press charges. I would have... Hell, I wanted to, but they said to let it go. On top of all that, I have to hear about her going from guy to guy on campus. A constant reminder of what she's done."

I suddenly feel sick. *What does he mean, something happened that day? Did something happen that night with one of my teammates? Did one of them cause the scars?* Nothing he's saying makes sense. The only comment that feels true is the last one, and he just described half the college population. Stealing, really? *How did she steal from them? Did they keep their money in cash? And why would she stay around if she did?*

He pauses for a minute, something else in his eyes other than anger. "She ruined their lives, Dylan. They were happy before, but the money and Summer leaving drove a wedge between them, and she doesn't even care."

Sometime during Thomas's speech, I release my hold on him. If what he's saying is true, then why is Summer the one who's hurting? I can't actually believe he's talking about the same person. It's not possible.

"I know what you're thinking, Dylan, but you're wrong. She's good at showing you a different side of herself. A fake side. I'm sorry she sucked you in; I really am." He cuffs me on the shoulder and then walks away. Like he's doing me a public service by warning me off her. All he's actually doing is making me want to punch him in the face.

There is no way I'm going to believe the bullshit he's spinning until I hear Summer's side of the story. The fact that all his arguments were based on things his parents said happened doesn't sit well with me. Why the fuck wouldn't he ask Summer himself? I need another drink.

As much as I want to talk to her, I know I need to give Summer her space tonight.

En route to the kitchen, a hand grips my shoulder and pulls me back. I'm about to throw a punch, thinking it's Thomas, when Luke's voice filters into my mind. "I'm sorry, man, I overheard, and ah...shit," he says as I turn to face him. The look on his face tells me exactly what he's trying to say.

"You think he's right?" I ask. Of course, all my friends would take Thomas's side over Summer.

"Actually...no." My eyes shoot to his in confusion. "Well, yes...I mean, I think he *thinks* he's right, but I don't think it's the true story. Where were you running off to just now?"

"I need a drink. I can't be here with him while I'm sober."

"He's gone."

Thank fuck for that because Luke's words only make me want to punch Thomas even more. How is it possible he didn't even bother to find out the truth?

Chapter Thirty-Six

Summer

I usually love the silence, but right now, as I lie in bed staring at the ceiling, I need noise. Lots of it. Someone repeatedly hitting a pan with a wooden spoon or blowing a trumpet in my ear. *All of it!* t's going to take a lot to pull me from the thoughts I have running through my head.

As soon as I walked out of Dylan's room earlier tonight, I walked straight to my car and headed home. Obviously, seeing my departure, Cory called and offered to come home, even begged me to open up, but I told her to stay with Nate. That I was fine. I didn't need a babysitter. I just needed to get out of my head. I'm not even sure what I expected was going to happen when Dylan saw my scars. Did I truly believe he *wouldn't* react? That he wouldn't ask questions? *Stupidly, yes.* On reflection, I should have known he'd react that way, but at the time, I raised my guard and prepared to fight.

In that moment with Dylan, I'd wanted him to see every part of me. If only I'd mentally prepared myself for what that would mean. Maybe then I wouldn't have been as defensive as I was.

The feelings I have for him scare the hell out of me. I've never had romantic feelings for anyone. Never felt this way before. The fear that I have, because of that, is stifling. What if I'm not good enough for him? What if I hurt him? What if he hurts me? I want to be able to trust him and trust myself to open up to him; I just need time to do that.

Lying in my bed, with my hands tucked under my cheek, I stare at the door and think about the day Dylan and I first met...officially, anyway. I can still remember the look on his face when his eyes met mine. It was a look I'd dreamed about as a kid. As a ten-year-old girl with her first crush. I saw him from a distance, as we both grew up over the years, but never approached him after that day. I was too embarrassed about what he'd witnessed, not that he even knew who I was.

When I saw Dylan again early this year, I was momentarily shocked. The last time I'd seen him was at my family home, when my brother had his first and only college party. He may have changed, but I would never forget him. I should have left him alone. I should have stayed in my lane, but I had to say hello. That's all I wanted. All I had planned. And yet, here we are. I roll my eyes at myself. *Look how that turned out.*

My phone ringing interrupts my thoughts, and I welcome the distraction. Sitting up, I wipe under my eyes and run my fingers through my hair, as though the caller can see me and will judge me for being such a mess. "Hello?" I say hesitantly, releasing a quick breath.

"Summer?" *Thomas?*

I stiffen as my heart begins to race. *Why is he calling? What could he possibly want after all these years?* I close my eyes and answer. "Yes, this is Summer," I say confidently, pretending I don't recognize his voice.

"I thought I told you, begged you, to stay away from my friends." I grimace as he seethes, not even bothering with any pleasantries. "You've already ruined our family; don't ruin the one I have with the boys too. Dylan deserves better than you. We both know you'll never give up your *lifestyle*, so leave him alone. Leave them all alone. Do the right thing. Don't drag him down with you."

Seriously?! He hasn't spoken to me in four years, and this is what I get? How does he even know?

"My life is none of your business, Thomas. And your so-called *friends* can do what they like. So, you've spoken to Luke or one of the other guys on the team, and they've said what...that I'm *with* Dylan? Well, they're wrong. Even if they were right, it wouldn't matter. It's none. Of. Your. Business."

Putting the phone on speaker, I stare down at it, fuming. Willing it to explode in my hand so I no longer have to listen to this bullshit. I'm so furious I—

"It was Dylan."

Huh?

"Dylan said—"

"Dylan lied," I say, cutting him off. "Whatever he said was a lie." I should listen to what Dylan told him, but I can guess. Something heavy fills my chest, and I place my hand there to calm it. *Dylan. It was Dylan.*

Thomas scoffs. "That's what I thought. Scars...right," he mumbles, as if talking to himself, then, much clearer, he adds, "Just stay out of my life, and I'll keep out of yours. Oh, and stay the *fuck* away from my friends."

With those parting words, he hangs up, and I crumble to the floor. *Scars.* He said scars. *How could he?*

My mind feels foggy, my chest tight. I'm not sure what hurts more—that Dylan betrayed my trust or that Thomas knows about the scars now and still seems to hate me. He's not stupid. If Dylan mentioned a car accident, he'd know I've never been in one and yet...

I lie back on my bed and stare at the roof for hours, or maybe it's only been minutes. Either way, I can't get Dylan's words out of my head. "Do *you really think I'd do that?*" No, I didn't. I trusted you completely.

Chapter Thirty-Seven

Dylan

My eyes are rolling in the back of my head, and I'm seeing double by the time I stumble to the couch around five to settle in for the night. I'm not going to even bother trying to find a way home. I just fall down onto the soft cushions of the couch and tuck my arm under my head for a pillow. I'll definitely regret this in the morning, but right now, it's the best I can do, and at least I didn't knock out my friend.

A soft buzzing noise starts to annoy me as I'm drifting off to sleep. *What the fuck is that?* I swat at my face a few times, but the incessant sound continues. I thrash around on the couch, trying to get comfortable, annoyed that the noise won't stop.

"It's your phone, you nutsack," someone yells from the floor nearby. *Huh? What's my phone doing?*

"It's vibrating. For fucks' sake."

Did I say that out loud? Fuck! Something hard hits me in the head, and I catch it before it falls to the floor. My phone. *My phone!* I check the screen to see that Summer is the one causing all the buzzing. *Well, this is a pleasant surprise.*

"Hey, babe," I slur and cringe. Even in my inebriated state I know that sounded creepy. Clearing my throat, I try again. "Hi, Summer."

"What the fuck, Dylan?" she yells, and I cringe again. This time at the loud noise. Although I'm pretty sure this is just a dream, because Summer never says the word fuck.

"It's not a dream, asshole." *I don't think she says asshole either. Definitely a dream.*

"Are you drunk?" she asks. *I sure am. Fuck, is Summer actually on the phone?* Pulling the phone away from my ear, I stare down at it and try to focus on the screen. I'm ninety percent sure it says Summer, so it's probably real. I run my hand through my hair and then down my face, taking a deep breath.

"Sorry, yes. I've been drinking." That sounded pretty normal. I think.

I hear a sigh and then Summer stays silent for a minute. "Are you there?" I ask, and she sighs again.

"I'm here." She pauses, and it's silent except for the deep breathing of whomever I'm sharing the room with. "This conversation would be better if you were sober."

Ah, what? That doesn't sound promising. I clear my throat again, like that's going to miraculously sober me up. "I'm focused. I'm good." *Focus. Focus. Focus.*

"Thomas called."

Fuck. This just goes from bad to worse. "Okay..."

"You promised you wouldn't say anything. You were hurt when I thought that you might."

Burying my face in my hands, I whisper-yell "fuck" and shake my head. She's right. God, I'm an asshole. "Summer, I'm so sorry. Can I come and see you? I need to see you."

"Just give me some time, okay?"

"What did he say to you? If he hurt you—"

"It wasn't anything he hadn't said before. I'm okay, I just..." *Have trouble trusting people and letting them in and I just fucked up big time.*

"I get it. Take all the time you need."

Summer says good night and hangs up, leaving me staring at a blank screen. I throw my phone against the back of the couch and pull my hair in anger.

"That was brutal," comes from the floor, and I've somehow sobered enough to recognize the voice as our defensive tackle.

"You're not wrong, man." I laugh, but it's coated in sadness. "Not wrong at all."

When I wake the next morning, or afternoon, I can hear Cory and Nate in the kitchen. I'm still fuming from everything that happened last night, and since Summer's already pissed at me, I figure I might as well dig a bigger hole. Entering the kitchen, I find them cleaning up the mess the boys left, something poor Cory's done many times before. *If only you could clean up my life's mess, Cory.* As soon as I meet her eyes, I laugh at nothing and shake my head. "So, tell me, Cory, how old was Summer when she had her car accident again? I forgot."

My question throws her off guard. Her eyes widen, and she looks to Nate for the answer. *I'll give you the hot tip, Cory. He doesn't know.* "She was...ah...God, it was a little while ago...maybe..." Her stumbling doesn't surprise me in the least. Deep down, I was hoping that Cory was in the dark, just as much as the rest of us, but as I suspected, she's not.

"What accident?" Nate asks with a furrowed brow. *That's the million-dollar question, isn't it?*

"Great question, Nate. Who was it?"

"What do you mean?" Cory says innocently as Nate looks between the two of us in confusion.

I take a step forward before stopping myself. "Come on, Cory. You know *exactly* what I mean." Enough is enough. I know Summer has every right to keep secrets from me, but I can't stand the idea of someone hurting her and getting away with it.

"Hey, Dylan. Ease up," Nate warns. I don't blame him for protecting his girlfriend. I would do the same. But I can't drop this.

"Ease up? Ease up!? Tell me, Nate. Would you *ease* up if someone had hurt Cory so badly that she had permanent scars?" I look him in the eyes and watch the color drain from his face as he not only pictures something happening to Cory but also thinks about his mom.

"I...I... What's he talking about?" Nate looks to Cory for answers.

"I'm sorry, I can't." Cory puts her head in her hands and shakes. I feel for her, I do, but this is fucked-up, and they shouldn't be letting the responsible person get away with this.

"Dylan, I think you should ask Summer. It's not really Cory's—" Nate begins, but I cut him off.

"She's protecting him." I probably shouldn't assume it's a *he*, but I don't think I'm wrong.

"Who? Cory?" The question is for me, but Nate's eyes are on her.

"Both of them," I reply. My tone is now a little softer but still has some bite.

When Nate was younger, his mom was attacked by a random guy when she was out one night. She ended up in the hospital, and they never found the guy. Like me, Nate doesn't take abuse lightly. I know he'll be on my side when he has all the facts.

"What the fuck, Cory?" Nate stands up in front of her, looking down. Was I fighting fair? No. Did I care? Also, no. I know on some level it's wrong to cause a fight between them, but the only person I care about right now is Summer.

Cory sobs. "I'm sorry. I'm sorry. I can't."

"Does Logan know? I think I've got his number." I make a show of getting my phone out of my pocket, but it's a bluff. Yes, I know I'm an asshole. But I think this will work. Logan cares for Summer, a lot. There's no way he knows about this. Cory takes the bait.

"No. Wait!" She jumps to her feet and looks at Nate, then back to me and then to the ground, but still, she doesn't speak.

"Cory, I swear to—"

"Her father!" she yells, openly sobbing. "It was her father."

Fuck! I freeze and then we both drop at the same time. Cory into Nate's arms, and me to my knees on the hard floor. With a few simple words, Cory knocked the wind out of me. Literally knocked me off my feet. I'd expected her to say it was an ex-boyfriend or something. I never thought...How could a parent knowingly hurt their child?

My mind flashes back to the one day I've tried hard to forget and the little girl that I don't want to remember. It's so clear in my head that it feels like I'm reliving it every time I think about it. I see the man gripping the girl's arm in a bruising hold and throwing her to the ground. I remember the tight feeling in my chest when he dragged her to the car. Then there's the relief of seeing my father running toward them and the uncertainty of watching the two cars speeding away.

I will never forgive myself for what happened that day. If I'd run faster then maybe she'd be okay. If I'd left her alone and minded my own business, maybe he'd still be alive. I hate that when I think about that day, it's not just my dad's death that upsets me. He should be the *only* one on my mind. I don't even know the girl, and yet, she takes up so much real estate in my mind, the guilt is unbearable at times. Sometimes, I wish I'd never seen her, but then I also wish I could see her again. Just to make sure she's okay.

With my face in my hands, I shake my head and try not to spiral into dark thoughts. It's been nine years, and that day still tears me up inside, to think that anyone could hurt someone like that. I may not have been able to save her, but I sure as hell won't be sitting back when it comes to Summer. *Why was she protecting him? How could her father...How could Thomas...?*

"Thomas..." I pause, unable to bring myself to ask.

"He doesn't know." She answers my silent question, wiping the tears from her eyes.

"Why wouldn't she tell him?" My heart is breaking for her. For Summer. I want to wrap her in my arms and never let her go. Protect her from everything that's bad in this world. I want to kiss her head and tell her...Actually, I don't want any of that. I *need* it.

"She couldn't...Wasn't allowed...Please don't ask me anything else," Cory says, looking broken. "She's never going to trust me again." She breaks down, and Nate gives me a pleading look, causing my chest to tighten. I'm not sorry she told me, but I'm sorry for my behavior. Summer needs her friends, and Cory doesn't deserve the hurt I've caused her.

"I'm sorry, Cory." I get up off the ground and walk over, dropping down beside her. "I really am. I just..."

"You love her," she says between sniffs, the hint of a smile now shining through.

I don't have to think about my answer. It's been screaming at me for days, maybe even weeks or months. I take a deep breath and smile. "Yeah, I do," I admit out loud for the first time. "But that doesn't make—"

"I told her to report it. I tried to help."

I squeeze Cory's arm and smile. "She'll forgive you, Cory," I say, and hope to God that I'm right.

Nate pulls her tighter against his body and kisses her head. "He's right, Little Bit. She'll understand. And Dylan will take the blame. Won't you, Dylan." His eyes meet mine, telling me, not asking. *Little Bit? Never mind.*

"Absolutely. It's my fault. I'm sorry again."

A throat clears behind me, and we all look up to see who's in the doorway. Joel stares at me, looking as wrecked as I feel, and I'm guessing he's been here a while.

"Come on, I'll take you home, or..." he trails off, knowing I can't go home until I've seen her.

"Summer's, please," I say before squeezing Cory's hand and following Joel out the door.

Chapter Thirty-Eight

Summer

W hen I'd hung up from Dylan, I'd stared at the wall in front of me. Unmoving. Defeated. I trusted Dylan. I... My stomach twisted at the thought of Thomas's words—*"he deserves better than you."* That may be true but he wanted *me*. He chose *me*. And then *he* broke *my* trust.

Finally snapping out of it, I lay back on my bed and wiped furiously at my eyes as they filled with tears. *I refuse to cry about this. It's done.*

I spent the next few hours drinking, wallowing in self-pity, and then slept through most of the next day until something roused me at three in the afternoon. Frazzled and confused, the nagging sound starts again, and I realize that someone is beating down my door. *How long has that been going on?* My head throbs when I slowly pull myself out of bed and head toward the entry. The knocks get louder and more frantic the closer I get. "Jesus, I'm coming," I yell. *Did Cory forget her keys?* I open the door, expecting Cory, and jump in surprise when it's not.

Dylan stands before me looking like hell. His clothes are the ones I stripped from him yesterday, and he has dark circles under his eyes. Eyes that are boring into mine. His hair is so messed up, he must have run his hands through it a hundred times. To sum it up, he's broken.

A sharp pain radiates through me as I look into his eyes. I want to slam the door in his face, but the emotion in his gaze stops me. He may not realize it, but he's conveying so much with that one look. Heartbreak, sympathy, pity, concern. They all confirm my own fears. *He knows the truth.*

I open the door wider and gesture for him to enter, closing it behind him. I pause for a second, still facing the door. *Deep breath, Summer. Now turn.* I look up at Dylan's face, ready to speak, but before I can get a word in, he moves toward me and engulfs me in a hug, tucking me into his body. His cheek presses into my head, and his chest rises and falls at a fast pace against my own. We stay like that for a few minutes until Dylan pulls away. "I'm so sorry, Summer. Sorry for what you've been through, sorry that you have shitty parents, sorry that Thomas—"

"You don't need to be sorry. For any of that," I say, cutting him off. "I'm fine."

He stares at me for a moment, maybe trying to figure out how not-fine I really am. "Then I'm sorry I hurt you. It was never my intention, but, Summer...when you're hurting, *I'm hurting*. I needed to know the truth."

"I didn't want you to know!" I say, raising my voice, not ready to forget about him breaking my trust.

"I know," he rasps, and I have to give him some credit because he appears remorseful. He sighs and then runs his hand through his hair once more. "How many times did it happen?"

I could play dumb. We technically haven't discussed how much he knows, but...

"Only twice," I say softly.

"Twice! Only twice? Summer, it shouldn't have happened at all." Dylan starts pacing, giving me flashbacks to the last time I saw him doing that. He was hurting for me then too. *He really does care.*

"Did he hurt you because you stole from him?" he asks, and I wince. For some reason I believed that Dylan wouldn't buy into the rumors, even if they came from Thomas. I hoped he'd see through them, and if I'm being honest, his comment hurts...a lot. I drop to the couch and rest my face in my hands, silently begging for this nightmare to end.

I feel movement in front of me and lift my head to see Dylan crouched down, his hands itching to touch me, but he holds back. "I never believed you'd done that," he says, and I release a held breath, "but Thomas...and then...it's just not adding up. Help me understand, Summer. Please," he begs, and I soften a little at his obvious concern for me.

I sigh and then speak without thinking. "I've never stolen from anyone; my parents gave me that money so that I'd..." *Shit!*

The softness of Dylan's expression hardens in an instant, and I know he's worked out what my comment means. I blush with embarrassment, the heat of it traveling through me, scorching my skin, as my most shameful secret hangs in the air between us.

"Please tell me it wasn't *hush* money?" Dylan whispers, even though he knows the answer. "Please don't tell me your own family *paid* you to keep quiet. And you accepted it?" He stares at me, dumbfounded, but somehow stays calm. Too calm. I want him to yell. It's what I'm used to. I can't handle the raw emotion on his face. The hurt. The pain. For me. It's all too much.

He's right. *Of course*, he's right. This is why I don't deserve him or anyone else. I took money to cover up a crime. What if my father moved on to hurting someone else? That possibility, however unlikely, drifted into my mind from time to time, but I always pushed it back down. I have no excuse except... "I...I had to. I had nothing."

"So, you let him get away with it and just moved on with life?" There's disbelief in his voice, but he still hasn't raised it. He doesn't need to. His words do enough damage.

"Moved on with life? Are you kidding me, Dylan?" I glare. "I will never get over what he did to me. It's ruined me."

"And yet you leave him free to hurt someone else." This time his words feel like a stab to the heart. In a matter of seconds, Dylan has moved from being caring and sympathetic to bitter and cruel.

"You know nothing about the situation—"

"I know that no one deserves to be hurt like you were, and he could be...God, Summer." He shakes his head in disgust.

"You have no idea what I've been through, or how I feel. Of course, I worry about that. But it's unlikely considering it was only ever me that he hurt, and only when he was drunk. Why are you getting so worked up about this? It happened to me, not you—"

"Because I couldn't stop it," he yells, and I freeze.

What?

My gaze bounces from one of his eyes to the other as I try to process what he means. "You didn't even know me," I whisper before breaking our stare.

"I'm not talking about you," he says, his voice a little raspy from yelling. He runs his hands over his face and sighs. "When I was about twelve..." He trails off and drops his head. Realization hits me. Oh. Oh! He remembers? I wait a moment, but he's clearly not going to continue, so I move from the couch to the floor beside him, leaving a space between us.

"What happened?" I ask, desperate to hear his point of view of my strongest memory.

"The short of it is, I saw a man...maybe a father? I don't know. I saw a man forcefully drag a little girl away from our football practice one day. I watched as she was dropped to the ground and then picked up and thrown into a car. I ran. I ran as fast as I could, but I was too far away. Nobody did anything. I yelled, and...I tried to stop it, but...And then my Dad..." The pain in his voice is heartbreaking, bringing tears to my eyes.

Oh, God! My chest tightens, and I feel physically ill. *Has he been holding on to this since he was twelve?*

He stops talking for a moment and just stares at his hands, hands that are balled into fists and pressed into his legs. I know I should say something, but I can't seem to speak, my thoughts whirling as I watch him.

Chapter Thirty-Nine

Dylan

S ummer doesn't say anything at my confession, but I don't blame her. What can you possibly say to that? I only hope that she's not quiet because she's replaying her own abuse in her mind. I didn't set out to hurt her. That's the last thing I wanted to do, but I hate that she's protecting her father. She doesn't seem like someone who cares more about material things and wealth over right and wrong, and yet...maybe I don't know her as well as I think. I want to be there for her. I want to save her like I couldn't save that little girl, like I couldn't save my dad, but maybe she doesn't need saving. Or want it.

I take a deep breath and look up from my hands, realizing that for her to understand my feelings, I need to share the biggest weight on my mind. She notices my gaze and locks eyes with me before taking a deep breath herself. Her expression does nothing to hide her emotions. She's breaking as much as I am. "The worst part is that my father...my dad...he died that day, and it's my fault." Summer gasps, but I continue without acknowledging it. "He followed them because of me. He's dead, Summer. He died because of me, and yet, I still think about the fact that I'll never know if *she's* okay."

I never thought I'd tell anyone that story. I mean, my teammates were there and saw what was going on, but they never made the connection, and we never spoke about it. After my father died, that's all people remembered from that day. I love my dad, more than anything. I shouldn't be thinking about that girl. But I do, every day. I think about her because if that man hadn't hurt her or if I'd just ignored it like everyone else, then my father would still be alive. And I feel so guilty for thinking that, and guilty for sending him after her, and guilty for not being able to help either of them. I'll never know how badly she was hurt, or if she... I don't want to think about it anymore, but I can't get that day out of my mind.

Summer says something, breaking my thoughts, but I don't hear it. She's looking up at me from her position on the floor with tears streaming down her face. Her hand rests on my knee, and she gives it a light squeeze. I hadn't even noticed she'd moved closer.

"Sorry, I didn't hear—"

"She's okay," she repeats while wiping under her eyes. If she's trying to make me feel better, I appreciate it, but it's not working.

I shake my head slightly. "Thank you for saying that, but we don't know—"

"Dylan, she's *okay*." She looks me dead in the eyes, begging me to understand something. "At least, she's trying to be." *Huh?*

I stare back at her in silence, frozen in place, as my mind runs over and over her words. "*She's okay.*" I close my eyes for a second, and when I open them, everything's clear. Instead of seeing the grown woman beside me, I see a little girl with long blonde hair standing on the sidelines, the little girl I couldn't save. *Summer?*

"Summer?" I ask aloud this time.

She nods and smiles as another tear slides down her cheek. I catch it with my finger, and the touch burns me. I'm not sure how I feel about what's just been revealed, so I can't seem to smile back.

We're both quiet for a while until I remember the one thing I always wanted to say to that little girl. "I'm sorry." I leave off my reasons for the apology, because it's not what one would think. If I were to be completely honest, I'd say, "*I'm sorry for not reaching you in time, and I'm sorry for hating you when you did nothing wrong.*"

Summer shakes her head and then crawls into my arms, hugging me tightly before resting her forehead on mine. "You saved me, Dylan. He may have hurt me that day, but after that, it all stopped. The drinking, the anger... At least, until... Point is, you saved me."

I cup her face in my hand and pull her back slightly so I can look into her eyes. "God, Summer. I..."

She laughs, probably thinking I'm just in shock over what she's revealed, and that's part of it. But hell, this is a complete mind fuck. The best I can do is pull her into another hug. So I do. I hold her tight. Breathe in her scent. Feel her warmth. My hands are running up and down her back, like I've done many times before, only this time I'm thinking about what's beneath my fingers, beneath the clothes. Thinking about all that she's been through. I don't think I've ever met a stronger person. My chest fills with something I've never felt before, and *fuck*, I knew I loved her, but this is stronger than that. I really love her. I'm *in* love with her. I never thought I'd be feeling anxious and uncertain when I finally found someone to love, but I do.

I pull back and brush a hair away from her face. "Summer, you will always be the most beautiful, smart, caring, funny...most amazing person I've ever met." But...I'm the one who needs a moment this time. I press my lips to her head, and we both sigh.

I'm so wrapped up in the fact that Summer and the little girl are one and the same that I momentarily forget what that really means. Her father is not only an abusive asshole, but he's the reason my father is dead. I need to get out of here. She can't see me break. She'll blame herself, and she's already been through too much.

I lift Summer up and gently place her down beside me before standing and running a hand through my hair. "I just remembered Joel's downstairs. And he's got his family Thanksgiving tonight. I'm sorry the timing is bad, but I have to go." None of that's a lie. But there's nothing stopping me from staying. That's my choice. "Before I go, I need to say...I think you should tell Thomas."

She nods.

"And forgive Cory for telling me. I kind of forced it out of her."

"I will. Thank you."

I raise an eyebrow in question, and she laughs. "I will. I promise."

"So I'll...ah...see you soon?" I say, gripping the back of my neck. I'm not really sure where we go from here, but "see you soon" seems like a safe goodbye.

Summer smiles softly from her position on the floor but doesn't speak. Her parting wave and sad smile play on repeat in my mind as I walk away.

"How is she?" Joel asks as I jump in the car.

I run a hand down my face, shaking my head. "I'm sorry that took so long—"

"Come on, Dyl. I don't care about that. I thought you'd be longer. And I know I asked how Summer is, but man, you look worse than when you went in. What happened?"

"I...Fuck!" I yell and slam my hand down onto the dash.

Joel looks at me with concern and sympathy in his eyes. "I take it she ended things?" He cringes as the words leave his mouth.

I laugh because that would actually be easier to deal with right now. I know I could change her mind if that were the case. We've got something special, and she knows it. But this, the darkness in my head, is so much worse than that.

Joel's expression turns puzzled as his concern for my feelings morphs into worry for my mental state. "Have to say, you're scaring me a little."

I laugh again and then groan before dropping my face into my hands. Realizing the car hasn't started moving, I quickly look up to Summer's apartment, but I can't see her in the window. I don't even know why I thought she'd be there. "Can we drive, please? I'll explain on the way."

Halfway through my story, Joel pulls over to give me his full attention, and when I finally finish, he stares at me for a good minute before speaking. "You've been carrying that around all this time?"

I nod, suddenly all talked out.

"I wish I'd known; that would have made a great case study for one of my classes."

I punch him in the arm and huff out a laugh.

"In all seriousness, that's a lot for one person to hold on to. You know it's not your fault, right? They said his phone was found near the driver's door, so he was most likely using it. And the other driver said he came out of nowhere..."

Everything he's saying is true, but Dad wouldn't have been there if I hadn't sent him after that girl...after Summer. *Fuck.*

"I can't do this. I'm sorry. Can you drop me home?"

"You're not coming?"

I give him an apologetic grimace, and he smiles sadly in return. "Okay, I'll drop you home."

I'm barely home five minutes when Lucy calls. Fucking Joel...

"Hey, Luce," I say as I drop onto the couch.

"Little Bro, how are you?" *That's a good question. How am I?* I sigh and look to the roof for the answer. When I take too long to respond, Lucy fills the silence. "What's wrong, Dyl?"

"Nothing." I pause. "Everything."

"Okay. I'm going to need details if you want my help, sympathy, or advice."

I laugh but it's definitely forced. "Joel didn't fill you in?"

She half laughs in return and sighs. "No, just sent a text to say I needed to call you."

I exhale loudly into the phone. "Where do I start?"

"Wherever you want. I've got nowhere to be. Take your time."

Resting my face in one hand, I close my eyes and take a deep breath. I still don't really know how I feel or what to think, so I'm struggling with what to say. Lucy knows most of the story, so you'd think it would be easier than telling Joel, but it's not. This story involves her father, too, and I'm not sure how she'll react.

"Do you remember me telling you about the little girl in the parking lot?"

"I do," Lucy says slowly, unsure where I'm going with this.

"It was Summer," I whisper, my fingers drumming restlessly against my thigh as I wait for her to catch up, sort through the memories.

I can almost hear a gasp before she yells, "No freaking way!"

I huff out a laugh, though nothing about this is funny. "Yes way," I confirm.

"So, she's okay. That has to be a relief, right?" She pauses. "I mean, she's okay, right?"

"Far from it, I think, but if you ask her, she'd say yes."

"It wasn't a one-time thing, then?"

"No," I say as a sharp pain rips through my chest. God, I'm an awful person. I just left her there without really talking about it. She's been hurting for so long, and I left. I've been begging her not to run from us, and what do I do...

"Shit!" Lucy says, interrupting my thoughts and hitting the pause button on my downward spiral. "That's horrible. But in a way, you should be happy. You don't have to wonder about her anymore."

I squeeze my eyes shut and run a hand through my hair, preparing myself for what I'm about to say. "I hated that little girl, Luce."

She gasps at my words. "What? Why?"

"Because what I didn't tell you about that girl, that day. What I kept hidden from you was...that all happened the day Dad died. I begged him to stop it, to save her, and he drove after them and died. He died!"

"Oh, Dylan. You can't blame yourself for that. If anything, you and Dad are heroes. I can't believe—"

What? "Why aren't you upset about this?" I ask, now pulling my hair instead of just messing it up.

"Because I knew it was all the same day. I've always known. That's why I always told you it wasn't your fault. Plus, there's nothing we can do to change that day. It's done." *It's* done. Like it's that easy to move on. This has been ripping me apart for years. I can't just forget about it that easily.

I stand and pace the room as a thought comes to mind. "Do you remember where it was?" *I'm definitely spiraling.*

"What?" Lucy says incredulously.

"The accident." *She knows what I mean.*

"Dylan, you need to move on."

I grit my teeth, trying not to yell. "Just tell me, Luce."

I can picture her shaking her head as she sighs. "Over on Everest Street, near the park. Does it really matter?"

"Probably not. I'm just curious. I'm all kinds of messed up over this, Lucy. It was *Summer.*"

"I know." She sighs again. "Come home. I'm still at Mom's. I don't want you being alone right now."

"Thanks, but I'll be fine."

We talk for a bit longer, and then Lucy tries once more to get me to visit her at Mom's, but I have other ideas. I text Nate, hoping that I'm wrong about the thoughts swirling in my head.

Me: What's Thomas's home address again?

My knee bounces up and down as I wait for his response, and as soon as I get it, I grab my keys and dart out the door, his text still fresh in my mind.

Nate: You mean his parents' place? Everest Street. I think it's number 46.

Fuck!

Chapter Forty

Summer

I f I thought my life was a mess *before* Thanksgiving, then it must be catastrophic now. In the space of a few days, I've gone from finally taking a step forward with Dylan, to losing him, with more than I can handle thrown in between.

Watching Dylan leave was hard. Even though I'd been pissed at him when he arrived, I wanted him to stay. I *needed* him to stay. Seeing him like that, so broken, ignited a fierce protectiveness in me. I wanted nothing more than to hold him close and take away his pain, pretending I wasn't the cause of it.

I've never been on the receiving end of someone walking away before, and I gotta say, it's not a great feeling. For so long after he left, I sat on the floor, numb, staring at the doorway. When I finally managed to move to the bed, my current location, I lay down with my arms behind my head and stared at the ceiling instead. Not great progress, but here I am.

The events of the past twenty-four hours have been playing on repeat in my mind. There's so much to unpack and process, and yet, one thing sticks out in my mind—the look on Dylan's face when he mentioned his father. How did I not know his dad died that day? I mean, I was ten at the time, so really, how would I have known? I couldn't even tell you the date of that fateful day. I chose not to keep track of it.

But Dylan...Dylan had the weight of both those things on his mind. It was obvious he held some pretty deep feelings about that day and guilt was high on that list. I wanted to help him; I wanted to say something to ease his pain, but it didn't take long to realize I couldn't do that for him. He had to forgive himself.

When he excused himself to leave, I knew it had nothing to do with Joel. He was breaking. He'd held on to the memory of that little girl for so long, and to discover it was me...I can't even imagine what that would have felt like. Just like I'd asked for space the night before, I knew he needed it now. I could wait. If that's what gets us through this, I'll wait.

Somewhere in the back of my mind, I become aware of someone knocking on the door, but I can't even bring myself to lift my head. It's probably Logan, back from his sleepover with Lucy's friend. Cory will get it. If she's even home. It's hard to believe that Friendsgiving was only yesterday. So much has happened since then. Hell, today's the real Thanksgiving, and I couldn't care less. I don't even know how long I've been lying here. I blindly reach for my phone to check the time when my bedroom door flies open and smashes into the wall, causing me to flinch.

Thomas.

I quickly jump to my feet, nervous to see what he's going to say or do, but he doesn't move. He stands on the threshold, a mix of anger, hurt, and curiosity on his face. His eyes search mine like he's looking for answers. Answers I don't want to give him, but answers I feel he already knows. He looks down at my body, then back up to my face, and I know what he's thinking. He may not have believed Dylan the first time, but I'm guessing they've spoken again.

I don't know why I do it. I should just kick him out, but instead I slowly turn and pull my top up to reveal my back. The soft fabric brushes against my scars. "Happy now?" I snipe.

Thomas remains silent. I don't want to look at him, but I need to know he's still there. I glance back at him as his head drops into his hands, and his shoulders shake. *Is he...?*

"Fuck, Summer, I'm sorry. I'm so sorry. I—"

"Don't. I don't need your apologies. Or your pity. You've seen the truth. You can go back to ignoring me." I'm angry. I don't need *anything* from him.

"Summer, I...Fuck, I don't know what to say if I can't apologize, but I'm not abandoning you again. Are you even okay?"

"Thomas—"

"No, Summer. You can yell, or hit me. Or both. I deserve it. Just don't make me leave. Please. I know I've fucked up, but I'm here now. Please let me fix this. Can I fix this?" His voice breaks.

My heart breaks for the second time today. This is too much for one person to cope with. "I'm sorry," Thomas repeats and then drops his head back into his hands.

A tightness fills my chest as I move back to the bed and sit down, unsure of what to say. Thomas doesn't move for a few seconds, and when he looks up there are definitely tears in his eyes. I want to hate him but I can't. If I force him to leave now then I may never see him again. Taking a deep breath, I pat the bed beside me with a blank expression, my olive branch. Thomas runs a hand down his face, and after a slight hesitation, he sits down.

We're both silent for a moment before Thomas speaks. "God, Summer. I didn't know. I tried to talk to you, the day after, but you wouldn't see me. Cory said It doesn't matter. I should have tried again, tried *harder*."

He's right. He tried once to talk to me. I probably should have spoken to him, but it had just happened. I was scared, and I was homeless. At the time I thought he'd give me more than one shot, and then the money... "I'm sorry for not seeing you that day. I—"

"You have nothing to be sorry about. You were sixteen years old. You're my *sister*. I should have been there for you. I should have seen the signs. Dad was always good to me. He showered me with attention, but you...I knew he gave you less, much less, maybe even nothing. I should have stepped up. You never talked about it. You were always so strong. I guess, I just thought you didn't mind. I'm sorry...I...I'll never forgive myself." His face falls again as he openly cries.

My chest tightens, and a tear runs down my cheek. *When did I start crying?* I wipe my eyes and turn to Thomas, waiting until he looks my way. "You were a kid, too, Thomas—"

"I was nineteen."

"Barely an adult. I don't blame you for anything that happened to me. I just hated that you were gone. That you seemed to believe their story."

"Fuck! I wish I could go back to that time and do everything differently. I'm so sorry. I was selfish and hurt, but there are no excuses. Please tell me we can get through this?"

I shrug and then sigh. "We can only try," I say, offering a half smile through the tears.

He huffs out a laugh and then turns to me suddenly. "You have to tell Mom."

My shoulders drop, and I sigh. God, I wish I didn't have to say this. He's already going to look at Dad differently. I don't want to ruin things with Mom too. But... "I think she knows."

His eyes widen in shock. "She can't know. We didn't know. Dad told us you stole from them; he said—"

"I know what he said, but...do you really think she didn't know?"

"She loves you. I've seen her crying when she doesn't know anyone's looking. She thinks you left. I'm sure of it. Do you really believe she knew?"

"I didn't want to at first, but she never came looking. Thomas, I was right here, and she never came."

Thomas wraps his arm around me and pulls me into his side. "She was hurting. We were both hurting from what you did...what we were told you did," he corrects.

"I'm sorry; I should have tried to talk to you or Mom. I was just so angry at you all. And I couldn't..."

"I know. Nate told me about the money. He called me and told me everything. Said he heard it from Dylan. Guess I should have listened to Dylan when he tried to tell me." *Nate told him? Not Dylan?* "And it was us that should've come to you. You did nothing wrong. Let's go and see Mom. Dad's not home tonight. He's supposed to be meeting me in town for a drink to celebrate my good news," Thomas continues.

I wipe tears from my eyes and look up at Thomas. "What good news?"

"I'm going to be the starting quarterback in the next away game. Our quarterback's wife is having a baby, and things are complicated for her, so he's staying home. I worry for him, but it's good news for me." He shrugs.

A little string pulls at my heart. Despite everything we've been through, I'm so proud of him. "Congratulations, Thomas. That's fantastic news."

"Thanks, Sum." He smiles, but it doesn't meet his eyes. "Are we going home? I mean Mom and Dad's. I suppose it's not home for you now."

I cringe because he's right. It will never feel like home again. "Aren't you going to meet Dad?" I say, hoping for some way to avoid going back there.

"Nah, I'm coming with you. I'll be with you through this. From here on out." *Great.*

The drive over is quiet. Thomas has some techno shit playing softly through the speakers, and I almost laugh at the memories of hating on his music in the past. Thinking about the fun times we had and seeing Thomas beside me is both calming and throwing me at the same time. Either way, it's taking my mind off things. As much as I'm not looking forward to this confrontation, I know that it's unavoidable. At some point, I have to face her. I'll probably have to face Dad too, but let's not get too carried away yet. One step at a time. *Wasn't that step facing Thomas?*

I almost laugh again at my inner thoughts when we pull up at the house and a familiar truck comes into view. *Shit!*

I leap out of the car, not even waiting for it to turn off, and run up the long driveway. I spot Dylan the second the front door comes into view, and I scream out in fear.

"Stop. Get away from him!"

Dad has Dylan pinned to the house with his hands pressed into his shoulders. I know Dylan's stronger, so he must be holding back, but I also know the hurt my father can inflict.

Thomas curses behind me and starts to run. When I reach the front porch, I grip my father's hand and try to pull it away. He lets go easily, throwing me off balance, and then his back hand whips out to smack across my face.

We both freeze in shock before I raise my hand to my cheek. Someone yells, "what the fuck," but I couldn't tell you if it was Dylan or Thomas. What I do register is my mother's gasp. I turn to see her in the doorway as Dylan grabs the back of Dad's shirt and throws him into the wall.

"You told me you'd never hurt her again," Mom says in a quiet voice, barely above a whisper, but it's loud enough.

"You knew?" Thomas says as he leaps onto the porch and takes over from Dylan, pinning Dad against the house. Mom doesn't reply, so he turns his attention to Dad. "Why didn't you ever hit me? Was it because you knew I'd fight back? Was it easier to prey on an innocent girl?" he says, getting right up in his face.

"I had no reason to hurt you," my father replies, seeming perplexed that Thomas would even ask the question.

"And you had a reason to hurt Summer?" he yells, slamming him back a little, his knuckles going white from the tight grip on Dad's shirt. "Really, Dad, she was a teenager for fucks' sake."

"Child," Dylan adds bitterly. "She was a child." *Oh, no!* I wince and try to mentally prepare myself for what's to come.

"The fuck did you say?" Thomas turns his anger to Dylan.

"He hurt her as a child. She was ten," Dylan whispers, looking broken. *Shit!*

Thomas's face falls, and he turns toward me, never releasing his grip on Dad. "Summer?"

I can't talk, so I simply nod and look away. Despite being told over and over that it's not my fault, I'll always be ashamed of the situation.

Thomas roars in anger and pain before slamming our father into the wall again and pressing his forearm against his neck. "What reason could you possibly have for what you did?"

The smallest hint of regret crosses my dad's face as he whispers the words that shock me to the core.

"We never wanted another child. I wanted to focus on you. And your mother—" He speaks directly to Thomas, still acting like I don't exist.

Thomas rears back from Dad and focuses on Mom. "And Mom what? Did you know about this? Condone it?"

At seeing the anger on Thomas's face, my mother sobs. "Of course not, Thomas. I would never—"

"Your mother cheated on me," Dad yells, forcing Mom to stop talking. "Summer could be another guy's kid and yet I was forced to raise her. Chase her around whenever she ran off. I—"

Thomas's eyes shoot to Mom's again, and he visibly swallows. "Is that true?"

She looks to the ground and gives a tiny nod.

My gaze flits between my family in shock. *I was born. He might not be my dad. My mom cheated. I was born.* I never stood a chance. It was all beyond my control. Bile rises in my throat and my stomach churns. I can't watch this anymore. Can't be here anymore. "Enough." I find my voice. "I'm going home." This is too much to process right now.

I turn to walk toward Thomas's and Dylan's trucks, not caring who follows to take me home but hoping at least one of them does. After a few seconds, I hear multiple sets of footsteps and sigh in relief.

"This is all your fault, Summer. It all happened because of your stupid crush on those boys. On him. That was the last straw," my dad calls out, obviously needing to get it all out of his system.

I stop and turn around to see him pointing at Dylan. He must be feeling more confident now that Dylan's stepped away. He looks me dead in the eye as he speaks. "You embarrassed our family by sneaking out and drooling over them. You always rebelled and I had to deal with it, time and time again. I'd had enough. And don't tell me you were there because you wanted to play; come on, you can't expect me to believe that. You were always nothing but trouble."

"Are you serious right now?" Thomas asks, his face full of disbelief. "She *was* watching the game because she wanted to play. We talked about it. She wanted to watch so she could learn the game. So she could play with us, with *you*. She just wanted your attention. Why would you think she was there for Dylan? She was ten, for fucks' sake."

"Then why didn't she watch *you* train, Thomas? Ever think of that? If she wanted to learn, she could have watched *you*."

"She—"

"She's a tramp, just like her mother. Sneaking out and making me find her all the time..."

He says the last part almost to himself and looks at me in disgust, causing me to flinch. *God, he's irrational. I was a kid. And he's wrong. I had wanted to play. I wanted to bond with him. At least in the beginning.*

Thomas begins to speak, but Dad cuts him off again. "And then you," he yells, turning his attention to Dylan, "you had to send your dad after me. You both ruined my life."

"How?" Dylan yells and I turn to look at him, seeing his face redden in anger. "You beat Summer. My dad *died*. How the fuck did *we* ruin *your* life?"

"Because I watched him die!" *What?* "He was my idol, and I watched him die. The guilt ate me up inside." *Jesus.*

Dylan's jaw drops, and he starts moving toward my dad with a menacing gaze. "Did you cause the accident? Was it your fault?" he yells as his pace increases.

Thomas grabs him at the last second. "It's not worth it. He's not worth it. Hurting him won't change a thing." Thomas then turns to Dad. "But you better answer him, or it won't be Dylan you have to worry about."

"I didn't. I..."

"He just told him to leave, chased him off our property. That's all," Mom adds, defending Dad and confirming she knew *everything* all along.

I stare at Dylan in shock. Despite what they're both saying, I'm sure my dad had a hand in the accident, even if not directly.

Dylan stands behind Thomas. He's looking up to the sky and gripping his face in obvious anguish. I want to move toward him, but I'm frozen in place.

"If all this is true, why the fuck did you hurt Summer again and kick her out at sixteen?" Thomas says, and until this point, the thought had never occurred to me. After the first incident, which we now have a reason for, Dad sobered up. So while our relationship never improved, I'd at least been living without fear. Then when I was sixteen, Thomas brought his college friends over, and everything changed. I hadn't even realized he'd seen me watching them. But was that it?

Dylan's eyes snap to mine and then Dad's, and then he lets out a string of curses I'd rather not repeat. *What's going on?*

He drops to the ground with his face in his hands.

"Oh, fuck." Thomas curses before crouching beside him, gripping his shoulder. "Don't. Don't blame yourself. She won't."

"What the hell am I missing?" I question, but it's loud enough for them to hear.

Dylan looks up at me with bloodshot eyes. "I was at the party, Summer." *And?* "He beat you because of me. Because of the guilt over my dad." *Oh, hell.* My heart breaks for him, not me, *him* as I stare into his shattered, soulful eyes. None of this is his fault. I'm even starting to realize none of this is my fault either. Seems we were all holding on to something from that dreadful day.

I ignore my mother and father and walk over to Dylan and Thomas. I drop beside Dylan and frame his face with my hands. "This isn't your fault. The only person to blame for all of this is my father. I'm sorry for his part in your father's death. I'm sorry for the guilt you hold over the day you saw him hurting me, and I'm sorry for the extra guilt that I know you've now added to the pile."

I rest my forehead against his and block out the world around us. "Dylan, when you hurt, *I hurt*," I say, repeating the words he once said to me, because they're one hundred percent true. That's when it hits me. *God, how did I not see it sooner?* How did it take so long to figure out that *Dylan is my person.* He's the one. He's my everything. "*I'm falling—*"

"Don't. Please," he says, cutting me off. I hadn't even realized I'd said those words out loud. *Was I about to say I was falling in love with him? Am I?*

I feel a warmth spread up from my chest until it hits my face, and I'm thankful it's now dark, so no one can see me blush with embarrassment.

Dylan lifts my face up with his thumb and looks into my eyes. His eyes hold so much pain that I want to look away. "Not here, not now," he pleads.

I give a small nod and then stand to my feet, brushing myself off. Dylan and Thomas stand too, and the three of us head toward the trucks. We've barely made it halfway down the driveway when my mother's sobs ring out in the silence. "Thomas, baby, wait. Don't go. I can't lose you too. Please!"

My heart breaks even more, something I didn't think was possible. Hearing my mother's cries for my brother and the love and fear in her voice is too much. My knees buckle, and I start to fall, but Thomas catches me, holding me up. *Why couldn't she have cared for me like that? How could her heart be so full of love for her son and hold nothing for her daughter? And why?*

"We're done," Thomas yells back, holding me tightly.

I shake my head furiously. "Thomas, no."

"Thomas!" Mom yells again, stopping me from saying more. "Please, just come back. Thomas!" She continues to call his name as we walk farther away. When we're almost at the trucks, her desperate tone changes into one of anger.

"Summer, this is all your fault. I hope you know what you've done."

Thomas's strong arms wrap around me as I start to shake. "I'm so sorry," he whispers. "They will never hurt you again."

Turning me around, Thomas pulls me into a hug, and it's then that I notice Dylan standing right behind us, his expression doing nothing to hide his emotions. I never thought this mess would affect others so badly. All I ever wanted to do was forget that chapter in my life and move on. I can't be the reason for Dylan's hurt, or for Thomas to lose his family.

"Thomas, I appreciate all you've done tonight, but you can't cut ties with them. They've been good to you—"

"The hell I can't." Thomas cuts me off with an angry glare. "They're both dead to me."

"Thomas—"

"No, Summer, I know I've got a long way to go before I earn back your trust, but I need you to know...I would never condone this. Despite the fact that it could have just as easily been me, they hurt my baby sister. Their lies made *me* hurt my baby sister. I will never forgive them for that. I will never forgive myself for that either."

He pulls me into another hug and then moves to open the passenger door of his truck, not letting me respond. "Let's get you home."

"Mind if I have a word with Summer first?" Dylan asks, speaking for the first time since we got up off the ground.

Thomas's eyes find mine in question, and I give him a small nod. "Okay, but we're going to have a chat about the 'no dating my sister' rule," he jokes, and I flinch, not sure where Dylan and I stand.

Dylan smiles, but it's missing its usual warmth. My heart clenches at the sight of it.

Without noticing the tension in the air, Thomas gives me a kiss on the cheek and then heads to the driver's side. "I'll be in the truck."

I step away, out of earshot, and wait for Dylan to follow. He takes a deep breath when he reaches me and then speaks. "I'm so sorry for everything you went through. For my part in it, for your shitty parents, and the even shittier hand you were dealt."

Instead of highlighting that he had nothing to be sorry for, I simply say, "thank you," and nod.

"I want you to know that I'll always care for you, Summer. I'll always be your best friend."

Oh God!

My heart beats rapidly in my chest, and I can't bring myself to look at him. I knew that something was seriously wrong when he stopped my earlier confession. This feels like goodbye, and I'm not at all ready for that.

"I'm sorry, Summer. I—"

"It's okay. I get it."

"I just need time. That's all."

"I understand." I pause and take a breath. "Friends until we both work things out," I say, and I mean it. He's given me so much time in the past that I need to return the favor. I could say something more or try to change his mind. I could even ask him how much time he thought he might need. But I don't do any of that. Instead, I do what I do best, what he expects me to always do—I walk away.

"I'll see you around," I say as I move to get in Thomas's truck. "Thanks for...everything, I guess." I shrug and then slam the door shut. When I look back through the windows, I catch Dylan running his hands down his face before violently pulling on his hair.

Thomas and I are silent on the way home, leaving me to my thoughts. The farther we drive away from the place I grew up, and from Dylan, the more my heart breaks, and by the time I've made it to my apartment building, I'm not sure I have anything left.

When we pull up, Thomas offers to come inside but I decline. I need to be alone. I move to leave, but he stops me with a gentle touch to my arm. "I love you, Summer. I'm sorry that I haven't acted like it for a while. I was angry. I wanted to hate you, but I always loved you."

I smile at that, not entirely sure how I feel. I know I love him, but I'm not ready to believe that anyone truly loves me just yet. We will get there, though; of that, I'm sure.

"Can we talk tomorrow?" he asks, still so unsure of our relationship.

"I'd love that," I say honestly and then wave as I leave.

Chapter Forty-One

Dylan

Lying back on the grass, I stare up at the clouds and let my mind drift. I should be focused on my future, but like always, my thoughts land on Summer. It's been a month since the last time I locked eyes on her. A *fucking month*. I always thought if we ended up in this situation it would be Summer's doing not mine. I was wrong. So, so wrong. This is all on me.

When Summer's dad hinted that he'd hurt her…no, hurt isn't a strong enough word. That he'd physically assaulted her to the point of scars, because he'd seen me at his house. It broke something inside me. And I don't just mean my heart. Something flipped a switch in my brain, and all I saw was darkness. I'd been holding on to so much guilt already, and that…that tipped me over the edge.

I wanted to be with Summer. I *want* to be with Summer. But right now, I'm struggling to find my way back to her.

After watching her drive away with Thomas, I had to force myself to get in my truck and not go back and beat the shit out of her dad. I tossed and turned all night between my worry for her and the fog that was taking up space in my mind. As soon as the sun came up, I sent her a message.

Dylan: I meant what I said last night. Summer, I will always be here for you, if you need me. I know you're a strong, independent woman, but even the strongest need someone in their corner. I'm sorry that I'm messed up. You deserve the world and right now I can't give it to you. I hope you understand.

And from there I messaged almost daily to check in. Just because I needed time to sort out my shit didn't mean I wasn't thinking about her and desperate for any kind of connection. Summer's replies were fast and detailed in the beginning, but the last few messages had been short or single words—until today. Today, Summer's texts were long and exactly what I needed. On a day when I'm struggling, she reached out.

Summer: I couldn't let today pass without touching base. Right now, you are probably going through an internal battle with advice coming at you from all directions. So here's mine—shut it out, all of it. Only you know what you want for your future. If playing makes you happy then go for it, but if that's not where your heart lies, then that's okay too. No matter what you decide, you have nothing to be guilty about. Whatever you choose IS the right choice.

Summer: And for what it's worth. You're a helluva football player, but I have no doubt you'll market the shit out of the sports industry too. If that's still the plan.

The more I think about Summer, the more I hate myself for reducing our relationship to solely text messages. But I hold out hope that I can still fix us, once I fix myself. I know Joel speaks to her on occasion, but he never mentions it to me, and while I still visit the Ball House, there isn't much chance of running into her since Nate and Cory broke up before Christmas. Something a friend would have asked about. Guess I'm not even good at that anymore either.

With my eyes closed and arms locked behind my head, a feeling of déjà vu hits, and I'm overcome with sadness. Summer's right; I do have a big decision to make, but I can't get her out of my head long enough to think it through.

The reason this has all come up now is because a local radio station caught wind of the fact that a few teams have shown interest in me, and I've been hesitant. That led to a few news outlets approaching me for a comment, and now I'm here, lying on the football field, trying to decide my future. No one would care if my father hadn't been the great player he was. But not much I can change about that. I met with Coach earlier to talk through my options, and while I technically don't have to declare anything, he seems to think I need to make my intentions clear, now that they're in question.

I was prepared to walk away. If they'd asked me last year, I would have said I was hesitant because I wasn't interested, but now... God, I have no idea. After everything happened with Summer, I kind of lost myself in football. It became my savior. The only time I felt alive was when I was on the field. When the season ended, I was lost again, and for the past week I've been a wreck. And now, New Year's Eve, a time I should be celebrating, I can't seem to get past the guilt I feel, and every time I think about Summer, I spiral even more. I want to see her, be with her, but I can't. She deserves someone who's whole, and I'm barely a fragment of my former self.

A whistle sounds somewhere to my left, and I turn to see a few of our school's cheerleaders run onto the field, possibly trying to sneak in an extra practice. Jumping to my feet, I pick up my ball before heading to the coaches' offices. *Guess my thinking time is up.* When I reach the head coach's room, I knock my knuckles against the door and then enter before awaiting a reply. His head rises, and he gives me a questioning look.

"Okay, I'm ready to talk," I say and then plop down on the seat in front of him.

When the evening rolls around, the boys drag me to Reilly's Place for a typical booze fest. I haven't been able to bring myself to drink since the night Summer confessed about her dad. Every time I so much as smell alcohol, I think of a ten-year-old Summer being hit by her drunk old man. Actually, it's probably safe to say *everything* reminds me of Summer these days. I can't seem to escape it. So, *why the fuck can't I sort myself out?*

The night plays out around me, and I do my best to act as a happy participant. I smile and nod during stories, I laugh at obvious jokes, I even buy a round of beer, but mentally, I'm checked out.

When talking gets too much, I head to the bar to drown my sorrows in water and proceed to spiral even further. I do want to snap out of this but can't for the life of me figure out what to do. The look on Summer's face when she tried to comfort me that night flashes into my mind. Her dad abused her because of *me*, and she thinks *I'm* the one who needs support.

Even in that moment of pain, I remember thinking about how beautiful she was. With her hands framing my face and her stunning green eyes wide with worry, pleading with me to understand, I wanted to be able to wrap her in my arms, forget about our trouble and kiss her tears away. Then she got that adorable startled look on her face as she was lost in thought, mumbling that she was falling... *Summer was falling in love with me and I cut her off. God, what the fuck is wrong with me?*

I knew loving her was going to be dangerous; it was a big risk to my heart, a risk I was willing to take. I'd prepared myself for Summer to run, and I was ready to fight for her. For us. I never once thought *I'd* be the one causing *her* pain.

I impulsively pull my phone from my pocket and send her a text. It's wrong on so many levels because nothing's changed, but I need her to know.

Dylan: I miss you.

A couple of hours later she still hasn't replied. It's the longest I've ever had to wait. Even if I can fix this mess, maybe I'm too late. *Am I? Have I ruined everything? Of course, I have, it's been a month.*

"I saw Summer yesterday," Joel says, joining me at the bar and catching me off guard.

"Oh...uh...how is she?" It's the first time he's mentioned her in a few weeks. I told him I couldn't hear about her. That I needed time, and he actually respected that—at least he had until now. Talk about timing.

"She looks like shit if I'm being honest, but as always, she says she's fine."

I don't know what to say so I just nod. Joel shakes his head at me. "Something she said confused me, and I need you to clear it up."

"Okay..."

"She seems to be under the impression that it's you avoiding her, not the other way around."

Shit!

"But that's not the impression *you* gave *me*. She's a mess, Dylan. A *mess*. Anyone would think she was in love with you by the heartbreak written all over her face, but..."

Joel stops mid-sentence when he notices me flinch. *Dammit.*

"What?" he asks, raising an eyebrow. I shake my head, about to tell him nothing, when he raises a hand in my face. "Don't bother bullshitting me. You've been keeping me in the dark for too long. What was that look about?"

I sigh and run a hand through my hair. I haven't been keeping this from him because I don't trust him with it, I've just been trying to avoid spiraling even further. Talking aloud makes everything more real, so it's been easier to keep my mouth shut.

He takes a sip of his beer as he waits for me to answer. I don't want to tell him, but I also do. Gripping the back of my neck, I stare down at my shoes "I think..."—*I know*—"Summer was trying to tell me she was falling for me that night at her dad's, but I cut her off."

He chokes on his drink and coughs for a second, shaking his head in disbelief. "Um, what?"

"You heard me." I shrug, like that piece of information isn't eating me up inside.

"Fuck! Poor Summer. Serial dater Dylan strikes again."

My eyes widen in shock, which quickly turns to anger. "What the fuck, Joel? You know that's not what this is."

"It's not? Then why aren't you together? If she's falling in love with you, and you love her...why aren't you together, right now?" A heavy lump forms in my throat, and I feel a bit sick. I'm going to assume that the bitter tone in his voice has everything to do with seeing Summer. He doesn't generally get this worked up over my issues, and he's become quite protective of her. What he doesn't understand is that so I am I. I would do anything to keep her from more harm.

"I'm doing it for her," I say through gritted teeth. "She knows I still care; *we message*. But, I'm messed up. I'm lost. I feel so guilty for everything that happened to her that I can barely sleep. She doesn't need me dragging her down into this deep ocean of pain."

Joel rolls his eyes as though I'm talking shit. "Very poetic. But don't you think that's exactly what she's been telling herself about you for your entire friendship. From the first time I saw you together, I knew there was a spark. Hell, everyone could see it, even you. Summer's been fighting it this whole time, trying to not only protect her heart, but to also protect you. From what? I don't know. But someone, probably her father, put it into her head that she wasn't worthy, and she didn't want you caught up in that."

I open my mouth to argue, but Joel starts shaking his head.

"I'm not finished. When she finally opens up and lets herself not only accept love, but feel it...you ran. *You* fuckin' ran. So, you shouldn't be asking *me* 'what the fuck?' You should be turning that question on yourself. And you've been messaging...Who cares? You need to talk to her."

I stare at him in silence, because fuck, he's right. I panicked when she started to say she was falling for me. I thought it was because I wanted to clear my head before hearing those words. He's right; I should have talked to her instead of messages. *Fuck, am I a commitment phobe?*

"Yep, you absolutely are. But I thought it was different with Summer," Joel says, breaking into my thoughts. *I've really gotta stop saying them out loud.*

"Why have you waited until now to tell me all of this?"

"Because I thought she was avoiding you, too, and I kinda hoped you'd get there on your own."

Fuck! What have I done? I need to fix this. Without pausing for another word, I push off from the bar and hear my stool crash to the floor as I leave Joel shocked behind me. I sprint toward the front door, pushing my way through the crowd, accidentally elbowing a few people in the process, but all I can think about is getting to Summer. Only a little bit farther. *Almost free.* I pull out my phone as I step into the hallway, not even caring to look up as I start dialing for a cab, and run smack into the most beautiful woman I've ever seen. She's breathtaking, even in her flustered state. I grip her elbow to balance her just as she looks up to meet my eyes. I watch as recognition registers and her face shatters. *I fucked up. I really fucked up. But I can't lose her.*

My heart beats out of my chest, and there's no doubt in my mind that it's love. *I love her.* I've been so stupid. She brushes a loose strand of hair behind her ear and takes a step back. "I'm sorry, I was just..." she trails off and looks behind her, like she's going to run.

So many things fly through my mind simultaneously as I watch the heartbreak on her face. I've lost my chance. She's it. She's all that matters and I've lost my chance. I can see it in her eyes. But I have to try.

"Please, wait."

Chapter Forty-Two

Summer

Dylan: I miss you.

I miss you. I stare down at the message and then exit from the screen so I don't reply. I can't do this anymore. I'm stronger than that. While he's kept his promise of being a friend, albeit through messages, I can't sit around and hope that things are going to change. The last couple of weeks have been hell for me. I've been going through the motions, *existing*, while inside I'm falling apart because *I freaking miss you too, Dylan*. But I need to move on.

Ugh! I have no idea what happened. What went wrong. Okay, so I know *a lot* of things went wrong. Some might even say we both have too much baggage to ever make it work, and maybe they're right. But, Dylan *never* said it was the end. He said he needed time. I gave him time but enough is enough. Even after keeping my last few messages curt, he still hasn't called me or given me anything to suggest he wants more than a friendship.

I'm hurt, and I'm angry. I trusted him. I opened up my heart to him, after he practically begged me to, and then he walked away. *He* walked away.

I had held out hope for the first few days, especially after his first few caring messages. Obviously stupid and naive when it came to love. I even started thinking about what our future might look like, not marriage and babies, but next year, after graduation, even a few years from now. Like I said, stupid and naive. I knew loving someone gave them the power to hurt you. I'd experienced it. So why would I put myself through that again?

I probably should have called him out, rather than just diminishing my replies, but is it wrong to want him to approach me? I deserve that. And just because I went and fell in love with him doesn't mean I can't be strong and cut ties when it's needed. Even thinking those words sounds strange. *I love him. Ugh!* It's because of that I can't seem to hate him, even if I want to.

If it wasn't for the news breaking today about Dylan's football career, I never would have contacted him. I'm done. But, I knew he'd be struggling. I warned myself to leave him be. Reminded myself that I'm the one who would wind up hurt again. But did I listen? Nope. I sent him a text to help him through and then decided that was it. That would be my last communication with him until he got his head out of his ass. *I miss you. Pfft. Whatever.* I need action.

As soon as it hits eight thirty, I jump up and start getting ready for bed. Eight thirty seems like an acceptable time, and I would rather be snuggled with my blanket in bed than lost in my thoughts elsewhere. I've spent a few nights in a daze, and despite it being New Year's Eve, I can't bring myself to leave the apartment. I'm a mess.

I've just finished brushing my teeth when Cory texts.

Cory: I need you.

She better not mean now. Ugh! I know she does. God, I hope she just needs a ride.

Cory: Nate's here.

Shit! Nate and Cory broke up just before Christmas. It's safe to say the two of us have not been fun to be around. In the last week there's been a lot of movies watched, tears cried—over said movies of course—and a hell of a lot of Ice cream consumed. We've both been a little crazy, but at least we've had each other.

Cory finally decided to leave the house to socialize tonight, for New Year's. She was determined to try and move on, but I guess that backfired completely.

I move around the room collecting things that I'll need, because we both know I'm going to help her no matter what she says or where she is. I pick up a pair of sweats and raise them to my nose. *Clean, perfect. Surely, I'm only picking her up...*

Summer: Where are you?

Cory: Reilly's

I mentally facepalm and shake my head. Well shit, of course, Nate's there. She had to have guessed he would be. They go there every weekend.

I grab my jeans instead of sweats and quickly put them on, even though I'm not too keen on leaving the car. I'm just pulling a clean tank top over my head when she texts again.

Cory: Dylan's here too. He's miserable without you.

"*Fuck!*" I cover my mouth in shock at my curse and sigh, because honestly, it's not helpful at all to know that. In fact, now that I've made my decision to move on I'd prefer to be kept in the dark for all things Dylan.

Me: Cory, we've talked about this...

Cory: He can't stop staring at his phone. Has he messaged you?

My heart picks up a little, but I'm not sure if it's left over from my anger or because Dylan might be upset. Why couldn't he have called me? *Would I have answered it? I can't say for sure.*

It would be easier to lie to Cory. Pretend I don't know what she's talking about, but I don't.

Me: Yes, he messaged.

Cory: Did you reply?

Me: No

Cory: Why not?

Good question, Cory. Why not? Maybe because he's an asshole, and I may not be perfect, or even close to it, but I deserve better.

Me: He misses me

I choose to ignore her question.

Cory: And you miss him. So, what's the problem?

Me: It's complicated.

Cory: Summer, you should see his face.

Me: I can't. I need to get over him. I don't want to keep feeling this way.

Cory: Please just meet me here. Maybe you'll feel differently when you see him. If not, it's crowded. He won't even know you're here. And I need you.

An hour later, I'm dressed, my hair's neatly styled, and I'm wearing makeup for the first time in weeks. I spot Dylan as soon as I walk in, but Cory's right; I could easily go unnoticed in this crowd.

Nate and Cory sneak a few glances at each other, and an idea forms to lock them in a room together to sort out their shit. Maybe then she'll let me leave. Having said that, they're not the only ones sneaking looks. I'm guilty of that. Dylan hasn't left the bar since I arrived. He has a revolving door of guests keeping him company but has never once engaged someone first. *Is Cory right? Is he miserable?*

My heart sweeps with emotion but cracks at the same time. I can't do this. I need a minute. I need to stare at myself in the mirror and remind myself that I'm okay. I've never needed a man before, and I don't need one now.

I walk casually through the bar, picking up speed when I'm in the hallway, but then decide I don't want to be here. At all. I don't need air. I need to leave. I turn back at the last second to talk to Cory and run straight into a hard chest. The impact hurts, and it takes a second to get my bearings. I smell him right away but hope that I'm wrong. His hand steadies me as I look up into his eyes. Dylan. *Shit! I'm not...I can't...* My head is a mess.

"I'm sorry, I was just..." *What?* I don't even know how to finish that sentence.

I look over my shoulder, fully prepared to walk away.

"Please, wait," Dylan begs. He reaches out to touch me but seems to reconsider when I glare back.

"What do you want, Dylan? I can't be your friend right now. I'm leaving."

He cringes and runs his hand down his face. "Fuck! I messed up, Summer. I know that. I'm not here as your friend. I'm..." He trails off and grips his neck. "I'm sorry, Summer. So fuckin' sorry."

I swallow a lump in my throat. This is what I wanted, isn't it? For him to step up. For action. I sigh before looking toward the exit and then back into the bar. I've got several ways to escape, but something keeps me in place.

"Please," he begs again and this time it's desperate. I can hear the panic in his voice. I look into his eyes and break at the pain I see there. He's trying. It's what I wanted. Giving him a small nod, I cross my arms over my chest and wait.

"I know this has taken me too long, and you have every right to be upset, but please hear me out." He looks around the hallway, noticing, as I do, that we've drawn a crowd.

Lightly grabbing my hand, he walks down the hall toward a storage room and pulls me inside. When the light flicks on, he cringes at the mess surrounding us. "Sorry, I wanted privacy."

I shrug, because, let's face it, the mess is fitting for our current situation.

Dylan sighs and runs a hand through his hair and then down his face. "I fucked up, Summer. I have no excuse, except that, apparently, I'm a commitment phobe in denial," he says with a sigh, shaking his head. "I'm thinking it stems from losing my dad and not wanting to lose someone else I love."

Okay. My eyebrows scrunch in confusion, but I remain silent. *Surely that's not all he has to say.*

"I have the tendency to hold on to issues, letting them fester and take over my thoughts, rather than allowing myself to work through them. I blamed that little girl, *you*, for taking up space in my mind that should have been reserved for my dad. I blamed myself for what might have happened to you, *and* I blamed myself for Dad's death. Then to find out you have those scars, because of me..." His voice wavers, and his eyes close in obvious pain.

I know what he's trying to say, because I do the same thing. I internalize rather than sharing the load, and as a result, I never work through my issues. The two of us make one helluva train wreck. Is it even possible to move past this? I want to. I really do, but...

Dylan sighs again and looks to the roof for a moment. When he looks back, he has a soft smile. "Remember when you stupidly tried to jump in a lake in the middle of the night, and I saved you?" Dylan says, completely off topic. *What?* I stare at him in confusion and shake my head. Not because I don't remember, but because I don't know where he's going with this.

"What about the night we spent an hour talking about the movie *Ghost* only to discover I was picturing the movie *Casper?*" *I won't be forgetting that anytime soon. It had me laughing for hours.*

"Or, how about that time we threatened to soak Luke's bed in beer if he outed you as a Backstreet Boys fan?" *Yep, he still decided to share that little tidbit.*

I know what Dylan's trying to do, and it's sweet, but...

He raises his hand to tell me to wait, sensing my reaction. "I remember *every* moment we've shared and even the ones we faked. I'm so sorry for the way I've treated you since Thanksgiving. You deserve so much more than a text message friendship.

"Summer, you've been my best friend since we were kids..." He pauses for a laugh, and he gets one, albeit small.

He smiles in return and continues. "Summer, we may have begun our friendship as a game, but everything I feel for you is one hundred percent real. I can't stop thinking about you. I want to be around you all the time. To hear you laugh, to see you smile, to kiss you... Point is, I'm sorry. I'm sorry I made you think that I didn't want that when I did...I do...so much. I'm sorry I ran. I don't have an excuse for my behavior, but I can promise that it will *never* happen again." He finishes and then shakes his head. We both stare at each other, and when I don't speak, his face falls, and his Adam's apple bobs. "Please, say something. *Anything*."

I don't know what to say. I've missed him and the way he makes me feel. But he walked away, he broke me when I thought I was already beyond repair. I know I'm not blameless; I haven't exactly been perfect. After all, my issues kept us apart for months. We've both made mistakes and both have a lot to work through. Can we really come back from everything we've been through, both together and separately? Right now, it doesn't feel like something we can get past. But God, I want it to.

Dylan steps forward and wipes his thumbs under my eyes. It's only when they come away wet that I realize I'm crying. He gently kisses my forehead and then takes a step back, a look of absolute devastation crossing his face. "I'm too late, aren't I?" he rasps.

My heart cracks in two, and I'm pulled from my own torment. I can't bear to see him like that...ever. His question put everything into perspective. The thought of never being with Dylan again pains me. I can't imagine not being able to kiss him or touch him. So is he too late? No. He's not. And if he's not too late, then why delay the inevitable?

I'm marginally aware that I should be saying something, but all I can think about is if I should put everything aside and kiss him. Dylan's eyes search mine for answers, and when I bite my lip, he groans and clenches his hands by his sides. He stares at me for a few more seconds and then shakes his head. "Fuck it," he says, and before I have a chance to question what he means, his hands cup my neck, and his lips meet mine in a scorching kiss.

Chapter Forty-Three

Dylan

I pour everything I have into this kiss. I'm not sure if it's goodbye or I've missed you too. Whatever it is, I need to make it unforgettable.

Summer moans the second our lips touch, and the sound vibrates through my entire body. Her hands rest on my waist. She's not pulling me closer but not pushing me away. With one hand still on her jaw, I run the other down her neck, over her breast, to her hip and then back up. When I reach her arm, I follow it down to her hand and then pull it away from my body before linking our fingers. She gasps at the gentle touch, and I slip my tongue into her mouth, deepening the kiss.

I take a step back, remembering there's a wall behind me, and pull Summer's body flush to mine. This is the moment. If she wants me, now is when she'll make it clear. She hikes up her leg and wraps it around my waist, strengthening our connection, and moves her spare hand into my hair. *Thank fuck!* I groan and pull my mouth from hers. "Please tell me I'm not too late?" I beg. I need to hear the words.

She shakes her head and pulls me back into her, sucking my bottom lip into her mouth. It's not exactly an answer, so I break the kiss again and prepare to lay everything on the line.

Raising our linked fingers to my lips, I hold them there and look into her eyes. The most beautiful eyes I've ever seen, eyes that I want to see every day, eyes that I want my children to have. *Fuck!* This is my last shot. "Summer, I need you to tell me we're going to be okay. I need to hear the words because I'm so in love with you that I can't bear to stay in any kind of limbo."

She stares at me in shock, but I continue. "I know it might take time to trust me again, to trust in us. But I need to know you haven't given up. That I have a shot. Please, Summer, I love you."

She blinks a few times, and a lone tear runs down her cheek. "But, you can't..." Her words trail off as she drops her chin to her chest. The look on her face as she speaks is heartbreaking. She's not saying "you can't" because she doesn't want me to love her, she's saying that because she truly believes no one could. God, I'm such a fuckup. I should have been showing her *every day* that she deserves love, that she's worthy.

I frame her face with my hands and lock eyes with her. I need to know she's listening, really listening to my next words. "Summer, you are perfect to me. Everything about you is perfect *for* me. When I look at you, I see my future. I'll admit that at first, these intense feelings scared the hell out of me and kept me away, but it didn't change the fact that the feelings are there. I love you. I'm *in* love with you. I should have focused on that instead of everything else we had going on. Because Summer, *nothing else matters*. I love you and—"

"Stop, please." She looks away, refusing to meet my eyes, and my shoulders sink. I'm too late. I thought I'd felt something in our kiss, but maybe I'm wrong. *God, is this the end? Are we done?* I'm so stupid. I should have taken her in my arms at her parents' house and told her how I felt. Actually, I should have let her tell me how she felt when she wanted to. Why did I have to freak out like that? I don't deserve her. She needs someone strong, someone who'll fight for her from the beginning. I know that now, but that information might be useless.

Summer remains quiet while I free-fall into hell. It's clear she's struggling with the right words, so I make it easy for her. "It's okay," I begin, ready to help her end it. "I un—"

She places a finger over my lips to shush me and smiles shyly. "I love you too."

Fuck! My heart stops at her words and then beats again in double time. I've heard those words many times before, but this time it feels like my entire world has shifted, and now everything's in its rightful place.

I smile back at her and grab her face again, kissing her nose, her forehead, her cheeks before ending back at her lips. "God, I love you so much, Summer," I say against her mouth.

She giggles and grips my shirt, deepening our kiss and showing me exactly how she feels.

After checking in with Cory, we walk hand in hand through the bar and out into the cold night. I pull Summer close to me when she shivers and wrap my arm around her neck. We've had moments like this before, but something feels different. It feels real. "Just so you know, I'm going to be calling you my girlfriend now," I say with a smile.

Summer cringes beside me. "Ugh, really? Isn't there something better than that?" she says, and I bite back a laugh.

"Partner?" I ask, trying to remain serious.

"Uh...no."

"Significant other?" I say with a straight face, turning in time to see Summer's reaction, and it's priceless.

She scrunches her nose and shakes her head, unimpressed with my suggestions. I laugh and gently flick her nose. "Unless you're ready to upgrade, then I think—"

Her eyes widen in alarm. "Girlfriend sounds perfect," she says, interrupting me. I knew that would get her across the line.

I laugh. "It does sound perfect, doesn't it?"

She shakes her head and smiles up at me, lighting up her entire face. My heart flutters in my chest as I realize that, for the first time, we're actually on the same page. We still have things to work through, but this beautiful, intelligent, playful, and loving soul is mine, and every part of me is hers.

When we're almost to her car, I squeeze her arm, pulling her close. "Remember that time I carried you honeymoon style all the way home?" I say, because I can't help myself. It's us; it's what we do.

Summer throws her head back and laughs, and fuck, I've missed that beautiful sound. "If you're referring to now, it's not going to happen."

"What about the time we snuck down an alleyway and..." I waggle my eyebrows suggestively.

Summer tries, *unsuccessfully*, to hide her smirk. "Nope," she says, but I can see she's not entirely against the idea. *I'll bank that information for later.*

"Oh, I know!" I say excitedly. "Remember the time..." I've got nothing, but it's fun to see her squirm.

The second we get inside, I pull her into my arms and kiss her with every part of my soul. This kiss isn't like the one in the storeroom. This one is raw, sloppy, and not the direction I want us to go in.

We've only been kissing a minute when Summer reaches down to the button of my jeans and pops it open. It takes everything that I have to pull away and take a step back, but I do. My back presses into the kitchen counter, stopping me from further separation. "I want to take this slow," I say, keeping a close eye on Summer's reaction. Her eyes widen for a second before she seemingly realizes what I mean, and a soft smile plays on her lips.

"We've got plenty of time for *slow*," she says, taking a tentative step toward me. "Right now..." Another step. "I need you." Another step. "Fast." Her final step places her body flush with mine. With my arms on the counter, I lean back in an attempt to create space. She's wrong. We have plenty of time for *fast*.

Summer doesn't relent; instead she leans closer until her lips are only a breath away from mine. She may be suggesting fast, but her movements are slow. She's nervous and dealing with it the only way she knows.

I straighten my body and stand tall before gripping her waist and holding her still. Staring into her bright eyes, I silently beg her to trust me, to trust us.

Her breath quickens, and her eyes search mine before she gives me the tiniest nod. *Yes.*

I slowly reach for her top and lift it up over her head, and her whole body shivers as it drops to the floor. I desperately want to touch her, but that can wait. I undo her jeans and slowly pull them down her legs, feathering kisses as I go. When I stand back up, my breath hitches at the sight of her. God, she's breathtaking. I feel like a deer in headlights as I marvel at the wonder in front of me. I couldn't look away if I wanted to. The blush pink bra she's wearing blends with her smooth porcelain skin, and the black lace panties might be my undoing. I bite my lip to suppress a groan, and Summer giggles, drawing my attention back to her face. The sound relaxes me, knowing she's okay.

She raises an eyebrow, and I shrug. I'm not ashamed of staring. She's beautiful; I'm not going to hide the fact that I want to see her.

Summer grips my shirt in her hands and pulls it over my head as I make light work of my jeans and briefs. I want her to feel comfortable, so I go all in. She bites her lip and then surprises me by turning around and reaching for her bra. Scars and all, she's perfect. Her panties follow the bra to the ground, and she stands before me completely naked, stripped bare in every sense of the word. Her clothes, her heart, her soul, all there for me to see.

Without thinking, I step forward and wrap my arms around her, kissing from her neck, down her spine, kissing each shoulder blade. Sometimes my lips meet her scars, sometimes they don't. Summer remains still without even a flinch, assuring me she's okay. When I reach her ass, I take a gentle bite and then spin her around so my mouth lines up with her core. When I look up at her, her eyes are glassy, but she's smiling, and I can see the heat in her gaze.

Without wasting another second, I slowly run my tongue along her folds and enjoy the feeling of her melting into me. I tease her slowly, and when her breathing increases, and she starts to wriggle against me, I stand up, lift her into my arms, *honeymoon style*, and walk her to my room. Tonight's not about a quick release. I'm going to show her everything that I feel.

I sit down on the bed, and Summer adjusts herself so she's straddling my lap, our bodies as close as physically possible. We stare at each other in silence, our breathing rapid, love in our eyes. I reach for protection and sheath myself before lifting Summer slightly and pushing myself inside her, causing us both to moan at the deep connection.

An intense feeling takes over my chest, and my heart beats harder than it ever has before. This is it. She is it for me. I'm going to marry this girl. Breaking our stare, I lower my lips to hers and make love to the girl I adore more than anything else in the world.

"That was..." Summer sighs midsentence.

"Us," I whisper, finishing for her, still a little out of breath.

"Us," she repeats, and I can hear the smile in her voice.

She's curled up in my arms, head on my chest, mindlessly running the tip of her fingers up and down my abs. Her fingers stop moving, frozen in midair, and it's a few seconds before she speaks. "You've loved me for a while, haven't you?" she asks, without raising her head.

"I have," I answer, my voice coming out a little raspy.

Summer lifts her head and rests her chin on my chest, looking into my eyes. "I'm sorry it took me so long to realize it."

"I should have been clearer. How I felt about you should never have been in question."

She's shaking her head as I speak. "No, I mean, I'm sorry it took me so long to realize I felt the same."

I smile and pull her hand up to my lips, kissing it gently. "You got there in the end."

She scrunches her nose. "Actually, I think I was there somewhere in the middle. I just put up a hell of a fight." She giggles, and the sound of it runs right through me.

I roll, flipping her onto her back to hover above her. "Would you believe me if I said I knew? That I felt it?"

"I would. I may have been blind to some things, but I didn't miss the fact that you have me all figured out."

I have to laugh at that, and I do, loudly. I *wish*. "I don't think I ever had you *figured* out, but I wanted to. From the moment I met you, I desperately wanted to know everything about you. I guess I just paid attention."

She blushes a little and smiles shyly up at me. "Thank you. For seeing me."

"Summer, you're all that I see. God, I love you." My mouth descends on hers, and she moans when our lips meet.

When I pull back to look her in the eyes, the most beautiful and genuine smile lights up her face. "Remember that time we—"

I crash my lips back down to hers without letting her finish. As much as I love our game, it's time we focus on making new memories. Summer wraps her legs around me and pulls my body into her, molding us as one. "I love you," she whispers against my lips, kissing along my jaw. I can't stop the smile from spreading across my face, because I know this is a moment I'll be reminding her of for years to come.

Game. Over.

Epilogue

Dylan – Six Months Later

S ummer's lifting a small box up into the top of the closet when I enter the room. If I wasn't carrying four extremely heavy boxes this would be the perfect time to take advantage of her. Her long, toned legs and perfect ass are screaming to be touched, and it's killing me to know I'm running out of time to do that.

When she turns around, I'm still staring, which isn't easy because I have to peek around the boxes I'm holding.

"If you stare any more intently, I'm going to actually feel it."

"I'm trying to commit it all to memory for when you're gone," I say, while blatantly scanning her body from head to toe.

She shakes her head and laughs. "I'd like to state for the record that it's *you* that's moving away." I groan because she's right. Maybe it's not too late to change my mind. Summer smiles warmly as though reading my mind. "And, we have a pact to see each other every couple of weeks. Denver's not far. It's going to be okay."

My shoulders sag, and I want to pout like a child who's not getting their way, but I can't. This is all my doing.

Summer walks forward and takes the boxes from me, one at a time, before wrapping her arms around me. "I'm going to miss you too."

I kiss her hair and pull her tight against me. "Am I crazy? I'm doing exactly what I said I wasn't going to do. I'm leaving my family for football."

"You're not leaving anyone. Plus, I encouraged it, remember?"

I sigh and shake my head. "Practically forced me into it," I joke. Summer was ready to support me with whatever decision I made and even asked me what she could do to help either way. Not that she accepted any of my ideas, which included moving away with me, moving away with me, *or* moving away with me. All valid options in my mind.

"And I'm in safe hands back here. I'm moving into this great house with an awesome deck and yard, and..."

"The best damn roommate anyone could ask for," Joel says, walking into the room.

"Don't you ever knock? You better knock when Summer's here alone," I say with a stern look on my face, and I'm not kidding. Ever since Summer decided to move in here, Joel's been making my life hell. He's lucky I trust him with my life, and yes, I mean Summer—she's my life.

"Relax, Dyl. I'll wait for her to invite me in before I jump into her bed."

I punch him in the arm without letting go of Summer and feel her laugh against my chest.

"I meant, walk into her room, obviously," Joel says with a smirk. *He's going to be the death of me.*

Summer pulls back and gives me a chaste kiss on the lips. "Okay, I'm going back to my apartment for two more boxes and then I'm done. Don't kill each other while I'm gone," she says as she moves toward the door.

"Want me to come with you?" The thought of being away from her for even a second kills me now that I'm so close to leaving.

Summer smiles sympathetically, completely understanding my feelings. "I was kind of hoping you'd stay and unpack. The sooner that's done, the sooner we can do other things." She winks and heads out to her car.

"Well, that wasn't subtle at all," Joel says, walking up beside me and patting me on the shoulder. "Please wait until I'm gone before you start your goodbye love fest."

I punch him in the arm for a second time before pushing him out of my room. I mean, Summer's room.

Going pro was one of the hardest decisions I've ever made, and though I'll never give him too much credit, knowing Joel's here, with

Summer, and that she has him close by when she needs someone, has made it slightly easier.

Don't get me wrong, I know Summer can handle herself. I will never doubt her again after the numerous arguments we've had over that very topic, arguments she *always* wins. It's just nice to know he's there, just in case. It also doesn't hurt knowing she's in my bed every night. *Her bed! It's now her bed.* I'll never tell her this but, in my mind, she's moving in with me; I'm just not always around to enjoy it.

I finish unpacking the boxes left in my room and make my way out to the kitchen where Joel's making a sandwich. He notices my miserable expression and sighs. "For what it's worth, you made the right call. You're meant to be out on that field. Your dad would be so proud. Hell, I'm proud of you. And Summer...she looks at you like you hung the moon. It's going to be okay. Go do your thing. Let us support you from here and know that everything will be fine."

I smile in thanks before pulling Joel into a hug. I needed that. He's right. Everything's going to be okay. Doesn't mean I'm not going to miss everyone like crazy.

Epilogue Two

Summer – Eighteen Months Later

I t's Thanksgiving again—at least, it was two weeks ago—but since our Friendsgiving is now a yearly tradition, it's better late than never.

Most of the same crew from the previous two years are smiling and laughing around the table, and a couple of new faces have joined our little gang. One of which is staring at me with a raised eyebrow and a smirk. *Thomas.* Our relationship is finally back on track and I'm so happy to have him in my life. He kept his promise to distance himself from our parents, even though I never asked him to, and has only been back once, to question Mom about my father, my *real* father. While she maintains that my dad is my dad, Thomas got the impression she was lying. In fact, he was so convinced of it, he said he'd help me find out the truth. I'm just not sure I'm ready for that yet.

I smile at him and shake my head before he turns his attention to the girl he brought as his date. A different girl than the one that came with him to the last Friendsgiving. In fact, she's a different girl to the one we saw a few weeks ago. While I will say they've all been nice enough, I can tell that they're only stepping stones as he looks for the right girl. Reminds me of the beautiful man sitting beside me. I squeeze Dylan's hand and meet his smiling eyes as Joel takes his turn in sharing what he's thankful for.

"I'm thankful that everyone was happy to postpone our Friendsgiving catch-up for two weeks so we could work around not *one* but *two* hot shot footballer's schedules," Joel says and everyone at the table laughs as both Dylan and Thomas shrug in a "what can you do" manner.

Dylan was starting wide receiver in his first game three weeks ago and has started ever since. Though we've had our ups and downs and have both struggled with the distance between us, he knows he made the right decision to go pro. He loves his team; he's found his calling. And despite missing the hell out of me and his family, the people sitting around this table, he's happy. And I have plans to make him even happier.

Joel's eyes find mine and I know instantly he's up to something. I shake my head and silently pray that he's not going to push Dylan too far today. In the beginning, the fact that I moved in with Joel, and into Dylan's old room, put Dylan's mind at ease when he moved away. If anyone was going to protect me as much as Dylan, it was Joel. These days he says he regrets it because Joel doesn't make things easy on him, as I'm sure we're about to witness. Deep down I know that he's grateful his friend is there for me, keeping me safe, *his words not mine*, even if he does occasionally want to knee him in the balls.

"I'm also thankful for my beautiful hosting partner, Summer. We've been through so much, and living together the past year and a half has definitely strengthened our relationship," Joel adds, staring at me, his eyes alight with mischief. *And here it comes.* "Summer, I love you, and I'm so thankful that, just today, you promised to never leave me." He winks and I shake my head. He knows about my plan but poor Dylan has no idea.

"You should also be thankful that I haven't kicked you in the nuts after that comment," Dylan says under his breath, pulling a giggle from within me.

He turns his head slightly to look at me with a devilish grin, and I bite my lip to stop myself from attacking his mouth.

"Joel who?" Logan says, in a voice I can only assume is meant to be me, as he also adds, "I didn't even realize I had a roommate with my mind always on my superstar boyfriend."

I've never been so happy to have him sitting next to me, because it allows me to slap him in the chest before I turn my attention back to Joel. "I'm thankful for you too, Joely boy."

Dylan rolls his eyes and then it's his turn to give thanks. He thanks me and his friends—well, mostly me with an "and I guess I should be thankful for all of you too" at the end.

When we've finished with the formalities, and have all had way too much food, we make ourselves comfortable for a few games and a lot of alcohol.

After dominating Jenga for the past hour, I decide it's time to tell Dylan my news. It's been killing me to keep it a secret, and I can't wait any longer. Linking my fingers through his, I pull him to his feet and walk him to the porch connected to our room. I say *our* room because in my head I didn't take over Dylan's room. I moved in with him and he just works away from home.

He looks so peaceful looking out at the stars. I'm not sure how he's so relaxed when it's freaking freezing out here, but he's comfortable and loves this spot, so I let it be without comment.

"I have an early Christmas present for you," I say, my eyes pinned in the same direction as Dylan.

He looks my way with a small smirk. "Oh yeah? Is this one of those situations where I should've had an early present for you too?"

I shake my head and laugh. "No, definitely not. This isn't something I bought; it's actually news." His face pales slightly, flashing to my stomach, and I have to work hard to bite back my smile. *He thinks I'm pregnant?* I'd love to see how his mind got to that conclusion.

Dylan swallows and puts on a smile. "Well, don't keep me in suspense."

He's trying hard to act happy and excited rather than nervous and apprehensive, and he's not quite succeeding. I know he wants kids and he wants them with me, but he wants us to live together first. To get engaged and then married. I'm definitely not ready to be a mom, either, but the order of things doesn't bother me as much. Either way, I'm *not* pregnant, but why not have some fun and mess with him a little.

"You might want to sit down," I say before sitting down on the outdoor lounge and patting the spot beside me.

Dylan drops to the edge of the seat and stares straight ahead. *Oops, I've really messed him up. I think he's broken.*

"Dylan, I—"

"Wait! Before you say anything, I need you to know that I love you more than anything, and I know you think I have plans in my head of how I want our future to be, but I would happily do life any way, in any order, as long as it's with you."

Gah! I love him so much. Now I feel bad.

"I'm not pregnant," I state and raise an eyebrow.

"You're not? I mean...I knew that. We're careful." He runs his hand through his hair and silently sighs.

I can't stop the laugh his reaction brings as I jump into his lap, brushing his lips with mine. "You are one hell of a guy, Dylan Mathers," I say when I finally break away.

"And I'm all yours." He winks.

"Always." I smile. "Now, while I'm not pregnant, I am still changing our future plans a little." I look into his crystal-blue eyes and can almost see that future staring back at me.

Dylan's brows furrow in confusion, but his gaze never leaves mine.

"I'm graduating early. I'm finishing up my final subjects as we speak and then I'm officially done."

His eyes widen in a mixture of shock and awe. "Seriously?"

"Yes." I laugh. "Seriously. So...I'm thinking about moving to Denver. Do you know anyone that needs a roomie?"

As soon as the words are out of my mouth, Dylan flips me on to my back and kisses me with everything that he has. "Fuck, I love you," he says between kisses, before pulling away and staring down into my soul.

"Marry me."

"W...What?" I stammer and my heart rate spikes.

He doesn't answer me but instead pulls us both up until we're standing and then drops down on one knee. "I was going to wait and do this on New Year's Eve. I don't even have the ring, but right now it feels even more perfect. Summer, I knew there was something about you the second I laid eyes on you. I had this intense need to protect you and I never even knew who you were. When I met you again over two years ago, I had the strongest feeling of déjà vu, like we'd met before, and an even stronger desire to never let you go. I may have fought it, but deep down my heart knew it was you. You were the one.

"I used to think that becoming your fake best friend was the best thing to ever happen to me, but now that I'm on one knee, looking into your eyes and seeing our future, I know that the best is yet to come. Every day with you is better than the last. Summer, I love you. Will you marry me?"

My pulse quickens and my heart almost beats out of my chest because...*Holy shit!* If you'd asked me six months ago if I thought I'd get engaged this year I would have said absolutely not. Hell, I'd have said that yesterday. But now...now that Dylan's asking me, I suddenly want nothing more. We've been through so much, and I know he's my end game. We might still be young, but why does it matter when you know it's going to happen at some point, probably soon. I love this man with all my heart.

"Yes!" I cry, dropping down onto my knees in front of him. My arms wrap around his neck as his own hands hold my face. "You just made a ten-year-old me very happy. How many people get to marry their first crush?" I say with a wink.

Dylan's eyes light up and he laughs before pulling my face to his and smothering me in a bruising kiss.

And just like that, I'm engaged to my best friend, and there is nothing fake about it.

Also by Katherine Jay

AIN'T NO SUNSHINE
A Heartstrings Novella
Cory and Nate's Story

Nate Edwards is hot. So freaking hot.

And kind. And supportive. And caring. He's worlds away from the other college guys I've dated and exactly the type of guy I need in my life. He's the real deal.

Loving him should have been easy. And yet...

Our story isn't that straightforward.

It took three seconds to feel a connection, three weeks to fall in love, and three people to ruin it all.

The worst part...one of them was me.

NOW AVAILABLE ON AMAZON

Acknowledgments

Gah!! It's finished. My debut novel, my *baby* is out in the world. This story has been inside me for a long long time. Dylan and Summer mean the world to me and I'm so grateful to you for taking the time to read their story and for all of those that made publishing this book possible.

Keelan Storm – without you this novel would not exist. Plain and simple. Sure, I had ideas and a draft, but your guidance and support helped to get the story to where it is today. I couldn't ask for a better Alpha writing buddy. Special thanks to you for putting up with my random questions or freakouts at all hours due to our time difference. Thank you. Bring on book two!

Brittanee Nicole – thank you for allowing me to Beta read for you when I had no experience and thank you for trusting me. Because of that, I've gained an amazing friend in you and am so grateful to have you on this journey with me. Your ongoing support has been invaluable and I appreciate your willingness to answer every question I throw your way.

Cass – thank you for your encouragement, for believing in me, and for keeping me accountable. I wouldn't have actually started writing it it wasn't for you.

To my amazing Beta Readers, Ree, Cass, Brittanee and Lydia... Thank you for loving Dylan and Summer as much as I do and for helping to shape this book into the story it is today. I could not have done this without you.

My super awesome, supportive and fun street team. I know I wrote this in the novella but I still feel the same... The support you've shown me from the moment you all signed on to the team is incredible. Your excitement for Dylan and Summer has meant the world to me. I will forever be grateful for the friendships I've developed with each and every one of you.

To Elle Thorpe... you replied to a email from a fan writing her debut novel and probably didn't even realise that the advice you gave would lead to her (me) becoming a published author. Thank you for being so willing to share your tips and to guide me the right direction so this dream could become a reality. You were the first person to help me on this journey and I will always be grateful.

Emily Wittig... Ahhh, I can't believe I have an Emily Wittig designed cover. I can't express how happy I am with Dylan and Summer's cover and am so thankful that you were able to fit me, a newbie, into your insanely busy schedule. Thank you.

To Ann and Ann, my editors, your suggestions made the world of difference to this story and I'm so grateful to have worked with you on this book. Thank you for your patience and for helping to bring my book baby to life.

Thank you to my family for all that you do and for supporting me on this crazy endeavour. You may never get to read my books and yet will always be my number one fans. Love you.

Finally, to my readers, thank you so much for following me on this journey and taking a chance on a newbie author. I'm so excited to bring you more stories for the Heartstrings world and hope that you love my characters as much as I do. I love hearing your thoughts on my stories and characters, so feel free to reach out and share. You are the reason I write. Thank you!

WANT MORE FROM THE CHARACTERS IN WHEN NOTHING ELSE MATTERS?

Cory and Nate's book, Ain't No Sunshine, is a novella set in the Heartstrings world and is now available on Amazon. Book two is also in the works with a release planned for September. I have six stories in this series and can't wait to hear your thoughts on who you want to get their own book.

Interested in keeping up to date on all things Katherine Jay? Follow me on Instagram and TikTok, and sign up to my newsletter to get first access to covers and blurbs, exclusive teasers and giveaways. You can find all of these on my linktree account – linktr.ee/KatherineJay

Thank you again for supporting indie authors. If you enjoyed this book, please shout it from the rooftops and leave a review on Amazon or Goodreads.

About Author

Katherine lives in Australia with her three awesome boys-Hubby and two kiddies. She spends her days partaking in role play, building fortes and dancing. While her nights are spent reading and writing.

Her debut series, Heartstrings, is an emotional new adult romance with love that's worth fighting for and characters full of heart.

Printed in Great Britain
by Amazon

87454418R00185